BUSINESS

Affairs

He's impatient…

He's impossible…

But he's absolutely irresistible!

She's in love with her boss!

In this extra-special collection of three
brand-new short stories, three talented,
bestselling Modern Romance™ authors
bring to life the thrill and passion of
finding the man of your dreams — at work!
From 9 to 5; sensual chemistry takes over —
but does it carry on after hours, too?

First published in Great Britain 2003 by
Harlequin Mills & Boon Limited,
Eton House, 18-24 Paradise Road,
Richmond, Surrey, TW9 1SR

BUSINESS AFFAIRS © Harlequin Enterprises II B.V. 2003

The publisher acknowledges the copyright holders of the
individual works as follows:

Her Secret Valentine © Helen Brooks 2002
The Boss's Valentine © Lynne Graham 2003
Rafael's Proposal © Kim Lawrence 2003

ISBN 0 263 83676 2

024-0203

Printed and bound in Spain
by Litografia Rosés S.A., Barcelona

BUSINESS
Affairs

Helen Brooks

Lynne Graham

Kim Lawrence

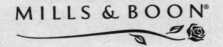

MILLS & BOON®

CONTENTS

HER SECRET VALENTINE

by

Helen Brooks

Helen Brooks lives in Northamptonshire, and is married with three children. As she is a busy housewife and mother, her spare time is at a premium, but her hobbies include reading, swimming, gardening and walking her two energetic, inquisitive and very endearing young dogs. Her long-cherished aspiration to write became a reality when she put pen to paper on reaching the age of forty, and sent the result off to Mills & Boon®.

Out this month!

THE PARISIAN PLAYBOY by Helen Brooks
Mills & Boon® Modern Romance™
February 2003.

CHAPTER ONE

'WHO was the bright spark that suggested Jim's retirement presentation should be followed by drinks and food all afternoon? Whoever it was has a lot to answer for if you ask me.'

Jeanie glanced up from her littered desk and smiled at the tall dark figure standing in the doorway of her private office. 'Do I take it you aren't enjoying yourself out there?' she asked mildly, her warm amber-brown eyes focusing on Ward Ryan's handsome and distinctly irritated face.

He grimaced, stepping inside and shutting the door, and as ever the steady thud-thud of her heart went crazy for a few moments before settling into the regular even beat one would expect of an experienced and highly respected junior partner in a large thriving solicitors' practice in the heart of London.

'What makes normally reserved and sensible people suddenly go crazy when someone mentions the words "office party" anyway?' Ward walked across to Jeanie's desk and perched easily on the edge of it, raking back a lock of black hair as he did so and frowning darkly. 'It was the same at Christmas... Jenny and Stephanie were practically paralytic then and the other two secretaries weren't much better which doesn't set much of an example to their juniors.

Did you know Bob's been ensconced in the stationery cupboard with Catherine for the last twenty minutes, and John and Michael are taking bets on who gets to take Kim home?'

Jeanie shrugged. She had been with Eddleston, Breedon and Partners for five years now and the two senior partners—Joseph Eddleston and Dan Breedon—looked after all their employees hand-somely, *too* handsomely at times. It was right that Jim Hatton's long years of service should be acknowl-edged and celebrated, but some individuals just weren't too good on handling free drink.

She glanced more closely at Ward and then said drily, 'You might want to wipe the lipstick off your cheek but I don't think you can do much about the pink shade on your shirt collar.'

'Damn women!' It was a low growl, and as Ward extracted a crisp white linen handkerchief from his pocket and scrubbed at the chiselled cheekbone Jeanie had indicated, she had to bite back a bitter-sweet smile.

All the women in the practice—from the nineteen-year-old office junior, Kim, with her fluffy blonde hair and come-to-bed blue eyes to Mildred Robinson, the two senior partners' sergeant-major type personal as-sistant—had a crush on Ward Ryan to varying de-grees. And Ward's cool, distant manner at the office, his unwritten law about keeping work and play totally separate, seemed to make some of the more predatory females desperate to be noticed when office protocol was relaxed a little, like today.

'That looks like Jenny's colour?' Jeanie was deter-mined to keep things light but ridiculously, after all the years of loving him from afar, it still hurt to think Jenny had actually done what she would give her eye teeth to do and kissed Ward. But then that would ruin the closeness between them that her self-control and reticence had been rewarded with, she reminded herself.

She knew he regarded her as his buddy, his close friend, probably the only woman friend he had because he never continued seeing the women he dated after he finished with them. The Ice-Man. That was his nickname among the female staff but it didn't stop them all fancying him like mad, she thought ruefully.

But he wasn't an ice man, not really. You only had to see him with his six-year-old daughter to know that, but then apart from herself she doubted if anyone at Eddleston and Breedon had had that privilege.

'Jenny!' Ward made an exclamation of extreme irritation. 'I was hoping to finish off the Bakerson report before we closed tonight but she seemed to think I'd asked her to come into my office for quite another purpose.'

'You're just an old meanie.' Jeanie had long since decided what tack she was going to take when some female or other threw herself at Ward—she'd had to, it wasn't an uncommon occurrence. 'Jenny just likes to flirt a little, that's all.'

The piercingly blue eyes surveyed her for a moment and then the hard handsome face relaxed in a smile that always had the power to make Jeanie go weak at the knees. 'Jenny's attractive enough,' he admitted easily, 'but she's my *secretary* for crying out loud.' That, in Ward's opinion, said it all.

Jeanie nodded briskly. She always found, with these

sort of conversations, that her limit of endurance was reached fairly quickly and now she changed the subject as she said quietly, 'All ready for Bobbie's birthday party? It's this weekend, isn't it?'

'Uh-huh. The twentieth of January,' Ward agreed.

She loved his voice; it was part of his overall attraction and of a deep smoky quality that was pure dynamite on the hormones. And now, as he stretched his neck and shoulders and powerful muscles flexed and bunched Jeanie found she had to take a deep hidden breath and let it out steadily before she could trust herself to speak.

'I suppose Bobbie is excited?' she said with as much casual warmth as she could manage considering she wanted to leap over the desk and devour him. She should never have had those couple of glasses of wine earlier, she thought grimly. It was vital to have one hundred per cent control around Ward at all times.

'Off the wall,' he agreed with another 24 carat smile. 'Going from six to seven is an event of supreme importance apparently, and I don't think there's a kid in the neighbourhood who hasn't been invited. Add to that the repeated pleas for a hamster for her birthday and she's worked herself up to fever pitch.'

'And is Daddy going to deliver said hamster?' It was a purely rhetorical question. If Bobbie had asked for the moon it would have undoubtedly been parcelled up and placed with Bobbie's cards and gifts on her birthday morning this Sunday.

Ward's wife had died six and a half years ago when the car the beautiful redhead had been driving had been hit by a falling tree in the middle of a freak storm and ended up in a ditch. Bobbie had been strapped in a baby seat on the back seat of the vehicle which had undoubtedly saved the infant's life, but the nine-hour operation which had followed to save the tiny child's crushed legs had left the little girl with the slightest of limps.

'It's been living in Monica's bathroom for the last two days,' Ward admitted with a mocking twist to his firm mouth. He was well aware his tiny daughter was able to wind him round her little finger. 'Which is an act of extreme heroism on Monica's part considering she is antirodents of any description.'

Jeanie nodded. She wasn't at all surprised. Ward's stout housekeeper worshipped the ground Bobbie walked on, and as Monica had never married and was now well over sixty, Ward and Bobbie were her family and she filled the role of indulgent grandmother perfectly.

'And you?' Ward drawled comfortably, leaning across the desk slightly and pouring himself a glass of wine from the bottle Jeanie's secretary, Stephanie, had brought in earlier when she'd given up trying to persuade her workaholic boss to come and join the 'fun,' as Stephanie termed it. 'What are you doing this weekend?'

It took a moment—well, more than one, Jeanie conceded crossly—for her to pull herself together sufficiently to think coherent thoughts. She always felt a terrible fascination grip her in Ward's presence, but today, with the warmth and scent of him filling her air space and his hard powerful thighs outlined under his trousers which had stretched taut as he balanced nonchalantly on the end of her desk, she felt positively liquid.

She had hoped, over four years ago now when she'd finally admitted the awful truth to herself and acknowledged that she was crazily, madly, *irrevocably* in love with one of her fellow partners, that she'd get a handle on coping with this thing that had hit her like a ton of bricks the first time she'd set eyes on Ward Ryan. She was still hoping.

The truth was she should have left the practice then, or in one of the four years which had followed. It would have been the sensible thing to do, something she would have told someone else in her position was the only sensible course of action.

Ward never discussed his late wife, but it was common knowledge he had been like a living, breathing robot for months and months after her untimely death, and even when he had seemed to return to the human race it was with an air of rigid autonomy where members of the opposite sex were concerned.

He had started dating occasionally a couple of years after Patricia, his wife, had died, but any woman who got involved with him had to accept the relationship would only be semi-permanent and with no strings or commitment on either side. The only female who had a place in his heart was his daughter and he had no intention of changing the status quo.

'What am I doing this weekend?' she said after a moment or two. 'Meeting a friend for lunch tomorrow and then driving up to York afterwards to see my family. I haven't seen them since Christmas and that was hectic with all my nieces and nephews gathered en masse.'

She wished he'd remove those lean hips from her eyeline. The fact that Ward was totally unaware of the

impact of his sex appeal didn't make it any the less
difficult to deal with.

He nodded thoughtfully. 'I sometimes think it's a
pity Bobbie hasn't got any cousins or family other
than my parents in Oxford,' he said slowly, leaning
forward again and offering her a sip from the glass in
his hand. 'What do you think?'

She *thought* that his aftershave ought to be banned
as being downright dangerous to a woman's state of
mind, Jeanie told herself, as she squeaked a refusal to
the wine and wondered how that tanned hard male
chin with its faint stubble would feel beneath her lips.
'I... I think Bobbie's fine,' she managed eventually
when she realised he was waiting for an answer to his
question. And then she nerved herself and broke the
silent code which underpinned her friendship with
Ward as she added, 'Hadn't your wife any brothers or
sisters, then?'

It was the first time she had mentioned Patricia—
no one but *no one* ever did unless they wanted a granite stare and a frosty put down—but apart from stiffening slightly he showed no reaction as he said
quietly, 'No, she was born to a single mother and
brought up in a succession of foster homes.'

And then he shrugged himself off her desk, his impossibly blue eyes narrowed and remote and the hard
angles and planes of his face closed against her as he
walked across to the window and finished the glass of
wine in one swallow. 'It looks like it's going to snow,'
he said evenly as he stood with his back to her looking
down into the busy London street beneath.

She was just opening her mouth to reply when a
gust of high riotous laughter mingled with raised

voices and the sound of a champagne cork popping reached them.

Ward swung round, his face and voice dry as he said, 'I think I'll disappear to my office and work on that report after all. I've already toasted Jim when Joseph and Dan presented him with his gold watch and his secretary got all emotional. I can't stand any more discussions about how he and his wife are going to spend their retirement. See you later, Jeanie.'

Jeanie nodded but didn't say anything as Ward left her office. He hadn't liked her mentioning his wife. It was the one thought which kept returning all through the darkening afternoon as Jeanie worked on, long after the others had begun to dwindle off home in their ones and twos. Obviously his pain was still as fresh, as raw as it had ever been. What must it have been like to have been loved like that by Ward?

It wasn't the first time she had brooded along these lines, and she let her imagination have free rein for some time which was stupid, she told herself sternly, miserable minutes later. She knew full well such rumination always left her feeling rotten. She had given up dreaming that one day Ward would glance at her across the desks and filing cabinets and Cupid's arrow would hit ages ago. It was time to count her blessings again!

She was thirty-two years of age, hugely successful in her own particular field of family law as her position at Eddleston, Breedon and Partners, and her nice fat pay cheque each month confirmed.

She owned her own little mews property, a small car; she had no financial worries and heaps of good friends. Her social life wasn't the stuff the tabloids liked, but it was full and active and she didn't have to spend one evening alone unless she wanted to. She was lucky. She *was*. She was very, very lucky, she reiterated grimly, springing up and walking over to the window in a flurry of irritated frustration and dissatisfaction.

It was quite dark outside, the lights from the offices and shops below her office on the third floor of the building, vying with the headlights of the busy, rush hour traffic snaking along the road. Well, it was the weekend again, something most people anticipated with some delight. For her, however, it just meant two days when there was no possibility of seeing Ward.

Oh, she was pathetic! A really sad case. She glared at the reflection in the glass, and dark eyes set in an oval face with delicate, elegant bone structure stared back at her. She smoothed her thick, sleek hair in its tight coil at the back of her head absently, suddenly aware she had a headache. It was probably more due to the amount of wine she had slowly consumed during the afternoon than the army of hairpins holding her hair in place, but suddenly she rebelled against the severe hairstyle she always wore for work and attacked the pins determinedly, combing her hair through with her fingers once it was hanging in a heavy shining blue-black curtain to below her shoulder blades.

That was better. She lowered her chin as she shut her eyes, rotating her head round and round as she massaged bunched muscles at the base of her neck. It had been a long day and in spite of remaining glued to her desk she hadn't done half of what she wanted to do, and no doubt she was the last one here as usual.

And then she caught at the self-pity, hating it and herself and this whole situation with Ward that had no hope of ever turning out as she would like. She groaned softly, biting her lip hard.

And then she nearly jumped out of her skin as an urgent, concerned voice behind her said, 'Jeanie? Are you feeling unwell? What's the matter?'

And she was turned round by a large pair of strong hands and found herself an inch or so away from Ward's broad chest staring up into the never ending blue of his eyes.

Whether it was her previous thoughts, or the wine, or the fact that she'd assumed he'd already left and she wouldn't be seeing him for a lifetime, or just the fact that his unexpected appearance brought home just how much she loved him, Jeanie wasn't sure, but the next moment she had horrified them both by bursting into tears. And not ladylike, controlled, solicitor-type tears either, but great loud wails complete with streaming eyes and a runny nose and the whole package.

Neither was the flood stemmed at all when she found herself enfolded tenderly into the haven of his arms, her wet cheeks resting against the magnificent male chest she had dreamt about so often, and his voice warm and smoky above her head as he murmured soothing nothings.

It was torture. Exquisite, heavenly, worth dying for torture admittedly, but torture nevertheless.

Jeanie went for gold and cried until there were no more tears left, and to be truthful she was amazed where they had come from in the first place. She hadn't been aware she'd been so low or so despondent, but perhaps five years *was* a long time without one hug or loving caress from the man you loved, she comforted herself weakly.

Whatever, she had made a mammoth fool of herself. As the knowledge dawned she felt more bereft. Whatever was she going to say to him? she asked herself dazedly as the sobs faded to soft hiccups and he still continued to hold her against him.

She couldn't tell him the truth and Ward being Ward would detect a lie a mile off. What had she done? Oh, what had she done?

CHAPTER TWO

JEANIE would have been happy to stay in his arms for ever. For all eternity. Locked against him so closely she could hear the steady slam of his heart, and feel surrounded by his male warmth and smell which was partly expensive aftershave on clean tanned skin and something else which was purely Ward. Even if he *was* holding her as a friend if this wasn't heaven it wasn't far off.

She sniffed carefully and then, as she felt herself moved away from her nesting place and felt a hand-kerchief dabbing at her wet eyelids, she almost whimpered with disappointment.

She opened her tear-drenched eyes and saw Ward was looking down at her with speculative concern, and for the life of her Jeanie couldn't think of a single thing to say to ease the excruciating awkwardness of the moment.

Not that Ward seemed to find it so. His sexy cynical mouth was twisted wrily and his blue eyes narrowed and intent on her hot face as he said, with a soft huskiness that produced a riot of sensation in her stomach she could have well done without in the present circumstances, 'Want to tell me what that was all about?'

No, she didn't. She stared up at him helplessly as she tried to brace herself for more questions. Because they would come. Oh yes, they would come all right. Ward was a brilliant lawyer with an almost scientifically rational and probing mind. He had a formidable reputation among his colleagues, not least for his tenacity and strength of will, and she had heard the other partners refer to him more than once as a genius. And now every cell of that frighteningly intelligent brain was homed in on her. It was a daunting thought.

'Why didn't you tell me something was wrong before?' he probed softly. 'We're friends, aren't we?'

Oh, God, please don't let me humiliate myself any further, she prayed frantically, as the last words hit home. Please let me extract myself from this with a little bit of dignity at least. I promise you I'll never ask for anything else in the rest of my life if you do!

She reached out and took the handkerchief from him, utterly unable to meet his eyes as she turned away and walked over to the seat she had vacated earlier, sinking down into the soft leather as her legs gave out completely. 'I... I'm sorry,' she managed at last, and then froze in horror as he walked across to crouch in front of her, taking both of her hands in his.

'Don't be sorry,' he said gently, 'and don't be embarrassed either. We've been friends too long for that. And all the others have gone so don't worry about them.'

The others? She hadn't given them a thought!

And then her heart turned right over as his voice gentled still more, like warm velvet, as he murmured, 'It can't be the job. Dan Breedon was singing your praises only the other day and saying he is constantly amazed by the amount of work you get through in any one week. And you said you had a great time with your parents and your sisters and all their kids at Christmas, and you're seeing them this weekend again. So, call me old-fashioned or just plain presumptuous, but could this unJeanie-like despondency have anything to do with a man?'

She had been fighting the hot prickles of sexual awareness that had flushed her cheeks and were threatening to make her tremble, but now she jerked her hands free, a mixture of surprise and—amazingly for her where Ward was concerned—anger sending adrenalin pumping fiercely round her bloodstream.

Surprise firstly at his intuition, and anger because it had suddenly dawned on her with his last words that for years Ward had only seen what he wanted to see regarding her. How did he know whether despondency was one of her natural traits anyway? He'd always demanded the same old steady, uncomplaining, reliable, friendly Jeanie be there for him. No complications, no messy emotions, no hysterics; he probably didn't view her as a *woman* at all. Just a dependable, predictable pal who happened to wear skirts and speak in a falsetto range!

Well she *was* a woman, a woman whose biological clock was ticking and who wanted a proper family home, babies, a husband. No, not just a husband—him; she wanted *him*. 'Yes, it is about a man.' She heard herself speak the words with a feeling of acute amazement and regretted them immediately, but it was too late. They were out and there was no going back.

She forced herself to meet the clear, darkly lashed blue eyes and saw they were soft with sympathy. Sympathy but nothing more. And it was only in that second that she realised she'd been hoping for something—*anything*— else. A spark of disquiet. The faintest trace of jealousy. Just a smidgen of disturbance in that cool, controlled, orderly freezer he called a brain box, where he thought he'd got everything wrapped neatly in little parcels.

And then she felt horribly, wretchedly guilty as he stretched out a tender hand and stroked one cheek gently, his voice warm with sincerity as he murmured, 'I don't know anything about it of course but I can say without any doubt that he's not worthy of you, you or your tears.'

Probably not but that didn't exactly help right now! And she had no right to expect anything at all of Ward, she reminded herself miserably. He couldn't help how he viewed her any more than she could help loving him.

She watched him crouch back on his heels again for a moment before rising slowly to his feet, and as she raised her eyes to his face she saw the sympathy was still there but threaded through with what she could only describe as faint surprise. 'Do you know I've just realised I don't know anything at all about you with regard to your relationships with the opposite sex,' he said thoughtfully. 'You've never talked about that area of your personal life with me, have you?' His eyes wandered over the shining, blue-black curtain of her hair as he spoke as though that was another thing she'd kept from him.

Jeanie shrugged carefully. She suspected there was the faintest touch of pique in this somewhere, but it wasn't quite the moment to remind him that he'd never had the interest to ask. That razor-sharp mind that made him a force to be reckoned with was already busy compiling data, and she had certainly said far too much as it was. She would die, shrivel away to nothing if he even so much as remotely suspected how she really felt about him. 'I could say the same about you,' she said quietly.

He nodded. 'True.' He seemed to digest that for a few moments and then said tentatively, 'Have you known him long?'

'A while.' She shifted uncomfortably in the chair.

'And you've had a row or something?'

She hadn't had so much as a something but she couldn't very well say so! Aware she had to be very wary indeed she said cautiously, 'Not exactly a row. It's just that he doesn't want to settle down and I do.' That much at least was true, she comforted herself guiltily finding it was much harder than she'd thought to lie to Ward. Although if she considered what she *had* said she really hadn't lied at all, more...misled him?

'He'll change his mind, Jeanie. Give him time. Men need to work into responsibility sometimes.''

'No, he won't change his mind,' she said very steadily. 'He doesn't feel the same way about me as I feel about him, you see. His feelings aren't the forever kind.'

'He's *told* you that?' He sounded so shocked she almost could have smiled. Ward had run his love life on that theme for the last six years but apparently heartily disapproved of this man doing the same!

'Oh yes.' Well, he had in a way.

'Hell!'

That was it in a nutshell, she thought soberly. Sheer hell, especially when he was looking at her as though he wanted to take this other man and strangle him. 'It doesn't matter.' She forced a smile which considering she must look like she'd been pulled through a hedge backwards probably made her appear more pathetic, she thought on reflection.

And this seemed to be borne out when he said urgently, 'Dump him, Jeanie, if you haven't done so already. If it can't go anywhere and you're eating your heart out, it's better to cut and run.'

'I can't do that.' She spoke from her eaten-out heart and with an intensity that caused him to stiffen. 'He might not want to marry me and can't love me like I love him, but he's my world until he chooses to step out of it.'

He was staring at her as though he had never seen her before, his eyes narrowed and almost navy-blue with a dark emotion that made him seem more handsome than ever.

He shook his head, raking back his hair in a gesture she knew meant irritation or worse. She knew lots of little things like that about him; she'd had five years to absorb them into her being. 'As big a fool as he is, you're a worse one to waste your life on such an ungrateful swine,' he ground out harshly, making her eyes widen with surprise at his fierceness. 'You're not getting any younger, Jeanie.'

The adrenalin pumped harder, and her voice carried an acidic note that wasn't lost on the big tall man watching her so closely, when she said, 'Oh thank you, Ward. I really needed you to point that out. That makes me feel a whole lot better.'

He had the grace to look discomfited. 'I didn't mean... Hell, you know you're a beautiful woman,

Jeanie, in the prime of life. It's just that—' He stopped abruptly, aware he was making it worse. 'I just don't like to think of you being used like this, that's all,' he said finally, his voice soft.

If this wasn't the height of irony she didn't know what was! Jeanie managed a fairly offhand shrug, and her voice carried a cool note that indicated the conversation was at an end when she said, 'I'm not being used, Ward. He never made me any promises and I went into it with my eyes wide open. It takes two to tango after all. Normally I can handle it just fine but you caught me at a low ebb tonight. Perhaps it's because this has been a particularly strenuous week and I'm tired, or the wine I've consumed on an empty stomach, I don't know. But I'm fine. Really.'

He didn't look at all convinced, surveying her thoughtfully from eyes which had taken on a steely hue. And she knew what that meant too, Jeanie thought ruefully. He had had a situation presented to him, had decided upon a logical and straightforward solution and the other party wasn't seeing it his way. She'd seen this look before in business when a client was being difficult or obtuse. That undeniably brilliant mind was now considering what other tack to take.

'Right.'

He'd clearly come to some decision, she noted with dark hidden amusement which was tinged, as always, by overwhelming sexual attraction. Both his tone and the enigmatic quality of his smile proclaimed it.

'You've just said your stomach is empty and all I've had today is a few nibbles from the buffet out there, so I'm taking you home for one of Monica's excellent lasagnes,' he said in a tone that brooked no argument.

'And then afterwards, once Bobbie's in bed and we've got the sitting room to ourselves, we're going to have a good chat, you and me.'

His expression was understanding but for once Jeanie felt—quite irrationally she admitted silently to herself—like kicking him. This was Ward in supremacy mode; manipulation by the iron hand in the velvet glove. He meant well, she knew he *meant* well, but she really didn't feel like discussing her bruised heart any further with the shredded tatters of her dignity pulled tightly round her. It was also far too dangerous an undertaking in the circumstances.

'I'm sorry, Ward, I can't, but thanks for the offer,' she said politely.

'Why not?' The piercing gaze fastened on her face. 'Are you seeing him tonight?'

Like a terrier with a bone, as always! 'No,' she managed fairly calmly, 'but I've heaps to do before I go to York tomorrow.' She dropped her eyes to her desk as she spoke, more to shut out his disturbing presence than because she needed to tidy it before she left.

Ward's charcoal-grey suit jacket was unbuttoned revealing a blue shirt tucked into the flat waistband of his trousers, and at some time during the afternoon he had loosened his tie and undone the first two or three buttons of his shirt. He looked less than his normal impeccable self and twice as sexy, and she really couldn't take it.

'Sorry, but that won't do.' Her head shot up at his words and whether it was because he'd seen her jaw set and her mouth tighten she wasn't sure, but his voice took on a distinctly soothing tone as he said,

'I'll be worrying about you all weekend if we leave it like this. At least come and have a hot meal and relax for a couple of hours, and we won't discuss it at all if you don't want to. And Bobbie would love to see you again. She still talks about the lady from my office who played snap with her all evening even though it was a few weeks ago.'

'She's a sweetheart.' Ward had been ill with the flu and had called her to bring some urgent papers round to him after work, and once there Monica had insisted on feeding her and Bobbie had pounced on a playmate. Jeanie hadn't minded; Bobbie was a naturally funny and truly lovable little girl, but seeing Ward in a home setting with his daughter had upset her equilibrium for the next twenty-four hours... For days... Well, ever since then really.

They had often had business lunches together or popped in the local wine bar after a stressful day for a drink to unwind, and on those occasions she knew Ward relaxed and emerged from the mask he normally wore, but that evening at his home she had seen him as a father and it had blown her mind.

In spite of feeling like death he had been gentle and patient and so tender with the small child it had been a revelation, and Bobbie herself had tugged at Jeanie's heartstrings. She'd gone home and cried all night. A repeat of that was the last thing she needed. She opened her mouth to refuse again but got no further than, 'Ward—'

'Please, Jeanie, if not for yourself then for friend-ship's sake?' he asked silkily with a winsome smile. 'It will put my mind at rest.'

He had turned on the charm and although she knew

it—had watched him use every trick in the book and charm the birds out of the trees in various situations in the past when it had suited him to do so—it was different when the full force of that magnetic personality was coming her way. Jeanie floundered 'I... I really don't want to talk about...him if I come.'

'Fine. No problem,' he gentled.

'And I shan't be able to stay long. I need to catch up on some chores at home and tonight is the only chance I'll have this weekend,' she said nervously, wondering how on earth she had managed to put herself in this ridiculous position.

'I understand perfectly. Finish off in here and we'll leave in...what? Ten minutes?' he asked cheerfully.

Jeanie nodded a touch bewilderedly, feeling as though she had just been run over by a steamroller.

Ward slanted a look at her troubled face from under half-closed lids and clicked his tongue with genuine irritation. 'No more brooding about this worthless idiot, not tonight,' he said briskly. 'Okay? You won't be able to give Bobbie's birthday your full and undivided attention if your mind's elsewhere,' he added with an obvious attempt to lighten the charged atmosphere. 'What's in the parcel you gave me for her anyway?'

'A doll,' Jeanie said shortly. She didn't add that it was a bride doll in full wedding regalia because she had the nasty feeling it was something of a revealing gesture, and was regretting her choice of present bitterly. But she knew Ward's daughter would adore the sweet-faced doll, and since the day she had met Bobbie she had thought about her often and felt terribly sorry for the small scrap of humanity who had been forced to grow up without a mother's love. 'Right, ten minutes you said?'

Ward took the hint and left, but Jeanie sat for another two minutes in a state of blind panic, her mind racing back and forth, before she took hold of herself. Enough, she told herself silently. Everything's okay. He doesn't know it's him and he's not going to know unless you tell him. So, calm. Calm, girl.

By the time Ward poked his head round her door Jeanie's desk was clear, her private filing cabinets locked and everything was spick and span.

'Ready?' he smiled from the doorway. He had pulled on his big black overcoat which accentuated his particular brand of dark maleness, and the blue of his eyes was riveting as he glanced over at her, quite unaware of his air of arrogant sophistication.

The man who had everything. Even as she smiled and nodded her mind was working quite independently. Everything except the one thing he really wanted, his dead wife. What had she looked like, Patricia? What had she *been* like, as a person, to capture his heart so completely?

Office gossip had related that she had been a tall, slim redhead and stunningly beautiful, but when Jeanie had visited his home that time there had been no photographs of Bobbie's mother as she had expected. Bobbie herself was tiny for her age, with delicate pixie features and dark brown hair and eyes, but, adorable as the little girl was, she couldn't be termed beautiful or even particularly pretty, which was surprising with her parentage...

'Jeanie?'

She gave a guilty start, suddenly aware she had been

miles away, and then flushed hotly at the expression on his face. 'Sorry,' she apologised weakly. 'I'm not myself today.'

'Quite.' It was terse, and she realised—with a little dart of painful amusement—that Ward wasn't used to women day-dreaming about another man in his presence, which was what he'd obviously assumed.

She had already slipped into her coat before he'd arrived and now she flicked her hair back over her shoulders where it shimmered like raw blue-black silk against the cream material.

The movement caught his eye, and again the faint surprise she'd read earlier on his face was there, along with something else she couldn't place, when he said quietly, 'Why don't you usually wear your hair like that? It's a crime to hide such beauty.'

'I don't think it's formal enough for the office.' The compliment—the first one she had received from Ward on a personal level and unconnected with her work— had totally thrown her, and she was concentrating on appearing matter-of-fact but it was hard.

He was still staring at her for one thing, and although he was leaning nonchalantly against the open door and appeared perfectly relaxed and cool—his normal self in fact—something had changed. There was electricity in the air.

And then she admonished herself silently for being so ridiculous. Pure imagination, she told herself sharply. Just because he had given her a compliment! The thing was, sexual provocativeness had never been part of her nature and she wasn't the sort of woman who blatantly invited flattery or even dealt with the occasional compliment very well.

She was the youngest of five sisters, and had always felt very much the odd one out. The others all had a couple of years separating them, but there was a six-year age gap between herself and Charlotte, her mother's fourth child, although that wasn't the only reason she'd always felt like the cuckoo in the nest. Lizzie, Susan, Miranda and Charlotte were all small and fair-haired—the colour ranging from blonde to golden brown—and on the voluptuous side.

She was tall and slender and had felt like a stick insect beside them through her teenage years, and her different colouring had been striking enough to emphasise the contrast even more and was invariably commented on when relatives and friends called by. She loved her sisters, every one of them, but had never really felt she *belonged* somehow, and the fact that they had all married fairly young and settled down to have large families within the same little community hadn't helped.

She moved quickly now, switching off her desk lamp and walking across the room as she said, 'I hope my turning up unexpectedly won't put Monica out.'

'Of course not, she'll love to see you again.' The expression of thoughtful gravity was gone and the blue eyes were smiling at her now, and as they walked out of the office and towards the lift at the end of the shadowed corridor, Ward's hand was in the small of her back in the normal friendly protective manner he always adopted with her. And as always his faintest touch was sending heat waves into every nerve and sinew.

Jeanie had long since given up feeling guilt and embarrassment and a hundred and one other similar emotions at her body's secret reaction to him, but to-night was different somehow, and she was glad of the sleek curtain of hair swinging forward to hide her flushed cheeks.

It was the unequivocally tough maleness of his body that always set the juices flowing, she thought silently as the lift doors opened in answer to Ward's finger on the control button on the wall. He exuded masculinity from the top of his head to the bottom of his feet; it was in every look, every gesture, the deep smoky sexy voice, even the way he walked with an easy, loping, almost animal-like grace.

She stepped quickly into the lift, glad his hand was gone from her back and yet at the same time regretting its loss. But then she was always like that around this man, she thought ruefully. Like a cat on a hot tin roof. It was a miracle he didn't know, although the years of hiding her feelings and pretending everything was all right through her childhood and youth had stood her in good stead for Ward Ryan.

Once she had met him she'd understood why she'd never felt overly tempted to fall into bed with previous boyfriends; she'd been waiting for Ward without knowing it. If only she'd met him before Patricia had come into his life, but then he would never have looked twice at her anyway. She only had to look into the mirror to be told quite frankly that she was aver-agely attractive, no more, and the women Ward dated were stunners from all accounts.

'I didn't bring the car, knowing I'd have a drink today,' Ward said easily as the lift doors closed. 'But there'll be plenty of taxis about at this time of night.'

Jeanie nodded, trying to match her tone to his as she said, 'I had the same thought.'

'There's the odd flake of snow in the wind and it's bitterly cold, so you wait in the foyer till I stop one.'

Jeanie was just opening her mouth to reply that she was more than capable of standing on the pavement beside him for a few minutes, cold or no cold, when the lift jerked violently to a halt between floors. One moment she was standing on her feet, the next she had been catapulted straight into Ward's arms which had opened automatically to receive her as he himself stumbled back against the carpeted walls.

The shudder the lift had given along with the momentum of her body sent him on to his knees, his arms still cradling her against his chest, and now Jeanie lay across his lap, her face uplifted to his and the silk of her hair like a fan across his arms.

It had all happened in a split second, and along with the panic and fright she felt about being trapped in what suddenly had become a frighteningly fragile little metal box, Jeanie was aware she was in his arms for the second time that evening and it felt wonderful!

The lights had flickered and dimmed for a moment but then, as the lift recovered from its hiccup and began to whirr downwards again, they were shining composedly on the two figures beneath them. Ward had made no attempt to move and neither had she; she couldn't. The blood was pounding through her veins with excitement not fear now, and she was breathless in his arms.

'It's all right, we're moving again.'

'I know.' She responded to Ward's soft husky voice without taking her eyes off his face. His eyes were very blue as they stared down into the wide amber depths of hers, and although they were breathing and talking it was as though they were both frozen in time, she thought dazedly.

Heady hot sensation had pervaded every single part of her and she knew, she just *knew* he was going to kiss her. She began to tremble deep inside as her eyes left his to focus on the hard, sensual lips which were coming closer.

His mouth closed over hers, warm and stunningly sweet, and now her heart was thudding wildly as through the explosion of her senses a little voice was saying, I told you, I told you it would be as good as this.

A burning insistent flow of desire was taking hold as the kiss deepened, his lips and tongue exploring her mouth as she quivered against the hard, steady beat of his heart. Her hands were still gripping his shoulders where they had clutched as they had both fallen, and she couldn't believe—she simply couldn't *believe* how he could make her feel with just his mouth alone. And yet she had always known...since the beginning of time.

And then—almost before it had started she thought despairingly—the kiss had ended as the lift stopped again and Ward raised his head sharply, as though he had just realised what had happened between them. He rose to his feet a split second later, taking her with him, and she was aware of him reaching up and removing her fingers from his shoulders as the door glided open.

'I'm sorry, Jeanie.' His voice was grim and controlled. 'That shouldn't have happened. I don't normally take advantage of damsels in distress,' he added with an attempt at lightness, obviously because he had realised the extent of his withdrawal, she thought with excruciating mortification.

She had invited him to kiss her. No, she had all but *begged* him to, she admitted painfully. And after all she had said earlier. He would either be thinking this great love she had spoken of wasn't worth her breath, or—and please, *please* don't let him go down this avenue, she pleaded silently—he'd suspect that maybe the object of her affections wasn't a million miles away.

'I'm sorry too.' She forced the words out through stiff lips and was amazed how normal her voice sounded considering how she was feeling inside. 'I think we had better put it down to Dan and Joe's generosity with the wine, don't you? Perhaps we should have eaten and partied more instead of working and drinking?' She'd *thrown* herself at him, nothing more or less.

'Perhaps.' They had stepped into the deserted foyer, and now he turned her round with a careful hand at her shoulder as he said, 'But you were extremely vulnerable tonight and I knew that.'

He was taking all the blame and they both knew she had been there every inch of the way. What could she say, what could she do to remedy this horrific situation? 'I don't know about the vulnerable bit,' she said quietly, 'but it was good to know that life still goes on even when your heart's taken a bit of a bashing. I'll survive him, Ward, in time, so please don't worry about me. And the kiss—' she forced herself to go on in the same soft understanding voice '—was because one friend was feeling sorry for another. I know that.'

And it was true, she thought as humiliation made her stomach muscles clench. Five years and not so much as a peck on the cheek, but then after she had finished crying all over him and telling him her story of unrequited love, she had all but asked him to confirm she was still attractive to the opposite sex. What was the poor man to do but kiss her?

She saw Ward open his mouth but whatever he might have said was lost in the next moment when the night security guard opened the door to his cubby-hole off reception. In the following exchange of 'Have a good weekend and see you Monday', they exited into the bitterly cold London street which was already dusted with a light coating of snow, and then Ward was hailing a black cab in his normal authorative manner which guaranteed one drew up immediately.

Once they were tucked into the back of the vehicle Ward set the tone by engaging in small talk for their journey across the city to Harrow where his home was situated, but Jeanie was well aware of the care he was taking not to touch her and the feeling that he was keeping her mentally and physically at arm's length intensified as the journey progressed.

She had shocked him tonight. Disgusted him even. She could hear herself conversing quite naturally through the maelstrom of her thoughts and blessed the inner strength that was keeping her tears at bay. And if nothing else the whole wretched episode had brought one thing home with unmistakable clarity. After tonight, she was going to have to do what she should have done a long time ago, and resign her position at Eddleston, Breedon and Partners.

There really was no other way out of this agonising mess than to take Ward's own advice and cut and run.

CHAPTER THREE

IT WAS gratifying that once the taxi pulled up on the big sweep of drive outside Ward's large and secluded detached house in a very quiet part of Harrow, and the front door immediately swung open indicating the occupants inside had been watching for the car, it was Jeanie who was the focus of Bobbie's attention.

Jeanie was deeply touched by the little girl's open delight in seeing her again, and as she was led into the house by Bobbie's small hands pulling her along, the child was chattering nineteen to the dozen. 'Monica said you're going to stay for dinner tonight,' Bobbie finished happily, after she had informed Jeanie that it was only one more night after this one—*one*—and then she would be seven years old.

Jeanie assumed—rightly—that Ward had phoned his housekeeper from the office, and now she flashed Monica a quick rueful smile. 'Only if Monica has enough food to go round.'

'Enough to feed an army,' Monica said stoutly. 'Give me your coat and then go and sit by the fire, dear, and get warm. Enough to freeze you out there, isn't it.'

It was nice to be fussed over for a change, very nice, and as Jeanie allowed Bobbie to lead her into the large and luxuriously furnished sitting room she had seen on her previous visit, she saw an enormous log fire burning in the fireplace sending warm flickering shadows dancing about the room, and she remembered the time before—a couple of weeks before Christmas—there had been a huge Christmas tree in the corner of the room. She smiled to herself as she recalled her conversation she'd had with Bobbie.

'What a beautiful tree.' Jeanie had been truly entranced.

Bobbie's face had been bright with excitement as she'd dragged Jeanie across the room, saying, 'Look at the fairy on top of the tree. I made her all by myself.'

Jeanie had looked up at the paper fairy and it had stared back at her stolidly, its squint eyes lopsided and its matchstick arms sticking out of its stomach.

'Daddy says she's the best fairy he's ever seen,' Bobbie had said with earnest pride.

'Oh, I agree, absolutely the best,' Jeanie had agreed. 'What's her name?'

Bobbie had looked up at her steadily, her brown eyes enormous in her heart-shaped face. 'Jeanie,' she'd said expectantly, in the manner of one bestowing an enormous favour.

Jeanie had glanced up at the gargoyle face topped by tinsel hair and then back to the little girl. 'That's my name,' she'd said in tones of great delight and surprise, 'but I'm not as pretty as she is.'

'I think you are,' Bobbie had replied, and then, overcome by sudden shyness, had galloped across to her father and hidden her face in his legs.

Jeanie watched now as Ward lifted the tiny child up into his arms, planting a kiss on the tip of the little snub nose with a naturalness that brought an ache of tenderness to her sore heart. Thin little arms wound immediately round his neck in a fierce bear hug, before Bobbie drew back a fraction and said beguilingly, 'I ate all my tea, Daddy, so can I come down again after my bath?'

'Hmm.' Ward pretended to consider and then glanced across at Jeanie. 'What do you think?' he asked lightly.

'I think that would be great,' she responded just as lightly, wondering if he had any idea of how it made her feel to see the ruthless, cynical, hard lawyer of business hours manoeuvred so willingly by this tiny scrap of nothing.

Monica had appeared in the doorway as they had been speaking, and now she held out her hand to Bobbie as she said, 'Bathtime, young lady.'

'Off you go.' Ward placed his daughter on the floor before ruffling the little head of sleek brown hair. 'I promise Jeanie will still be here when you come down,' he added teasingly as Bobbie scampered out of the room, Monica shutting the door behind them both.

'She's a darling.' With the shutting of the door the atmosphere had changed, the new and disturbing unease that had been in the car on the drive home back with renewed force. She had been so stupid, so utterly *stupid* to invite that kiss, Jeanie chastised herself for the hundredth time, regretting more than she could bear the loss of Ward's past comfortable and relaxed manner with her.

'Yes, she is,' Ward agreed quietly. 'The first couple of years of her life were spent going back and forwards to hospital, and right up until a few months ago the doctors weren't sure how her legs would develop with the injuries she suffered being so severe. But all is well, so they say, so that's good. Some kids would have either become terribly precocious or whiny, or just plain fearful, but she's quite amazingly well-adjusted.'

It was the most he had ever said about what had happened and Jeanie endeavoured to hide her surprise. 'She's had a solid base here with people who love her and a devoted father,' she managed after just the slightest pause. 'That's made a difference I'm sure.'

'Thank you.' He smiled at her but she was aware of a reserve, a distance in the riveting blue eyes that hadn't been there before and again sick self-reproach clawed at her stomach. His friendship had been the most precious thing in her life and now she had lost it through her own foolishness. And yet... Her thoughts raced on as Ward suggested a sherry before dinner and she smiled her acceptance. And yet maybe this was what had been needed to force her to take stock of her life and move on? But how *could* she move on if it meant a life in which she wouldn't see Ward, be able to watch him, hear him, even share a little in his triumphs, and occasionally, the odd case that didn't go quite the way he would have liked it to?

And then she raised her chin a fraction in defiance to the defeatist thoughts. The decision had effectively been taken out of her hands, she reminded herself harshly. Something precious had been lost during those heady moments in the lift when all the longing of five years had come together and she had been in his arms, his mouth on hers. They couldn't go back to how it had been but there was no going forward either. The writing was on the wall. She needed to leave Eddleston and Breedon, and *soon*.

Bobbie had what must have been the fastest bath in history, and was back downstairs in record time looking adorable in matching puppy-dog pyjamas and dressing gown, her tiny feet bare. The limp was more noticeable as she ran across to the sofa where Jeanie was sitting—Ward having seated himself in a chair some feet away—whether due to tiredness or the fact that the child was wearing no footwear, Jeanie wasn't sure.

Whatever, Jeanie found she was more than a little relieved when the small girl appeared; the last few minutes had verged on the painful, and the child's physical vulnerability took away any diffidence and made her open her arms wide as Bobbie wriggled up beside her on the sofa and onto her lap.

Bobbie smelt of talc and baby shampoo, and the overall sweetness of the little girl brought a lump to Jeanie's throat as she cuddled her before saying, 'That was a quick bath, wasn't it?'

'I know,' Bobbie agreed solemnly. 'Monica said Daddy will have to bring you home every day if it makes me so quick.'

Oh yes please.

'An' guess what I've got in my pocket?' Bobbie continued, bringing her packet of cards out of her dressing gown with the air of a conjuror performing a trick.

'Bobbie.' Ward's voice was cautionary. 'Jeanie's worked hard all day and she is tired. She doesn't want to play snap.'

'I don't mind.' Jeanie smiled down into the hopeful little face. 'But if it's anything like last time I shan't win, shall I. You are very good at this game.'

'It's only 'cos I practise,' Bobbie explained earnestly. 'You'd be as good as me if you practised too. You can come and play with me lots more if you want can't she, Daddy?'

The disturbing blue eyes rested lightly on Jeanie and then smiled at the little figure snuggled on her lap. 'Jeanie is a very busy lady,' he said easily.

Yeah right. Well that had told her all too plainly she was as likely to get another invitation to Ward's home as a snowball in hell. Jeanie smiled brightly, refusing to dwell on the hurt as she said to Bobbie, 'Come on then. You deal and we'll see how I get on.'

They played until Monica called them through to the dining room for dinner, Bobbie immediately pleading to be allowed to sit at the table rather than be sent upstairs to bed, her brown eyes beseeching. Jeanie added her own entreaties to that of the child's, and they both received a mock stern glance from Ward as he said, 'Ganging up on me, eh? Okay, if you're good, young lady, because I, for one, don't want indigestion.'

This was too cosy, too intimate, too altogether painfully wonderful to be bearable, Jeanie told herself silently as they walked through to the dining room; Ward carrying Bobbie on his shoulders and making her giggle with delight as he had to bend almost double to fit through the doorways.

Since she had met Ward she had come to heartily despise the person who coined the phrase 'It's better to have loved and lost than never to have loved at all.'

This—tonight, seeing him in his home with his family—was bad enough, but if she'd actually been *loved* by him and then he had walked away or been taken from her, she wouldn't have been able to go on. Perhaps the person in question had never really loved someone with every fibre of their being? Or perhaps it was simply that they'd never come into contact with Ward Ryan? she reflected with dark, self-derisory humour.

By the dessert stage Bobbie was sitting on Ward's lap, settled comfortably in the crook of one arm as he ate his food with a practised ease that told Jeanie Bobbie being allowed to stay up while he ate wasn't an unknown occurrence.

The little girl was fast asleep by the time he finished his last mouthful and Monica came and picked Bobbie up in her arms. 'I'll settle her down and then put the coffee on,' she murmured softly to Ward. 'Why don't you and Jeanie go through to the sitting room and I'll bring you yours in there before I clear up in here?'

'Thanks, Monica.' Ward's voice was relaxed and even, and Jeanie glanced at him with a thread of resentment.

She had been dreading this moment all through Monica's delicious meal, especially in view of the earlier atmosphere when they were alone, but he clearly didn't give a fig. He might have found the incident in the lift briefly embarrassing, and he perhaps was faintly annoyed that the result of it meant he'd lost his staunch ally and dependable, no-nonsense—and most important of all—completely platonic co-worker and friend, but *he* hadn't got his insides turning cartwheels. If she didn't love him so much she'd hate him!

Jeanie drew herself up straight and stared steadily across the table as Monica bustled out with her precious bundle, drawing in a deep breath and letting it out silently before she said calmly, 'That was a wonderful dinner, Ward, and I appreciate your kindness tonight but I really do need to get off home as soon as possible. Perhaps I could borrow your phone and call a taxi?'

He had been in the act of rising from the table and apart from a slight pause continued, walking round to her and drawing back her chair as she stood to her feet, before he said quietly, 'I want to talk to you first, Jeanie.'

Jeanie was taken aback for a moment. She'd expected him to be only too pleased to get rid of her as soon as possible. Her observations through the years, heightened by her love for him, had told her that once something was over for Ward it was over. Be it a personal relationship, a client, a case or whatever, he never indulged in sentiment or futile regrets but finished the matter swiftly and incisively, like the surgeon's scapel. Messy entanglements or complications were not an option with this man; certainly not for himself and where others were concerned she knew it brought irritation at best and scathing condemnation at worst.

The incident in the lift apart, he would be considering her attitude regarding this other man to be the height of folly and her emotional weakness would appal him. She should never, *never* have started this ball rolling. She still could hardly believe she'd been so incredibly stupid.

'I thought you said back at the office that we didn't

have to discuss anything further if I didn't want to?' she reminded him carefully, keeping a check on the tone of her voice. There had been enough emotion flying about for one night and he wouldn't appreciate any more.

'I lied.' It was so unrepentant that for a moment all she could do was to gape at him.

Then her mouth shut with a little snap before opening to say, 'You don't mean...' She took another hidden breath before continuing, 'You aren't saying you got me here under false pretences, are you? That you always intended to question me whether I wanted it or not?'

If she was hoping her terminology would shame him—it didn't. 'That's exactly what I'm saying, Jeanie,' he agreed pleasantly. And he had the audacity to try one of his charming smiles. But she had noticed the hard twist to his mouth and the way the blue eyes were unblinking and as piercing as a razor-sharp blade and she wasn't fooled.

And it was only in that moment that she realised she didn't know Ward as well as she had thought.

CHAPTER FOUR

JEANIE kept a very dignified and cool silence until they were seated in front of the roaring fire. She had found this form of self-protection early on in life when she'd felt out of things and hurt and vulnerable, so it wasn't hard to retreat into the shell now.

The shell cracked a little when, instead of Ward reseating himself in the chair he had vacated before dinner, he chose to sit by her on the sofa. But almost immediately the edges closed again and she presented a calm and neutral face to Ward when he said, his voice carrying what in anyone else but him she would have considered a petulant note, 'All these years we have been friends and I've just realised I don't know you as well as I thought I did.'

It was on the tip of her tongue to tell him she'd just had the same thought about him, but then she bit it back quickly. She knew better than most that Ward was a dangerous adversary and somehow, over the last hours, that was what he had turned into. She had to remember that or suffer the consequences.

Secretly stiffening her spine she forced a cool, faintly surprised smile as she said, 'I'm sure that's not so, Ward.' This was the manner to adopt, she assured herself. The Jeanie he was used to was businesslike and competent; a confident, organised and practical career woman who knew where she was going and how she was going to get there.

The other Jeanie, the one who cried herself to sleep every time she knew he had a date and who was a shivering lovelorn mess inside with passions and desires of such an erotic nature that they even shocked her, had to be kept hidden from him.

'I'm sure it is. Take this boyfriend of yours for instance.'

He was frowning, she noticed, as she risked a quick glance at the hard handsome face before returning her focus on the red and gold flames licking at the partially burnt logs on the fire. Pine logs if the smell was anything to go by. They, added to the warm dancing shadows which gave the room an unbearably intimate, cosy feel, and emphasised hearth and home and everything enduring, didn't help her hammering heart an iota. Neither did she trust her voice to sound anything but weak and trembling.

'Can I ask if this relationship has been going on for a matter of months or longer?' he asked after the seconds had stretched into a minute and neither of them had broken the screaming silence.

'Longer,' she admitted, her voice a study in control.

'*Longer?*' His explosive expression confirmed it was not the answer he had been expecting. 'And you say I know you? Hell, Jeanie, why haven't you mentioned him before, especially if you're so unhappy? And you are unhappy, aren't you,' he added more softly.

'Sometimes.' He was half turned towards her in the semi-darkness, one arm resting on the top of the sofa at the back of her shoulders. He had discarded his suit

jacket and tie before they'd gone in to eat and his shirt
was unbuttoned at the collar, showing a smidgen of
body hair at the base of his throat. The blue silky
material cloaked the powerful male shoulders in a way
that brought his aura of brooding masculinity frighteningly to the fore, emphasising the tough, sensual
quality to his attractiveness in a way that told Jeanie
she didn't dare to look at him again. She just didn't
trust herself not to demand a repeat performance of
the kiss in the lift.

'Sometimes.' It was caustic and her skin shivered
at the tone. 'Most of the time more like. Are the few
hours you spend with him in the average week really
worth all the pain you suffer the rest of the time?'

'Yes.' It was one simple word but he couldn't doubt
the sincerity, and his mouth tightened, his eyes glittering angrily in the flickering firelight.

'He's *using* you, Jeanie. Can't you see that?' he
snapped furiously, before breathing deeply and pat-
ently taking a hold of himself. 'Look—' his voice was
almost insultingly patient '—just try and step back a
pace and look at it reasonably. Bring logic to bear.'

It was so utterly Wardish she could have laughed.
Or cried. Or both. 'Logic has no place in this,' she
said with total honesty. 'And before you say anything
more, I know you're right. He cares about me in his
way, but he'll never marry me, I know that. He doesn't
want commitment or promises of undying love, and
he's not the sort of man to send me a Valentine card
or buy me chocolates or flowers. In fact in all the time
I've known him he's never even remembered St.
Valentine's Day.'

'Valentine's Day?' He stared at her as though she

was mad. 'We are not talking about Valentine's Day for crying out loud. We're discussing you wasting your life on some—' He stopped abruptly, dragging in a hard pull of air. 'On a man who isn't worthy to lick your boots,' he finished grimly.

'How can you say that when you don't know him?' she shot back quickly. 'Surely you know me well enough to realise he must be pretty special if I love him?'

'Jeanie, I don't know you at all,' he ground out angrily. 'You seem to have made up your mind that this man is the be all and end all. You're a young woman, you'll fall in love again if you get rid of him now and give yourself a chance. I hate to talk in clichés but there really are plenty more fish in the sea.'

'There haven't been for you.' It was out before she realised what she had said and she froze immediately, knowing even before she looked at his face that she had gone too far.

He had stiffened, the blue of his eyes arctic, and his lips had a white line of rage round them when he said, 'What exactly does that mean?'

She could have backtracked, made some sort of faltering excuse and played for the sympathy vote, but in the last few moments a spirit of recklessness had taken her over. She was going to go out of his life soon, she had to, she'd made up her mind about that, but suddenly she rebelled against the years of always putting Ward and his feelings first. Of hoping she would become indispensable in some way.

Okay, so soon her time at Eddleston and Breedon would be history, along with her friendship with him, but she was darned if she was creeping out of the picture like a small whipped puppy. If she had to go it was going to be with a bang, not a whimper! She'd had enough of watching what she said and treading on eggshells: he'd asked for the truth and he was going to get it!

'Your...your wife,' she said tremblingly, her voice shaking in spite of all her noble thoughts. 'Since she died it's been like part of you died too.'

'Rubbish,' he grated tightly.

'It's not rubbish.' She knew she should stop but somehow she couldn't.

'I've dated since Patricia died.' It was the first time she had ever heard him say his wife's name and, ridiculously, it hurt hearing it on his lips.

'You might have dated but always strictly on your terms,' she said, hearing the starkness of her words with something like disbelief at her own temerity. 'And you've always chosen a certain type of woman, ones that are on your emotional wavelength and just want a good time for a while with no strings attached.'

'I can't believe I'm hearing this.' She had never seen him so angry and although she longed to stand up and put some distance between them she didn't dare move an inch. 'What gives you the right to think you know anything about me?' he bit out with such fury she actually winced.

'The same right you had when you talked to me about the man I love,' she said bitterly, his words piercing her through like tiny, poison-tipped arrows. 'You think he just wants sex from me with no commitment or responsibility, but you're just the same with your women friends so don't play holier than thou, Ward.'

'Why, you—' His hands tightened on her shoulders as he ran out of words, his blue eyes threatening to burn through her head with the force of his blazing anger. What would have happened then Jeanie didn't like to think, but in the next second there was the unmistakable sound of crockery rattling and then a thump on the sitting room door a second before it swung open.

'Here we are then, a nice pot of coffee,' Monica enthused happily as she trotted in with a trolley. 'And I've put out a plate of those brandy snaps I made to-day, and some shortbread.'

It took a moment more but then Ward's voice was amazingly composed when he said, 'Thank you, Monica. We'll serve ourselves in a minute or two.'

'Right you are. I'll see about clearing the dining room and tidying up in the kitchen, and then I'm to bed if that's all right. I'm a wee bit tired. Bobbie was up at the crack of dawn this morning and I was worried she might come into my room and see the hamster, so we were downstairs having breakfast at six o'clock!'

She beamed at them, completely oblivious to the electric atmosphere, and from somewhere Jeanie found the strength to say fairly normally, 'Before you go I must say thank you again for that wonderful dinner. The ready meal I was going to pop into the microwave tonight can't even begin to compare with it.'

'Go on with you!' But Monica was plainly pleased by the compliment, bustling off with a cheery, 'Good-night then.'

Jeanie waited until the door had closed again and then she said quietly, 'Do you want me to go, Ward?'

A muscle knotted in his cheek. 'Not until we've got a few things straight,' he growled.

In Ward language that meant the other party capitulating and seeing things his way. Five years in close proximity to this man had left her with few illusions, Jeanie reflected wrily, as she poured them both a coffee, handing Ward's to him black and adding sugar and cream to her own before she took a reviving sip. If ever she had needed a shot of caffeine it was now!

'You seem to have a pretty low opinion of me on the whole,' Ward said grimly after a moment or two. 'Could it be that this man is souring you towards the male sex in general?'

The male ego in all its arrogant glory! It couldn't possibly be that there was anything wrong with him or his actions, oh no. 'Not at all,' Jeanie said evenly, holding on to her temper with some effort. 'And I haven't got a low opinion of you, merely a realistic one.'

He glared at her, draining half the cup in one angry swallow without taking his eyes off her pale face. 'How come you haven't given me a list of my failings before super lover came on the scene?' he asked acidly.

'Perhaps because you didn't ask?' she returned succinctly.

'I resent being compared to this low life and found wanting.'

For a moment, a crazy moment, she almost thought there was a thread of what sounded suspiciously like jealousy in his voice before she told herself that was impossible. It was pride she was hearing, injured male ego, a powerfully destructive force all on its own.

'Look, Ward, we seem to have wandered off the beaten track,' she began tightly, only to be interrupted with a startlingness that was as dramatic as it was chilling. There was the sound of a high, drawn-out scream from outside the room followed by the unmistakable bump of a body falling down the stairs amid what sounded like crashing crockery.

Ward was across the room and out of the door before Jeanie had found her feet, and by the time she joined him in the hall it was to see him kneeling by a distraught Monica, who was surrounded by the wreckage of what had obviously been her supper tray which she was taking up to bed. Fragments of china were everywhere, along with thick splashes of what looked like cocoa and bits of shortbread, and a crumpled book with a somewhat lurid cover.

'Where have you hurt yourself?' Ward had one arm under the elderly housekeeper's shoulders, and Jeanie noticed with some concern that Monica's face was as white as a sheet.

'Everywhere.' Monica tried to smile but her lips were quivering too much. 'Oh, Ward, I'm so sorry. I was almost to the top and the wretched book began to slip off the tray and I tried to save it, and the next thing I knew my foot had slipped and I was falling.'

'I've always told you love and romance are more trouble than they're worth.' Ward stroked a strand of grey hair off Monica's brow. 'Just lie still and Jeanie's going to call an ambulance.'

'Oh no, no, please.'

Jeanie ignored Monica's protests and did as Ward had directed, and once the ambulance was on its way hurried upstairs to the airing cupboard on the wide landing and fetched a blanket which she tucked round Monica, blessing the fact that Bobbie seemed to be sleeping through all the trauma.

Monica was crying in earnest now, as much with worry about the proposed birthday party on Sunday as with the pain in her legs, one of which was obviously broken by the look of its twisted position. 'He…he doesn't know how to boil an egg,' Monica sniffed, clutching at Jeanie's hand once she had finished folding the blanket in place, 'let alone sort out food for twenty children and organise a party.'

Ward was trying not to look put out at his housekeeper's marked lack of faith in his prowess as a domestic, but the more he tried to assure Monica all would be well, the more upset the old woman got. 'I've ruined Bobbie's birthday,' she said tearfully. 'That's what I've done.'

'Of course you haven't.' Jeanie added her assurances to those of Ward. 'And please don't worry about Ward and Bobbie any more. If you tell me some of the things you still need to do I can delay leaving London tomorrow until I've helped out here.'

'I thought you had a lunch date,' Ward said softly at the side of her, and it was only then, as she looked into the challenging blue eyes, that she realised he'd assumed her date was with her supposed lover.

'I do but I can cancel it,' she said shortly, some perverse emotion stopping her from disillusioning him. And then she turned to Monica, adding, 'I'll come to the hospital with you while Ward stays here with Bobbie, and you can fill me in on everything I need to know. And it might be that you'll be home again before the night's out anyway,' she said encouragingly, although she didn't think there was any chance of that.

'Bless you, dear.' Monica was white-lipped with pain, but as they heard the ambulance draw up outside Jeanie saw the small plump housekeeper had relaxed slightly, now she knew things were a little more under control again. 'You're heaven sent.'

Jeanie didn't know what made her glance at Ward at that precise point but in the seconds before he rose to go and open the door she saw the narrowed sapphire gaze was very clear and very cold. And she got the impression—probably understandably so in view of their earlier conversation—that 'heaven sent' was not the way Ward would have described her tonight.

But then it never would be. On the ride to the hospital Jeanie found Ward's words to Monica about love and romance being more trouble than they were worth, along with the cavalier way he had dismissed Valentine's Day, burning in her mind. Okay, so perhaps the card industry and the rest of the commercial world made a killing out of Valentine's Day, but that didn't mean it still wasn't great for one to be told how much they were loved on that special day once a year, did it?

She'd had the odd card or bunch of flowers from an admirer in the past of course, and that had created a nice warm feeling, but for the man you adored, the man who meant more than life to send you a card or present, that would be... She ran out of words in her head to express what it would mean if Ward did just that.

But he wouldn't. He didn't even lust over her for a

start, let alone love her, and without the first the second had no chance.

Oh why was she thinking like this now of all times? She came out of her musing with a very real flash of guilt, glancing across at Monica lying on the other side of the ambulance with a paramedic crouched at her side.

There was a time and a place for everything, and right now this was *not* the time to be thinking about Valentine's Day!

CHAPTER FIVE

X-RAYS confirmed the worst. Monica's right leg was broken in two places but the main problem, the consultant in charge of Accident & Emergency explained, was that the breaks were such that Monica would need an operation. It would certainly be a day or two before she was able to go home.

Jeanie telephoned Ward several times to keep him up-to-date with progress, and by the time the long night was over and Monica had been wheeled away to theatre from the little room off the women's surgical ward where she and Jeanie had spent the night, a pale sun was well and truly up in a white, wintery January sky.

Somehow—and Jeanie still wasn't quite sure at what point this had occurred—she had found herself promising an emotional and pathetically vulnerable Monica that she'd step into the breach regarding both the preparations for the birthday party and the organising and running of the actual event. She could see her family the following weekend, she assured the housekeeper.

'I'm going home to crash out for a couple of hours,' she told Ward as she telephoned him for the last time, 'but I'll be back later to do some cooking and ice Bobbie's birthday cake, and I'll come again Sunday and stay to help with the party.' He might not love her, or even be aware of her as a member of the opposite sex, but she was going to take this weekend and savour every moment of it for the rest of her life.

'We'll come and pick you up.' He hadn't made a murmur to the effect of, 'I can't possibly let you do this,' or 'You mustn't alter your arrangements for me,' but—selfish and undeserving ingrate that he was—she didn't care. Somehow, by some miracle, she was going to share part of a special weekend with him, and just the thought of it was intoxicating.

However, once Ward's sleek and very presentable Mercedes drew up on the cobbles outside her little mews house later in the day—after Ward had popped into the hospital and ascertained the operation had been a complete success and the patient was sleeping off the effects of the anaesthetic—Jeanie discovered it wasn't just part of the weekend she was going to share, but all of it.

'It's ridiculous you travelling backwards and forwards when there's a perfectly good guest room,' he said determinedly, Bobbie dancing round them excitedly, utterly beside herself at the prospect of Jeanie coming to stay. 'You must be worn out as it is after last night, I know I am.'

He didn't look worn out, Jeanie reflected silently. He *looked* fantastic. Apart from the time he had had the flu, she'd never seen him dressed casually before, and even then he'd been ensconced on the sofa wrapped in a huge blanket with papers strewn about him, refusing to give in to the virus and go to bed like any normal sensible person would have done.

Today the smart formal suits had given way to black

jeans and a dove-grey turtleneck sweater, a heavy black leather jacket completing the picture of good-enough-to-eat masculinity. Even his hair looked different, the odd curl or two falling across his forehead and softening the severe everyday office formality.

The ruffled hair style was probably due to the weather though, Jeanie reflected, glancing out at the whirling snowflakes before shutting the front door and following Ward and Bobbie into her small open-plan living room cum dining room.

'This is very nice.' Ward was standing in the middle of the light maple wooden floor, and Jeanie had to swallow hard before she could respond. How many times had she imagined the pair of them in here, wrapped in each other's arms on her sofa or lying in front of the fire on her luxuriously soft rug making wild passionate love until the dawn broke? Hundreds. *Thousands.*

'Thank you.' It *was* nice. Tiny, but nice. Because of the smallness of her compact one-bedroomed dwelling place she had kept the colour scheme light and bright, the maple flooring which ran throughout the house being perfectly complemented by the pinky terra-cotta and poppy red shades in her living room and the cream of her small kitchen off the minute hall. The charming bay window and exposed beams in the living room gave a real cottagey feel to the property, and Jeanie had been happy here from day one.

'I wish *I* lived here.' Bobbie was clearly enchanted by the little house which was more her size than Ward's large, five-bedroomed detached house. 'And I like that picture.' The little girl pointed to the framed print over the small fireplace of a polar bear cradling its infant in the warmth of its fur. Little of the mother bear could be seen but the way she had curled round her tiny baby, who was picked out with exquisite detail, had captured Jeanie's heart from the moment she had seen the picture in a frighteningly expensive art gallery a couple of years before.

It had somehow encapsulated all her dreams for the future, of cherishing and being cherished, and in spite of the price tag she had bought it that minute.

She saw Ward staring at it now, and after a few seconds he turned to face her, penetrating blue eyes looking into her soul—or that's what it felt like. And it was extremely uncomfortable.

To cover her confusion Jeanie wrenched her gaze from his and directed it at Bobbie instead, lifting the little girl into her arms as she said smilingly, 'How about you help me decorate your birthday cake when we get home? First we'll ice it, and then you'll have to tell me what you want on the top of it. Your name and your age for sure, but what else?'

Bobbie considered for a moment. 'A hamster.'

'A hamster?' It wasn't what she had expected and she wasn't at all sure she could do rodents!

'Uh-huh, a hamster.' And then Bobbie hugged her tightly. The small, slight body felt terribly fragile and vulnerable in her arms, and as a fierce flood of maternal protectiveness swept over her with shocking suddenness it was all she could do not to close her eyes and groan.

She didn't want to fall in love with this delightful little scrap; she had enough heartache coping with her feelings for Bobbie's father!

By the time Jeanie's small suitcase and overnight

bag had been loaded into the car she had regained her composure. This Good-Samaritan thing probably wasn't the cleverest decision she'd made in her life, but she'd really had little option, she comforted herself silently, as Ward's Mercedes nosed its way through heavy London traffic towards Harrow.

Monica had been so distraught and in such pain she would have promised the elderly woman anything to make her feel better, but besides that she wanted to make sure Bobbie had a good birthday.

And Ward? the honest probing voice of her conscience challenged. He didn't have anything to do with this act of self-sacrifice then?

Well yes, she admitted weakly, and then, in a rush of emotion, he was *everything* to do with it. Her eyes were fixed on the fat swirling feathery flakes of snow falling on the windscreen which the wipers were labouring to sweep away, and which were sending Bobbie—strapped in the back seat—mad with delight, but Jeanie was acutely aware of the big muscled body at the side of her.

The broad shoulders, lean hips and long legs were on the perimeter of her vision but crystal clear on the screen of her mind, every plane and angle of the powerful male anatomy forcing her to acknowledge her overwhelming sexual desire where Ward was concerned.

It was inconvenient and unwelcome as well as downright dangerous, but it was there and she couldn't do a darn thing about it.

'I hope your parents weren't too upset that you had to postpone until next weekend?' Ward said quietly at the side of her.

Jeanie flashed a quick glance at the hard handsome profile before she said, 'No, they understood you needed a hand when I explained the circumstances.'

He nodded slowly. 'And your dinner date?' he asked silkily. 'I trust they weren't too disappointed?'

She didn't answer immediately and his eyes narrowed, but she was contemplating whether to tell him the truth or continue to let Nicki be a man. She decided on the latter. Ward had jumped to conclusions but it was better to let him continue to think what he liked rather than get an inkling of the truth—that *he* was the man she was in love with. 'Not too disappointed, no,' she said finally, her voice dismissive.

He gave her a hard look. 'Good.' The word belied the tone.

'Me an' Daddy made your bed this morning,' Bobbie piped up from the back seat into the awkward silence which followed. 'Daddy let me choose which duvet cover an' I picked the one with poppies on. Do you like poppies?' the little voice asked anxiously.

'Love them,' Jeanie answered warmly. 'They're my favourite flowers along with freesias because freesias smell nice.' She was pleased her voice was so natural because the thought of Ward making her bed had sent a shiver straight into the core of her.

'An' Daddy put the 'lectric blanket on to make the bed nice and warm,' Bobbie added earnestly.

'Thank you.' The car had just pulled up at red traffic lights and she glanced at him as burdened shoppers staggered across the crossing in front of them.

'You're welcome.' The devastating blue gaze had been waiting for her. 'Please feel free to call on any personal services you'd like me to perform during your stay,' he said smoothly, his mouth curving slightly as blue eyes witnessed the startled widening of brown.

He was *flirting* with her? Jeanie's brain suddenly scrambled and she couldn't think of a single thing to say in reply. No, she must have been mistaken. Or did he think—now she had told him about this other man and then responded to him like she had in the lift— that she was in the market for a little sexual comforting? A cosy weekend in every sense of the word? Poor Jeanie, I'll do her a favour type thinking?

And then she immediately felt mortified. Ward wasn't like that; he would no more take advantage of someone in her situation to satisfy his own needs and desires than fly to the moon. He might date women who knew the score and were as tough as he was in the no commitment regard, but he wasn't cruel or selfobsessed.

Over the years she had watched him choose women who would leave him with a smile and maybe just a smidgen of brief regret when the affair ended. And from what she had revealed about this 'other man' he knew she was a woman who desired much more than that.

He was merely being gallant, she decided at last as they neared the outskirts of Harrow. And after the caustic conversation of the night before she ought to be glad he had resorted to teasing friendliness. It was her wicked mind that had taken his attitude a step further; the longings and desires of her subconscious taking over. She'd have to watch that over the next few days.

Nevertheless, she couldn't quite quell the faint un-

easy excitement that had started deep inside however
much she reproached herself for her carnality. Just being within three feet of Ward had always had the
power to turn her into a fluttering sixteen-year-old
schoolgirl inside, but with wants and needs that were
very grown-up!

Their relationship had always been one of calm and
friendly courtesy but over the last twenty-four hours
that had been blown to smithereens. He had seen a
side to her that obviously annoyed and appalled him,
and she had seen her normally smooth, controlled and
rather cold work colleague so angry she'd thought he
was going to strike her in those moments before
Monica had brought the coffee last night. Not that he
would have, she was sure.

As they drew into the driveway of Ward's home
Jeanie realised she had been lost in thought for miles
and that Bobbie was fast asleep in the back seat. 'Poor
little mite.' She drew round from glancing at the sleeping child with a tender smile still softening her lips.
'She's already worn out with excitement. Oh to be that
age again when a birthday has the power to thrill so
much.'

'Thanks for doing this, Jeanie.' His voice was deep
and sincere, and as her eyes met his he turned off the
engine and twisted in his seat to face her. 'You've
made Bobbie's day—in fact her weekend—in coming
to stay. 'You know that, don't you.'

Bobbie's, but not his. Jeanie smiled brightly. 'What
else are friends for?' she said steadily.

Why did he have to look so gorgeous? Why was
she such a mess inside? *Why did she love him so
much?* It wasn't fair, none of this was fair. Why

couldn't she have been born a beauty, the sort of woman who would send him crazy with desire? Like Patricia, his dead wife, who still had claim to his heart and his life, and whom he had loved so utterly that it had spoilt him for anyone else.

'This is beyond the call of friendship but I do appreciate it.'

She stared at him, her eyes dark as she struggled to hide what his closeness was doing to her, and then, like that time before in the lift, they were in another world.

'Your eyes are like warm honey. Why haven't I noticed that before?' he murmured softly, his hand lifting to take a lock of her hair before letting the blue black strands slip through his fingers like shimmering silk. 'And your hair, it's the most beautiful thing I've ever seen. Any other woman would flaunt such an asset every day, but you hide it away. Why, Jeanie?'

'I... I told you.' It was too breathless but she couldn't help it. Her stomach was going over and over and her heart was thudding so hard she felt faint. 'It's not suitable for the office loose.'

'Do you wear it loose for him?'

'What?' To her mortification she felt herself blushing furiously.

'Him. The rat. The damn fool who doesn't know what he's got,' he said huskily. 'Do you wear it loose for him? But of course you do,' he answered himself softly. 'It must make him feel like a sultan, a god, to see what other men are not allowed to see.'

'You're seeing it,' she managed faintly.

'Yes I am, aren't I.' His smile was crooked. 'Would he mind?' His voice dropped an octave as his eyes narrowed still more. 'And did you tell him that we kissed when you said you couldn't see him today, Jeanie? And that you'll be living in my house—with me—this weekend?' he asked with silky intent.

Jeanie felt utterly trapped, and she shielded her panic by lowering her thick black lashes as she realised, too late, that she should have ended this conversation firmly and politely aeons ago. 'He knows exactly what happened.'

'And he still let you come here with me?'

'Of course,' she said, nervousness making her voice stiff. 'He knows we're friends, nothing more.'

'He either trusts you to the point of stupidity or his ego is jumbo size,' Ward pronounced flatly. 'Either way he doesn't deserve you. And you know that, you must know it deep, deep inside even if you won't admit it to me. I've seen you with Bobbie; you'd make a wonderful mother and if you hang around for this guy you're going to lose any chance of having a marriage and a husband who really loves you.'

She swallowed hard. If he didn't stop she was going to cry, she thought brokenly.

'You accused me of being like him yesterday and of acting holier than thou,' Ward went on as the snowflakes settled like a thick white blanket over the windscreen and windows and locked them into a silent silvery world. 'But you forgot one important thing, Jeanie.'

'What?' From somewhere inside she didn't know existed she found the strength to raise a composed face to his.

'The women I date know the score,' he said roughly, 'from day one. I make sure of that. I also make sure that if there's the slightest indication their feelings are changing, that they're getting attached to me, I finish it immediately. This guy isn't playing fair, Jeanie, whatever you say in his defence. If he can't love you like you want and deserve he should let you go for someone who can. *Make* you accept it. Sometimes you have to be cruel to be kind.'

She couldn't take any more of this. 'It's me who wants to keep things the way they are,' she said flatly. 'Not him. I'm the one who won't let go.'

'Then I'll have to make you see that however good he is in bed and however much you think life after rat doesn't exist, you're wrong,' he rasped suddenly. 'If you can kiss me like you did yesterday, I know you can learn to love someone else. Oh, okay, you might have been tipsy and emotionally exhausted with every defence down, but hell, I was there, Jeanie, and I've got enough experience to know what I'm talking about.'

She knew that. She knew *that* all right.

She was still reflecting on his last words when his mouth came down on hers, and in a second it was too late to even think of resisting. She was taking in the scent of him, the feel of his lips as he stroked hers open and then plunged into the territory beyond and it was heady, thrilling, absolutely mind blowing. And crazy and stupid and dangerous...

The need inside her was so sharp, so hungry that it was part pain, part pleasure but totally unstoppable. He was holding her closely and securely but not so tightly she couldn't have jerked away if she'd a mind to, but her mind was his. It always had been.

His tongue was probing her mouth and sending

flickers of fire radiating into every nerve and sinew, melting her limbs and causing her to become fluid in his arms. She could feel the warmth of him through the rough wool of his sweater, the sensation of leather as her hands moved up and over his shoulders to tangle in his hair as she hungrily searched his mouth for more.

And then they heard Bobbie stir behind them and his mouth rose slowly, regretfully from hers, before he dropped one last lingering kiss on the tip of her nose and settled back in his seat.

'See?' he said very softly, his gaze holding her wide dazed one in the second before he turned to his daughter. 'You underestimate your power of survival after rat, Jeanie.'

CHAPTER SIX

CONSIDERING the state of her emotions Jeanie thought she did very well throughout the rest of the day.

It had been just after three when they had arrived back at Ward's house, and after her brief nap Bobbie was twice as excited and virtually on springs.

The snow had settled well and was coming down even thicker and Bobbie was desperate to build a snowman in the garden, so while Jeanie fixed a quick mid-afternoon snack of hot chocolate and muffins before the three of them went out, Ward telephoned the hospital again for news of Monica.

The sister on the housekeeper's ward informed him Monica was still sleeping and wouldn't really rouse until later that evening, but Ward was more than welcome to pop in for just a few minutes then if he liked? Ward did like and said so. 'And tell her not to worry when she's compos mentis, would you,' he added quietly. 'And that we love her and miss her of course.'

'I think she'll realise that when she wakes up, Mr. Ryan,' the sister said drily. 'We can barely find the patient for the amount of flowers surrounding her bed.'

Ward was grinning as he put down the receiver and when Jeanie asked why and he repeated the conversation, she smiled too. But inside she found she was envying Monica, poorly as she was, with all her heart.

Ward obviously cared deeply for the elderly woman and looked on her as part of his family, a second mother in effect, and when she said as much Ward nodded slowly.

He glanced at Bobbie who was eating her muffin perched on a stool by the kitchen window as she looked out at the snow, and seeing his daughter was oblivious to them he said quietly, 'Monica has been more of a mother to me, and more of a grandmother to Bobbie, than my own mother has even been. She and my father never wanted children... I was the pro-verbial 'mistake,' and although they were never un-kind and very supportive in their own way, there was no natural parental warmth there.'

She stared at him, sensing the well of hurt beneath the brief explanation. 'I'm sorry, Ward,' she said softly. 'I didn't mean to pry.'

'I know that.' He shrugged slowly. 'And it doesn't matter now. I make the odd duty call two or three times a year to show them their granddaughter, and they are very patient and polite until we're gone. There's no animosity on either side.'

So he had always had to rely on himself from a small child. This explained so much about him, Jeanie thought, not least the total devotion and love he had given his dead wife.

'What do they do? Does your mother work?' she asked carefully, struggling not to show what the thought of Ward as a lonely, isolated bewildered child and self-sufficient, independent teenager did to her.

'Very much so,' he said cynically. 'My mother is a quite brilliant chemist involved in food science research, and my father is an ophthalmic medical practitioner with his own private practice.'

Two highly intelligent and gifted individuals who obviously hadn't had the first clue about bringing up their equally intelligent and gifted son. How tragic. Jeanie could have cried.

'*Daddy.*' The childish treble was irate. 'You haven't even *started* on your muffin and it will be dark soon. *Hurry up.*'

They both turned to look at the diminutive figure perched by the window and Jeanie saw Ward's expression change as he surveyed the little face frowning back at him. How he loved Bobbie, Jeanie thought with a big lump in her throat. And what a blessing the child must have been to him when his wife was killed so tragically. The little girl must be a precious reflection of the brief year or two of happiness he had with her beautiful mother, a pocket-sized reminder of the seemingly perfect union that he'd enjoyed with Patricia. How could she—how could *anyone*—begin to compete with a relationship that memories would have enhanced with an even rosier glow?

And then she shook off the dark cloud that was threatening to settle with a determination that was an integral part of her character. This was a special weekend and even the elements had conspired to make it magical; the white scene outside the window unbearably lovely. She was not going to mope for one minute throughout what was left of it, but take every precious moment as a gift. She'd cope with the aftermath—when she walked out of heaven—when she had to.

They had great fun building a snowman, partly because the snow wasn't really deep enough for the job and Ward made Bobbie shriek with feverish excitement as he made a great play of scraping up every morsel; shaking the branches of the trees so a cloud of white descended on them all and sent Bobbie wild with glee.

At one point, as the tiny child rolled in the snow like a small puppy, they both stood looking at her convulsed with laughter. When Jeanie felt Ward's arm slip casually round her shoulders she steeled herself to show no reaction and treat it as the natural, friendly gesture he meant it to be, but immediately the moment heightened with painful poignancy.

The winter wonderland of the garden, the hundreds and thousands of big fat feathery flakes descending from the laden sky, the small snowman with his borrowed hat and scarf and the excited child, and Ward— *Ward*—became bitter-sweet.

They could be any old married couple standing here like this, she couldn't help torturing herself by thinking. Standing close together and linked by the tenderness of the moment as they watched their child playing so happily in the snow. But Bobbie *wasn't* her child and Ward—what was Ward exactly?

Not just a work colleague—they had gone beyond that some time ago, but friend? She couldn't think of him in that light, she never had. She wanted more, much more than mere friendship from this man, and she could never go back to the months and years before that breathtaking moment in the lift. So what was he?

Everything she had to leave behind.

'I think we've done our stint out here, don't you?' He grinned down at her, stunningly handsome with his hair wet and daring to curl slightly and as far removed from the Ward of office hours as the man in the moon. 'Hopefully that's worked off some of her excess energy,' he added wrily, nodding at Bobbie, who had stood to her feet and was now brushing the snow off the frozen bird bath with one encrusted mitten.

Jeanie smiled back but she didn't trust herself to speak. Not with his arm still round her. And then he bent and deposited a swift kiss on her surprised lips. 'Sorry but you look like a small abandoned Rudolph with your red nose,' he said lightly as she stepped back a pace in instinctive retreat.

'It's...it's cold,' she said breathlessly.

He nodded, the somewhat disparaging content to his words negated by the look in his eyes as they wandered over her flushed face and bright eyes beneath the scarlet woollen cap she'd pulled over her ears. And then he reached out and drew her against him again, tucking her hands inside the warmth of his jacket as he said softly, 'Let me warm you.'

She could feel the hard steady beat of his heart beneath the wool under her nerveless fingers, the faintly delicious smell of him surrounding her intoxicatingly. 'My gloves are wet,' she protested weakly.

'I don't care.'

His face was quite unreadable but then it mostly was. 'We ought to get Bobbie in for a hot bath,' she managed at last, knowing if she stayed for one more second in this position with his arms round her waist and her hands against the wall of his chest, all her resolve would melt and she'd be virtually begging him to kiss her again.

'It's all right, Jeanie, you're quite safe,' he said

mockingly. 'I'm not about to drag you into the under-growth and have my wicked way with you. Bobbie is a small but very adequate chaperone.'

More's the pity. 'I didn't think for a moment any-thing like that had entered your mind,' she said with an indignance which carried the unmistakable ring of truth. Now the possibility of it being the other way round...

'No? Why?' He was suddenly put out and she was astonished.

'Because you're not like that,' she said innocently.

'Like what? Red-blooded, virile?'

'I didn't mean—'

'Is *he* like that, Jeanie? Macho man? A vigorous Ramboesque type whose brains are situated consider-ably lower than his head?' he snapped tightly, his eyes taking on an arctic silveriness which made the blue all the more amazing.

She stared at him, utterly astounded. Why was he taking this tack and was it—could it possibly be—*jealousy* in his voice? she asked herself faintly. But no, that was ridiculous and she knew it. She had known Ward for five years and in all that time he had invariably treated her as a friend, a pal, a buddy. He liked her, cared for her even in his way and he didn't want to see her hurt by this other man, but jealousy? Jealousy was a whole different ball game. And the emotional undercurrents of such imaginings were far too dangerous to risk even putting a toe in.

She took a deep hidden breath and tried to answer him as calmly as she could considering he was still holding her, and his touch always had the power to make her melt. Even sharing a coffee break at work had been fraught with danger due to it resulting in her being a quivering wreck for minutes afterwards. '*He* is a very intelligent and articulate human being,' she said reprovingly. 'And I only meant that we're friends, Ward, and I trust you implicitly,' she added, fully expecting that to do the trick.

Instead his frown deepened to a scowl. 'You're still locked into this guy like a nuclear missile, aren't you,' he ground out irritably, 'unable to see the wood for the trees.'

Yes, yes, yes. Always had been, always would be. 'Not at all,' she lied decorously, and then felt bereft when he unceremoniously moved her away from him, swearing softly under his breath as he turned away and began to walk towards Bobbie who was now busy wiping every little single flake of snow off the remnants of the muffins Jeanie had put on the bird table.

She stood where he had left her, a great heaviness on her heart. Control. That's what all that had been about. And there was more than a touch of the machiavellian to Ward at times. The more she got to know him away from the office the less she knew him it seemed. And now he was in a filthy fit and the evening would be ruined—

'Come on, dreamer.' He was standing in front of her again, Bobbie in his arms and the crystal eyes as clear as a blue sky, his mouth smiling. 'This one needs a bath, and while I'm seeing to the little Snow Queen you're going to put your feet up in front of the fire with a nice glass of wine, and relax.'

She stared back into the enigmatic face in surprise, aware however much he was smiling there was more going on behind that lethal blue gaze than Ward was

prepared to let on. He was inscrutable, she decided
with a touch of anger. Inscrutable and perplexing and
unfathomable, and if she didn't love him so much he
was just the sort of man she would loathe!

'I need to do some things for the party,' she said
flatly. 'And then organise dinner for tonight. And
there's the cake—'

'We'll sort out the cake and stuff later, but Bobbie
and I have been talking, haven't we, sweetheart?'
Ward added to the little girl in his arms who nodded,
her face bright as she giggled. 'And we have decided
it's baked potatoes in their jackets with sour cream
and cold meats for tonight, all of which we are quite
capable of dealing with. So, go and relax for a while,
Jeanie. Okay? I'll bring you a glass of wine before we
go up.'

Why did he have to do this? Why did this big, definitely ruthless and often aggressive male have to
stroke and soothe her frayed nerves with that sexy,
smoky voice? It made her forget to be annoyed and
want to purr like a kitten instead. 'I don't think—'

He slanted an amazingly sensual look at her from
under half-closed lids, that she was sure he was unaware of but made her toes curl into tight little pads.
'It's an order, not a suggestion,' he said silkily.

'But—'

'Bobbie and I are aware of how you've had to alter
your plans at a moment's notice to look after us, and
we intend to do our share, okay? You can be the general and we'll obey orders.' He turned his glance from
her to Bobbie. 'Right cupcake?'

Bobbie nodded vigorously, her arms tight round her
daddy's neck. Jeanie gave up. She knew when she was

defeated and actually the thought of a few minutes relaxation after the turmoil and pace of the last twenty-four hours was incredibly tempting. She had tried to catch a few hours sleep after leaving the hospital earlier that morning, but her mind had been a seething mass that just wouldn't turn off and she had only managed an hour or two of light dozing that had left her feeling more tired than before she'd gone to bed.

Once seated in front of the roaring log fire on one of the beautifully deep and soft sofas in Ward's gorgeous sitting room, a glass of deep red wine at her elbow and her head resting on plump cushions, Jeanie stretched luxuriously. Ward had switched on the TV before he'd taken Bobbie for her bath, and now the low drone of some quiz show or other provided a backdrop to her thoughts.

She had never dreamt, not even in her wildest imaginings, that something like this weekend would ever happen. But it had, it had. She was here, in Ward's home, sharing his daughter's birthday and that was a miracle for a start. Why couldn't another miracle happen, that of Ward falling in love with her?

It wouldn't happen, it could never happen given Ward's slant on the female of the species since Patricia's death, but she could pray for a miracle nevertheless, couldn't she? Nothing else had worked! 'Please, God,' she whispered softly into the gently flickering shadows of the darkened room, lit only by the fire and the light from the TV screen, 'please *please* make him love me. I don't care how long it takes—' She stopped abruptly. 'Well, yes I do, God, I can't help it. Please let it be soon.'

She took several sips of the blackcurrant wine that

smelt richly of spices and oak, and surveyed the tiny orange flames licking round the pine log which Ward had helped Bobbie place on the fire with due ceremony before they had disappeared.

She loved him, unequivocally and absolutely, and for the moment she was too tired to think beyond that. The future, with its looming goodbyes and black hole of desolation was far away and tonight there was just warmth and colour and a numbing lassitude. Jeanie closed her eyes, her lids too heavy to fight the exhaustion a second longer, and within moments she was fast asleep.

The kiss was coaxing and persuasive, teasing her lips open with a lazy eroticism that spoke of experience and finesse before moving to her eyelids and then her throat in burning hot, feathery kisses that sent her blood racing through her veins in a flood of hot sensation.

She had been dreaming, she knew she had been dreaming but she also realised that the kiss was not part of the dream. It was real. And if she opened her eyes it would finish. So...she didn't open her eyes. She just kissed Ward back with a hunger and a passion she could never show normally.

She heard him make a sound of pleasure low in his throat and her body echoed the sound, responding to the age-old mating call with a desire that would have shocked her if she'd been thinking rationally. But she wasn't thinking rationally; that had stopped the moment his hard firm lips had met her mouth.

He could arouse her so easily without touching her; one look, one glance often bringing her senses to fever pitch at the office where she was supposed to be prim, respectable Miss Potter, and it hadn't helped her feeling of humiliation that he'd been completely unaware of her body's traitorous response to his sensual attraction.

His mouth was covering hers again and she knew she couldn't hope to make the moment last any longer; it would be taking credibility a mite too far and Ward was no fool. She stirred, shifting on the sofa and moving her hands and the lips lifted from hers. She opened her eyes.

'Sleeping Beauty.' His face was just an inch or so away from hers and he was making no effort to pretend he hadn't kissed her. 'I could never understand why the prince would bother to fight his way through all the snares and perils just for a kiss, but I think I understand now. Years ago when I was a boy, before life and the ugliness of the real world got in the way, I used to think what it'd be like to kiss this girl or that, and in those innocent days the imaginings never went beyond that first kiss.'

'And then?' she asked softly.

'Then I grew up,' he said quietly. 'I learnt all about the games lovers play, about how there is always a winner and a loser, and that gentleness and consideration and love can be seen as weakness and used as weapons.'

So he had been hurt by a woman in the days before he had met his wife. Which would have made him love Patricia and their child even more. Jeanie couldn't speak at all. She was afraid that if she even breathed he would withdraw again. She was seeing a side to Ward she had always suspected was there and it was as fascinating as it was disturbing.

And then light running footsteps sounded outside and Ward straightened just as Bobbie came bursting into the room calling, 'I'm in my 'jamas, Daddy! And I was *really* quick. I'm a good girl, aren't I?'

'Pretty good,' Ward confirmed lazily with a teasing smile.

'Good enough for a hamster?' Bobbie asked fervently. 'A golden one with little hands and everything, like Gemma Prichards at school?'

'Ah, now that's for you to find out tomorrow.' Ward ruffled Bobbie's hair before adding, 'But now we need to serve dinner, yes? Let's go and see how the baked potatoes are getting on, shall we, because you can't be too late to bed tonight. It's going to be a busy day tomorrow, and you know why, don't you?'

'My birthday party!'

Jeanie managed to catch Ward's eye as Bobbie danced out into the hall in front of him, and to her mouthed 'Golden?' he replied with a nod and a pursing of his lips which denoted extreme relief.

How would she be able to bear all the weekends which followed this one? Jeanie asked herself when she was alone again. She sipped at her wine, looking deep into the fire.

But perhaps, just maybe, this new relationship with Ward might lead to something else? Especially when she left Eddleston and Breedon and they weren't work colleagues anymore? Ward was scathing about office romances, but if she had left…

Pipe dreams. She sat up straighter as the words hammered home. Born of the circumstances, the wine, and not least her low defences. Just because he'd kissed her as though he enjoyed it she couldn't forget what he was like. Commitment or a long-term relationship was not on Ward's agenda, and she would have no excuse if she tried to convince herself otherwise on the strength of a couple of kisses.

Earlier today in the car when they had been sitting talking outside the house, he had made it as clear as ever how he saw things. 'The women I date know the score from day one.' The words had burnt into her subconscious and were now crystal clear without any mind searching.

'I also make sure if there's the slightest indication their feelings are changing and they're getting attached to me, I finish it immediately.' That was what he had said just hours ago and she forgot it at her peril.

And he'd also said something about making her see that life would go on if she finished with this man. His kisses, the way he'd looked at her once or twice, were just to prove she could be sexually attracted to someone other than her lover and therefore back in the market for a new relationship in the future which would possibly provide her with the degree of commitment she needed.

Such reasoning would be perfectly logical and acceptable to Ward, Jeanie thought bitterly. A successful solution to a problem which had been presented to him. But she wasn't one of his cases waiting to be stamped, concluded and locked away in his filing cabinet.

She narrowed her eyes at the dancing flames and finished the last of her wine with one big gulp. She was flesh and blood with a mind of her own, that's what she was, and if she thought about it it was downright insulting of Ward to assume she could fall out of love so easily, even if he was acting—as he thought—in her best interests.

Oh, she was sick of thinking about the whole thing! She frowned ferociously into the inoffensive fire, sighing irritably. And she was not going to do it any more. Once the meal was over and Bobbie was tucked up in bed, she would sort out a few things regarding the party but make sure she was upstairs in her own room before Ward returned from visiting Monica at the hospital. Her mind didn't feel as though it belonged to her today, and she needed some solid uninterrupted hours of rest to steady her shaky equilibrium.

She loved Ward, she would always love him, but he had to be the most annoying, arrogant, *unshakable* man in the whole wide world!

CHAPTER SEVEN

ALMOST eight hours of deep dreamless sleep worked wonders, and when Jeanie awoke early the next morning to the sound of excited shrieks from Bobbie's room next door to the luxurious guest room she was occupying, she found herself smiling at the sound. The next moment the door to her room was flung open and a small, brown-haired and wide-eyed human missile launched itself onto the bed, Bobbie's whole body wriggling in ecstasy as she cried, 'Come and see! Come and see my hamster. Oh I love her, I just love her.'

'She's the colour you wanted then?' Jeanie sat up against the pillows, brushing the hair out of her eyes as Bobbie bounced on the bed at the side of her with enough energy for ten children. The question was rhetorical; once Bobbie had been fast asleep the night before and just before Ward left to see Monica, they had crept into Bobbie's room, positioning the cage and its precious occupant on the small chest of drawers in a corner of the room. But Jeanie didn't want to spoil Bobbie's pleasure in showing her the new pet by letting the child think she had already seen it.

Bobbie had looked impossibly angelic the night before, curled under the covers and fast asleep with one arm round her teddy bear. Jeanie had stood with Ward and gazed at the sleeping child for a moment or two, and when she'd thought of all the little girl had gone through in her short life—not least losing her mother before she had ever known her—she'd found she'd had tears in her eyes once she and Ward were outside on the landing again, and the door to Bobbie's room was shut.

She had struggled not to show her emotion, gulping once or twice and breathing deeply as she'd endeavoured to keep the tears at bay, but the sight of the small child cuddled up to the frayed, somewhat shabby and obviously well-loved bear was heart-wrenching.

'What is it?' Ward had lifted her chin in the subdued light as he had caught the glitter of tears in her eyes.

Jeanie had almost shivered as his flesh had made contact with hers but had controlled the instinctive response of her body to his just in time. The little heart-to-heart she'd had with herself before dinner was still with her and strengthened her resolve, and now she spoke quietly as she stepped back a pace away from his body warmth. 'I was just thinking how vulnerable she is and how brave she's been. You must be very proud of your daughter, Ward.'

'Yes, I am,' he said softly, watching her with that penetrating gaze that was so much a part of him, and which was more than a little unnerving at times. 'Bobbie is one in a million.'

Like her mother had been. The thought brought Jeanie's chin up and stiffened her spine, and her voice was even and flat when she said, 'Thank you for letting me share such a special moment in there. Now I mustn't keep you. You must be wanting to get off and see Monica.'

'Must I?' he asked slowly, a quirk to his mouth.

'And I've got masses to do for the party,' Jeanie said briskly, taking another step backwards and then turning for the stairs. She spoke over her shoulder as she said, 'There are all the party bags for the children to take home to make up for a start. Monica has bought little bead bracelets and sweets and party blowers and all sorts to put in them.'

'Clever Monica.' They were downstairs in the hall now, and he smiled in the slow, sexy way that always sent her hormones flying into confusion as she glanced at him. 'Never mind, there's always tomorrow night to look forward to.'

Jeanie's eyes jerked away from his. She was sure he hadn't meant his words the way her sinful heart had taken them, but suddenly the wonderfully seductive image of the big plump sofa pulled close to the flickering fire and two naked bodies entwined on the soft cushions had been so real it had turned her face scarlet. 'Yes. That's…that's all right then. I…' She made a huge effort and pulled herself together. 'I'll see you in the morning, Ward,' she managed fairly coherently.

Ward was surveying her thoughtfully when she met his eyes again but he had said nothing more, merely nodding, his crystal blue gaze silvery and unblinking and his uneven mouth curved in a way that made her wonder what he was thinking.

Jeanie had got ready for bed in just a couple of minutes, too tired for more than just a cursory wash, and immediately her head had touched the pillow she had been asleep. And if she had dreamt at all she couldn't remember it, she thought now, as Bobbie tested the springs of the bed with gusto, knocking off Jeanie's little travel alarm in the process.

'Hey, where are the herd of elephants that I can hear stampeding around?'

Jeanie was just throwing back the covers to reach for her robe on a chair nearby when the deep male voice from the doorway made her give a little squeak of surprise and drag them up to her chin.

Bobbie immediately threw herself off the bed and sprang over to her father, whereupon she was whisked up into his arms in a way Jeanie could only envy as she stared over the top of the duvet, letting her tousled hair fall about her face to hide the hot tide of sensation flushing her cheeks.

As Bobbie thanked Ward over and over again for the hamster, Jeanie drank him in, eternally grateful she didn't have to trust her legs to hold her up. Clothed Ward was pretty amazing but clad only in black cotton pyjama bottoms and an open matching robe, he was out of this world for pure, flagrant and uncompromising maleness.

He'd obviously just got out of bed, his black hair ruffled and the sexy stubble on his chin indicating he hadn't had a shave yet, but it was the acres—or that's what it seemed like to Jeanie's feverish mind—of bare flesh beneath his chin that was causing problems with her breathing.

The open robe showed his torso to be thickly muscled, the black body hair on his chest narrowing to a thin line as it disappeared into the pyjama bottoms, and he was lean and tanned and magnificently pow-

erful. He looked tough and sensual, his body possessed
of a lithe, hard masculinity that was a fascinating challenge in itself.

Jeanie swallowed hard. She hadn't bargained for
this. Stupid maybe, but she'd expected—if she'd
thought about it at all which she had to admit she
hadn't really—that they would all leave their rooms
dressed and groomed for the day. A nice, tidy, no one
infringing on anyone else's privacy type of affair. She
might have guessed Ward wouldn't play by the rules.
What was she saying? The man wasn't even aware
there *were* any rules!

'Good morning, Jeanie.' His voice was mortifyingly
casual which made her lobster red face all the more
embarrassing. 'Did you sleep well?' he asked over
Bobbie's urging to come and see Suzy—as the small
rodent was now named.

'Fine, thank you.' It had taken a moment or two but
she was rather pleased how normal her voice sounded
when she at last got her vocal cords in working order.

'Excellent.' He smiled, and she wondered if he
knew how sexy the fullness of his bottom lip was.

'Can we open the rest of my presents and cards
now, Daddy?' Bobbie clearly wasn't in the mood for
social pleasantries. 'I can bring Suzy and we could sit
on your bed.' The child turned to Jeanie with a bright
innocent smile, holding out one little hand invitingly.
'Come on, there's room in Daddy's bed for you.'

Jeanie raised her drowning eyes to Ward and saw
he was looking vastly amused. She thought she heard
him murmur, 'Out of the mouths of babes,' as he bent
down and placed the small child on her feet, but decided in the next moment she must have misheard

when he sent Bobbie skipping off to her room with a promise that he'd be along directly, but they would be opening the presents and cards downstairs.

'I hope it isn't broken.'

'What?' She knew she was still staring at him mesmerised but she couldn't help it, and then, when he indicated the alarm clock on the carpet at the side of the bed she nodded weakly. 'Oh, I'm sure it's all right,' she said quickly, wishing he would just *go* so she could come out from under the covers and at least have the protection of her thick fleecy robe between those devastatingly experienced eyes and her gossamer-thin nightie.

And then her heart stopped beating, every muscle in her body tensing as he stepped inside the room and walked across the floor towards the bed, his stance easy and relaxed and his bare feet sure-footed. She watched him as he retrieved the small clock and placed it on the bedside cabinet, her eyes wide and the blood racing and roaring in her ears. And then she was conscious of the blue eyes surveying her, his voice husky as he said, 'You're a different woman to the one I've known for five years.'

She had dreamt of him saying something similar for all the years she'd been in love with him. She had pictured them at a small, discreetly elegant restaurant seated in a quiet alcove, and Ward looking at her and seeing her with new eyes. Or maybe at some function or other which all the junior partners were expected to attend now and again. Or— Oh, the list was endless, she admitted desperately, but never, not once in all her wildest imaginings, had she thought it would be when she was without a scrap of make-up and looking like something the cat had dragged in! No wonder he thought she looked different to the perfectly groomed, cool and very controlled Jeanie Potter of business hours!

'Different as in a mess?' she said with as much lightness as she could muster.

'No, different as in beautiful,' he corrected softly. 'A real fairy tale Sleeping Beauty.' He lifted up a lock of her silky hair, his eyes slumberous.

'I'm not beautiful,' she said flatly, forcing her voice to betray none of the panicky excitement and longing that was gripping her. This was just Ward being nice, that's all. He probably assumed that her ego had taken something of a beating in the last little while. 'And I'm wide awake.'

'Don't argue.' He bent and took her lips, and right from the moment his mouth touched hers this kiss was as different to the others as chalk to cheese. It was hot and heady and urgent, a fierce assault on her senses that took without asking permission and with a deep passion that spoke of arousal and need.

He had sat down on the bed, his hands firm and strong as he'd reached out and pulled her against his bare chest so she was half lying across him, and as the duvet fell away to expose the soft creamy swell of her breasts under their flimsy covering of pale jade silk, the kiss deepened abruptly.

She could feel his heart pounding like a sledgehammer and in the position in which she was lying his body told her all too plainly he was aroused, the thin cotton of his pyjamas hiding nothing.

This wasn't pity. It might not be for everness or a passion that would last beyond the few months which was Ward's normal time span for involvement with a member of the opposite sex, but whatever, pity wouldn't have him breathing hard and his body tense and rigid against her softness. The knowledge swam in her mind, and as his hands moved over her slender shoulders, stroking the pure clean line of her throat before moving to the rounded globes beneath, she answered his desire with passion equal to his own.

'Now do you believe me when I say you're beautiful?' he said roughly a second after Bobbie's voice had called them again. 'Prim and proper at the office with not a hair out of place and looking as though butter wouldn't melt in your mouth, and now... Now...'

'What?' she asked shakily, knowing he would have to leave in a moment, that they would both have to share the morning with Bobbie.

'Now you're a black-haired siren who's threatening to send me mad,' he said huskily. 'I want you, Jeanie. I can't help it. It might not be what you want to hear right now but it's the truth, so help me.'

Want. Sexual need. An animal kind of hunger. All those but not a word of love. But of course there wouldn't be, she knew that—*she knew it*. This was Ward for crying out loud. And maybe, when she had first started loving him and she had been just another business colleague to him and then later a friend, maybe then if he had seen her as he was seeing her now, in a sexual way, she might have risked her heart and gone for the sort of affair Ward indulged in, hoping that her love would *make* him love her back in time.

But she couldn't do that now, she dare not. The last

long lonely years of loving him from afar had taught her one thing; she would love him until the day she died. And the last few days had taught her something else. If she let him into her body as well as her heart, got to know him intimately and became part of his life—and Bobbie's too—for the length of time the affair lasted, she would never survive the aftermath when Ward finished it.

It had only been a couple of days ago that he had spelled out how he saw the women in his life, had emphasised that at the first signs of an affair getting serious it was ruthlessly terminated.

She couldn't do this, couldn't be what he wanted, she thought feverishly. He thought she was in love with someone else and that physical attraction and yes, friendship, would be enough for her at this time. Perhaps he even thought to wean her away from the other man so she could go out into the big wide world again? She didn't know. How could anyone know what a man like Ward was thinking? All she did know was that *she couldn't do this*.

'You can't deny the chemistry between us?' he murmured. 'I want you and your body tells me you want me too.'

She straightened in his arms, moving away from him and back against the pillows and then watching him as he rose slowly to his feet.

'Wanting isn't enough for me, Ward,' she said very softly. 'Can't you understand that? I could never live with myself if I had an affair or a relationship just on that level. I have to love too. I should never have responded to you like I have over the last day or two, I know that. It was just that...' She floundered. How could she explain the unexplainable? She couldn't tell him the truth but she couldn't think of a feasible lie. And then Ward did it for her.

'You were miserable and upset about this other guy,' he said evenly, the imperturbable mask telling her nothing.

She stared at him helplessly, not knowing what to do or say, the situation utterly beyond her.

'It's okay, Jeanie, I'm not about to throw a tantrum or scream and cry.' The dark voice was faintly mocking with what she felt was an amused quality, and that was all the confirmation she needed to know she had done the right thing. This would always be a dangerously unequal relationship with all the cards stacked on Ward's side, because his heart wasn't really involved.

If she was stupid enough to be tempted into some sort of an affair with him she would tear herself apart trying to be what he wanted, and she would never succeed. She had been playing with fire and she'd got burnt, but there was no one to blame but herself. Ward had always been very clear on how she fitted into his life and he had assumed she saw things the same way. Now, somehow, everything had got tangled and messy, and so she had to set it back on a level footing and be the calm and cool woman he thought he knew.

'I never thought for a moment you would throw a tantrum, Ward,' she said smoothly, 'and I'm flattered you're attracted to me of course, you know that. Maybe if things had been different...'

He surveyed her for a moment more, and then as they both heard little feet come skidding along the landing he nodded abruptly. 'Maybe,' he said laconically as he turned and walked towards the door, meeting Bobbie in the doorway.

He picked the child up before he turned to face Jeanie again, and then his voice was its normal self and the only expression on his face was one of warm indulgence when he said, 'We'll meet you downstairs in a minute, and I'll put the kettle on for a cup of coffee. I've got a feeling the day has well and truly started.'

CONTRARY to what Jeanie expected following the cataclysmic start to the morning, she actually enjoyed the rest of the day.

Once she had heard Ward and Bobbie go downstairs she had shot out of bed and into the en suite, having a quick sixty seconds under the shower with her body shampoo before towelling herself dry. She pulled on a well-washed pair of jeans and a thick baggy sweater she'd brought with her, bundling her hair into a ponytail and hurrying downstairs just in time to meet Ward in the hall carrying a coffee tray.

The black brows rose at the sight of her, but beyond his mild, 'Why do I suddenly feel underdressed?' he'd made no comment on her appearance.

Ward—of course—had had no such scruples with regard to modesty, as the pyjama bottoms and robe proclaimed.

Bobbie had just a few presents and cards to open—most of her presents would be arriving with her friends later that afternoon—but she went into transports of delight over the bride doll, hugging Jeanie hard and then kissing her. She was a truly sweet little girl.

After breakfast preparations began in earnest for the

birthday party that afternoon. Monica had already done a certain amount of cooking, but there were still some sausage rolls and other child-sized nibbles to do, and of course the finishing touches to the birthday cake which Bobbie had helped Jeanie ice the evening before.

The two of them had great fun piping out the shape of a hamster on the top of the cake, which Jeanie then filled in with honey-coloured icing, adding currants for the eyes and a large sultana for the nose. Jeanie wasn't sure if it looked more like a dog than a hamster, but Bobbie was thrilled and that was the only thing that mattered.

They were just transporting the very last remnants of the icing from the bowl into their mouths with the tips of their fingers, and giggling guiltily, when Jeanie happened to glance over to the doorway. Ward was standing there, a very strange look on his face as he stood surveying them both.

'Daddy! Come and see what we've done.' Bobbie was off her stool and over to her father in a moment, and by the time Ward had reached her his face was so normal Jeanie told herself she had been seeing things. But that was what this man did to her, she told herself silently. Turned her inside out and back to front until she didn't know what day it was, let alone anything else.

'That's a terrific hamster.' Ward gave due homage which satisfied his small daughter, and once Bobbie had disappeared to the bathroom to wash her hands, Jeanie began to clear the sticky dishes away after placing the cake carefully to one side.

'Thank you so much for doing this, Jeanie.' Ward's

voice was low and husky and brought her turning to look at him. Suddenly the easy companionship of the time spent with Bobbie was gone and the atmosphere took on an electric quality that caused her throat to dry up.

'You don't need to thank me, I've had a great time,' she managed fairly normally. 'Bobbie is a lovely little girl and fun to be with.' She smiled in what she hoped was a buddy-buddy type way, trying to disguise what the vivid blue eyes did to her. He was so gorgeous, she thought despairingly. That was the trouble. Too sexy, too handsome, too overwhelmingly male to ever be truly comfortable with, given their present circumstances. She just hoped he kept a fairly low profile when all the other children were here; she needed to be totally on the ball then with an army of small infants invading the house—distraction wasn't an option.

It wasn't as if he was even trying to look good today, but he really couldn't look anything else. The long lean legs were encased in old faded blue jeans, and the massive chunky cream sweater he was wearing might look perfectly ordinary on any other man but on Ward's powerful frame it turned into something dreams were made of. The hard tanned face, jet-black hair and vivid blue eyes were heart stoppers all right, but she couldn't dwell on them now. Not now.

With that thought firmly at the forefront of her mind she turned back to loading the dishwasher, saying quietly over her shoulder, 'If you want something to do there's a couple of loaves of bread to be buttered for sandwiches. Okay? And then we really need to decide

what games we're having and when; I'll leave that to
you.'

She had expected him to say something more, but
when she next turned round he was tackling the
mound of bread with single-minded determination.
She stared at his bent back and rolled up sleeves with
a feeling akin to despair. Why was it that the touch of
domesticity increased his lethal appeal a thousandfold?
This just wasn't *fair*.

The party went as smoothly and happily as one
could wish for with twenty plus little girls to control,
and when the last child had gone Bobbie announced
she wanted Jeanie to give her her bath. Once un-
dressed, the tiny body bore evidence to the tragedy
which had claimed the life of her mother although
Bobbie seemed quite oblivious to the scars on her legs,
giggling and splashing as they played a game with the
child's wind up frog and blowing countless bubbles
into the air from a bubble-making kit one of her
friends had bought her.

Jeanie was glad of the little girl's happy disposition
and ability to entertain herself without too much input
from Aunty Jeanie as Bobbie had decided to call her.
The afternoon had been bitter-sweet and she was more
tired than she had thought she would be. It wasn't the
party or the children which had exhausted her though;
it was the strain of playing happy families with Ward.
Seeing him playing games with the small tots and just
generally being in Daddy mode had been a real killer
on her already taut heartstrings, and she had had to
come to terms with the fact that she cared far too much
for Bobbie too.

Bobbie's bath finished, Jeanie began to towel the

child dry, her thoughts racing on. She loved this little girl. The feeling she had been subconsciously fighting from the first time she'd been introduced to Ward's daughter, and which had grown over the last few days as she'd got to know Bobbie better couldn't be denied any longer.

The knowledge was not welcome; loving Bobbie was another complication in the already tangled mess her pseudo-friendship with Ward had become. But— and this was a hard one to face—she had no one to blame for this development but herself.

Once Bobbie was in her pyjamas they went downstairs, where the small mite ate her tea of crumpets and strawberry jam sitting on Jeanie's lap. She was already asleep on the last bite.

Jeanie felt as though her heart was being wrenched out by the root when Ward disappeared upstairs with his small offspring. This was the last full day she would ever have with Bobbie, and once she had left Eddleston and Breedon she probably would never even see Ward again, let alone his daughter. But for now all she could do was to cook them both dinner and continue the act. The last thing in the world she wanted was for Ward to guess the truth.

She had half expected—or was it hoped? she asked herself caustically as the evening progressed—that Ward would refer to what had happened between them that morning, but he seemed to all extent and purposes to have slotted their relationship back into its previous mould of mutual respect and friendship.

He sat and chatted to her at the breakfast bar in the kitchen while she prepared a stir-fry for them both, and Jeanie found she had consumed two large glasses of a particularly rich, fruity, mature Rioja before she had even served the food. They ate off trays in front of the log fire, and although Jeanie knew the meal was good it could have tasted like sawdust for all the impact it made on her senses. Because she suddenly realised what had happened in Ward's mind after the episode in her room that morning.

That cool, logical, relentlessly male brain had considered his brief lack of control, dissected all the data including the implications a relationship with her would involve, and had come to the conclusion after all she had said that an affair was definitely more trouble than it was worth. He was probably breathing a heartfelt sigh of relief at this very moment that she had reacted as she had, thus letting him off the hook that his uncharacteristic and temporary lack of control could have made if her response had been different.

'That was delicious.' He had eaten his food with every appearance of rapt enjoyment, which was a further nail in his coffin as far as Jeanie was concerned considering she'd had to force every mouthful past the dry leaden lump of misery in her throat.

'Good.' Her smile was brittle and bright. If there was any justice in the world it would have choked him.

'And now I'll make the coffee,' he said easily, stretching his long legs comfortably for a moment before rising to his feet. The action had lit an immediate fire in her as hard muscles had flexed and then relaxed, and she was furiously angry with herself that she couldn't deny what he could do to her. He didn't have to touch her, he didn't even have to *look at her to make her liquid with desire, and it just—was—not fair!*

'You haven't tried my coffee before, have you,' he drawled lazily, smiling down at her with those incredible blue eyes. 'I'm told it's slightly wicked but you'll have to judge for yourself. It includes malt whisky and whipped cream and one or two spices, so it has to be savoured slowly.'

Jeanie hadn't got past the 'I'm told' bit which meant—*of course,* she told herself sourly—his other women. 'None for me, thank you,' she said with a brilliant smile. 'It's work again tomorrow, and I think I have had quite enough alcohol for one night. In fact I'm dead beat, Ward, so I'll call it a night if you don't mind.'

'It's only nine o'clock!'

His amazed face told its own story, and if she'd had it in her she would have laughed. The great Ward Ryan, the epitome of the love 'em and leave 'em brigade and lover extraordinaire having a woman finish the evening at nine o'clock. If nothing else she would stick in his memory for this, she told herself with silent dark humour.

'Maybe, but the last few days have been pretty wearing on the whole,' she said with a firmness that was born of desperation. If she stayed with him she would make a fool of herself, she knew it. She had always faintly despised women who allowed themselves to be walk-overs with the opposite sex, but she was in danger of behaving far worse than that. She wanted to recant everything she had said to him that morning, to beg him to make love to her, to tell him that she would accept any criteria he wanted to lay down as long as he let her be close to him. She didn't want to leave him—couldn't he see that? Couldn't he *see* how much she loved him?

'I see.' They stared at each other for a second and Jeanie watched the warm, smoky look in his eyes freeze to the arctic crystal hardness he did so well. She had seen him intimidate people with that look many times before in the past, but until this moment it had never been directed at her.

Well, there was a first time for everything, she told herself with excruciating bravado as she forced herself to stand up and reach forward to kiss him coolly on the cheek. 'Goodnight, Ward.'

'Goodnight, Jeanie.'

He just stood there as she walked across the room to the door and she had opened it when his voice caused her to pause, still with her back to the room. 'Do you think he is thinking about *you* right now, Jeanie? Do you?' he snarled softly.

And she could answer with absolute conviction before she walked out and closed the door behind her. 'Yes, Ward. Yes, I do.'

And it gave her no pleasure at all.

CHAPTER EIGHT

THE next few days were possibly the worst of Jeanie's life. Ward had been more than a little grim-faced the morning after Bobbie's birthday party, when Jeanie had insisted on calling a taxi rather than letting him drive her into work. She knew he had spoken to one of the partners over the weekend to explain the circumstances and they had urged him to take a day or two away from the office to organise things at home, so there was no need for him to go into the heart of London, she'd maintained with desperate firmness. She had hugged and kissed Bobbie, marched out to the waiting taxi with her overnight bag and case, and then fought back the tears all the way to the office.

She hadn't heard from Ward over the next couple of days but she hadn't really expected to. However, on Wednesday morning he dropped into her office with two cups of coffee mid-morning like he often did when he wanted a chat, and once she'd got her pounding heart under control she was able to ask quite naturally, 'How's Monica doing? Is she home yet?'

'Last night.' He smiled at her, and—quite irrationally on her part, Jeanie admitted—she wanted to slap him. It was just that he seemed so totally *normal,* and, her breaking heart asked, how *could* he be that way after the weekend when they had nearly... Nearly what? If she thought about it they hadn't nearly anything!

'That's good.' She forced a bright smile.

'Yes, it's all worked out very well,' he said cheerfully. 'Monica's sister was at the hospital when I called to see her on Monday along with her daughter who, it turned out, is a qualified nanny and has just recently left her last position when the family decided to move abroad. She's more than happy to fill in for the time being, and if she works out I might just offer her a job permanently. I've been thinking for some time that Monica needs help, and this girl has her own car and so on.'

'It sounds perfect,' Jeanie agreed, the mental image of a gorgeous, eager, exuberant young thing causing her stomach muscles to knot.

'We'll see. It would certainly cut out the sort of panic that occurred this weekend,' Ward said quietly.

And would mean his home life was as well planned and constructed as his working life, Jeanie thought. All possible complications anticipated in advance and intercepted. The man who didn't need anyone. Well, she could no more make him need her like she needed him than she could force him to love her. Patricia still held the key to his heart and she'd taken it to the grave.

He continued to talk a little more, leaning against the wall of the office and apparently relaxed and totally at ease. Jeanie, on the other hand, was a quivering mess inside. He stayed longer than usual that day, and on Thursday longer still until Jeanie—terrified she was going to betray herself in some way—made it clear she had some urgent correspondence to deal with.

The 'urgent correspondence' ploy didn't work so well on Friday morning, but knowing she was going to take off and flee the capital to the sanctuary of her parents who, it had transpired on the phone the previous night, had organised a big family dinner with all her sisters and their families for Friday night, enabled her to maintain the efficient Miss Jeanie Potter facade until he left. She hadn't expected to see Ward again that day, so on Friday afternoon when he opened the door of her office she stared at him in surprise.

'You're going to your parents this weekend, yes?' And at her nod, he added quietly, 'Give me a call when you get there.'

'A call?' she repeated faintly. 'Why?'

'Isn't it obvious?' he said a touch testily, raking back his hair as he spoke which always did the weirdest thing to her equilibrium. But then *everything* about him did the weirdest things to her equilibrium!

'Not to me, no,' she answered truthfully. Obvious was not a word that reared its head in Ward's presence. There were enigmatic men and there were enigmatic men, and then there was Ward Ryan.

'I want to make sure you have arrived safely,' he said shortly. 'The weather's foul again and high winds are forecast.'

It shook her. She hadn't expected him to be that bothered once she'd gone—out-of-sight, out-of-mind type reasoning she supposed, she admitted silently—and in spite of all the warnings she had drummed into herself over the last few days her heart turned over as a ridiculous little seed of hope sprouted. Was it remotely possible he was beginning to see her as something other than just another female? she asked herself.

They had been friends for a long time—something she knew was unique for Ward with regard to the opposite sex—and perhaps he had meditated over that in the last few days, along with the fact that he now found he could actually fancy her too?

And then hard reality hit. She had stayed in London to step into the breach and do him a favour; he was just feeling beholden to her, that was all. Added to the fact that the way his wife had died must always be there at the back of his mind, and it had been bad weather conditions which had caused Patricia's car to end up in a ditch.

She had to stop reading what she wanted to see into anything he said or did. He might like her and not want to see her hurt, but that didn't mean he was beginning to fall in love with her. She knew this man very well and she had faced facts a long time ago regarding the hopelessness of her feelings for him.

'I'll ring,' she said quietly.

'Good.' They looked at each other for a moment, and then he walked across the room to where she had risen from behind her desk when he had opened the door. 'Drive carefully.' He bent his head, brushing her smooth cheek with his lips, and the subtle scent of his aftershave sent the usual flickers of desire coursing through her bloodstream.

A hopeless case, that's what she was, Jeanie thought mordantly, watching the way his body moved as he turned and walked back to the half-open door. A totally hopeless case. She managed a fairly neutral smile as he turned and raised his hand before shutting the door behind him, and then stood for some seconds with her hands clenched and her head back as she willed herself to calm down.

She wished she'd never come to London; she wished she'd never trained to be a solicitor; she wished she'd never taken a position at Eddleston and Breedon, but most of all—*most of all*—she wished she had never set eyes on Ward Ryan.

Deep breath. Deep, deep breath. She relaxed her fingers one by one. At the end of the month she was going to give notice to the partners and from that point she could start taking control of her life and emotions again. This was not the end of the world. It might feel like it, but it was *not* the end of the world.

Right, she was leaving early for the drive to York so now was a good time to exit. All her things were in her car situated in the underground car park, so she could be on her way within minutes. She cleared her desk by the simple expedient of bundling everything into a drawer, slipped into her coat, picked up her briefcase and left the office, and she was halfway through the larger outer office when one of the secretaries called to her, waving what looked like a wad of tickets in one of her hands.

'Jeanie? Are you doing anything for Valentine's Day, only my husband's cricket club has got up a dinner/dance and we've managed to get a terrific band.'

Valentine's Day. If there was one thing she didn't need to be reminded of just at this precise moment it was that torturous event—or rather it had been torturous since she'd fallen in love with Ward—which occurred with grim monotony on February 14th each year.

Jeanie forced a smile to her lips. 'Sorry, no can do,

I'm afraid. Perhaps another time?' And as Ann subsided back into her seat Jeanie made swiftly for the door.

ONCE in the car she purposely slid a CD of dance music into the car's CD player rather than one of the romantic ballads she usually favoured, determining to concentrate on the road and nothing else.

It was snowing again but not too thickly by the time she reached Lincoln, but it had been dark for over an hour and the weather was really setting in when she eventually drew up outside her parent's big sprawling semi in York. She could see from the cars parked on the drive that her sisters were already in residence, and after turning off the engine she stretched a little, easing aching neck muscles before she got out of the car.

She was just pulling her bags out of the boot when the front door opened and her sisters piled out into the drive, calling out as they came.

'Jeanie! At long last. Come and have a drink.'

'What happened last weekend then?'

'We've missed you, kiddo! Seems like ages since Christmas.'

'Who's the lame duck you've been ministering to anyway?'

This last was from Charlotte and as Jeanie opened her mouth to reply, she horrified them and herself by bursting into tears.

It was the warmth of their greetings that had done it, that and the genuine love and pleasure at her arrival that had been shining out of the four pairs of blue eyes that were now looking at her with such concern.

'Fledgling! What is it? Whatever has that brute done

to you?' This was from Lizzie, her eldest sister, and Lizzie's use of her nickname for Jeanie only made Jeanie cry the harder. Four pairs of arms were patting and comforting her and for the first time it dawned on Jeanie that her four sisters loved her just as much as they loved each other, but differently—in a protective, maternal way rather than the provocative and often competitive feeling they displayed one to another. And right at this moment it felt wonderful.

She sniffed and snuffled for a bit, insisting she didn't want to go in the house until she was herself again and that their parents definitely mustn't have their weekend spoilt by her problems, and then she quickly told the four women the gist of the dilemma.

They were all sympathetic, fiercely indignant on her behalf and to a woman called Ward every name under the sun, and then they all gave different opinions as to what she should do from this point. The heart-to-heart finished with Jeanie laughing helplessly as the four of them vehemently took each other to task. And laughter was something she hadn't expected to indulge in at all this particular night, she reflected warmly, when her parent's arrival in the lighted doorway of the house cut the discussion short.

She was so glad she had come home. It might be pathetic, and it certainly wasn't in keeping with the successful, smart, quick-witted and bright career woman she now purported to be, but it felt indescribably good to be held so dear and loved so unconditionally. She would phone Ward now, a brief friendly call and nothing else, and then put him out of her mind! She *would*.

'Ward Ryan.'

The telephone was picked up immediately the other end barely before it had had time to ring, and in spite of all her good resolutions Jeanie's stomach lurched as the deep cool voice sounded down the wire. His hard handsome face with its piercing blue eyes was instantly on the screen of her mind, and she had to take a deep breath to prevent her voice from shaking before she said, 'Ward? It's Jeanie. I'm just phoning to say I've arrived safely as promised.'

There was a moment's pause before he spoke again, and then the husky quality to his voice was emphasised when he said softly, 'I was getting worried. I'd worked out you should have arrived some time ago.'

'I drive a Polo, Ward, not a Mercedes,' she said drily. She was rather pleased with that response, and added, 'How are things your end? Give Monica and Bobbie my love, won't you.'

'Bobbie's missing you.'

Jeanie held the receiver away from her ear for a moment and stared at it, her heart thudding. How was she supposed to take that? she asked herself silently. And that note in his voice... Had she imagined the deep throaty tenderness?

'Jeanie? Are you still there?'

She pulled herself together sufficiently to answer, 'Yes, I'm here. Look, I've only just got here so I need to say hallo to everyone. See you Monday, okay? Goodbye for now.'

'Take care, Sleeping Beauty.'

She was still standing holding the telephone moments after Ward had replaced the receiver the other end, and then she forced herself to logically examine everything which had been said.

He had been worried when she hadn't kept to the time-scale he had worked out. That was friendly concern, and she knew full well his past had probably made him more sensitive to journeys in bad weather conditions and so on; it was perfectly natural. He had said Bobbie was missing her—Bobbie, not him. That was hard cold fact.

And Sleeping Beauty? her ridiculous heart asked. What did that mean? In view of all the rest nothing, plain common sense answered. She couldn't keeping hoping, seizing on the odd word or inflexion in his voice and building it up to mean something quite different to what he meant. She had to stop this now, finish it in her mind once and for all. If she didn't she would go stark, staring mad.

That talk to herself set the tone for the rest of Jeanie's weekend in York.

She immersed herself in her family, saturating herself in being nothing more complicated than daughter and sister and aunty, and in spite of the deep well of regret and longing that enveloped her whenever her thoughts strayed to Ward and Bobbie, she discovered a strength in herself she hadn't suspected was there. It didn't stop the tears in the dead of the night when she was alone, but it did help her face each day with a smile and a bright and cheerful countenance as she determined she would *not* cast a shadow over everyone else's weekend and wear her heart on her sleeve.

Lizzie, Susan, Miranda and Charlotte vied for her company and she was always at one or other of their homes, causing her long-suffering mother to bemoan the fact that even when Jeanie was here, she wasn't *here*.

By the time Jeanie drove back to London very early on Monday morning, she was congratulating herself on how clear-headed and rational she was about Ward, and about what she had to do in the immediate future.

Her first mistake had been in remaining at Eddleston and Breedon for so long after she had realised the extent of her feeling for him.

Her second, in allowing and even encouraging a friendship that was all pain and no gain on her side.

And her third, and—she had to admit with hindsight—the one that knocked the others into a cocked hat, in listening to her heart and Monica's entreaties, and agreeing to stand in as temporary housekeeper-cum-cook-cum she wasn't quite sure what, last weekend.

But she was realisitic now. Calm, practical, even dispassionate? She had come to her senses at last, and she accepted she had to remove herself completely from the pull of Ward's dark orbit which sucked all her reasoning and common sense and emotions into it like a great black hole.

She would tender her resignation this very day, and would begin looking for another job at once. She was tied to a three-month contract with Eddleston and Breedon, and even if she didn't find another position within that time she knew it was still the right thing to do.

Her bank account was very healthy, and if necessary she would consider a radical change of direction, even of career. Perhaps it was time to get out of the capital for pastures new? Miranda had mentioned an aid organisation her husband knew of which had recently advertised for a solicitor in the north of England, or she might even look for an opening abroad? The world was her oyster, that's how she had to look at this, and the little voice in the back of her mind that kept whispering a world without Ward in it would be a very grey and empty place would learn to die in time. It would have to.

There were a string of messages on her answering machine when she let herself into the house, but nothing from the one voice she wanted to hear. Not that she had expected it, she told herself firmly as she quelled the sick disappointment in the pit of her stomach, and she wasn't going to start going down that road either. She'd made a promise to herself on the way home that her days of crying were over, and she intended to keep to it even if it killed her!

Jeanie had left York long before the rest of the world was awake knowing she needed to give herself enough time to go home and shower and change, and still get to the office before anyone else arrived. She needed to look good today—it wasn't every day one tended their notice—and she also needed to feel in control of herself, her workload and the whole situation with Ward. The latter might be an illusion, but she still needed to feel it.

She had dressed with an eye to boosting her confidence, and the wildly expensive cream suit and equally expensive gold silk blouse was an outfit she had only worn once before, when an important function had necessitated lashing out with very little thought of cost. But the amount she had balked at then now seemed worth every penny. The cut of the suit and the pencil-slim skirt was smart but extremely feminine, and the soft gold blouse brought out the amber shade to her eyes and made them seem enormous.

She had put her hair up but not so severely as usual, leaving a few silky wispy tendrils curling about her neck to soften the style. She didn't want to look *too* obvious but she did need to look good, and as she was meeting Nicki for their postponed lunch date she could always use that as an excuse if anyone commented.

She felt better once she had typed out her resignation, printing it in duplicate and then putting the copies into envelopes. It had become fait accompli somehow, and seeing the physical evidence in black and white made her all the more determined to go through with it. She sealed the envelope addressed to the senior partners and put her own copy in her handbag, and then set about sorting out her priorities for the day.

Half an hour later, her mind given over to the intricacies of a particularly ugly custody battle, she felt her stomach jump and turn over when she heard her door open.

'Morning.' Stephanie grinned at her from the doorway and Jeanie had to stop herself sagging as a feeling of anticlimax made her spine fluid as she smiled at her secretary. And then Stephanie gave a little whistle of admiration before adding, 'And you look like you've had a great weekend if you don't mind me saying. Can't you twist his arm and come to the St. Valentine's dance?'

'What?' And then as understanding hit Jeanie blushed slightly. 'I've a lunch date,' she said, 'and it's still no to the dance.'

'Boy, he must be pretty special. You look sensational.'

Jeanie smiled that aside before saying, 'Shut the door, Steph. I've got something to tell you and I'd prefer to keep it private at least for the next couple of hours.' Stephanie had been her secretary since Jeanie had first started at the firm and had been a great support to her, and Jeanie felt it was only right to explain she was leaving before she popped along to see Joseph and Dan.

Jeanie was gratified at how genuinely upset Stephanie was at the news, and when she spoke to the senior partners half an hour later they too expressed deep disappointment and regret at her decision, but after seeing how determined she was they reluctantly accepted her resignation.

Once back in her office she worked for a couple of hours in seclusion as she prepared the way forward for her client on the custody case, and when Stephanie brought her coffee at eleven was able to ask fairly casually, 'I don't think I've seen Mr. Ryan today. Is he in?'

'It appears he's in court all morning.' Stephanie now glanced behind her and shut the door before she continued, her tone confiding, 'Jenny told me his housekeeper had an accident recently and Mr. Ryan's now taken on a nanny permanently for his kid. Now that's a job I wouldn't mind; living with Mr. Ryan!' She winked cheekily at Jeanie, who just managed to bite back the comment that the nanny wouldn't be living in before it left her lips. Office gossip needed little fact at the base of it at the best of times, and it was better to just play dumb and nod than let on she knew more than Ward's secretary apparently did.

Obviously Monica's niece had worked out okay

then. Jeanie sat musing for a few minutes while she
drank her coffee, and then forced herself to put the
image of a fresh-faced, modern and undoubtedly
lovely—knowing her luck—girl out of her mind. It
was no business of hers what Ward did or didn't do,
or whom he did it with. And cradle snatching wasn't
Ward's style anyway. It was just mortifying to know
she would have given the world to be in that girl's
position, and not just to be near Ward either. Bobbie
had touched her heart in a way that was both permanent and painful.

She frowned irritably, annoyed at the way her rogue
thoughts kept focusing on Ward in spite of herself. But
it would be easier when she had left here, she reas-
sured herself firmly, pulling a file out of the pile at the
side of her and opening it. And now she was going to
concentrate on this case and nothing else.

Just after half past twelve she heard her door open
again. She had asked Stephanie to remind her of the
time about twenty to one so she wasn't late for Nicki,
and now, her eyes glued on the list of figures she was
checking, she said absently, 'Thanks, Steph, I hadn't
forgotten, but I just need to finish this first. I promise
I won't keep him waiting though!' adding the last on
a teasing note after Stephanie's earlier comment.

'Hallo, Jeanie.'

Her head shot up at the deep, cool voice, and as she
saw Ward framed in the doorway her heart went haywire. 'Oh, I'm... I'm sorry,' she managed breathlessly.
'I thought you were Stephanie. She...she's just keeping a check on the time.' She swallowed hard. 'I've a
lunch date,' she finished weakly.

His eyes narrowed slightly. 'I'd gathered that,' he

said softly, his gaze taking in the cream suit and focusing on her hair. 'Anyone I know?'

'No.' She didn't know why but somehow she didn't like his tone of voice, or maybe it wasn't his voice but the way he was looking at her? She forced herself to show no reaction and said carefully, 'Successful morning? I understand you were in court for most of it.'

'Yes, I had a successful morning,' he ground out tightly.

She stared at him. If this was how a successful morning left him she would hate to see him when a case went wrong! 'Good.' She smiled dismissively, indicating her desk as she said, 'Well, I must finish this, so...'

He completely ignored the hint, pinning her to her chair with his lethal blue eyes as he kicked the door shut behind him.

He looked fantastic. She didn't want to think it and she tried not to dwell on how seeing him again was making her feel but it was hopeless. He was wearing a pale silver-grey shirt and matching tie and a deep grey suit, and for some obtuse reason the very formality of the clothes reminded her how he had looked half-naked, and she felt herself blushing a burning crimson.

'When did you get back?' he asked evenly. 'I called round last night to tell you Monica's niece has worked out great and she's now permanent.'

He'd called round? But only to tell her about Monica's niece, she reminded herself fiercely in the next instant. And—surprising though Ward might find it—she didn't want to know about Monica's apparently ideal relation! 'I came straight from York this morning,' she said coolly.

'Hence the lunch date?' he bit out grimly.

What on earth was the matter with him? Jeanie stared at the very masculine, cold face in surprise for a moment or two, before a healthy dart of anger made itself felt. Whatever it was she didn't have to put up with this. She hadn't expected him to fall on her neck but this was the other extreme. Someone had obviously upset him this morning, and it must have been something bad for Ward to show his feelings so blatantly, but there was absolutely no reason for him to take it out on her! She wouldn't be treated as though she'd done something wrong.

'Is something the matter, Ward?' she asked frostily.

'Yes, something's the matter,' he bit out savagely as he glared at her, his eyes like two chips of blue ice in a granite hard face. 'Don't you value yourself at all, Jeanie? Haven't you any self-respect?'

'What?' She stared at him in amazement.

'This bozo lets you come and stay with me—*in my house*—without so much as the whiff of a protest from what I can make out, and then you dress yourself up to look absolutely fantastic to go out to lunch with him, and don't bother to deny that it's him you are seeing because I know it is. I *know*.'

Jeanie's soft mouth tightened. 'Now look, Ward—'

'No! *You* look. Damn it all, Jeanie, I can't believe you're letting yourself be treated this way. Can't you see he wants you for one thing and one thing only? What are you going to do this lunch-time? Disappear into a hotel room somewhere for dessert? You're away for a weekend, and the minute you're back and he snaps his fingers, you jump.'

'How dare you!' Her voice rose and she checked it with an effort, reminding herself the thin partitioned walls only gave a limited amount of privacy. 'You have absolutely no right to talk to me like this.'

'Why the hell don't you tell him to take a running jump?' he rasped testily. 'What's this guy got that makes him so damn irresistible anyway?'

Black hair, blue eyes and a smile to die for, not that the smile was anywhere in evidence today. 'I'm not discussing this with you now, Ward. Not with you in this mood,' Jeanie snapped angrily. She rose to her feet, gathering her handbag and long cream lambswool coat before marching over to the door and exiting her office before he could say another word. She knew she had surprised him with her sudden departure; she'd seen the brief widening of the beautiful blue eyes a second before he had narrowed his gaze.

She stopped for a moment in the main office to tell Stephanie she was taking a long lunch, and then continued into the lift without a backwards glance, her cheeks fiery with righteous indignation. Maybe she should take Ward's advice and tell him to take a running jump? she thought furiously as the lift took her swiftly downwards. Maybe that's *exactly* what she should do!

She caught sight of her reflection in the mirrored walls, gazing at her flushed cheeks and flashing eyes for a moment before all the anger evaporated and she leant limply against the side of the lift. What a tangle. What a 24 carat mess. Even though she hadn't actually told Ward any lies she had twisted the truth to the point where they were at each other's throats, she thought miserably. And there was no easy solution to the web of prevarication and falsity either. She couldn't tell him the bald truth, so she had no option but to see the whole ghastly charade through to the bitter end.

He thought she was sleeping with a man who was using her for his own pleasure, who was unprepared to make any sort of commitment or show her any loyalty or devotion, and he despised her because she was letting herself be used in this way. It would be funny if it wasn't so tragic.

And she had nobody but herself to blame for all of this. She should have at least made it plain she was meeting Nicki for lunch and not her supposed lover, but he had made her so *mad*.

Irritating, blind, obstinate, intractable man that he was!

She sighed deeply and then straightened as the lift doors opened, emerging with her head held high and her back straight. She could hardly believe that a sensible, thirty-two-year-old woman who had been in charge of her destiny for years and knew her own mind to the point where she had used to drive her parents mad, had contrived to get herself locked into this present checkmate. But she had. What fools love can make of the most sane people.

And the last thing she felt like right now was meeting an old university friend and being bright and cheerful all through lunch!

THE lunch went far better than Jeanie had expected, mainly because it turned out Nicki was having man trouble of her own and they spent most of the time agreeing the world would be a far better place with just females in residence.

Jeanie arrived back at the office at just before three, and as she passed Stephanie's desk on the way to her office her secretary grabbed her arm, saying urgently, 'Mr. Ryan is in your office and he's in a real temper over something or other. I thought I ought to warn you. He's been waiting in there for the last half an hour although I said you were going to be late back.'

Great. The day was getting better and better, Jeanie thought derisively, but apart from a brisk, 'Thanks, Steph,' she didn't delay the dreaded moment.

As she opened the door Ward swung round from the window to face her, for all the world as though he hadn't budged since she had left two hours ago. He certainly looked just as mad. 'What's all this about you resigning?' Never one to beat about the bush he went straight for the jugular. 'And why the hell didn't you tell me you were thinking of leaving?'

She stared at him for a full ten seconds and then said crisply, 'From what I can recall of our conversation before lunch you didn't give me much chance to say anything.'

He didn't even have the grace to look slightly shamefaced. 'Is it to do with him? The rat?' he growled angrily. 'Don't tell me he's had a change of heart and asked you to marry him or something.'

Oh for goodness' sake! Jeanie glared at this man she loved with all her heart and soul and mind, and snapped, 'Yes, it is to do with him and no, he hasn't asked me to marry him or even suggested ''something.'' I've decided to finish it once and for all if you must know, and make a completely fresh start in every area of my life, my job included.'

'Have you told him? Is that why you went to lunch with him today?' he asked suspiciously.

'I didn't say I was going to lunch with him, you assumed that,' she said tightly. 'I was actually having lunch with an old friend, a female friend.'

'You said you wouldn't keep *him* waiting, when you thought I was Stephanie.'

'It was a joke...something Steph had said earlier—' She stopped abruptly. 'Look, Ward, I don't have to justify myself to you. I had lunch with a big buxom blonde called Nicki, all right? Believe me or don't believe me, it's up to you. And yes, he does know, and while we're on the subject...' She took a deep breath, her eyes flashing, 'Why would I resign anyway if he *had* asked me to marry him? This isn't the Dark Ages you know. Modern, independent women do still work if they want to once they are married, and I am both modern and independent,' she finished with a flourish.

He walked over and perched himself on the side of her desk, never taking his eyes off her flushed defiant face. 'How did he take the news?' he asked softly.

She shrugged. 'I've made up my mind and that's it.'

'And how do you feel?' he asked even more softly.

'Determined, resolute, upset.' Desperately, desperately upset, you unfeeling swine.

He nodded. 'Have you got another job lined up?'

'No.' This was hard, it was so, so hard. She took a ragged pull of air and said abruptly, 'I might go abroad for a while actually, have a year or two working in the sun. A sort of legal sabbatical. I might even do waitressing or bar work, or maybe apply as a holiday rep. Something completely different.' The thought had only just occurred to her but it suddenly seemed right somehow. 'Financially I wouldn't struggle if I didn't find something straight away.'

He was pinning her with the steady, unrevealing stare she'd seen him adopt so often, so when he hitched off the desk and walked over to her, lifting her chin to gaze into the velvet amber depths of her eyes, she didn't know what he was going to say. 'You seem to have it all worked out.' He traced a path down one silky cheek with his finger. 'But I'm sorry you are upset, and just for the record never for a moment did I think you're anything other than modern and independent.'

She didn't trust herself to say anything, she was too emotionally shattered, and after gazing at her for a moment more he shook his head slightly, turning and walking to the door.

'But you aren't going to sit and brood for the next three months until you fly out to your Utopia,' he said silkily over his shoulder. 'I won't let you. So I'll pick you up for dinner tonight at eight, okay? And dress up. I'm taking you somewhere nice.'

And her mouth was still open in dazed surprise when he shut the door behind him.

CHAPTER NINE

If JEANIE had had to describe the next two weeks, only one word would have done—unreal.

Ward wined and dined her, took her to the theatre, art galleries and the like, but the times she enjoyed the most were quiet meals at his home once Bobbie was in bed and Monica had gone to her quarters, because that was when he really talked. For the first time in the five years she had known him he had totally opened up to her, and she found it amazing. And perplexing. And incredibly frustrating. Because not once during all the evenings out and the heart-to-hearts at his home did he make any sort of move on her.

Oh, he'd sit with his arm round her; hold her hand when they were out together; kiss her lightly on the lips now and again and stroke her face with that tender, gentle way he had at times, but *never* did he try to take things any further. For two weeks she didn't have one evening to herself, and he didn't try to hide the fact he was taking her out at work either.

Jeanie had lost count of the number of people who had asked her when, exactly, she and Ward had started dating, and when she gave her stock response—that they weren't dating but just seeing each other as friends—she knew, however polite they were, no one believed her. And she couldn't blame them for being incredulous. She felt that way herself. And confused and bewildered and utterly at a loss.

They had some wonderful days out with Bobbie at the weekends, and Jeanie met Henrietta, Monica's niece, who was sweet and funny and resembled a little wise owl with her big black-rimmed spectacles and enormous brown eyes.

Jeanie was happier than she had ever been and more miserable than she could bear—sometimes in the same hour—and through it all Ward never once referred to her decision to leave Eddleston and Breedon, or asked her not to go.

The whole thing was surreal, Jeanie thought one night towards the middle of February. She and Ward had just finished a meal she had prepared and cooked—Monica still being unable to do much, and Henrietta having cooked for herself, Bobbie and her aunt earlier before Jeanie and Ward had got home— and were now taking their coffee through to the sitting room where a roaring fire greeted them.

'This is nice.' Jeanie sat down on the sofa which had been pulled close to the hearth and stretched out her toes to the red and orange flames. It had been raining and sleeting all day and now a fierce wind moaned about the house, sending the icy drops of rain lashing against the windows and splattering down the chimney now and again. 'There's something so *elemental* about a real fire on a night like this. You can imagine people sitting in their caves thousands of years ago and feeling exactly the same satisfaction. Do you know what I mean? It's like—'

She turned to glance at Ward sitting by the side of her and then stopped abruptly, the words dying on her tongue as she met the sapphire eyes trained on her face.

'I need to talk to you, Jeanie. *Really* talk to you,' he said very quietly, and the look on his face frightened her.

'I thought we *had* talked tonight, and all the other nights,' she managed fairly lightly. Whatever this was, whatever he was going to say, she didn't want to hear it. If he was going to tell her that he considered her time of nuturing and support over, or that he had met a new woman and would have to curtail seeing her, or *whatever,* she'd rather it be in the cold, clinical light of day at work, where she couldn't disgrace herself by throwing herself on his chest and refusing to let go.

'Yes, we have,' he agreed evenly. 'In fact I think I've told you more than I've ever revealed to another living soul, but there is something you need to know. Something…difficult for me to talk about because it feels like a betrayal of Bobbie.'

'Bobbie?' She stared at him, totally taken aback. Whatever she'd expected it wasn't this. 'I don't understand?'

He shifted sharply, his eyes leaving her bewildered face and turning to look into the flickering flames, and when he spoke it was in a flat, expressionless voice. 'Bobbie's mother was a very beautiful woman,' he said quietly, 'and she had charisma. She drew men to her like moths to a flame. I was fascinated by her, everyone who came into contact with her was, and when she told me she was pregnant with my child we married within the month. I felt like I'd captured an unbelievable prize.'

He rose from the sofa, but not before she had been

shocked by the way his eyes had narrowed and hardened, his mouth setting in a grim, uncompromising line. 'Ward, you don't have to say anything more,' she said quickly, watching him as he strode across the room and drew back the heavy drapes at the window to stand looking out into the dark, storm tossed night. Her heart was thudding wildly but she wasn't exactly sure what was happening. He had loved his wife totally and utterly, everyone knew that, but how could that relate to a betrayal of Bobbie?

'I knew Patricia needed attention,' he continued steadily as though she hadn't spoken, 'and she was an outrageous flirt, but I thought it was just her way. It didn't mean anything. She had had a rotten childhood, pushed from pillar to post and never really settling in any of her foster homes. So, I put up with the sulks and tantrums her hatred of being pregnant caused, although I think I knew within the first week of marriage that the woman I thought I'd loved was a figment of my imagination.'

'But... But I thought—'

'That we were the perfect couple?' he said harshly, turning to glance at her for a moment. 'I'm not surprised you've heard that, we played our parts very well. Then Bobbie was born and Patricia found there was something she hated more than being pregnant and that was being a mother with a child to care for. Monica took over Bobbie lock, stock and barrel. By then I suspected there were other men but Patricia was clever and cunning.'

Jeanie had her hands to her mouth, her head whirling as she tried to grasp the reality of what he was revealing. She couldn't have spoken to save her life.

'The only time Patricia had contact with her daughter was in the afternoons when she would take Bobbie in the car and visit friends,' he went on bitterly. 'Or that was where she told Monica she went. And Monica encouraged her to take the child, feeling she needed to bond with the baby and that then things might be different. In reality Bobbie spent the time strapped in the car seat in hotel car parks while her mother was inside with her lovers. Patricia used her as a smokescreen, that was all. It was when my wife was on her way home from one such liaison that she crashed the car, and it was the subsequent police investigation which revealed the truth. They were very good,' he finished grimly. 'Very discreet.'

'Oh, Ward.' Jeanie wanted to put her head down on a cushion and cry her eyes out, but knowing how much he'd hate it she forced herself to say, through the tightness in her throat, 'I'm so very sorry. I don't know what to say.'

'Oh the best is yet to come,' he said with a crispness that spoke of rigid control. 'Patricia died instantly in the accident and it was touch and go with Bobbie. She needed blood transfusions galore and a whole load of stuff, and to cut what is a very unsavoury story short she has a rare blood group. A blood group which means I couldn't possibly have been her biological father. Note I said biological, Jeanie, because in every other sense Bobbie *is* mine.'

Through the stunned disbelief a separate part of Jeanie's brain had accepted the truth instantly. It explained so much. Ward's total withdrawal from the human race after his wife's death, his repudiation of further commitment with another woman, his cynicism and overall coldness regarding the opposite sex...

'No one knows,' he said tightly, 'not even Monica, and Bobbie will never know. She is mine. If you had seen the way she fought for life—' He stopped abruptly, and when she saw the tears in his eyes she would have gone to him but he waved her back down in the seat. 'No, let me finish. She is mine, Jeanie. I couldn't love a child of my flesh more. She has nothing of her mother in her and I don't care who the hell her father was. I know what *she* is and that is my daughter.'

'I know.' Why had he told her this? Could it be that he had fallen in love with her? She thought back to all the little tender moments over the last weeks and her hopes soared, and then plummeted when she reminded herself that not once had he asked her to stay, not once had he spoken of the future or *really* kissed her, like he had those couple of times before. Surely a man in love would try to stake his claim? He didn't love her. He would never love her. Patricia might not have his heart like she had thought, but his ex-wife had seen to it that it was buried along with her nevertheless.

'Ward, why have you told me all this?' she asked at last, knowing she had to put what she was feeling into words however he might answer.

His eyes were quite unreadable. 'Because it was time you knew,' he said simply.

'I see.' No, no, she didn't see, so why had she said she did? she asked herself silently. 'Well, thank you for trusting me.' She couldn't exactly cross-question him on his motives after all.

'That's all right,' he said softly. He had changed his clothes earlier whilst Jeanie had sat and chatted with Monica and Henrietta in the kitchen, Bobbie snuggled contentedly on her lap, and now in the shadowed room the black jeans and dark grey shirt he was wearing made him seem all the more darkly masculine and alien.

She thought back to what he'd told her about his parents and what a lonely, unhappy little boy he must have been. Patricia's betrayal must have been his worst nightmare coming true. *Oh, Ward.* Her love brought her to her feet and she had crossed the room to him before she even thought about it, reaching up and touching his face like he had done with her several times in the last weeks, as she said very softly, her eyes wide and liquid with the tears she dare not let fall, 'I think Patricia was mad not to realise what she had got in you and Bobbie.'

He smiled, a twisting of his mouth, taking her hand and holding it to his lips for a brief moment before he said quietly, 'Don't pity me, Jeanie. Whatever else, don't do that. I know you've been in love with this other man for years and being the sort of person you are it'll take time to get over him, but even if you do still love him you can't deny there's something between us.'

He was talking physical attraction again…wasn't he? She stared at him, unsure and uncertain of where he was coming from.

'And why have you told people we aren't dating?' he asked very evenly.

'What?' She felt she was in danger of losing her grasp on reality here.

'People at work,' he said quietly. 'You've told them we aren't dating according to the office grapevine.'

'Well we aren't, are we?' she asked confusedly.

'The hell we aren't.'

She was startled by his vehemence, her eyes opening wide as she saw the blue eyes spark.

'Obviously this idiot you've been involved with has confused you as to how a real man goes about courting,' he said tightly, 'but there is a right way, believe it or not. And that's what we're doing. Got it?'

The old-fashioned word had delighted Jeanie more than he would ever know, but she forced herself to keep control of her wayward emotions which were threatening to go haywire. He still hadn't said a word about commitment or love or anything that really mattered, she warned herself fiercely, and after all he had said in the past—*emphasised* in the past—she couldn't assume anything, not feeling about him the way she did. She'd never survive further disappointment.

'Joe and Dan wouldn't like the complication of two of their junior partners dating,' she said weakly.

'Ah, but you aren't going to be an employee of Eddleston and Breedon much longer,' he said triumphantly, 'so in my opinion that negates that one. Added to which I don't give a damn what Joe and Dan like. Come and drink your coffee.'

'What?' She was saying that far too much but she just couldn't keep track of this evening.

'Come and drink your coffee,' he repeated with a coolness that deflated Jeanie utterly.

Surely, if he was serious about having anything more than one of his temporary affairs he would at least say *something?* she thought dazedly. Not necessarily a vow of undying love or eternal devotion—that wasn't Ward's style any more than Valentine cards and chocolate hearts—but he'd been more controlled and correct since the moment he found out she had finished with her supposed lover than before, at least on a sexual level.

She didn't understand this. She didn't understand *him*. And he hadn't even asked her not to disappear out of his life to pastures new. She had said she was planning to go abroad once she had worked out her notice. Didn't he *care* about that? Obviously not.

Jeanie was very quiet on the drive home and Ward seemed disinclined to break the silence in the car which couldn't possibly have been described as comfortable.

Once in the mews he saw her to the door as always, and if she was hoping for a sign to let her know what he was thinking it didn't come. 'Good night, Jeanie.' He bent and kissed her briefly on the lips, his mouth warm and firm but constrained. 'See you in the morning.'

She nodded, too flat and miserable with an overwhelming sense of anticlimax to speak.

'And don't worry,' he said huskily, holding her for a second longer before stepping back a pace and looking at her with glittering blue eyes, his black hair ruffled by the wind and damp with the rain. 'All men aren't blind morons although experience might have led you to think so. Some of us have our eyes opened in spite of ourselves.'

He had turned and walked back to the car in the next moment, leaving her—as always where Ward was concerned—with a sense of things left unsaid and unfinished business. And she was fed up with it, she told herself as she stepped in the house and closed the door without waving him off as usual. Sick and tired and fed up.

All that about his wife had upset her more than she could have believed, considering the final line meant he hadn't loved Patricia like she had thought he had. But his pain and desolation, and not least the fact that Patricia had robbed him of his biological parentage of Bobbie, had cut deep enough for Jeanie to realise she'd have gladly spared him all that heartache at the cost of him loving Patricia to the day he died.

What was she going to do? *What was she going to do?* She prowled about the house for a good hour as her mind continued to whirl.

Hang around and hope that he would learn to care for her, even if it wouldn't be the grand, for everness she felt for him? Hope that she could become part of his life and Bobbie's to the point where he couldn't do without her? Or would it be better for everyone concerned if she did what she'd said she was going to do—what he might be expecting her to do for all she knew—and disappear abroad for a few years?

Why had he so determinedly swept her into his orbit the last few weeks anyway? And he had, he had. He had done all the chasing, all the insisting on seeing her every night and drawing her into his and Bobbie's lives.

And she had been so *clear* about what she'd got to do when she had arrived home from York, she wailed silently to herself as she stood under the shower some time later. And then somehow, as soon as she had seen

Ward again, it had all snowballed into a bigger tangle than ever.

She was still debating the issue when she lay down in bed and closed her eyes, weary in mind and body. She couldn't take much more of this hot and cold from Ward, that was for sure, she told herself just before she drifted into a restless, troubled sleep. She'd start seriously making plans to go abroad tomorrow and let him know what she was doing. And then, if he still didn't at least ask her to stay, she would know.

But she didn't want it to be like this—her forcing him to say something if he didn't really mean it...

For the first time in years Jeanie overslept the next morning, and it was only when she was sitting eating a hasty breakfast of toast and coffee that the disc jockey on the radio reminded her it was St. Valentine's Day.

St. Valentine's Day. She shut her eyes as one solitary tear slipped through the defence barrier she thought she had erected in the last weeks. For years this day had been a subtle torture with the one person in all the world she cared about not even knowing she existed as a woman, let alone sending her a card. Not that all that romance stuff was Ward's forte, she knew that, and a piece of folded card with a few fancy words on it meant nothing in the overall plan of things, she knew that too. But nevertheless...

She sniffed disconsolately, feeling very young and very small as she sat at her tiny breakfast bar and glanced miserably at the electricity bill the post had brought. Just one bill. Nothing else.

After that she couldn't hurry to get ready somehow,

and it was well past nine o'clock and verging on the half past dot on her dainty gold wristwatch when she passed through the doors of the building which housed Eddleston and Breedon and entered the lift for the third floor.

She had to pass through the main office to her own office, and as she opened the door and stepped into the room an immediate hush fell over the place. Jeanie glanced round at the faces dotted about in surprise, feeling her face flush in spite of herself. She wasn't *that* late, she told herself uncomfortably, besides which the junior partners worked very much on a flexi-time basis owing to the amount of extra hours they were expected to fit in to the average week. Everyone knew that.

She pitter-pattered down the centre aisle towards Stephanie's desk at the far end which was situated just outside her office, trying to ignore how loud her high heels sounded in the sudden quiet, and when she reached her secretary's desk she paused for a moment. 'Everything okay, Steph?' she asked quietly.

'Fine.' Stephanie was looking at her strangely, almost excitedly but definitely oddly, and now Jeanie felt a slight sense of alarm grip her which she struggled not to betray.

'Nice card,' she said lightly, nodding at the big satin number propped on Stephanie's desk. Every year the desks in the outer office were full of them, but it had never grated quite so much as this year.

'Thanks.'

Stephanie wasn't usually monosyllabic; something was definitely wrong but she couldn't for the life of her imagine what it was.

She looked at Stephanie for a moment more and Stephanie stared back at her, not at all her normal chatty self, before saying, 'Coffee?'

'Great, thanks.' She nodded brightly and walked on, opening the door to her office and then finding herself rooted to the spot. She was conscious of the immense quiet behind her in which you could hear a pin drop, and she knew she ought to step inside and close the door, but that was only on the perimeter of her consciousness. Her whole being was taken up with the sight in front of her.

Her desk, her windowsill, the filing cabinets, the floor—every single bit of available space was filled with flowers leaving just a pathway for her to walk through. The scent and colour was heady, the main source of the perfume emanating from the hundreds upon hundreds of freesias that dominated the display, and on her desk in the middle of a circle of freesias and poppies in little wicker baskets was the most enormous bouquet of red roses.

Her heart was thudding so hard it was a physical pain but she was too dazed to actually think as she closed the door behind her and walked to the desk purely on automatic.

Delicately tinted orchids and lilies of every hue, violets, Michaelmas daisies, ostrich plume asters, vibrantly coloured chrysanthemums, cornflowers, dahlias, baby's breath, various kinds and colours of poppies; the list was endless as her unbelieving gaze struggled to take it in, and intermingled throughout were the freesias.

She bent over and lifted up the bouquet of red roses—at least fifty or more enclosed in a cloud of fern—but then she found she had to sit down suddenly before she could take the little card attached to the cellophane.

When the door opened in the next moment and Ward stepped into her office, his handsome face expressionless and his piercing blue eyes fixed on her face, she knew Stephanie had told him she was in. 'Happy Valentine's Day,' he said softly, his voice holding a note she hadn't heard before.

'This…' She couldn't speak through the strange emotion in her throat, and had to swallow hard before she could try again. 'All this; is it you?' she said faintly.

'Haven't you read the card?' He nodded at the flowers in her arms and when she shook her head dazedly, walked across to her, taking the little card off the bouquet as he said, 'Then let me tell you what it says.'

He opened the small envelope but looked at her rather than the little card. 'You said he never sent you flowers but I want to fill your life with them. He doesn't want commitment or to hear promises of undying love, but there is nothing I want more. I love you, Jeanie. With all my heart, for ever, and if it takes the rest of my life to make you love me then so be it because I'm not going to give up. Do you hear me? I'm not going back to the way it was and I'm not going to let you leave my life. And even if you love him still, you're beginning to love me too. I know you are.'

'That's…that's an awful lot for such a small card,' she whispered.

'I don't understand why I didn't see it before but that weekend it was like a light turning on in my understanding,' he said softly. 'But you loved someone else. And then when you said you'd made the break I knew I had to be patient, to give you time to get used to the idea of being with me. I had to show you that whoever he is, I'm far better for you than he is. And so I've been patient,' he said with touching arrogance.

'But…but it's only been a few weeks,' she protested faintly, terrified of letting herself believe for a moment this was real.

'We've known each other for years and we've been friends first; there's hardly anything we don't know about each other, Jeanie.'

He pulled her to her feet and into his arms, capturing her mouth with urgent, burning lips and kissing her until she was dizzy and fluid in his arms. 'You see?' He raised his head to look down into her flushed face. 'You couldn't respond to me like you do unless you are halfway to loving me. You need me, Jeanie, I know you do. I don't care whether you understand that yet, you'll just have to trust me on it.'

It was so Ward at his most arrogant and imperious that Jeanie shut her eyes at the flood of love that swept into her heart. The hot tide of emotion melted the frozen disbelief that had taken her over and she knew, instantly, she believed what he was saying. She might be being terribly naïve here, credulous and trusting, but for the sort of man Ward was to do what he had done this morning…

'Don't shut your eyes against me,' he said huskily, 'and don't start thinking you are responding to me on the rebound. This is real, I promise you it's real.'

She opened her eyes then; her love intuitively telling her that the rebound comment was a secret fear of his. She had to tell him the truth and then do exactly what he had urged her to do and trust him. If he loved her, really loved her, knowing there was no other man lurking in the background to tempt her away from him would be a joy and a relief but it wouldn't make any difference to the urgency of his feeling.

If his desire was a composite of sexual attraction and the challenge this other man presented, then she would know from his reaction.

'Ward, I have to tell you something,' she said shakily, straining back a little in his arms and looking straight into his dear beloved face. '*You're* the man I've loved for years, and there isn't anyone else. I... I would never have told you because I knew you didn't feel that way about me, but then that day at the office I said too much and the whole thing just seemed to snowball. I resigned because after being with you for that weekend I knew I couldn't take any more.'

He stared at her, and she had the unique privilege of seeing Ward Ryan utterly stunned and silent.

'There...there has never been anyone else,' she said softly, wishing he would say something—*anything*. 'I knew as soon as I met you I'd been waiting for you all my life.'

'Me?' he whispered dopily, the brilliant, instinctual, frighteningly intelligent lawyer. '*Me?*'

'You.'

And she saw his face light up and become radiant. '*Me?*' he shouted at the top of his voice, picking her up off her feet and swinging her round as baskets of flowers and posies were knocked everywhere. 'All this time, when I've been tearing myself apart you loved *me?*' he said huskily when she was on her feet again, giddy and trembling.

'I had five years of torment, remember?' She reached up and cradled his face in her hands, loving him so much it was a physical pain.

'Then you'll marry me straight away? As soon as I can get a special licence? Or do you want a white wedding with all the trimmings?' he added quickly, uncertain again.

It was a revelation to Jeanie that Ward could be unsure about anything, and as she looked up into his hard handsome face that was quite literally shining with the love he had kept hidden for the last agonising, excruciatingly precious weeks, she knew if she lived to be a hundred she would never forget the intensity of this moment. The heady smell and colour of the flowers, being held in Ward's arms, the look on his face and most of all—*most of all*—the miracle of his proposal.

'I'd marry you today if I could,' she said very softly, 'but a couple of days will give me time to buy a white dress for myself and a bridesmaid's dress for Bobbie.'

'I love you, Jeanie. With all my heart. You believe that, don't you?' he said passionately, gathering her to him with a sensuousness that made her weak at the knees. 'By the end of the week you'll be Mrs. Ryan whatever strings I have to pull to make it happen quickly.'

She stared back at him, her heart too full to say anything but her shining eyes speaking volumes to the tall dark man looking down at her so lovingly.

And when Ward kissed her she responded with such

unbrindled desire and deep unashamed hunger that it was some time before he could bring himself to stop, and only then because of where they were.

'I think you'd better look for those dresses this afternoon,' he said unevenly as he adjusted her rumpled clothing with hands that weren't quite steady. 'If tomorrow night isn't your wedding night it won't be for the lack of me trying.'

'I can't believe this is happening.' She smiled tremulously, overwhelmed with the swiftness with which her life had changed.

'It's happening all right,' he said with the fierce intensity she recognised, kissing her once more before reluctantly drawing away. 'And now, my love, we had better go and put all those people out there out of their misery, and announce we're getting married.'

'Oh, Ward.' She clutched hold of him, suddenly shy.

'Come on,' he said softly, drawing her into the side of him where she fitted as though she'd always belonged there. 'I want the world to know I've found my perfect valentine, and you are, my love, you are. I'm going to spend the rest of my life telling you so.'

And Ward Ryan was a man of his word.

Lynne Graham was born in Northern Ireland and has been a keen Mills and Boon® reader since her teens. She is very happily married, with an understanding husband who has learned to cook since she started to write! Her five children keep her on her toes. She has a very large dog, which knocks everything over, and a smaller Highland terrier. When time allows, Lynne is a keen gardener.

Don't miss the first book in Lynne's
Brides of L'Amour mini-series:

THE FRENCHMAN'S LOVE-CHILD
on sale July 2002 in Mills & Boon®
Modern Romance™

THE BOSS'S
VALENTINE
by
Lynne Graham

CHAPTER ONE

IT HAD been a hideous day at work.

On the way home, Poppy called into the corner shop and the first thing she noticed was that the big valentine card she had admired over a month earlier was still unsold. She couldn't understand why nobody had bought it for she loved its glorious overblown pink roses and simple sentimental verse. She wondered why all the cards her more fortunate friends received were joke ones with comic, cruel, or even crude messages.

On an impulse, Poppy lifted the card and decided to buy it. Why shouldn't she send a valentine card? True, nobody had ever sent *her* one, but that didn't mean that she couldn't use the card as a means of brightening someone else's day. As to the identity of that special, lucky someone, there was no doubt in her mind about who would receive the card...

Poppy had fallen head over heels in love with Santino Aragone in her first week working at Aragone Systems. She was all too well aware that Santino was as out of her reach as the moon. Santino was a hugely successful entrepreneur, blessed by spectacular sleek, dark Italian looks, and he had a never-ending string of gorgeous women in his life. But in an emergency Santino Aragone could also be incredibly kind. On her first day at work, when she'd got her finger trapped in a door, Santino had taken her to the hospital himself. When he had fainted dead away at the sight of a needle, Poppy had known he was the man for her…she had thought that was so sweet.

Starry-eyed over the idea that her small, anonymous gesture of a card might at least bring a brief smile to Santino Aragone's brooding dark features on what she knew would be a difficult day for him, she was unlocking the door of her bedsit before her thoughts roamed uneasily back to her own horrendous day at work.

Desmond, the slick new head of marketing, had asked her if she had been born stupid or perhaps she'd got that way with effort? Having spilt coffee on his keyboard, Poppy had cleaned it up without telling him and in the process somehow wiped his morning's work from his computer. Although she had made grovelling apologies, Desmond had still put in a complaint about her to Human Resources and she had been issued with a formal warning.

Her colleagues would have been surprised to learn that Poppy, famed for her laid-back nature, was even angrier with herself than Desmond had been. If she had not been so busy chatting, the coffee would never have been spilt. Time and time again, a lapse in concentration led to similar mistakes on her part. Sometimes she wondered if the problem had started when she was at school and her parents had, without ever meaning to, managed to undermine her every small triumph.

'I'm sure you've done your best,' her mother would say with a slight grimace when she scanned Poppy's school reports. 'We can't expect you to match Peter's results, can we?'

Her elder brother, Peter, had been born gifted and his achievements had set an impossible standard against which her more average abilities sank without trace. Punch-drunk with pride over their son's academic successes, her parents had always concentrated their energies on Peter. Poppy would have liked to go to university, too, but when she was fifteen, her parents had told her that, as further education was so expensive and Peter would still be completing his doctorate, she would have to leave school and train for a job instead. It had seemed to her then that there was no point in striving for better grades. But it had been a conviction that she had since lived to regret.

Now painfully conscious that she didn't have much in the way of academic qualifications and that she had been lucky to get a position in a slick city business, Poppy worked hard as a marketing assistant. She was willing, enthusiastic and popular with her colleagues, but employees who made foolish mistakes were frowned on at Aragone Systems. In addition, the warning she had received that day was her second in six months and if there was a third, she could be sacked. Ironically, it was not so much the fear of being fired that sent a chill down her taut spine, it was the terrifying knowledge that if she was fired she would never, ever set eyes on Santino Aragone again...

'Is this someone's idea of a joke?' Santino Aragone demanded with incredulous bite when he opened the giant envelope two days later and found himself look-

ing at the most naff of valentine cards awash with
chintzy roses in improbable clashing pinks.

'I'm as surprised as you are.' His PA, Craig Belston,
thought with considerable amusement that no woman
could have chosen a worse way of trying to impress
his sophisticated employer. Or indeed a worse day or
even year to make such a declaration.

The staff Christmas party had been postponed after
the sudden death of Santino's father, Maximo, and re-
scheduled to take place as a Valentine's Day event this
evening. As bad luck would have it, Santino was attending another funeral of an old schoolfriend that
very afternoon. Furthermore, it might be a little-known
fact but Santino loathed Valentine's Day in much the
same way that Scrooge had loathed the festive season.

Lean, strong face grim, Santino opened the card. A
faint whiff of an eerily familiar perfume made his nostrils flare and he frowned. Floral…jasmine? An old-
fashioned scent, not the type of fragrance worn by a
stylish woman. But so taken aback was he by the candid message on the inside of the card that he forgot
about the perfume.

'As always, I'm thinking of you and loving you
today,' ran the screed.

Had he become the unwitting target of some dreadful schoolgirl with a crush? Wincing at the very idea
while he mentally ran through the very few teenage
girls within his social circle, he made no demur when
Craig took the liberty of turning the card round to
peruse it for himself.

'Tinkerbell…' Craig pronounced in a tone of raw
disbelief.

'I beg your pardon?' Santino prompted drily.

'That dippy redhead in marketing. We call her Tinkerbell because she's always flying about and putting her feet in it noisily. Well, Poppy's certainly stuck her silly head above the parapet this time,' the younger man remarked with an unpleasant smile. 'I'm certain she sent this card. That's her scent. She always wears it and guess who loves pink and flowers as well?'

Poppy Bishop, the marketing junior, hired six months ago by his late father in total defiance of HR's choice of candidate while Santino had been on vacation. Why? Maximo had felt sorry for her because she had confided that it was her first interview after fifty-odd job applications. Poppy with her shy but sunny smiles, explosive Titian corkscrew curls and her comical penchant for floral prints and insane diets. Even in a large staff, Poppy was hard to ignore and calamity did follow her around.

'Some women just *live* to embarrass themselves,' Craig remarked thinly. 'Shouldn't someone have a word with her about this? The cheek of her too...a little nobody like her making up to the boss!'

Summoning up a recollection of how Poppy behaved in his vicinity, Santino decided she very probably *was* the culprit. He knew he made her nervous. Around him, she was more than usually clumsy, tongue-tied to the point of idiocy and enveloped in a continual hot blush. She also had a way of looking at him that suggested that with very little effort he might walk on water. Other women treated him to the same look but where they were concerned it was deliberate flattery, whereas Poppy's expressive face paraded her every thought like a banner. He was relieved that she had not signed the card. She would not have appre-

ciated that her trade-mark perfume and love of flowers
might be a give-away and would undoubtedly cringe
if she realised that she was even under suspicion.
Instantly, Santino regretted allowing Craig to read the
card.

'I doubt that Poppy Bishop sent it,' Santino murmured in a bored tone of dismissal as he dropped the
card straight into the bin. 'She's just not the type. I
imagine it's more likely to have come from some
schoolgirl, possibly the daughter of one of my friends.
Now, since we've had our entertainment for the day,
could you get me the MD of Delsen Industries on the
phone?'

Later that morning, Santino's attention wandered
back to the bin where the card lay forlorn and rejected.
A groan of exasperation escaped his wide, sensual
mouth. What on earth had possessed her? His PA
hated her guts and would do her a bad turn if he got
the chance. Why? Craig was famous for hitting on the
youngest, newest female employees, treating them to
a one-night stand and then dumping them.

But when his PA had tried his routine on Poppy,
she had turned him down and admitted that she had
been told that he was the office romeo on her first day,
a put-down that had hit Craig's ego right where it hurt.
Craig would have been more humiliated, however, had
he realised that Santino had been the one to issue that
warning. He still didn't know why he had bothered.
Maybe it was the fact that his father had warmed to
the girl; maybe it was the sheer naivety he had seen
in her blue pansy-coloured eyes...

Around ten o'clock that morning, Poppy had to stock
up the stationery cupboard. She was glad that she had

to trek down to the floor below to get fresh supplies. Anything capable of taking her mind off the valentine card she had sent was welcome.

To say that she had got cold feet about that card would have been a major understatement. It had been an insane impulse and she hadn't stopped to think about what she'd been doing. Suspecting that Santino could hardly be looking forward to the staff party when it would only remind him of his father's sudden demise at Christmas, she had overflowed with sympathy for, as far as she knew, Santino had no other close relatives. And although her own family were still alive, they had emigrated to Australia and she rarely heard from them.

Even so, her far-too-emotional frame of mind the night before last was no excuse for the personal message she had inscribed on that card. She also had the sinking suspicion that Santino, who was the very image of ruthless workplace cool and efficiency, might very much have disliked receiving a huge pink envelope at the office. Surely some of the executive staff must have commented on that bright envelope? And possibly laughed, which was not something she felt that Santino would have enjoyed either.

That idiotic declaration of love had been her biggest misjudgement of all. Why had she let herself get so carried away? Why hadn't she had the wit to just sign it with only a question mark? Then the card might have been interpreted in a dozen ways and even as a harmless joke. But her statement of undying love had put that crazy card into an entirely different realm and might well rouse much greater curiosity.

Clutching a sheaf of paper and several bags of pens, Poppy headed back towards the lift, her steps slowing when she saw Santino chatting to several other men in the reception area. Her heartbeat quickened, her chest tightened, her mouth ran dry, symptoms that always assailed her when Santino Aragone was in view or even within hearing. The dark, deep timbre of his honeyed, accented drawl sent a positive tingle down her backbone. Santino could voice the most prosaic statistics and make them sound like poetry.

While pretending great interest in the supplies she was carrying, Poppy glanced up and stole a look at him. *Bang*...the full effect of Santino just exploded on her. She was entranced by the commanding angle of his dark head, the gloss of his black hair beneath the lights, the sheer height and breadth of him in a dark formal business suit that exuded classic designer tailoring. Yet when he moved he was as fluid as a big cat, and as graceful. As he turned his head to address someone she caught his profile, strong and distinctive from his lean, sculpted cheekbones to the proud jut of his nose and the aggressive angle of his jawline. His golden skin was stretched taut over his superb bone structure.

He made her ache. Just looking at Santino made her ache. As one of the bags of pens escaped the damp clutch of her nerveless fingers and fell to the floor Santino swung round and she collided with his incredible eyes, black as sloes below these harsh interior lights but the same shade as polished bronze in daylight. His gaze narrowed, spiky black lashes curling down to zero in on her. Then, instead of looking away again as she expected, he stared almost as if he had never seen her before.

It was as if time stopped dead for Poppy. Her heart was pumping blood so hard, she was as out of breath as if she had been running. There was a singing sound in her eardrums and her whole body felt oddly light and full of leaping energy. She looked back at him, wide, very blue eyes steady for possibly the very first time, and sank without trace in the glittering golden intensity of his appraisal.

Someone stooped and swept up the bag she had let fall, blocking her from Santino's gaze and breaking that spell. She focused with dizzy uncertainty on Craig Belston, absorbed the sneer etched on his self-satisfied features and almost recoiled, her fair skin reddening.

'You're making a patsy of yourself,' Craig murmured very low. 'The old dropped hanky routine went out with the ark!'

Her face tightened in shaken disconcertion. 'Sorry?'

Faint colour demarcating the hard slant of his cheekbones, Santino strode into the lift, hit the button to close the doors and left all his companions behind without even thinking about it. Poppy Bishop's hair was a vibrant golden auburn and very unusual. Just for a moment under the lights her hair had looked quite dazzling and she had beautiful eyes. For once, although he was quite certain that it would have been something that would have jarred on him, he had not noticed what she was wearing. But he was not attracted to her; of course, he wasn't.

Poppy was an employee, he reminded himself with relief. Not even if Cleopatra joined the staff would Santino have allowed himself to be tempted into an unsuitable liaison. That stupid card was still on his mind, that was all! He began with cool logic to list all Poppy's flaws. She was only about five feet three and he preferred tall blondes. She was twenty-one and he liked women closer to his own age. She had such dreadful dress sense that she stuck out like a canary bird among the suits at a meeting. She talked too much, knocked things over, messed up royally on the computer on a regular basis. He was a technical whizz, a perfectionist, she was an accident that just kept on happening. She was also the kind of woman men married and he would die single. The prospect of the funeral he had to attend that afternoon was stressing him out. What he ought to have was a drink.

Poppy hurried back to the marketing department and went to fetch Desmond's coffee. She was in turmoil. Why had Santino stared at her that way? Or had that just been her imagination? She was so ridiculously obsessed with him that her mind had probably played tricks on her. Why had she got this horrible suspicion that he knew she had sent that card? How could he *possibly* know? He couldn't read minds, could he?

And why had Craig attacked her that way when he usually behaved as though she was beneath his lofty notice? For goodness' sake, what had got into him? Craig Belston never deigned to speak to her, at least not since that first week when he had asked her out and badgered her to the point where she had been tactless enough to say that she had been warned about him. 'The old dropped hanky routine'? Did Craig suspect her feelings for Santino? But how could he?

It was madness to let her discomfiture about that wretched card work her up into a state, Poppy told

herself in annoyance. Short of dusting the card for
fingerprints and matching them to hers, there was no
way that anyone could identify the sender. As for
Craig, well, he had few friends at Aragone Systems
and was pleasant to even fewer. Brainy he might be,
but he had a nasty tongue and a habit of smirking at
other people's misfortunes. So it would be foolish to
read anything into those snide comments of his...
Wouldn't it?

CHAPTER TWO

'NO…NO…NO!' Desmond urged Poppy in loud dismay. 'Just leave the coffee over there. I prefer to stretch my arm out!'

Although Poppy smiled like a good sport at the tide of amusement that those pointed instructions roused, she was cut to the bone. Hadn't she suffered enough yet for the episode of the spilt coffee? A lecture about safety measures with liquids from the HR manager had set the seal on her shame while she had also been reminded of her first formal warning, which had resulted from poor timekeeping in her very first month at Aragone Systems. 'One more strike and you're out,' had been the message she'd received after the coffee incident and she really was determined not to make any further blunders.

'What are you wearing to the party tonight?'

Grateful for the interruption, Poppy glanced up with a smile from the unexciting graph she had been tinkering with on her monitor. It was Lesley, a tall, slim brunette on the market research team. 'Nothing special. Just a dress.'

She listened while Lesley described her own outfit. She knew that without a doubt it would enhance every slender curve of the other woman's enviable figure. As Desmond informed her that he wanted the graphs she had been working on for a meeting, she hurried into printing them, relieved that she had finished the last one in time.

'I heard that Santino got a valentine card,' Lesley continued, and as Poppy tensed she added, 'I was more surprised to hear he didn't get a whole sackful! I bet it was from his ex trying to get back in with him.'

'Ex?' Poppy queried, relaxing again.

'Don't you read the gossip columns? He dumped Caro Hartley a month back,' Lesley informed her with authority. 'I didn't think that would last long. She's quite a party girl and I suspect Santino got bored fast. He's a very clever guy.'

'I'm sure he'll not be on his own for long,' Poppy remarked, anxious eyes on Desmond, her boss, as he treated the printed graphs to a cursory appraisal. Had she changed the colouring of the one she had first done in pink for her own amusement? Yes, she was sure she remembered doing so. Even so, she didn't lose her tension until he had slotted them into a folder.

Never, ever again would she play around with the colours of the graphs, she swore as she went into the cloakroom to freshen up at lunchtime. If it killed her, she was going to erase her every bad habit. She gave herself only the most fleeting look in the mirror. At least she had grown out of the spots and her skin now looked great. But her rippling auburn curls were a constant source of aggravation, for the little tendrils that gathered round her face ensured that her hair never looked as tidy as other women's. However, cut short her riotous curls were even harder to handle, so she kept her hair long and wore it clipped back at the nape of her neck.

Her unfashionable curves were the biggest challenge, she conceded ruefully. She was in dire need of a new, inspiring diet. The banana regime had put her off bananas for life, and the cabbage soup one had ensured that she felt queasy just passing vegetables on a market stall. No, it was back to boring old salad and yogurt, which worked but meant that she spent most of her time fantasising about food and feeling so hungry she could have munched on wood.

When she returned to her desk, the email icon was flicking on her monitor and she opened it, hoping it was a cheering communication from a friend.

'Pink graphs are inappropriate in a business environment,' ran the email.

Poppy looked at the message in shock and then glanced around herself to see if anyone was looking at her, but nobody was. Who had seen her mucking about with that graph before lunch? Who was pulling her leg? It was unsigned and the address was a six-digit number and, as such, anonymous.

'Says who?' she typed in and sent the email back.

'I like graphs in dark colours.'

'That's boring,' Poppy told her correspondent.

'Rational. Pink is a distraction.'

'Pink is warm and uplifting,' she protested in reply, typing at full tilt.

'Pink is irritating, cute, feminine…inappropriate.' That awful word, inappropriate again. Her correspondent was a guy, she decided, and certainly not Desmond, who regarded email as a time-wasting exercise and who would surely have gone into orbit the instant he saw a pink graph.

'How did you see my graph?' she typed.

'Stick to the issue.'

Poppy grinned at that rejoinder. *Definitely* a guy.

'One more warning and you could be out of work. Be sensible.' That next message came in fast on the previous one without having given her the chance to respond.

Her grin fell off her lips at supersonic speed. 'How do you know that?' she typed.

But this time, infuriatingly, there was no answer. Thinking about her mystery correspondent, Poppy conceded that quite a few people would be aware of those warnings on her employment record. The very first time it had happened she had been so upset, she had talked about it herself and, after the coffee episode, Desmond had been so furious that he had announced his intent to complain about her in such ringing decibels that most of the department had heard him.

Intrigued by those emails, scanning her busy colleagues with intense curiosity, Poppy sent several more to the same address that afternoon but still received no further response. Then she began thinking about the party that evening and wondered what she would wear, since pink had become such a controversial issue...

'I'm *amazed* that you're still laying on large supplies of alcohol for your employees.' Jenna Delsen's exquisite face emanated shocked disapproval as she scanned the low-lit noisy room full of party revellers. 'Daddy used to help our staff to get sloshed at our expense, too, but not since *I* joined the company. Now we have a nice sober supper do. No loud music, no dancing, no drink and everyone behaves.'

'I like my staff to enjoy themselves. It is only one night a year.' Santino suppressed the ungenerous thought that the blonde could be a pious, penny-pinching misery, for she had been welcome company at the funeral that afternoon and he had enjoyed dining with her and her father at their home afterwards.

'I suppose that's the extrovert Italian in you. You threw some very riotous parties when we were at Oxford together.' Jenna gave him a flirtatious, rather coy look as she reminded him that they had known each other since university.

In receipt of that appraisal, all Santino's defensive antenna hit alarm status. 'Let me get you a drink,' he suggested faster than the speed of light, already mentally listing the unattached executives present on the slender but hopeful thought that she might take a shine to one of them instead. They had always been friends, *never* anything else.

Jenna curved a slender hand round his arm when he returned to her side. 'I have a confession to make…for the whole of the time we were at uni together, I was in love with you.'

Santino conceded that what had started out as an unusual day, and had gravitated into being a very long day, was now assuming nightmarish proportions. 'You're kidding me.'

'No.' Jenna fixed her very fine green eyes on him in speaking condemnation. 'And you never noticed. In four *long* years, you never once noticed that I felt rather more for you than the average mate.'

In one unappreciative gulp, Santino tipped back an

entire shot of brandy meant to be savoured at leisure. He was transfixed and trapped by that censorious speech. There was no polite or kind way of telling her that, beautiful and intellectually challenging as she was—for she had a first-class brain—there had been no spark whatsoever on his side of the fence.

'And I had to sit back and watch you chasing girls who couldn't hold a candle to me,' Jenna continued with withering bite.

'Oddly enough, I don't recall you sitting home alone many nights,' Santino countered sardonically.

'Once I understood that I was in love with a commitment-phobe, I trained myself to regard you only as a friend—'

'Jenna...when you first met me, I was eighteen. Most teenage boys are commitment-phobes.' Santino groaned, thinking what an absolute pain she seemed to have become, still nourishing her sense of injustice over the unwitting blow he had dealt to her ego so many years after the event. 'I was no better and no worse than most—'

'Oh, don't be so modest,' Jenna trilled in sharp interruption. 'All the girls were crazy about you! You were spoilt for choice but you deliberately chose women whom you knew would only be short-term distractions. You always protected yourself from the threat of a steady relationship and you're *still* doing it!'

When Santino went back to the bar for another drink, Jenna was so taken up with her discourse that she accompanied him. Santino's temper was on a very short leash and his second drink went the way of the first. He was cursing the innate good manners that had persuaded him that he ought to invite the blonde to accompany him to the party. He was thinking of what a very much better time he would have had mixing with his staff. Then he glanced across the room and saw a figure hovering in the doorway and the remainder of Jenna's barbed criticisms washed off him because he no longer heard them.

Noticing that she had lost his attention, Jenna followed the direction of his gaze. She saw a youthful redhead with a vibrant mane of curly hair. Small, very pretty, but not at all Santino's style. Yet Santino was so busy watching the girl that he had forgotten Jenna was there.

Scanning the crowded room, Poppy finally picked out Lesley in her distinctive white and silver dress and began to move towards her, an apologetic smile on her lips. She was a little late but then some of her colleagues had opted to stay on in the city centre and warm up in a bar before attending the party. But Poppy loved getting ready to go out at home and had known that she didn't have enough of a head for drink to have sustained a lengthy pre-party session.

'I really like that dress,' Lesley said warmly as she flipped out a seat for Poppy's occupation. 'Where did you buy it?'

'It's not new. I got it for my brother's wedding,' Poppy confided, and then added in an undertone. 'To be honest, it's my bridesmaid's dress—'

'I wish my best friend had let me wear an outfit like that for her big day. At least I could have worn it again afterwards.' Lesley admired the strappy green dress that flattered Poppy's shapely figure and slim length of leg, then drew Poppy's attention to the drinks already lined up in readiness for her, pointing out that she was very much behind the rest of them, before continuing, 'It must have been an unusual wedding.'

'My sister-in-law, Karrie, wanted a casual evening do. She wore a short dress, too.'

Poppy's attention, which had been automatically roaming the room in search of a certain tall, dark male, finally found Santino where he stood by the bar with a spectacular blonde woman clinging to his arm. She lifted the drink that Lesley had nudged into her fingers and sipped it to ease her tight throat, but she resisted the urge to ask the chatty brunette if she knew who Santino's companion was. After all, what was the point? Did it make any difference who it was? And it was none of her business either.

Indeed, she should not even be *looking* at Santino Aragone, Poppy told herself guiltily, because looking was only feeding her obsession. Having thought over Craig's sneering remarks earlier that day, Poppy had finally faced the unhappy fact that he at least suspected that she was rather too attached to their mutual employer. That conclusion had unnerved her for Craig's reputation for making others the butt of his cruel sense of humour was well-known. So, she would have to be more circumspect in the future, for languishing like a lovelorn teenager over Santino could easily make her a laughing stock at work. In fact, she would be much better devoting her brain to sussing out the mystery identity of her email correspondent, who had to at least *like* her to have gone to the trouble of trying to give her a warning word of advice, she reflected.

'Who is she?' Jenna enquired very drily of Santino.

'Who are you talking about?' Santino asked with a

magnificent disregard for the direction of his own gaze.

'The little redhead with the pre-Raphaelite hair… the one whom you've been watching for at least *three solid minutes*,' Jenna completed between gritted teeth.

'I'm not watching her,' Santino murmured with cool disdain.

'But even though you employ hundreds of young women you know *instantly* who I'm referring to,' Jenna noted with rapier-sharp feminine logic.

'Did you get out of the wrong side of the bed this morning?' Santino drawled with his sudden flashing smile. 'Exactly *why* are you trying to wind me up?'

'Before I tell you—' Jenna gave him a grudging smile of approbation for finally registering that she had been set on evening the score for past injuries '—you tell me who the redhead is and I will give you ten very good reasons why one should never, ever date an employee.'

Santino drained his drink again and dealt her a mocking glance. 'I don't need them, Jenna. All ten of them are in my mind right now.'

Returning to her table after chatting to various friends, Poppy sat down again. Lesley and two other women were chatting about Santino's date, who was evidently the daughter of the owner of Delsen Industries.

'What do *you* think of Jenna?' another, less welcome voice enquired.

Poppy's head swivelled, her startled gaze only then registering that Craig Belston had joined their table during her absence. That question had been directed specifically at her and she was gripped by discomfi-

ture. 'Why would I think anything of her?' she answered with a determined smile. 'All the boss's girl-
friends are incredible beauties.'

'Now why did I get the idea that you mightn't have
noticed that?' Craig rested his pale blue probing eyes
on Poppy and her mouth ran dry.

'Santino's leggy ladies are rather hard to miss.'
Lesley shot a frowning glance at Santino's PA and
added, 'Come on. You've been keeping us all in suspense since we finished work. Who sent Santino the
naff card?'

Poppy froze and then gulped down her drink as her
colour heightened.

'Did I mention that it was an *inside* job?' Craig
murmured with tormenting slowness and Poppy's
heart skipped an entire beat, her every tiny muscle
pulling rigid.

'No, you darned well didn't!' one of the other
women piped up in exasperation. 'Who on earth working for Santino would be daft enough to send him a
valentine card swearing undying love? I mean, come
on, *yes*, he's hugely fanciable, but he's the last guy
around who would respond to that kind of blatant invitation from a member of staff.'

'You said the card wasn't signed,' Lesley reminded
Craig. 'So how could you know it was sent by someone in Aragone Systems? It didn't come through the
internal mail, did it?'

'Just assume that in this particular case we're talking about someone who's not very bright,' Craig invited, and Poppy's tummy began to churn where she
sat. 'Someone who assumed that only a name would
expose her identity.'

'You recognised the handwriting!' someone exclaimed.

'I really don't think I like this conversation very much,' Lesley remarked suddenly. 'Valentine cards are just for fun.'

'It wasn't the handwriting. It was a combination of errors,' Craig explained to the table at large. 'A distinctive perfume, a predilection for a particular colour and a love of flowers.'

Poppy was now as pale as milk and feeling physically ill with humiliation. She could not bring herself to look at any of her companions and silence greeted Craig's last explanation, an awful uneasy silence that left Poppy's nerves screaming and her skin clammy.

'Now who do we all know who wears jasmine scent?' Craig murmured.

'I don't know anyone who wears that,' Lesley chimed in, and the two other women followed her lead to say the exact same. Painfully conscious that her companions were trying to throw sand in Craig's eyes and deflect him from his target, Poppy had to grit her teeth to prevent herself from lifting her drink and throwing it at her tormentor.

At the other side of the room, Jenna was still in full confiding mode, but Santino was having a hard time dragging his brooding scrutiny from his PA's smug expression and Poppy's pale, rigid face.

'So, I hope you'll forgive me for giving you a rough time tonight,' Jenna murmured in dulcet continuation, 'but I always promised myself that some day I would tell you the truth and make you sweat for a few minutes. Will you still come to my engagement party?'

Taken aback, Santino frowned. '*Engagement party?*'

'I'm so grateful I'm not in love with you any more.' Jenna sighed. 'Didn't you hear me telling you that I'm getting engaged to David Marsh and that he's picking me up here in five minutes?'

It had been a long time since Santino had heard that much good news in one sentence; he was genuinely fond of Jenna and relief on his own behalf and pleasure on her behalf sliced through his growing tension. Realising that the blonde had merely been set on claiming a small slice of revenge for his past indifference to her, he flung back his handsome dark head and started to laugh with genuine appreciation.

The sight of Santino splitting his sides with laughter, and Jenna equally convulsed and holding onto him for support, filled Poppy with paranoia. Immediately, she assumed that Santino had told the blonde about her pathetic card and that they were laughing at her, for if Craig had guessed that she was the culprit he was certain to have told Santino. Feeling as if she had just had her heart ripped out while she was still breathing, Poppy nonetheless rose from her seat with as much dignity as she could muster, for she could not bear sitting there playing poor little victim for Craig's benefit any longer.

'You're a real Sherlock Holmes, Craig,' she said flatly. 'I'm very impressed.'

Poppy walked away fast. Tears were stinging her eyes and blurring her vision, but she kept her head high and that was her final undoing. She didn't see the small table laden with drinks in her path. She hit it with such force that the table tipped over with an enormous crash that seemed to turn every head in the room. For an instant, Poppy hovered, staring in horror at the smashed glass and liquid everywhere, not to mention the startled dancers leaping back from the mess she had created. Then her control just snapped and she fled.

'Now,' Lesley said icily to Craig, who was sniggering at Poppy's noisy exit, 'while you're wondering why Poppy's friends aren't rushing after her to offer support, watch Santino and *learn*...'

'What are you talking about?'

'Upsetting Poppy is not a career-enhancing move in Aragone Systems. You see, if you were a woman and in touch with the *real* newsbreaking gossip in this building, you would already *know* that Santino fancies the socks off Poppy, too—'

'Rubbish!' Craig snapped. 'He binned the card!'

'Did you check the bin at the end of the day?' someone enquired drily.

'Santino doesn't know what's hit him yet,' one of the other women commented with immense superiority. 'He's more at home with his keyboard than his emotions.'

'But when a bloke like Santino, who likes everything done by the book, starts telling poor Desmond that pink graphs are fresh and creative, he's in *very* deep,' Lesley completed.

In companionable and expectant silence, the three women then focused pointedly on Santino, who had stridden forward the instant that Poppy had sent the table flying. He swung round to speak to Jenna Delsen and not thirty seconds later left in the same direction as Poppy. Witnessing that demonstration, Craig turned the greyish colour of putty and groaned out loud.

CHAPTER THREE

WHEN Poppy emerged from the function room at full tilt, several women were entering the cloakroom across the foyer and she wheeled away in the opposite direction.

Finding herself by the lifts, she stabbed the call button with a frantic hand and gulped back a sob. She had to find a quiet corner to pull herself back together again. Selecting the marketing floor, she slumped back against the lift's cold steel wall as the doors closed. Wrapping her arms round herself, she hugged herself tight. But it was no help, no comfort, because all she could think about was what a fool she had made of herself.

When she saw the dark reception area on the marketing floor, it looked eerie and she hit the door button again in a hurry and tried another floor. Her eyes flooded with burning tears. Of course, Santino Aragone would have laughed when he was told who had sent that card. Everybody would be laughing! After all, she was just a junior member of staff, the plump little redhead Craig had nastily labelled, 'Tinkerbell' and hardly competition for the gorgeous women Santino specialised in. Why on earth hadn't common sense intervened before she'd posted that stupid card to Santino at the office? Didn't she *have* sense like other people? Her throat aching, she could no longer hold back the tears and a sob escaped her. How could she have exposed herself to that extent?

In the foyer below, Santino was watching the lights that indicated which floor the lift was at. The light flicked through the levels in descent again, made several brief stops and then sank as low as the floor above before beginning to ascend again. When the lift finally reached the executive level, he waited in taut suspense to see if it moved on again.

When the doors opened on the top floor, Poppy blinked in confusion for she had lost track. But low lights were burning and the floor was not in darkness like the others. Dimly recalling that Santino's secretary had a private washroom, Poppy stumbled out. She needed to tidy herself up and fix her face before she could go home.

But shock was still setting in hard on Poppy. Only when it was far too late to change things did she see her mistake. She *should* have toughed out Craig's insinuations. Instead she had fallen right into his trap and confirmed his suspicions. He couldn't have proved anything, yet she had virtually confessed by saying what she had and leaving the table.

Taunting, wounding images were now bombarding her mind, increasing her distress. She had left the party with all the cool of a baby elephant let loose in a drawing room. She saw Craig's self-satisfied smile, Santino laughing, the stiff, disapproving faces of the other women. Craig might as well have stripped her naked in public. Her trembling hands braced on the edge of the washroom vanity unit and, letting her head hang for she couldn't stand to look at herself in the mirror when she hated herself so much for her own stupidity, she began to sob.

Santino had never made it from the lift to his secretary's office so fast. But then those heartbreaking sobs acted on him like a shriek alarm. He would usually have gone quite some distance to avoid a crying woman, but the curious automatic pilot now overruling his normal caution ensured that he strode right through the open door of the washroom and gathered Poppy straight into a comforting embrace.

The sheer shock value of a pair of masculine arms closing round her when she had believed that she was alone provoked a startled cry from Poppy. Then she looked up and focused on Santino and even more shock froze her from head to toe. Bronze-coloured eyes set below lush black lashes were trained to hers, the lean, dark contours of his handsome features taut with concern.

'It's OK,' he soothed in his gorgeous accented drawl.

'Is it?' Poppy's voice emerged on the back of a breathless sob, for she could not have got oxygen into her lungs at that instant had her life depended on it. What was happening should have felt unreal but, in actuality, being in the circle of Santino's arms felt very real and very right. Furthermore, it was something she had been dreaming of for so long that no power on earth could have sent her into retreat.

'Course it is,' Santino asserted, not really knowing what he was talking about, then deciding it was safer to confine himself to inconsequentials rather than risk reawakening her distress. Lifting a lean hand, he curved it round the back of her head to urge her face back into his shoulder where she had started out.

Poppy's tension evaporated and she subsided against him, feeling as boneless as a rag doll. The faint aroma of whatever shaving lotion he used assailed her and immediately became familiar to her: rather exotic, distinctively male. She sucked in a steadying breath, her fingers resting lightly against his broad shoulder, yet she could still feel the flex of his lean, powerful muscles beneath the expensive cloth of his jacket as he held her close. He could be so kind. How had she managed to forget how considerate he had been when she had hurt her finger and he had taken her to hospital? A little calmer, better able to think than she had been minutes earlier at the height of her distress, she saw how unlikely it was that Santino had been nastily indulging in a good laugh at her expense with his ladyfriend. He wasn't like that.

'Let's get out of here,' Santino urged with a faint quiver of wry amusement edging his deep voice. 'This is my secretary's inner sanctum and I feel like an intruder.'

In a jerky motion, she peeled herself from him again, her colour high, her eyes lowering, for she was sure she looked a total fright after giving way to all those tears. Her nose would be pink, her eyes swollen and her mascara might have run. Not that she felt that he would care either way, but she didn't want him seeing her at her very worst. He pressed a light hand to her tense spine and turned her back into the office beyond and on into what had to be his own office.

Abandoning her in the centre of the dark room, Santino strode over to the desk to switch on the light there and indicated a door to her left. 'You can freshen up in there if you like.'

Her eyes widened at the sight of the big luxurious office and then centred back on Santino where he was poised by his desk. The pool of illumination shed by the lamp shrank the large room to more cosy contours but simply emphasised his impact. He was so tall, so wonderfully dark and vibrant. Why was it that every time she looked at Santino he seemed more gorgeous than ever? As she encountered the onslaught of his mesmeric dark golden eyes her heartbeat thudded in what felt like the foot of her throat. She reddened, suddenly all too conscious of the emotions that had got her into such a mess in the first place. Dropping her head again, she went through the door he had indicated.

Santino released his breath in a slow, sustained hiss. He would chat to her for a while just to smooth matters over and then tuck her into a taxi to go home. Concerned employer? He grimaced, picturing her standing there in that green dress that defined her lush curves, the fiery luxuriance of her glorious hair tumbling round her face, bright blue eyes full of strain. He wanted to see her usual sunny smile replace that hunted look. He just liked her, that was all. There was nothing wrong with that that he could see.

Poppy winced when she saw her tousled reflection in the mirror on the wall of Santino's opulent washroom. Breathing in deep because her head was swimming a little, she repaired her eye make-up but didn't bother to refresh her lipstick, lest he think that she was getting tarted up for his benefit. Don't think about that valentine card, she warned herself fiercely. What was done was done and, whether he knew she had penned that card or not, he was hardly likely to mention it. Having dried her hands, she emerged again.

'Take a seat,' Santino told her.

'Don't you have to get back to the party?'

'No. I don't usually stay to the bitter end. My presence tends to inhibit people,' Santino advanced with a wry smile that lent his lean, dark face such innate charm that for several tense seconds she simply couldn't take her eyes from him. 'Would you like a drink?'

'What have you got?'

'Just about everything,' Santino informed her, deadpan. 'Come and have a look…'

Madly self-conscious of her own every move, but enervated by the novel sensation of being alone with him, Poppy moved closer, peered into the packed drinks cabinet and opted for what she hoped was the most sophisticated choice. She backed away with the glass until her legs brushed the low arm of one of the comfortable leather sofas that filled one corner. She sat down on the arm, too skittish to seat herself in the more normal way.

She watched him pour a brandy from a cut-crystal decanter, light burnishing his black hair, accentuating his hard cheekbones and the very faint blue cast of stubble already shadowing his strong jawline. She hadn't seen him when he needed a shave before and she decided that it gave him a very sexy, macho look. As he straightened he shot a glance at her and caught her staring.

'So,' Santino murmured on a casual note intended

to put her at her ease. 'Where did you work before you came here?'

'I was a nanny…that's what I trained for when I left school,' Poppy advanced, her face flushed, her voice tense as she strove to match his relaxation.

'A nanny.' Santino was initially surprised and then he saw her in his mind's eye surrounded by a bunch of children and it was like the missing piece of a jigsaw puzzle suddenly sliding into place for him. Kids would adore her, he thought. She would throw herself into their games, never mind when they got dirty, fuss over them and hug them when they got hurt. Thinking of the chilly, correct sourpuss of a nanny he had had to endure as a little boy, he felt positively deprived.

'How come you ended up in Aragone Systems?' Santino prompted.

Poppy sighed. 'My first placement was with a diplomat's family and I was with them for two whole years…'

'Did they make you work endless hours for a pittance?' Santino enquired cynically.

A brief smile blossomed on her lips at that idea. 'No, they were a lovely family. They treated me very well. The problem was all mine. I got far too attached to the children and when they left England and I was no longer needed, I was just devastated,' she admitted ruefully. 'So I decided it wasn't the job for me and signed up for an office skills course.'

Within an ace of remarking that he considered that decision a wrong move on her part, Santino thought better of it when he registered that he could not imagine the marketing department without her.

'The trouble is…the career change hasn't worked out very well,' Poppy commented rather gruffly.

Santino's ebony brows pleated. 'Everyone makes an occasional mistake—'

'I've managed to pick up two formal warnings in six months.' Poppy shrugged a slight shoulder, cursing her own impulsive tongue, her habit of being too candid for other people's comfort. All she had done was bring her own failings to his notice.

Santino had to resist a strong but unprofessional urge to tell her that her head of department had been guilty of an overreaction when he'd made a complaint about her on the strength of an accident with a spilt drink. She had been unlucky. Desmond Lines was in his first week in the job, keen to make his mark and show his authority, but he had chosen the wrong event and the wrong person to clamp down on. In fact, Poppy might not know it, but that misjudged warning had even been discussed in the boardroom with varying degrees of levity and incredulity. One of Santino's senior executives had looked in mock horror at the puddle of mineral water he had left on the table and had wondered out loud if HR were going to haul him over the coals, too.

Poppy tilted her chin. 'I didn't make mistakes as a nanny.'

'But people would miss you if you weren't here.'

Colliding with glittering dark golden eyes, Poppy felt dizzy. Did he mean *he* would miss her? For goodness' sake, what was she thinking? What difference would it make to him if she went off in search of another job and moved on? She was one very humble cog in a big wheel. He was just being kind again.

Quick to recognise when a subject ought to be changed, Santino asked, 'Do you have any family living in London?'

Poppy moistened her dry lips with her drink and sighed, 'Not any more. My parents moved out to Australia about eighteen months back. My brother, Peter, and his wife, Karrie, live in Sydney.'

'What's the connection that took them all to the other side of the world?' Santino enquired lazily, lounging back with indolent elegance against the edge of his desk.

'Basically...Peter. He's married to an Australian and he was offered a very prestigious teaching post at a university out there. He's a brilliant mathematician. He was doing algebra as a toddler.' A self-deprecating smile curved Poppy's lips. 'I was still struggling to do it at twelve years old.'

'There are more important things,' Santino quipped, opting for the sympathy vote and overlooking his own stratospheric success in the same subject. 'So why didn't you emigrate to Australia with your family?'

'Well...I wasn't *asked*,' Poppy confided with a rueful grin of acknowledgement at that oversight. 'Mum and Dad just worship the ground Peter walks on. They've bought a retirement home near where he and Karrie live. Mum now looks after their house and Dad keeps their garden blooming.'

'Free labour...not bad if you can get it. Does your sister-in-law mind?'

'Not at all. Karrie's a doctor and works very long hours. She's also now expecting their first child. As an arrangement, it suits them all very well.'

'Do you have any other relatives left in the U.K.?' Santino pressed with a frown.

'An elderly great-aunt in Wales whom I visit for the odd weekend. What about you?' Poppy questioned, emboldened by that dialogue.

'Me?'

'I suppose that if you have any relatives they live in Italy,' Poppy answered for herself. 'When did your mother die?'

Santino tensed, his jawline clenching. 'She's not dead. My parents were divorced.'

Disconcerted, Poppy nodded, thinking that that was a little known fact in Aragone Systems for most people had assumed that Maximo Aragone had been a widower.

Santino drained his glass and set it down. 'I haven't seen my mother since I was fifteen.'

'How *awful*!' Poppy exclaimed, her soft heart going out to him at the thought that he had been abandoned by some hard-hearted woman.

Santino shot her a look of surprise and then added drily, 'It was *my* choice to cut her out of my life.'

At that explanation, Poppy surveyed him in sincere shock, and when he went on with complete cool to ask her if she wanted another drink, she said no. Although she suspected that what he had just confided was rather private, she could not rest without knowing more.

'Was your mother cruel to you?' Poppy asked baldly.

'Of course not. She loved me very much but she was not such a good wife to my father,' Santino ad-

vanced on a forbidding note that would have warned
the more cautious off the topic.

'Oh...I see. You took your *father's* side when they
divorced.' Poppy spoke that thought out loud without
meaning to.

Raw exasperation currented through Santino. As if
it were that simple! As if it weren't possible that he
had reached such a decision on the strength of his own
judgement!

The silence seethed.

Recognising that she had got too personal, Poppy
turned pink with discomfiture. 'I'm sorry. It's
just...you said she loved you and yet you've been *so*
cruel to her.' As she registered what she had said she
actually clamped a sealing hand over her parted lips
and surveyed Santino's set features and flaring golden
eyes in dismay and apology. 'It's time I tucked my
big mouth up for the night,' she muttered through her
spread fingers.

'No...I will defend myself against that charge first!'
Santino countered forcefully. 'Let me tell you why I
hate St Valentine's Day...'

'You...*do*?' Her hand falling back to her lap, Poppy
stared at him in a combination of surprise and confusion.

'I adored my mother,' Santino grated. 'So did my
father. He flew her over to Paris to her favourite hotel
to celebrate St Valentine's Day and do you know what
she did?'

In silence and very much wishing she had minded
her own business, Poppy shook her curly head.

'That's the night she chose to tell him she'd been
having an affair and that she was leaving him for her

lover!' Santino ground out like an Old Testament prophet reading out the Riot Act, raw censure in every hard male angle of his striking features.

Poppy pondered that explanation. 'She probably felt so guilty that she couldn't help confessing...I bet she didn't choose that night or those circumstances deliberately.'

'Whatever...Maximo was *shattered*,' Santino stressed on a note of decided finality.

'Was he...?' Poppy compressed her lips on the question she was dying to ask, but then discovered that she was unable to hold it in. 'Was he always faithful to her?'

It was an issue that Santino had never before discussed and she was coming back at him on an angle he had actually never once considered. He stilled in angry unease, looked at Poppy's intent face and wondered why the hell he was suffering from a sudden need to justify a decision he had not once wavered from in fifteen years. It had been that little word 'cruel' that had shaken him, disturbed him in a way he could not have believed. Dark colour marked his superb cheekbones.

'You're not sure he was...are you?' Poppy whispered, recognising the rare flash of uncertainty now lightening Santino's dark gaze. 'Yet you still judged her and not him. But then I've heard that it can be harder for boys to forgive their mother's...er... mistakes.'

'Tinkerbell...the *oracle*?' Santino derided with all the cutting force of his own unsettled emotions. 'That's got to be a new one.'

Poppy flinched as though he had slapped her and

every ounce of her natural colour drained away. He had never utilised that tone on her before, much less looked at her with a pure dismissive contempt that bit right through her tender skin to her bones and made her feel about an inch high. And, of course, he was right, for what did she know about such a situation? Some of her friends had lived through their parents' breaking up but she had no personal experience. Who was she to tell him that he had been unjust and cruel?

'You're right...' Her voice emerged slightly thickened by the stark rise of tears threatening her again and she slid off the arm of the sofa in a hurried movement. 'I can't even solve my own problems, much less tackle other people's. A-and as you've already said,' she stammered in growing desperation as she turned round in a blind uncoordinated circle, 'you don't have a problem in the first place—'

'I'm sorry,' Santino bit out in a rather raw undertone.

'Never mind. I'm hardly the world's most diplomatic person...especially after a few drinks,' Poppy mumbled, narrowly missing a sculpture on a pedestal in her haste to reach the door. 'Maybe I was even a bit jealous.'

'Jealous?' Santino echoed in incomprehension as he tracked her the whole way across his office.

'Yeah...' Poppy had to force herself to turn back. 'You said your mother loved you very much. If mine had ever loved me like that she might answer my letters more often.'

Santino groaned something in Italian and reached for her hands to prevent her from getting any closer to the door. 'Come here...' he urged thickly.

CHAPTER FOUR

SUDDENLY extraordinarily short of breath, Poppy stared up at Santino and as she met his beautiful dark golden eyes she drowned there in her own reflection.

Santino inched her steadily closer until bare inches separated them. 'I want to kiss you...'

'Seriously...?' Her wide gaze clung to his.

'I want to take you home to my bed,' Santino confessed raggedly. 'In fact, I can't think of anything else...'

Poppy blinked. It was as if a little buzzer went off in her brain and allowed her to think again. But what he was telling her was still such an enormous surprise, she just ended up staring up at him again, dark pupils dilated, moist lips parted on her own ragged breathing. He wanted to *kiss* her? That revelation wholly enchanted her. But the second was too much to handle for as yet no man had contrived to persuade Poppy either to go home with him or allow him to come home with her.

'But I'll settle for a kiss...and then supper somewhere public, *cara mia*.' Santino noted the sudden anxious expression in her gaze and the rise of colour in her cheeks with the strangest, newest sense of protectiveness he had ever experienced. He didn't know what he was doing and, for the first time in his very structured life, he realised that he didn't care.

Poppy's heart was playing leapfrog with her ribs. He was attracted to her, too? She couldn't believe it. She was achingly conscious of his hands holding hers and such a flood of happiness filled her that she felt literally light-headed with it and her throat ached. 'Kiss…' she selected her favourite option, the one she could least bear to wait for.

Santino smiled, his heartbreaking, stunning smile that lit up his vibrant bronzed features and sent her pulses racing. 'Only one kiss…otherwise I might not stop.'

'One's a bit mean,' Poppy argued. 'I've been waiting a long time for this. Oh, good heavens, you've left your girlfriend downstairs!' she suddenly gasped, her expression one of comical horror.

'Jenna's just an old friend and she's already left,' Santino assured her with a laugh of appreciation.

As relief at that explanation travelled through Poppy, Santino was already drawing her back across the office towards the corner with the sofas. It was so cool and natural the way he did it, too, that she was helplessly impressed. She couldn't dredge her attention from his lean, strong face, couldn't quite accept that what was happening was really happening. Her legs went weak under her at just the thought of his wide, sensual mouth on hers and she was so keen for it to happen, she was ashamed of herself.

'What are you thinking about?' Santino murmured silkily.

'Kissing you…' Poppy told him, but in truth she was equally enthralled by the new and more intimate side of Santino that she was seeing. It occurred to her that he was in his element, she the one floundering and following his smooth, assured lead.

'Kissing me...' Santino repeated huskily as he tugged her down onto the sofa, wound long fingers through her hair, curving them to the nape of her neck to angle her mouth up to his.

'You're good at this,' Poppy muttered, trembling with the most wicked amount of anticipation.

'Ought to be...' Santino treated her to a slashing irreverent grin that acknowledged his own experience and her eyes clung to his lean, powerful face, her heart hammering. 'But I've never got this close to a woman in the office before—'

'No?'

'Feels forbidden and...*fantastic*,' Santino growled in a throaty purr of hunger.

Poppy quivered, every skincell leaping, and when he brought his mouth down on hers, when he hauled her close, fantastic was in her opinion a serious understatement. She fell into that explosive kiss as though she had been waiting all her life for it.

He captured her lips with intoxicating urgency and with sensual slowness let his tongue slide into her mouth in a darting, probing invasion that was unbelievably exciting. Poppy had never felt what she felt then, not that rise of inner heat or that sudden charged impatience for more that gripped her like a greedy vice. She couldn't get enough of his hot, hard mouth. Every so often sheer necessity forced them to break off just to breathe but they welded back together again fast, Santino groaning low in his throat and muttering fiercely against her swollen mouth, 'You blow me away, *cara*.'

He pulled back from her to shrug free of his suit jacket and wrench at his silk tie to loosen his shirt collar. Sucking in a shallow, shaken breath, Poppy slumped weak as water back against the arm of the sofa and just watched him. The tie was discarded on the carpet beside his jacket and as he straightened he swept her ankles up so that she was lying full length. He slid off her shoes and let them drop as well. Poppy collided with smouldering dark golden eyes and she had never been so electrified with sheer excitement in her entire life.

Santino ran deceptively indolent eyes over her as she lay there all of a quiver, his attention lingering with potent appreciation on her. 'I love your hair…it's incredible and you've got a very, very sexy mouth…'

'Don't stop talking,' Poppy whispered helplessly.

'If I talk, I can't kiss you,' Santino pointed out thickly, scanning her feminine curves in a more bold and intimate appraisal that sent the blood drumming at an insane rate through her veins.

'Problem,' she agreed, barely able to squeeze that single word out.

'Not an impossible one, *cara*,' Santino assured her in his wicked dark drawl, his intense bronzed eyes signalling pure enticement and sensual promise. 'I can think of several very interesting pursuits that I can talk through.'

The atmosphere sizzled. His smile flashed out once more and she just ached so much for contact again that she sat up, grabbed his shoulder to steady herself and found his passionate mouth again for herself. A low moan of response was wrenched from her as he suckled at her lips and then parted them to invade her mouth again.

'Thought I had to talk,' Santino teased as he lowered her back to the sofa and unbuttoned the rest of his shirt.

'No…' Her mouth ran dry as she stared up at him. He looked so big and powerful. A haze of short dark curls delineated his broad, muscular chest and his skin was the vibrant colour of bronze. Her body tensed, wild heat snaking up inside her again.

'Last time I was on a sofa with a female, I was sixteen,' Santino confided with dancing amusement in his dark golden gaze.

He lifted her up to him with easy strength and curved her round him. Cool air hit her taut spine as he unzipped her dress. He brushed down the delicate straps on her slim shoulders and released his breath in a slow, sexy hiss of appreciation as he bared her lush, pouting breasts.

'Superb…every inch of you is a work of art, *cara mia*,' Santino swore with husky fervour as a tide of shy pink washed up into her cheeks. 'Without a doubt you are the perfect reward at the end of a lousy day.'

Then he touched her and she was immediately lost in the passion again. All control was wrested from her by the seductive delight of his skilled fingers on her tender flesh and the even more intense excitement of his knowing mouth caressing the almost painfully sensitive rosy peaks. With a whimper of tormented response, she surrendered to that world of wild sensation…

CHAPTER FIVE

SANTINO wakened to the buzz of his mobile phone.

Disorientated in a way that was far from being the norm for him, he sat up, realised that he was still in the office and dug into his jacket for his phone. It was a very apologetic security guard calling up from the ground floor to ask if he was still upstairs working. *Working?* Santino stole a lingering glance at Poppy where she lay fast asleep beneath the suit jacket in which he had rifled for his phone. Shame and discomfiture gripped him.

'Yes, I'm here. I'll be a while, Willis.' Discarding his mobile again, he checked the illuminated dial on his watch. It was after four on Saturday morning. His teeth gritted as he attempted to come up with a viable plan that would enable him to smuggle an admittedly very small redhead past the security guards down in the foyer. Otherwise, Poppy's reputation was likely to be in tatters by Monday.

Santino swore under his breath. How much alcohol had he consumed yesterday? There had been the pre-dinner drinks with the Delsens, the wine over the meal he had barely touched and then several brandies in succession. That kind of boozing was not a habit of his. All right, he had not been drunk, but he had not been quite sober either. Alcohol had certainly released

all inhibitions and slaughtered his ethics, he conceded
grimly.

He looked at Poppy again. Her gorgeous hair was
a wild tumble spilling across the leather, one pale bare
shoulder and his jacket. She looked adorable, totally
at peace and innocent. Only, as he now had very good
cause to know, she was no longer *quite* the innocent
she had been *before* he laid his womanising hands on
her. In the midst of examining his conscience, Santino
was appalled to register a powerful temptation just to
grab her back into his arms again and kiss her awake.
Drink was supposed to be death to the average male
libido. *Dio mio*, so much for that old chestnut!

Raking angry hands through his tousled black hair,
Santino suppressed a groan. He was furious with himself. How could he have taken advantage of Poppy
like that? He struggled to work out how it had happened. They had almost had an argument. He had
thrown that vicious comment. She had been leaving
when he'd apologised. At that instant, it had somehow
seemed unbelievably important to him that she did *not*
walk out through that door. Then she had said that
about her mother not answering her letters and...?

Ebony brows pleated, Santino gave up on that confusing angle to concentrate on the logical facts that he
was more comfortable with. She *worked* for him.
Affairs between staff were officially frowned on in
Aragone Systems. And guess which smartass had laid
down that ground rule for the greater good of inter-
personal office relationships and morale? He grimaced.
She had been a virgin. He hadn't taken a single precaution. It dawned on him that the last time he had
been on a sofa with a woman he might only have been

a teenager, but he had exercised a lot more caution then than he had demonstrated the night before. He had screwed up, royally screwed up. In the midst of that lowering acknowledgement, which sat not at all well with his pride, he wondered whether there were still any valentine cards for sale. Finding himself wondering something so inane and out of character unsettled him even more. He breathed in very deep.

Poppy wakened to the sound of a shower running somewhere and her sleepy eyes opened only to widen in dismay when the first thing she saw was her dress lying in a heap on the carpet. A split second later, she realised that she was actually lying under...Santino's jacket! Her heart skipped a beat as she finally appreciated that she had spent most of the night in his office. In *his* arms. As the events that had led up to that staggering development unreeled in her blitzed brain like a very shocking film, she leapt off the sofa like a scalded cat. Praying that Santino would stay in the shower next door long enough for her to make an escape, she dressed at excessive speed.

Tiptoeing to the door, her shoes gripped in one trembling hand, she crept out and then raced for the lift. How could she have behaved like that with Santino? She hadn't even been out on a date with him! Sick with shame and embarrassment, she emerged from the lift and slunk out past the two men chatting at the security desk and mercifully behaving as if she were invisible. The buzzer went, though, to unlock the door and let her out, and her face was as red as a beetroot by the time she reached the street.

'She's a right little looker,' Santino's chauffeur remarked to Willis, the head security guard. A long night of playing poker together had formed an easy camaraderie between the two older men.

'She's a nice friendly kid. That's the first time she's walked out of here without saying goodnight,' Willis said. 'I suppose I can recall the rest of my team now—'

'They'll be getting suspicious if you don't. I'd better get out to the limo and look like I've been dozing. Still, at least you got them shifted before the cleaners come on. Like I said, the boss doesn't usually carry on like this.'

Minutes later, Santino strode from the lift out of breath, black hair still wet from the shower, stormy golden eyes sweeping the foyer in search of Poppy. He couldn't believe she had walked out on him without a word. As if he were some sleazebag of a one-night stand she didn't want to face in daylight! He was outraged. That kind of treatment had never come his way before. Indeed, the clinging habits of certain previous lovers had driven him near to distraction. He had never had one who'd evaporated like scotch mist the first chance she'd got.

He had had hardly any sleep…he was going home, he was going to bed and he'd call on her in the afternoon, he decided. She'd be glad to see him then. She'd appreciate him by then. He hoped she spent the whole lousy morning miserable because that was what she deserved and, in that self-righteous and ripping mood, Santino strode out of the building.

Late that afternoon, Poppy sat on the train watching the countryside fly by with eyes that were blank and faraway. In her mind all she could truly see was a lean, dark, handsome face.

It was amazing how little time it had taken to pack up her belongings and give notice on her bedsit. Everything she possessed fitted into two suitcases. But then she never had been one for gathering clutter, and money to spend on non-essential items had always been in short supply. A fresh start was the best thing, she reminded herself painfully. She could not go back to work at Aragone Systems again. Yes, she could have steeled herself to live down the gossip about that stupid card and her own silliness, but *no*, she could not put herself through the agony of seeing Santino again. She imagined he would be relieved when word of her letter of resignation finally filtered through to him.

Well, she had surely taught herself one good, hard lesson about what happened when a woman flung herself at a man. After all, wasn't that exactly what she had done? Humiliation and guilt engulfed her, for she blamed herself entirely: that childish card telling him that she loved him.

Once Santino had known who the sender was, he wouldn't have been human if that hadn't made him curious. Craig's malice, Santino's concern and her own distress had led to a physical intimacy that would never have developed in normal circumstances. There they had been all alone in the enervating quiet of his office. No doubt even the admiring way she had looked at him had been a provocative encouragement and invitation on male terms. And she might not have much experience with men but every magazine she read warned her that, while nature had programmed women to seek a relationship, men were programmed to seek something an awful lot more basic.

While the train was speeding Poppy towards Wales where her father's aunt, Tilly, lived, Santino was having a very trying dialogue with one of Poppy's former neighbours.

'Nah…haven't seen her for weeks,' the guy with an obvious heavy hangover groused, yawning in Santino's face. 'Maybe she's in there and just doesn't want to answer the door. I had a woman who did that to me. Do you mind if I go back to bed now?'

'Not in the slightest,' Santino breathed grittily.

Santino was now in what was totally unknown territory for him. Maybe Poppy didn't want anything further to do with him. Maybe she *was* in her bedsit not answering the door and praying that he would take the hint and leave her alone. It wasn't exactly a mature response, but a woman who had retained her virtue to the age of twenty-one might well hate his guts for having slept with her when she'd been in such a vulnerable state. If she was so keen to avoid him, and her flight from his office had already brought that message home once, did he have the right to crowd her? Or was he more likely to make a difficult situation worse by pushing too hard too soon? At the end of that logical internal discussion with himself, Santino was still fighting an almost irresistible urge just to smash the door down!

Three weeks later, Poppy was shouting at Tilly's pet geese for lurking behind a gate in an effort to spring a surprise attack on the postman. But the older man was even wilier than the web-footed watchdogs and he leapt into his van unscathed, honked the horn in cheerful one-upmanship and drove off.

Poppy went back into her great-aunt's cottage, clutching the post and the newspaper. Tilly, a small, spry woman with short grey curly hair, well into her seventies but very fit and able, set her book down in favour of the paper.

'Have you got some answers to that ad you placed?' Tilly asked.

'By the looks of it, several,' Poppy answered with determined cheer. 'With a little luck, you'll be shot of your uninvited house guest within a few weeks!'

'You know I *love* having you here,' Tilly scolded.

But her great-aunt's cottage was tiny, perfect for one, crowded for two. Furthermore, Tilly Edwards was one of those rare individuals who actually enjoyed her own company. She had her beloved books and her own set little routine and Poppy did not want to encroach for too long on her hospitality. Within days of her arrival at Tilly's rather isolated home, she had placed an advertisement in a popular magazine seeking employment again as a nanny.

She would take anything—short-term, long-term, whatever came up. The sooner she was working again and too busy to sit feeling sorry for herself, the happier she would be. In the minuscule kitchen, she made a pot of tea for herself and coffee for Tilly. Of recent, she herself had gone off coffee. But then she had pretty much gone off food, too, she conceded wryly, thinking of the irritating bouts of queasiness she had suffered in recent days. Obviously a broken heart led not just to sleepless nights, but poor appetite and indigestion as well. So out of misery might come skinniness. She couldn't even smile at the idea.

She was grateful that she had had enough pride and sense to leave Aragone Systems, but the pain of that sudden severance from all that was familiar and the knowledge that she would never see Santino again was unimaginable and far worse than she had expected. But then it was short, sharp shock treatment, exactly what she had deserved and most needed, she told herself.

'Poppy...' Tilly said from the sitting room.

Poppy moved a few feet back to the doorway. Her great-aunt held up her newspaper. 'Isn't that the man you used to work for?'

Poppy focused on the small black and white photo. Initially the only face she saw was Santino's and then right beside him, beaming like a megawatt light bulb she recognised Jenna Delsen. 'What about him?' she prompted as evenly as she could manage, for one glance even from a distance at Santino in newsprint upset her.

'Seems he's got engaged...an attractive woman, isn't she? Would you like to read it for yourself?' Tilly immediately extended the paper.

'No, thanks. I'll take a look at it later.' Poppy retreated back into the kitchen again and knew that the glimpse she had already had of that damning photo was more than sufficient. She felt incredibly dizzy and assumed that that was the effect of shock. Bracing unsteady hands on the sink unit, she snatched in a stricken breath and shut her anguished eyes tight. *Engaged?* To Jenna Delsen only weeks after he had referred to the beautiful blonde as 'just an old friend'?

Later she went out for a long walk. The strain of
trying to behave normally around Tilly had been immense. So, the man you love isn't perfect, after all,
she told herself heavily. Shouldn't that make it much
easier to get over him? His engagement put a very
different complexion on their night together. Santino
had *lied* to her. He had lied without hesitation. He was
a two-timing louse, who had simply used her for a
casual sexual encounter. Clearly he had already been
involved in a relationship with Jenna Delsen that went
way beyond the boundaries of platonic friendship.

Three days later, Santino arrived in Wales. Finding
out where Poppy's only relative lived had been a long
and stony road, which had entailed ditching quite a lot
of cool and calling Australia several times before
eventually contriving to talk to Poppy's sister-in-law,
the doctor. And if Karrie Bishop ever got tired of med-
icine, secret police forces everywhere would vie for
her services. Santino had not appreciated the interro-
gation he had received, and even less did he appreciate
getting lost three times in succession in his efforts to
find a remote cottage that he had even begun suspecting Dr Bishop might have only dreamt up out of a
desire to punish him!

But there the cottage was, a minute building hiding
behind an overgrown hedge, the sort of home loved
by those who loathed unexpected visitors, Santino reflected with gritty black humour. His tension was at
an all-time high now that he had arrived and he had
to think about what he was going to say to Poppy.
Oddly enough, Santino had not considered that con-
tentious issue prior to his actual arrival. *Finding* Poppy
had been his objective. What he might do with her

when he found her was not a problem for his imagination in any way, but what he could reasonably say
was something more of a challenge. He missed her at
the office? He couldn't get that night out of his mind?

Very unsettled by that absence of cutting-edge inspiration, but too impatient to waste time reflecting on
it, Santino climbed out of his sleek car in the teeming
rain. When a pair of manic honking geese surged out
of nowhere in vicious attack, Santino could happily
have wrung their long, scrawny necks, built a bonfire
on the spot and cooked them for dinner. The confident
conviction that the cottage might lie round every next
corner had prevented him from stopping off for lunch
and he was in a very aggressive mood.

Hearing the noisy clamour of the geese announcing
a rare visitor, Poppy hurried to the front door to yank
it open. The car was a startling vivid splash of scarlet
against the winter-bare garden. But it was Santino,
sleek and immaculate in a charcoal-grey business suit,
who knocked most of the air in her lungs clean out of
her body.

In the act of holding his feathered opponents at bay
with his car door, Santino caught sight of Poppy lurking in the doorway and stilled. The pink sweater made
her look cuddly and the floral skirt with the pattern
that made him blink was *cheering* on a dull day, he
decided, rain dripping down his bronzed features. He
just wanted to drag her into the car and drive off with
her.

Shock having made Poppy momentarily impervious
to his battle with the geese, she stared back at Santino,
only dimly wondering why he was standing in heavy
rain and getting drenched. What on earth was he doing

in Wales? How could he possibly have found out where she was? She met his beautiful eyes, dark as ebony and shameless in their steady appraisal, and she knew she ought to slam the door closed in his face. Seeing him in the flesh again hurt. It only served to refresh painful memories of how much that one night, which had meant so little to him, had meant to her. For just a few hours she had been happier than she had ever hoped to be, but her happiness had flourished in a silly dream world, not in reality, and punishment had not been long in coming.

'Are you planning to call the geese off?' Santino enquired gently. 'Or is this supposed to be a test that picks out the men from the boys?'

Forcing herself free of her nervous paralysis, Poppy lifted the broom by the door and shooed the geese back to allow Santino a free passage indoors.

'Grazie, cara,' Santino drawled, smooth as silk.

Her soft mouth wobbled. With an inner quiver, she recalled the liquid flow of Italian words she hadn't understood in the hot, dark pleasure of that night. She turned her burning face away, but not before he had seen the shuttered look in her once trusting and open gaze. She was ashamed of her own weakness. She knew she ought to tell him to go away, but she just didn't have the strength to do that and then never know why he had called in the first place. At least Tilly was out, she thought guiltily, and she wouldn't find herself having to make awkward explanations for his visit.

As Poppy led him into the sitting room Santino bent his dark glossy head to avoid colliding with the low lintel. The room was packed to the gills with furniture and so short of floor space he was reluctant to move in case he knocked something over.

She could not look away from him. Her entire attention was welded to every hard, masculine angle of his bold profile, noting the tension etched there but secretly revelling in the bittersweet pleasure of seeing him again. He turned with measured care to look at her, curling black lashes screening his keen gaze to a sliver of bright, glittering gold.

The atmosphere hummed with undercurrents. Her restive hands clenched together, longing leaping through her in a wildfire wicked surge. Lips parted and moist, in a stillness broken only by the crackling of the fire in the brass grate, she gazed back at him and leant almost imperceptibly forward. Santino needed no further encouragement. Body language like that his male instincts read for him. Without a second of hesitation, he reached for her. Tugging her slight body to him, he meshed one possessive hand into a coil of her Titian red curls and tasted her lush mouth with a slow, smouldering heat that demanded her response.

She was in shaken turmoil at that sensual assault, and a muffled gasp escaped Poppy. His tongue delved with explicit hunger into the tender interior of her mouth. The liquid fire of need ignited in her quivering body faster than the speed of light. She was imprisoned in intimate, rousing contact with his big, powerful length, and her spread fingers travelled from his shoulder up into his luxuriant black hair to hold him to her.

And Santino? In the course of that single kiss, Santino went from wary defensiveness to the very zenith of blazing confidence that he was welcome.

Indeed, he was totally convinced that everything was one hundred and one per cent fine. He would have her back in London by midnight. Mission accomplished. Simple, straightforward—why had he ever imagined otherwise?

Then, without the smallest warning, Poppy brought her hands down hard on his arms to break his hold. She wrenched herself free of him with angry tears of self-loathing brimming in her eyes. A wave of dizziness assailed her and she had to push her hands down on the dining table to steady herself and breathe in slow and deep. There was just no excuse for her having let him kiss her when he belonged to another woman. As for him, he was even more of a rat than she had believed he was. He was a hopeless womaniser!

'What's wrong?' Santino breathed in a tone of audible mystification and indeed annoyance.

Her back turned to him, Poppy finally managed to swallow the tears clogging up her vocal cords and she stared with wooden fixity out the window at his car. 'What are you doing in Wales?'

'I had a business meeting in Cardiff earlier.' Santino had decided to play it cool. He was a step ahead of her, he believed and he was already thinking of how to present his having phoned Australia as the ultimate in casual gestures.

But Poppy took the wind right out of his sails by saying, 'I suppose my landlady gave you my forwarding address.'

Infuriatingly, so simple a means of establishing her whereabouts had not even occurred to Santino, but, ignoring that angle, he cut to the chase. 'I wanted to see you.'

He had some nerve. Did he really believe that she was still that naive? In the area on business and at a loose end on a Friday afternoon, he had decided to look her up. Why? Well, she had been free with her favours before and why shouldn't he assume that she would be again? No man could think much of a woman who let him make love to her on his office sofa for a cheap, easy thrill. Poppy felt horribly humiliated.

'I would've thought that most men in these circumstances would've been glad *not* to see me again,' Poppy countered painfully in a small voice.

Santino wondered why it was that, when she had run to the other side of the country to avoid *him*, he was being accused of not wanting to see *her*. Suddenly he too was asking himself what he was doing in Wales. Suddenly he suspected that he could well be within an ace of making a total ass of himself.

'Why would you assume that?' Santino enquired.

'Well, if you don't know that for yourself, I'm certainly not going to be the one to remind you!' Poppy condemned chokily, for she refused to lower herself to the level of mentioning Jenna Delsen's name. She refused to give him that much satisfaction. No doubt his ego would relish the belief that she was heartbroken at the news of his engagement. Or maybe he imagined that she was still in blissful ignorance of the true nature of his relationship with the beautiful blonde.

Unable to work out exactly where the unproductive dialogue was going, Santino decided that it was time to be blunt. 'Why did you send me a card telling me that you loved me?'

If the window had been open at that moment, Poppy would have scrambled through it and fled without hesitation. Aghast at that loaded question, she went rigid.

'I don't think that's an unreasonable question,' Santino continued, tension flattening his accented drawl into the command tone he used at work. 'And I'm tired of talking to your back.'

Seething discomfiture flamed hot colour into Poppy's cheeks, but pride came to her rescue. Flipping round on taut legs, she encountered brilliant dark-as-midnight eyes and forced a dismissive shrug. 'For goodness sake...the valentine card was a joke!'

The silence that fell seemed to last for ever.

Santino had gone very still, his strong bone structure clenching hard. 'A joke...?' A flame of raw derision flared in his gaze as he absorbed that demeaning explanation. The most obvious explanation, yet one that for some reason he had never considered. 'What are you...fourteen years old or something?'

'Or something...' Her nails were digging purple welts into her damp palms while she struggled to control the wobble that had developed in her knee joints. 'It was just a stupid joke...and then Craig got hold of it and blew it up into something else and I ended up looking like an idiot!'

'I hope you don't also end up pregnant,' Santino framed with a ragged edge to his dark, deep drawl, wide, sensual mouth compressed, the pallor of anger lightening the bronzed skin round his hard jawline. 'I doubt very much that that would strike even you as a joke.'

Poppy gazed back at him in appalled silence, her tongue cleaving to the roof of her mouth, for not once since that night had she even considered that there might be consequences. She had, without ever really thinking about it, simply assumed that he had taken care of that risk for her.

'You mean, you *didn't*…?' she began shakily.

'I'm afraid not.' Brooding dark eyes acknowledging the level of her dismay and disconcertion, Santino released his breath in a slow speaking hiss of regret. 'But I do accept that, whatever happens, the responsibility is mine.'

CHAPTER SIX

AT THAT moment, Poppy wanted to curl up in a ball like a toddler and cry her heart out, for what Santino had just revealed shed a very different light on what had motivated his visit.

Since when had she got so vain that she believed Santino Aragone was so bereft of females willing to share his bed that he had sought her out in Wales? The idea was laughable, *ridiculous*! Now she was remembering his tension when he'd first arrived. Had she precipitated that kiss? Had that been her fault once again? Or just one of those crazy mishaps that occurred when people were all wound up and not really knowing how to react or what to say?

Well, it scarcely mattered now, Poppy conceded painfully. Santino had come to find her and speak to her for a very good reason, and indeed the fact that he had made the effort told her much more about his strength of character than anything else. He had been worried that he might have got her pregnant. That was the only reason he had taken the trouble to seek her out again. Most men, particularly one who had just asked or had been about to ask another woman to marry him, would have done nothing and just hoped for the best. But Santino had *not* taken the easy way out.

'The night of the party...' Santino caught and held
her swift upward glance '...we had both been drinking. I have never been so reckless, but then I don't
have a history of that kind of behaviour and I know
that you had no history at all.'

Feverish colour flared in Poppy's tense face. She
was still in shock at her own naivety, her own foolish,
pitiful assumptions about why he had come to see her.
It took enormous will-power for her to confront the
more serious issue. Might she have conceived that
night? A belated rethink on what might have caused
her recent bouts of nauseous disinterest in food froze
Poppy to the spot. And what about the little dizzy
turns she had written off as being the results of not
eating or sleeping well? *Was* it possible that she was
pregnant? She had never bothered to keep track of her
own cycle. How long had it been since the party? A
couple of weeks, *more*? Her brain was in turmoil, refusing to function. When had she last...? She couldn't
remember. It seemed like a long time ago. Santino had
just delivered what had to be the ultimate male put-
down. He had come to tell *her* she might be pregnant!

Poppy shifted her head in a dazed motion. 'I really
don't know yet if I'm...you know...I don't know...
er...either way.'

Santino took a slight step forward. She looked so
much like a terrified teenager. She couldn't even find
the words to talk about conception. He wanted to close
his arms round her, drive out the panic and uncertainty
clouding her eyes, tell her that she had nothing to
worry about and that he would look after her. And
then he stiffened, sudden bitter anger flaring through
him, making him suppress his own natural instincts.

The valentine card had been a joke, a childish, stupid joke with no sense that he could see, but then someone might have dared her to do it for a laugh. How did he know? He didn't feel as if he knew anything any more about Poppy.

In fact, the more Santino thought of how she had behaved, the more alienated he felt. She wasn't in love with him, never had been in love with him. Even a little dose of infatuation would have lasted longer than a couple of weeks. Maybe she had slept with him because she had decided it was time she acquired some experience. Whatever, her behaviour ever since had spoken for her: she didn't want to see him and preferred to forget about that night. In fact, she could not have made her feelings clearer. She had jacked in her job, left London. Exactly why had he gone to such extraordinary lengths to locate her? Had he become such an arrogant jerk that he couldn't accept a woman's rejection?

'Presumably you'll know whether or not you're pregnant very soon,' Santino drawled without any expression at all. 'If you are, please get in touch with me immediately and we'll deal with it together. Obviously I will give you my support. You know how to reach me.'

His beautiful dark eyes were still level but his detachment was noticeable and complete. Poppy could feel that change like a wall he had thrown up between them. He wanted to leave. She could feel that, too. But then why not? It hadn't been a very pleasant visit for him to have to make, she recognised miserably. It had been a waste of time too when she had been unable to tell him that he had nothing to worry about.

Naturally he would be praying that there would be no repercussions from that night and that awareness prevented her from sharing her own misgivings. Why say anything when she might well be fretting about nothing?

Santino strode towards his car and then swung back for one last look at her. 'Look after yourself,' he offered gruffly.

Feeling as if she were dying inside, Poppy stood like a statue watching the car reverse out. She had the most terrible urge to run after it and tell him that, even though she ought to hate him, she still loved him. But what would he want to know that for? He *had* to be in love with Jenna.

A couple of miles down the road, Santino brought the car to a halt, buzzed down the window and drank in a great lungful of the fresh, rain-wet air. *Mission accomplished?* A raw-edged laugh, empty of all humour, broke from him. Why was he chickening out of confronting the obvious: his success scores before the sofa, and on the sofa, had been nil. Everything that had struck him as fantastic and very special had left her distinctly underwhelmed. She hadn't even offered him a cup of coffee. All the way to Wales for the privilege of being shot down in flames in the space of ten minutes!

Thinking of the stupid, naff valentine card he had bought for her, a violent miasma of emotion lanced through Santino. He just wanted to smash something. He didn't want to think about her. In fact he was determined not to think about her. Of course, she wasn't going to be pregnant! Off the top of his head, he could have named three young, healthy married couples tying themselves in knots in a desperate effort to conceive a child. The chances of his having fathered a baby in one night were slim and surely she would have known by now? He would check into a hotel, get something to eat...only he wasn't hungry any more.

So he would check into a hotel and have a lost weekend. Why? He just felt like it! He wanted to drink himself into a stupor. He was off women, really, really *seriously* off women.

Three days later, Poppy learned that she was indeed pregnant.

During the weekend, she had had to content herself with purchasing a pregnancy test kit. When the test had come up positive, she'd barely slept for the following two nights. Unsure of how reliable a home test was, she'd made an appointment at her local surgery. When the doctor gave her the same confirmation and discussed options with her, she already knew that she didn't want a termination. She loved children, had always hoped that some day she would have some of her own, but that prospect had until then existed in some dim, distant future. Now that a baby, Santino's baby, was a much more immediate reality, she also knew she had some hard thinking to do about how she intended to manage.

At first, she believed that she could steel herself to phone Santino to tell him that she was carrying his child, but when it came to the point she couldn't face it. Santino was engaged to Jenna. Like it or not, what she had to tell him was very bad news on his terms. She had her pride too and she didn't want to risk getting all weepy and apologetic on the phone, did she?

As she wasn't prepared to consider a termination, she decided that it would be less painful all round if she wrote a letter spelling out her intentions.

So, Poppy sat in Tilly's narrow little guest-room bed and tried to write a letter. But she kept on sitting there and trying to write it and failing and scrunching up her every attempt and ended up in floods of miserable tears.

Finally, she stopped trying to save face and just let her own honest feelings speak for her in what she wrote. After all, did she really want Santino to go on thinking now that the valentine card had just been a cheap, silly joke? That their baby had been conceived as a result of such a joke? Poppy cringed at that image. Some day, she would want to tell their child that she had loved his father and that truth was surely more important than her own pride.

When it dawned on Poppy that she would have to send the letter to Aragone Systems because she *still* didn't know Santino's home address and he wasn't in the phone book either, she was careful to print 'Private and Confidential' in block capitals on one corner of the envelope. Once it was in the post, she tried not to think about it. The ball was in his court now. She would just have to wait and see what happened.

During the following week she was offered interviews with two families in search of a nanny, in fact *desperate* for a nanny. Qualified nannies, it seemed, were in even shorter supply than they had been when she had first emerged from her training. But did she admit she was pregnant or not? She decided that she would be happier being honest from the outset as she would need time off to attend pre-natal hospital ap-

pointments, and then of course she would have a baby
in tow. At the same time, on every occasion that
Tilly's phone rang, her heart would start banging like
a drum and she would think that it was Santino calling
her. But Santino *didn't* call and watching the post
proved to be no more productive.

But then, had she but known it, Santino never received her letter. He was in Italy when it arrived and
Craig Belston was working his last day at Aragone
Systems. An astute operator, Craig had recognised that
his promotion prospects were slim if he stayed;
Santino had been cold with him ever since the night
of that party. Although Craig had found lucrative employment elsewhere, his resentment at what a little
teasing of Poppy Bishop had cost him still rankled. He
examined the letter, his mouth twisting at the 'P.
Bishop' and return address printed on the back of the
envelope. Walking over to the tall drinks cabinet,
which had of recent contained nothing stronger than
soft drinks and mineral water, he dropped the letter
down between it and the wall and he smiled.

Within a month Poppy had left Wales and started
work as a nanny again. Initially shocked that Santino
had not responded to her letter, she grew more cynical
as time passed. After all, his silence was in itself an
answer, wasn't it? Confronted with the worst-case scenario, Santino had decided that he didn't want to know
about the baby. Why had she swallowed all that impressive guff about him being willing to take responsibility? Why once again had she begun thinking of
him as an essentially decent guy?

After all, Santino had lied that night about Jenna to

get her onto that sofa, so, why shouldn't he have lied again? She was on her own in *every* way and, for the sake of the child she was expecting, she reckoned that she had better get used to the idea.

CHAPTER SEVEN

'YES, that uniform looks the thing, all right. Turn round,' Daphne Brewett urged Poppy, her be-ringed hands clasped together, an approving smile blooming on her plump, attractive face. 'You look like a *proper* nanny now, luv. No chance of folk mistaking you for one of those au pair girls, who work for pocket change! What do you think, Harold?'

Her balding husband, Harold, removed his admiring gaze with reluctance from Poppy's slim black nylon-clad ankles. 'Does anyone but the Royals put their nannies in uniform these days?' he enquired in his refined public school accent, his tone apologetic.

Daphne stuck her hands on her ample hips and skewered him with one warning glance. 'Poppy's wearing a uniform...OK?' she rapped out loudly.

Harold nodded in submission and picked up his newspaper. Poppy, who had been toying with the idea of mentioning that she was afraid that the fussy white apron and the frilly little hat were *definitely* over the top, thought better of it. Daphne had a terrible temper and Harold might be a very astute and respected business tycoon, but he was terrified of his wife and knew when to keep quiet. Poppy reminded herself that she was earning an enormous salary. If pleasing Daphne meant dressing like a cross between a French maid

and a Victorian nurse, she would just have to put up
with it. After all, Daphne had been broad-minded
enough to hire a nanny who came with a very young
child of her own in tow. Indeed, Daphne had been
warmly accepting of what had struck other potential
employers as a serious drawback.

'Right…' Having vanquished Harold, Daphne
turned her attention on Poppy again. 'You have the
kiddies packed and ready for two this afternoon. We're
off to Torrisbrooke Priory for the weekend. That'll be
a treat for you. You can look forward to seeing some
real landed gentry there,' she said with unhidden satisfaction.

Poppy walked out of the drawing room. Three children were seated on the stairs: Tristram, aged ten,
Emily Jane, aged eight, Rollo, aged five, all blond and
blue-eyed and very unspoilt and pleasant children.
Daphne Brewett might be a very domineering personality but beggars could not be choosers, Poppy reminded herself squarely, determined to make the best
of her recent employment with the family.

'Well, did you tell Ma how dumb you looked?' Tris
asked with rich cynicism.

Poppy shook her head in wincing apology.

'I'm not going to be seen dead with you in that daft
get-up!' Tris warned her.

'It's very uncool,' Emily Jane pronounced in a
pained tone.

'You look funny!' Rollo giggled. 'I like your silly
hat.'

With a rueful grin, Poppy went over to the pram
parked below the stairs. Florenza was wide awake, big
blue eyes sparkling beneath her soft mop of tiny black

curls. Poppy reached in and scooped her daughter out to take her back upstairs again. Florenza was three months old, cute as a button, and the undeniable centre of her adoring mother's world.

'Who lives at Torisbrooke Priory?' Poppy asked Tris on the way upstairs.

'Dunno. But Ma thinks the invitation's really great, so it's probably somebody posh with a title. I wish she'd just leave us at home,' he grumbled. 'She's really embarrassing in other people's houses.'

'Don't talk about your mother like that,' Poppy reproved.

'I don't like people laughing at her,' Tris said defensively.

Ignoring that, for to deny that Daphne could be both vulgar and comical in her desire to impress all with the conspicuous extent of the Brewett wealth, was impossible.

At four that afternoon, the Brewett cavalcade of limousines drove at a stately pace up the long, wooded, winding drive to Torrisbrooke Priory. A vast and ancient building appeared round the final bend. It was built of weathered Tudor brick, winter sunshine glittering over the many mullioned windows, and Poppy gazed out at it with interest. Half a dozen big cars were already parked on the gravel frontage.

A venerable butler stood at the gothic arched front door in readiness. Daphne and Harold descended from the first limo. Florenza clasped in her arms and wearing the gabardine raincoat that went with her uniform, Poppy climbed out of the second limo in the wake of the children. The third limo was just for the luggage: Daphne did not travel light.

When a very tall, dark male strolled down the steps to greet her employers, Poppy's steps faltered. It couldn't be, it couldn't possibly be! But as her shattered eyes focused on the lean, devastatingly handsome dark features that still haunted her dreams on a shamefully regular basis, she saw that it truly was…it *was* Santino Aragone! Sheer, disbelieving panic afflicted her. Was he their host? Why else would he be shaking hands with Harold? Did that mean that the priory belonged to Santino?

Daphne summoned her children to her side to introduce them. In the background, Poppy hovered. There was no place to go, no place to hide. At the exact moment that Santino registered her presence, Poppy froze, heart thumping so hard she felt sick, her taut face pale as milk. His brilliant dark eyes welded to her and just stayed there, his surprise unconcealed.

'And this is our nanny, Poppy,' Daphne trilled in full swing. 'And little Flo.'

Her blue eyes achingly vulnerable, Poppy's chin nonetheless came up in a sudden defiant tilt. What did she have to be embarrassed about? Santino was the one who ought to be embarrassed! She noted that as his piercing gaze suddenly veiled, he did not succumb to the temptation of stealing so much as a glance at his own daughter.

'Poppy and I have met before. She used to work in Aragone Systems,' Santino remarked without any apparent discomfiture. 'Let's go inside. It's cold.'

While Daphne chattered cheerfully about what a small world it was, Santino was in shock but refusing to acknowledge it. A coincidence and life was full of them, he told himself. Poppy was the Brewetts' nanny and she would be busy with their children all weekend. It was almost a year to the day *since*... No, no way was he revisiting that memory lane. A baby wailed. As Santino hadn't noticed a baby in the party, he turned his head in bewilderment, following the sound right back to source: the small bundle cradled in Poppy's arms.

'I didn't realise you had a new baby,' he said to Daphne, struggling to act the part of interested host, endeavouring to force a relaxed smile to his taut features.

'Oh, the baby's not ours.' Daphne loosed a girlish giggle, flattered by Santino's misapprehension because she was pushing fifty. 'Three was quite enough for me! Flo is Poppy's kiddy.'

At the foot of the glorious oak carved staircase where the butler was waiting to show her upstairs, Poppy stared at Santino with very wide blue eyes. What on earth was he playing at? When his startled gaze zeroed in on her with sudden questioning force, she was at a complete loss. Why was he acting so surprised? Hadn't he appreciated that pregnancies most often led to births and little babies?

'Her name's Florenza,' Tris piped up. 'Flo's just what Ma calls her.'

'Florenza...' Santino repeated, ebony brows pleating.

'It's I-talian,' Daphne told him helpfully.

Santino angled a charged scrutiny at the little squirming bundle. He was suffering from information overload. Was Florenza his child? What age was the little girl? She was wrapped in a shawl and, the way she was being held, the shawl was all he could see.

She might be a newborn baby, she might be some other man's child. She *couldn't* be his daughter! Poppy would have told him, wouldn't she?

Fabulous cheekbones prominent below his bronzed skin, Santino dredged his attention from the mystery bundle, encountered a speculative look from Daphne Brewett's keen gaze and hastened to show his guests into the drawing room.

Poppy climbed the stairs in a daze, beneath which a growing turmoil of emotions seethed. Santino had been astounded when Daphne had informed him that the baby was her nanny's. He had stared at Florenza much as though she were a Pandora's box ready to fly open and cause a storm of catastrophe. A tremor ran through Poppy and her arms tightened round her tiny daughter. Why was she shrinking from facing the obvious explanation for Santino's incredulity? Evidently, Santino had assumed that without his support she would *not* continue her pregnancy. Well, how else could she interpret his shocked reaction to Florenza's existence?

Was Jenna waiting in that drawing room downstairs? Jenna in her gracious role of hostess as Santino's wife? Had they got married during the last year? At that awful thought, a cold, clammy chill slid down Poppy's spine and her sensitive tummy clenched in protest. For the first time, she regretted not having allowed herself to check out whether or not that wedding had taken place as yet. But refusing to allow herself to seek any information whatsoever about Santino Aragone's life had been a necessary defence mechanism. She had brought down a curtain on the past and disciplined herself to live only in the present.

'Is this Mr Aragone's home?' she enquired of the elderly butler, Jenkins, whose steps were slowing with each step up the stairs.

'Yes, madam,' he wheezed and, as he was so clearly in no fit state to answer any further questions, Poppy had to content herself with that.

Three hours later, having supervised a late and riotous tea with the children that had been served in a small dining room on the ground floor, Poppy set up Florenza's bright and cosy travel cot in the nursery and tucked her up for the night. Poppy was tired. Her days started at six when Florenza wakened and she was grateful that it was her night off. Although impressing that necessity on Daphne had been a challenge, she conceded ruefully. But she was painfully aware that live-in nannies had to define boundaries or she would soon find herself on call twenty-four hours a day.

The priory was a simply huge house. Poppy reflected that she might well contrive to stay the weekend without seeing Santino again. Unhappily, she was conscious of a dangerous craving to nonetheless throw herself in his path for a showdown. He *deserved* to be told what a rat he was! Removing her elaborate uniform with a grimace of relief, she ran a bath for herself in the bathroom beside the nursery and got in to have a soak.

In the library downstairs, undercover of having announced the necessity of making an urgent call, Santino was delving in frustration through a very old book on babies. All he needed to know was what weight the average baby was when it was born. Armed with that knowledge, he might then take a subtle peek at Poppy's baby and work out whether it was within the realms of possibility that Florenza was *his* baby, too. Why not just ask Poppy? That would entail a serious loss of face that Santino was unwilling to consider.

Convinced that Poppy would be down in the basement swimming pool supervising the Brewett children, Santino strolled into the nursery on the top floor. The grand Edwardian cot was unoccupied but the lurid plastic and mesh contraption set beside it contained his quarry. Breathing in deep, Santino advanced as quietly as he could to steal a glance over the padded rim. The first thing he saw was a downy fluff of black curls and then a pair of soft blue unblinking eyes focused on him. His first startled thought was that, for a baby, Florenza was remarkably pretty.

But it was hard to say which of them was the most surprised. Santino, who had paid only the most fleeting attention to friends' babies, fully believed that infants only operated on two modes: screeching or sleeping. He had *expected* Florenza to be asleep. Aghast, he watched Florenza's big eyes flash like an intruder-tracking device, her tiny nose screwing up as her little rosebud mouth began to open.

Santino backed off fast. But even though he was bracing himself, the threatened screech never came. Instead, Florenza turned her little head to peer at him through the mesh. When he dared to inch forward again, Florenza's tiny face tensed in warning. It dawned on him that lifting the baby to gauge her weight was not a viable option. She was a really sharp, on-the-ball baby, ready to shriek like a fire alarm at the first sign of a stranger getting too close, and he didn't want to frighten her.

Wrapped in a bath towel and barefoot, Poppy glanced into the nursery just to check on Florenza before she went to get dressed and could not credit what she was seeing. Her lips parted on a demand to know what Santino thought he was doing, but the manner in which her tiny daughter was holding him at bay was actually very funny. However, she only found it funny for about the space of ten seconds. For as she studied Santino's bold, masculine profile and switched her strained gaze to Florenza's matching dark eyes a wealth of powerful emotion overwhelmed Poppy without warning. Father and daughter didn't even know each other and never would in the normal way. Curiosity might have brought Santino to the nursery, but that did not mean he had suffered a sudden sea change in conscience.

As an odd choky little gasp sounded behind him, Santino swung round and caught only the merest glimpse of Poppy's convulsed face as she spun away and raced into the bedroom across the corridor, slamming the door in her wake.

Sobs catching in her throat, she sank down at the foot of the bed and buried her head in her arms. She hated him, she *really* hated him! She was thinking of every bad experience she had had in the months since that night they had shared, not least having been the only woman in the maternity ward without a single visitor. In addition, her parents' initially shocked and censorious reaction to the revelation of a grandchild born out of wedlock had increased Poppy's distress. Although relations had since been smoothed over and

gifts had been sent, Poppy remained painfully aware
that once again she had disappointed her family.

When the door opened and Santino strode in, Poppy
was astonished for she had not expected him to risk
forcing a confrontation in his own home. But there he
stood, six feet three inches of lean, powerful masculinity, apparently so impervious to remorse that he
could face her with his arrogant head high, his stubborn jaw at an angle and without any shade of discomfiture. For a timeless few seconds, she drank her
fill of looking at him. He was still absolutely gorgeous,
she noted resentfully, and she was ashamed to feel the
quickened beat of her own heart, the licking tension
of excitement and the taunting curl of heat slivering
through her. In despair at her own weakness, she
veiled her gaze.

'I only have one question…' Santino breathed in the
taut silence. 'Is Florenza mine?'

'Are you out of your mind?' Poppy gasped.

What was he trying to do? Portray her as some loose
woman, who might not know the paternity of her own
child? How much lower could a guy sink than to in-
sinuate that?

Taut as a high-voltage wire, Santino was endeavouring to make sense of the incomprehensible while
resisting what had become a predictable instinct when
Poppy was upset: a need to haul her into his arms that
was so strong only fierce will power kept him at the
other side of the room. He was also working very hard
at not allowing his attention to roam one inch below
her collar bone, where an expanse of smooth, creamy
cleavage took over before vanishing beneath the
tightly wrapped towel.

'You know very well that Florenza's yours,' Poppy splintered back at him, her bright tousled head coming up, her blue eyes angry. 'So don't you *dare* ask me a question like that!'

Knocked back by that accusing confirmation that Florenza was his child, momentarily blind to even the allurement of Poppy's exquisite shape in a towel, Santino could not immediately come up with a response. He was a father. He had a daughter. His mother was a grandparent. He was an unmarried father with a baby sleeping in a plastic playpen. His baby's mother hated him *so* much she hadn't even been able to persuade herself to accept his support, financially or in any other way...

Poppy collided with his stunning dark-as-midnight gaze and tensed at the sight of the pain and regret that he couldn't hide. 'You don't even know what to say to me, do you?'

'No...' Santino acknowledged hoarsely, lean hands coiling into fists and uncoiling only slowly again.

'I've turned up like a bad penny in the wrong place.' Poppy said what she assumed he was thinking. 'Is Jenna downstairs?'

'Jenna?' Santino echoed with a frown. 'Jenna who?'

Poppy flew upright and threw the first thing that came to her hand. A shoe thumped Santino in the chest. The second shoe caught him quite a painful clip on the ear. Poppy blazed back at him in a passion that shook him even more, 'Jenna...*who*? Jenna Delsen, your fiancée, whom you described as *just* an old friend when it suited you! You lying louse, Santino Aragone!'

Santino cast aside the second shoe, brilliant eyes

narrowed in astonishment. 'I'm not engaged to Jenna. She *is* an old friend and I was a guest at her wedding last summer.'

In wordless incredulity, Poppy stared back at him, but a hollow, sick sensation was already spreading through her trembling body. He had been a guest at Jenna's wedding? Such a statement had a serious ring of truth.

Lean, strong face taut, Santino moved expressive hands in a gesture of bewilderment. 'Where on earth did you get the idea that I had got engaged to Jenna?'

Poppy snatched in a stark, quivering breath. 'It was in a newspaper...a picture of you and Jenna. It said you were engaged...er...but I never looked at it that closely.'

Santino stilled then, black brows drawing together. 'An old friend did phone me to congratulate me on my supposed engagement last year,' he recalled with an obvious effort, his frown deepening. 'The newspaper he mentioned had used an old picture of Jenna and I together and he'd misread the couple of lines below about her engagement party. Her fiancé, David, *was* named but he hadn't picked up on it.'

Silence fell like a smothering blanket of snow.

Poppy was appalled at the explanation that Santino had just proffered. Tilly had only glanced at the item because she had recognised Santino and Tilly only ever skimmed through newspapers. When her great niece had failed to display any interest in the seeming fact that her former employer had got engaged, Tilly would, in all probability, not have bothered to look back at it again. And Poppy had been far too cut up, far too much of a coward, to pick up that newspaper and read exactly what it had said for herself.

'Tell me,' Santino asked very drily, 'exactly when did you see that newspaper and decide that I was an outright liar?'

Her breath snarled up in her throat. It had been too much to hope that he would not immediately put together what she had believed him capable of doing. Squirming with guilty unease and embarrassment and a whole host of other, much more confused emotions, Poppy admitted shakily, 'Before you came to Wales…'

A harsh laugh that was no laugh at all was dredged from Santino, bitter comprehension stamped in his brooding features as he turned sizzling dark golden eyes back on her in proud and angry challenge. '*Per meraviglia*…you had some opinion of me! You decided I'd been cheating on another woman with you. No wonder you were so surprised to see me in Wales, but you didn't have the decency to face me with your convictions, did you?'

Poppy gulped. 'I—'

'I didn't have a clue what I was walking into that day,' Santino framed in a low-pitched raw undertone, treating her to another searing appraisal that shamed her even more. 'But all the time that I was trying to make sense of your bewildering behaviour, you were thinking I was a two-timing liar with no principles and no conscience!'

'Santino…I'm *sorry*!' Poppy gasped.

His lean powerful face stayed hard and unimpressed. 'You tell our daughter you're sorry. Don't waste your breath on me!'

'No...you tell her you're sorry,' Poppy dared hoarsely. 'You're the one who decided you didn't want anything to do with her.'

'I didn't even know she *existed*!' Santino's temper finally broke free of all restraint. 'How the blazes could I have had anything to do with a child I wasn't aware had even been born?'

'But I wrote to you telling you I was pregnant,' Poppy protested.

'I didn't get a letter and why would you write anyway? Why trust an important and private communication of that nature to the vagaries of the post? Why not just phone?' Santino demanded, immediately dubious of her claim that there had ever been a letter.

Poppy closed her eyes and swallowed hard in an effort to pull herself together. It was obvious that her letter must have gone astray. Only then did she recall once reading that thousands of letters went missing in the mail every year. But why that one desperately important letter? Why *her* letter? She could have wept.

'Look, I have thirty-odd people waiting dinner for me downstairs,' Santino admitted curtly. 'I don't have time to handle this right now.'

'There *was* a letter,' Poppy repeated unsteadily.

Before he shut the door, Santino dealt her a derisive look. 'So what if there was?' he derided, turning the tables on her afresh. 'What kind of a woman lets her child's whole future rest on one miserable letter?'

CHAPTER EIGHT

STRIVING to look as though she had not passed a sleepless night waiting for the phone by her bed to ring or even the sound of a masculine footstep, Poppy knocked on her employer's bedroom door and entered. 'Tris said you wanted to see me.'

Still lying in bed, clad in an elaborate satin bed jacket, Daphne treated her to a rather glum appraisal. 'Yes. It's a shame about that uniform, though. I bet you it won't fit the next nanny.'

Poppy stilled. 'I'm sorry…er…what next nanny?'

With a sigh, Daphne settled rueful eyes on Poppy. 'Santino had a little chat with me last night. Didn't he mention it?'

Her colour rising, Poppy stiffened. 'No.'

'You just can't work for us any more, luv. Once Santino told me that little Flo is his, I saw where he was coming from all right,' Daphne continued with a speaking grimace. 'Naturally he doesn't want you running about fetching and carrying for my kids!'

'Doesn't he, indeed?' Her face burning fierily at Santino's most unexpected lack of discretion, Poppy was scarcely able to credit her own hearing.

'It wouldn't suit us either.' Daphne gave her an apologetic look. 'The point is, Harold and Santino do business together. You're the mother of Santino's kid and you working for us, well, it just wouldn't look or feel right now.'

It was obvious that the older woman had already made up her mind on that score.

'You don't even want me to work my notice?'

'No. Santino's arranged for an agency nanny for what's left of the weekend. He's a decent bloke, Poppy…' Daphne told her bluntly. 'I don't see why you should be angry with him for wanting to do what's right by you and take care of you and that little baby.'

A minute later, Poppy stalked down the corridor and then down flight after flight of stairs until she was literally giddy with speed and fury. She arrived in a breathless whirl in the main hall. Santino appeared in a doorway. He ran his lethally eloquent dark eyes from the crown of the frilly hat perched at a lopsided angle in her thick, rebellious hair to the starched apron that topped the shadow-striped dress beneath.

'Good morning, Mary Poppins,' he murmured lazily. 'Remind me to buy you more black stockings, but you can ditch the rest of the outfit.'

'Yes, I can, can't I?' Poppy hissed. 'Especially when you've just had me thrown out of my job!'

Striding forward, Santino closed a hand over hers and pressed her into the room he had emerged from. 'We don't need an audience for this dialogue, *cara*.'

'I'm surprised you care! You had no trouble last night baring my deepest secrets to Daphne Brewett!' Poppy condemned.

'Why should Florenza be a secret? I'm proud to be her father and I have no intention of concealing our relationship,' Santino stated with an amount of con- viction that shook her. 'And please don't tell me that you're breaking your heart at the prospect of taking off that ludicrous uniform!'

Poppy refused to back down. 'It was a good job, well paid and with considerate employers—'

'Yet the rumour is that the Brewetts still can't keep domestic staff. Do you know why?' Santino enquired sardonically. '*Daphne.* She's wonderfully kind and friendly most of the time. But she can't control her temper and she becomes much more abusive than the average employee is willing to tolerate these days. Haven't you crossed her yet? It doesn't take much to annoy her.'

Poppy paled, reluctant to recall the older woman's worryingly sharp reproof the previous afternoon when she had been five minutes late getting the children downstairs with all their luggage.

'But then you've only been working for them for a few weeks and she'll still be wary, but I do assure you that if you had stayed much longer, you would have felt the rough edge of Daphne's tongue. She's famous for it.'

'Well, I still don't think that that gave you the right to interfere,' Poppy retorted curtly. 'I can look after myself.'

'But unfortunately, you're not the only person involved here. I want what's best for all *three* of us.' Santino surveyed her with level dark golden eyes, willing her to listen to him. 'I don't see the point in a further exchange of recriminations. Life's too short. I also want to share in Florenza's life. For that reason, I'm willing to ask you to marry me...'

Shock held Poppy still, but the way he had framed that statement also lacerated her pride. He was 'willing' to ask her to marry him? Big deal! Her first marriage proposal and he shot it at her when she was seething with angry turmoil at the manner in which he had attempted to take control of her life. Now it seemed that he had taken away her security so that he could offer her another kind of security. That of being a wife. *His wife.* Her lips trembled and she sealed them.

'Possibly I messed up the delivery of that,' Santino conceded as the tense silence stretched to breaking-point. 'I *do* want to marry you.'

Poppy spun away to gaze out the window at the rolling parkland and mature trees that gave the priory such a beautiful setting. Of course, he didn't *want* to marry her! In Daphne's parlance, Santino was offering to do 'the right thing' by her. He had got her pregnant and he saw marriage as the most responsible means of making amends. He was really lucky that she wasn't the sort of female who would snatch at his offer just because he was rich, successful and gorgeous. Or even because she still loved him, she conceded painfully.

Poppy flipped round to meet Santino's intense dark scrutiny, her face tight with strain. 'Our relationship has only been an ongoing catastrophe,' she framed unevenly.

His jawline clenched. 'That's not how I would describe it—'

'When you called on me at Tilly's, you said pretty much the same thing,' Poppy reminded him. 'I ended up on that sofa because you had had too much to drink and you regretted it. That's no basis for a marriage and, anyway, I don't want to be married to some guy who thinks it's his *duty* to put a ring on my finger!'

'Duty doesn't come into this.' Santino groaned in sudden exasperation. 'We made love because I couldn't keep my distance from you, because I couldn't help myself, *cara*—'

'Yes, but—'

'Just looking at you burns me up. Always did...*still* does,' Santino intoned, striding forward to close his lean hands round hers. 'That's not a catastrophe, that's fierce attraction. If you hadn't worked for me, we would have got together a lot sooner.'

'I can't believe that...' But even so, it was an assurance that Poppy longed to believe.

Santino reached up and whisked the frilly hat from her hair and tossed it aside.

'What are you doing?' she whispered.

The sudden slashing smile that she had feared she might never see again flashed out, lightening his lean, dark features and yanking at every fibre of her resistance. He undid the apron, removed it with careful hands and put it aside, too. Then he unbuttoned the high collar of her dress.

'You want me to prove how much you excite me?' Santino enquired with husky mesmeric intensity, molten golden eyes scanning her with anticipation. 'Ready and willing, *cara mia*.'

A little quiver of sensual response rippled through Poppy's taut frame. 'Don't...'

'Don't what?' Santino asked, flicking back the collar to press his lips to the base of her slender throat, sending such a shock wave of instantaneous response leaping through her that she let her head tip back heavily on her neck, her untouched mouth tingling, literally aching for the hungry heat of his. 'Don't do *this*…?'

He discovered a pulse point just below her ear and lingered there. She trembled, heard herself moan and she grabbed his jacket for support, feeling herself drowning in the melting pleasure she had worked so hard to forget. Then, he framed the feverish flush on her cheekbones with spread fingers and kissed her just once, hard and fast, demanding and urgent, leaving her wanting so much more.

'Now do you believe I really want you?' Santino breathed raggedly.

Poppy stumbled back from him, lips still throbbing and body still thrumming from that little demonstration against which she had discovered she was without defence. He could turn her into a shameless hussy with incredible ease, but he didn't *love* her. 'It wouldn't work…us, I mean.'

'Why not?'

'Don't you know how to take no for an answer?' Poppy muttered shakily from the door.

'I took it the last time. It gained me a daughter of three months old whom I have still to meet.' As Santino made that raw retaliation Poppy's discomfited gaze slewed from his and she left the room and was relieved when he didn't follow her, for he had given her a lot to think about.

Getting changed into jeans and a sweater, Poppy put Florenza in her buggy and went out for a walk. She was starting to see that all she had ever done with Santino was think the worst of his motivations and run away as fast as her legs could carry her. Twelve months ago, she had still had a lot of growing up left to do. So many misunderstandings might have been avoided had she not performed a vanishing act after the staff party. She had reacted like an embarrassed little girl, afraid to face reality after the fantasy of the night. Scared of getting hurt, she had ended up just as hurt anyway. She had assumed that everything that had happened between them had somehow been *her* fault and had denied them both the chance to explore their feelings.

Poppy sat down on a fallen log below the trees. In the same way she had just accepted that Santino was engaged to Jenna Delsen and had hidden behind her pride rather than confront him. But what she could forgive herself for least was the conviction that Santino was a liar and a cheat when he had never been anything but honest and straight with her.

How much could she still blame Santino for effectively getting her the sack? She understood all too well his angry impatience and his need to take control when she herself seemed to have made such a hash of things. He had made it clear that if she conceived his child, he would stand by her. What good had it been for her to talk about a letter that he had never received? Had he got the chance, he would have been a part of Florenza's life from the start. And that was why he was asking her to marry him. Her wretched pride had made her too quick to refuse that option. After all, she loved Santino, could not imagine *ever* loving anyone else...

Fifty feet away, Santino came to a halt to study Poppy on her log and Florenza snuggled up in her buggy. Poppy did not look happy. The marriage proposal had not been a winner. But then he had not promoted his own cause by depriving her of her employment, had he? However, an ever-recurring image of Poppy sailing away in a Brewett limo the following day never to return had driven him to a desperate act. He had known exactly what he'd been doing, he acknowledged grimly. He had cut the ground from beneath her feet in a manoeuvre calculated to make her more vulnerable to his arguments.

Glancing up and seeing him, Poppy froze. Dressed in tan chinos and a beige padded jacket that accentuated his black hair and olive skin, Santino looked stunning. Her mouth ran dry. Should she admit that she'd been a bit too hasty in turning him down?

'Won't your guests miss you?' she asked as he dropped down into an athletic crouch to look at Florenza.

'Country house guests entertain themselves and most of them are still in bed. As long as I show up for dinner, nobody's offended,' Santino told her, resting appreciative eyes on his baby daughter. 'She's something special, isn't she?'

In a sudden decision, Poppy reached into the buggy and lifted Florenza free of the covers. Santino vaulted upright, looking ever so slightly unnerved. 'I've never held a baby before. It might upset her.'

'She's a very easy-going baby. Just support her head so that she feels secure.'

Santino cradled Florenza in careful arms. He looked down into his daughter's big, trusting blue eyes and then he smiled, a proud, tender, almost shy smile that made Poppy's eyes glisten. 'She's not crying. Do you think she sort of knows who I am?'

'Maybe...' Her throat was thick.

'And maybe not, but she can learn.' Santino studied Poppy with sudden, unexpected seriousness. 'Let's hope that Florenza never does to me what I did to my own mother. I'm in your debt for what you said the night of the party about me having taken my father's side when my parents divorced.'

Poppy blinked. 'How in my debt?'

'I went over to Italy to see Mama and found out what a pious little jerk I'd been,' Santino admitted with a rueful grimace. 'I blamed her for the divorce and she didn't want to ruin my relationship with my father by telling me that throughout their marriage he'd had a whole string of casual affairs. I just wish he'd been man enough to admit that to me, instead of going for the sympathy vote to ensure that I chose to live with him when they broke up.'

Knowing how close he had been to his father, Maximo, Poppy muttered, 'I'm sorry…'

'No. Don't be.' Santino smiled. 'Thanks to what you said, my mother and I are getting to know each other again.'

Poppy was delighted at that news. 'That's brilliant!'

'I would never be unfaithful to you,' Santino informed her in steady continuation, and then his wide sensual mouth curved in self-mocking acknowledgement. 'I'm even working on my narrow-minded response to pink graphs…'

Poppy froze at that teasing conclusion. 'That was *you*…that emailed me the day of the party?'

'Who did you think it was?' Santino glanced at her in surprise before hunkering down to settle their sleeping daughter back into her buggy with gentle hands.

It meant so much to Poppy to know that that teasing

exchange had been with him. Her heart just over-flowed, and when Santino sprang back up again he was a little taken aback but in no mood to complain when Poppy flung her arms round him and hugged him. 'I think I might just want to marry you, after all,' she confided. 'Is the offer still open?'

'Very much,' Santino breathed not quite levelly, unable to drag his gaze from her happy, smiling face and absolutely terrified that she might change her mind. 'How do you feel about getting married next week in Italy?'

Her lashes fluttered up on shaken blue eyes. '*That*...soon?'

'I'm really not a fan of long engagements,' Santino swore with honest fervour.

'Neither am I,' Poppy agreed with equal conviction, her heart singing, for there was something very reassuring about a guy who just couldn't wait to get her to the altar.

CHAPTER NINE

WALKING back towards the priory, Santino said with smooth satisfaction, 'I'll feel a lot more comfortable when you sit down to dinner with my guests this evening.'

At that prospect, Poppy's eyes widened in dismay. 'But I can't do that. I came here as the Brewetts' nanny and what are people going to *think* if I suddenly—?'

'That you're my future wife with more right than most to grace the dining table.' Impervious, it seemed, to the finer points of the situation, Santino exuded galling masculine amusement.

'Well, it can't be done. I didn't bring any dressy clothes. I've got nothing but jeans!' Poppy exclaimed.

'If that's the only problem...we'll go out and get you something to wear right now, *cara mia*.'

Nothing pleased Santino so much as solving problems with decisive activity. The village a few miles away rejoiced in a very up-market boutique. It took him only twenty minutes to run Poppy there, stride in, select a short, strappy, soft blue dress off the rail, which struck him as absolutely Poppy, and herd her into the changing room, paying not the slightest attention to her breathless and shaken protests.

Inside the cubicle, Poppy stared at her reflection

dreamily in the mirror and wondered how Santino had managed to pick the right size and a shade of blue that looked marvellous with her hair. Then she looked at the price tag and almost had a heart attack.

'Poppy...?' Santino prompted from the shop floor.

Poppy emerged. Santino had Florenza draped over one shoulder and looked for all the world like a male who had been dandling babies from childhood. Impervious to the sales woman oozing appreciation over him, he studied Poppy with shimmering dark golden eyes that made her cheeks fire with colour and her heart pound like a manic road drill.

'We'll take the dress,' Santino pronounced without hesitation. 'What about shoes?'

Before Poppy could part her lips Santino was requesting her opinion on the display, and within minutes she was trying a pair on. When she reappeared in her jeans, two women were clustered round Santino admiring Florenza and his deft touch with her. By the sound of the dialogue she could hear, he was showing off like mad. Both shoes and dress were removed from her grasp and paid for with Santino's credit card without her having any opportunity to speak to him in private.

'Do you have any idea how much that little lot cost?' Poppy whispered in total shock as they settled back into the limo.

Santino gave her an enquiring glance. 'No.'

Poppy told him.

Santino looked surprised. 'A real steal...'

'It's a fortune!' Poppy gasped.

'Allow me to let you into a secret,' Santino teased in the best of good humour. 'I'm not a poor man.'

Back at the priory, it was a further shock to discover that her possessions and Florenza's had been moved from the nursery wing to a magnificent guest suite on the first floor. 'Are you sure I'm supposed to be here?' she asked the butler, Jenkins.

'Of course,' he wheezed.

Poppy urged him to sit down. He looked shifty and muttered, 'You won't mention this to Mr Santino, will you?'

'Well, I…' Poppy felt the old man really ought not to be working in such a condition.

And then Jenkins explained. He lived alone and he had been in retirement for five years, but he'd missed the priory and his old profession terribly. At his own request, Santino had allowed the old man to come back to the priory and relive what he termed the good old days on occasional weekends and he very much enjoyed that break. Touched by that explanation and by Santino's understanding, Poppy said no more.

Dinner was not at all the ordeal she had imagined it might be. But then she had always enjoyed meeting new people, and from the instant she entered the drawing room and Santino's dark and appreciative gaze fell on her she also felt confident that she looked her best. Late evening, Santino came upstairs with her and went into the dressing room off her bedroom to look in on his sleeping baby daughter. His lean, dark face softened, his sensual mouth curving. 'It's extraordinary how much I feel for her already,' he confided.

A discomfiting little pang assailed Poppy and she rammed it down fast. How could she possibly be envious of the hold Florenza already had on her father's heart? After all, he was marrying her for their daughter's sake. Keen not to dwell on that painful truth, she said awkwardly, 'You know, I really can't see how we can possibly get married this coming week. It takes ages to organise even the smallest wedding.'

'The arrangements are already well in hand, *cara*,' Santino delivered with a slashing grin that made her mouth run dry. 'Early Monday morning we fly over to Venice where a selection of wedding dresses will await your choice. There is nothing that you need do or worry about. I just want you to relax and enjoy yourself.'

'It sounds like total bliss,' Poppy admitted, thinking of the weighty responsibilities and decisions that had burdened her throughout the previous year when she had had nobody to rely on but herself.

'I have a question I meant to ask you earlier,' Santino declared then. 'Exactly when last year did you write to me to tell me that you had conceived our child?'

Her brow furrowing in puzzlement, Poppy told him. His eyes flared gold and then veiled.

'What?' she prodded, unable to see the relevance of that information so long after the event.

Santino shrugged, lean, strong face uninformative. 'It's not important.'

Ultra-sensitive on that issue, Poppy was taut, and in receipt of that casual dismissal she flushed. She was convinced that he had to believe that there had never been a letter in the first place and that she was merely trying to ease her conscience and fend off his annoyance by lying and pretending that there had been. And how could she prove otherwise?

'I'm tired,' she muttered, turning away.

Lost in his own suspicions of what might have happened to that letter and determined to check out that
angle as soon as he could, Santino frowned. He could
not imagine what he had said to provoke the distinct
chill in the air, but caution prevented him probing
deeper. Once they were married, caution could take a
hike, but he was determined not to risk a misstep in
advance of the wedding. Saying goodnight, much as
if he had only been seeing an elderly grandparent up
to bed, he departed.

Disconcerted, Poppy surveyed the space where he
had been and her dismayed and hurt eyes stung with
hot tears. The very passionate male, who had sworn
she was an irresistible temptation earlier in the day,
had not even kissed her. Had that plea just been a
judicious piece of flattery aimed at persuading her to
marry him so that he could gain total access to
Florenza? Or was he just annoyed at the idea that she
might be fibbing about that wretched letter? And if
that was the problem, how was she ever to convince
him that she *had* written to him?

Made restive by her anxious thoughts, Poppy got
little sleep and, after feeding Florenza first thing the
following morning, fell back into bed and slept late.
Finally awakening again, she went downstairs to find
Santino surrounded by his guests. A convivial lunch
followed and then the visitors began to make their de-
partures. Only then appreciating that she still had to
pack up her possessions at the Brewetts' home, Poppy
slipped away to speak to her former employer and decided that it would be simplest for her to return home
with them and see to the matter for herself.

'I'm catching a lift with the Brewetts to go and col-

lect my stuff,' Poppy informed Santino at the last minute.

'I can drive you over there,' Santino offered in surprise.

'No, I thought it would be easier if I left Florenza
here with you,' Poppy confided with a challenging
sparkle in her gaze, although she rather suspected the
female domestic staff would soon help him out with
the task.

Santino was merely delighted that he would retain
a hostage as it were to Poppy returning again and
proud that she felt that he could be trusted. In fact, his
keen mind returning to a concern that had been nag-
ging at him all morning since he had called his secretary at her home and spoken to her, he knew exactly
what he intended to do during Poppy's absence.

Three hours later, in a triumphal mode, Santino
hauled his office drinks cabinet out from the wall and
swept up the still-sealed and dusty envelope that lay
on the carpet. He resisted the temptation to tear
Poppy's lost letter open then and there. He would surprise her with it. They would open it together. Maybe
that way, he would feel less bitter at the high cost of
Craig Belston's mean and petty act of malice.

'If it hadn't been for you being there, I'd have hammered that little jerk,' Santino informed Florenza,
where she sat strapped in her baby carrier watching
him with bright, uncritical eyes. 'Then maybe not,' he
acknowledged for himself in reflective continuance.
'He was so scared he *was*... I suppose I have to watch
my language around you. But then you don't know
any Italian curse words, do you?'

Florenza was asleep by the time he got her slotted

back into the limo. Santino was really pleased with himself. He was naturally good father material, he was convinced of it. She hadn't cried once, not even when it had taken four attempts to change her and his chauffeur, a long-time parent, had mercifully intervened with a little man-to-man advice on the most effective method. They had tea at the Ritz where she was very much admired. She glugged down her bottle of milk like a trooper and concluded with a very small ladylike burp that he didn't think anyone but him heard.

'We're a real team,' Santino told Florenza on the drive home, and around then it occurred to him to wonder how Poppy planned to get herself back to the priory. With a muttered curse, he rang the Brewetts only to discover that she had already gone.

Right up until Poppy had left the Brewetts' with her cases in a taxi, she had expected Santino to call and say that he would come and pick her up. Instead she'd had to catch the train. But when she saw him waiting on the station platform to greet her at the other end of her journey, a bright, forgiving smile formed on her lips.

'I ought to grovel, *amore*,' Santino groaned in apology, looking so gorgeous that there was little that she would not have forgiven. 'It didn't even cross my mind that you don't have your own transport.'

'I expect you were too taken up with Florenza.'

'We did have quite a busy afternoon,' Santino admitted with masculine understatement. 'And when we get back to the priory, I have a surprise for you.'

The very last thing, Poppy expected was to have her own letter set before her like a prize. She was gobsmacked. 'Where on *earth* did that come from?'

'I phoned my secretary this morning. She actually remembered your letter arriving the day before she went off on holiday last year because she noticed your name on the back of the envelope. That week, *I* was in Italy mending fences with my mother.' Santino's strong jawline hardened. 'And Belston was working his last day at Aragone Systems—'

'Craig?' Poppy was still transfixed by the sight of that dusty, *unopened* letter, and her fingers were twitching to snatch it up and bury it deep somewhere Santino could never find it. At one level, she was at a total loss as to what Craig Belston could have to do with the miraculous recovery of a letter that had gone missing almost a year earlier, but on another level she was already recalling with shrinking, squeamish regret the horribly emotional outpourings of her own heart within that letter. It was wonderful how what could seem right and appropriate in the heat of the moment could then threaten utter humiliation eleven months on...

'Yes, Belston. The minute I worked out that time frame, I was suspicious. So, I called at his apartment this afternoon and was fortunate enough to find him home—'

Poppy blinked in growing disconcertion, but Santino was far too caught up in his recital to notice her taut pallor. She was cringing at that very idea of him reading that letter while she still lived and breathed. Here they were on the brink of a marriage of very practical and unemotional convenience and pride demanded that she strive to match that challenge. But he would undoubtedly die of embarrassment *for* her if he was now confronted by those impassioned pages that declared how instantly, utterly and irrevocably she had once fallen in love with him.

'I really don't know why you would've thought Craig might remember anything about one stupid letter,' Poppy muttered abstractedly, regarding the item with all the aghast intensity of a woman faced with a man-eating shark.

'He had a grudge against you and he's a coward,' Santino informed her with expressive disgust. 'I had the advantage of surprise today. He was so taken aback by the sight of Florenza and I—'

'You took Florenza with you to call on Craig?' Poppy squeaked, her expectations of Santino taking yet another beating.

'I wasn't going to leave her behind when I'd promised to take care of her,' Santino pointed out with paternal piety. 'The minute I mentioned the letter and got tough, Belston spilled the beans about what he had done with it. He threw it behind a piece of office furniture where it's been ever since. Mind you, it shows you how the cleaners cut corners.'

Poppy winced. 'What a nasty, low thing to do…oh, well, all's well that ends well and all that,' she added breathlessly, snatching up the envelope and endeavouring to scrunch its fat proportions in one hand. 'I'm glad the mystery's been solved but time has kind of made this letter redundant.'

'I still want to read it…' Questioning dark golden eyes pinned to her, Santino extended an expectant hand.

Poppy turned very pale and bit her lip and closed her other hand round the crumpled envelope as well. 'I really don't want you reading it now…'

'Why?'

As the taut silence stretched Poppy chewed at her lower lip in desperation. Santino tensed, a cool, shuttered look locking his darkly handsome features. What the hell had she written? A total character assassination directed at him? The news that she hated him for taking advantage of her naive trust and overlooking contraception and never, ever wanted to lay eyes on him again? His taut mouth set hard. Self-evidently, the letter she had penned was of the poisonous and destructive ilk.

'So I won't open it, but it's still mine,' Santino heard himself counter with harsh clarity, and no sooner had that foolish offer left his lips than he regretted it.

Intimidated by the tone of that announcement, Poppy handed over the envelope with a reluctance that he could feel. Santino smoothed it out between long, lean fingers. 'I believed that we could read this together, that you'd be pleased I had the faith to believe that you'd sent it,' he continued in angry bewilderment. 'For the first time in my life, I feel pretty damned naive!'

Most unhappy to see him in possession of what was indisputably *his* letter, Poppy lowered her head. 'It's not the sort of thing we'd want to read together,' she mumbled in considerable mortification. 'What did you say to Craig?'

'Nothing repeatable but I didn't hit him.' Santino's dark drawl was rough-edged. 'I wanted to kill him…only not in front of Florenza.'

'Oh…' Poppy was shattered by that blunt admission.

'You see, I thought he'd cost us our chance of happiness.' Santino welded his teeth back together on the rest of what he had almost said, which was that, in his volatile opinion at that instant, *she* had just done that most conclusively. There was so much he had longed to ask and learn about those months they had spent apart, and that she could not be honest about her feelings then angered him and made him feel shut out.

'We have some forms to fill out to satisfy the wedding legalities,' Santino continued grittily. 'Then I've got some calls to make.'

He didn't even laugh when she confided that her middle name was Hyacinth. Before he went off to make those phone calls, Poppy shot a glance at his grim profile and gathered all her strength to ask, 'Are you still sure about this...sure you want to go ahead and marry me?'

'Of course, I am sure.' Having fallen still at that sudden question, Santino shook her by tossing the letter back on the table in front of her. 'Keep it. As you said, the passage of time has made it redundant.'

Poppy went up to her imposing bed and cried. What had gone wrong? Where had the wonderful warmth and intimacy gone? Surely a silly, outdated letter should not create such tension between them? And she knew that she had said and done the wrong thing. Even though it would have mortified them both beyond bearing, she should have let him have that letter...

CHAPTER TEN

AT FIVE the following afternoon after an incredibly busy day, Poppy stood out on a Venetian hotel balcony entranced by the magical scenes taking place on the quays and the canal below.

A group of masked men and women in superb medieval costumes were boarding a launch outside the imposing *palazzo* opposite. A Harlequin and a Pierrot passed by in a gliding gondola, their outfits blessing them with total anonymity. On the quay, a trio of children, dressed up as a clown, a milkmaid and a comic spotty dog were whooping with delight over the firework display streaking through the heavens above the rooftops. Venice at carnival time: noisy, colourful and so full of bustling, vivid life that the very air seemed to pulse with mystery and the promise of excitement.

'You are pleased to be here with us?' A designer-clad little dynamo of a lady of around sixty, Santino's mother, Dulcetta Caramanico, emanated vivacity and natural warmth.

'I have had the most wonderful day...' Poppy admitted with sincerity. 'And I can't thank you enough for the fantastic welcome you have given us.'

Poppy had not expected to meet her future in-laws alone, but urgent business had forced Santino at the eleventh hour to accept the necessity of his coming

out on a later flight. Greeted at the airport by Santino's
mother and Arminio, his charming stepfather, Poppy
and Florenza had been wafted on to their motor launch
and across the lagoon into the city of Venice. They
had brought her to their hotel but it had taken her most
of the day to work out that the older couple indeed
owned an entire chain of international hotels, famed
for their opulence, legendary customer service and ex-
clusivity.

From the instant Dulcetta and Arminio had laid eyes
on them, Poppy and Florenza had been treated as
though they were already a much-loved part of the
family circle. Florenza had been the star of the party.
The luxurious suite of rooms allotted to them would
have been at home in a palace. That morning, the
Caramanicos had taken them to St Mark's Square to
see the Flight of the Little Doves that officially opened
the carnival, and after lunch Dulcetta had escorted
Poppy to a fantastic bridal salon where a huge array
of glorious gowns and accessories had awaited her in-
spection.

Dulcetta was delighted by Poppy's freely expressed
gratitude, and her fine dark eyes shone with happy
tears. 'It is a joy to please you, Poppy. You brought
my son home to me and now you are even making
him smile again. When Santino first visited me last
year, he didn't confide in me but I sensed how very
unhappy he was at heart.'

Poppy hung her bright head, wondering how low
she would sink in the popularity stakes when Santino
arrived in Venice looking as grim and detached as he
had the night before at the priory.

'Santino may have inherited Maximo's looks and
business acumen,' his loving mother continued. 'But

inside, Santino is much more emotional and caring
than ever his father was. So will you wear the dress
for me this evening and surprise my son?'

Poppy focused on the utterly over-the-top eigh-
teenth-century-style silk, brocade and lace gown on
the dress form that awaited her and a rueful grin tilted
her generous mouth. 'Just you try and stop me getting
into the carnival spirit!' She laughed in spite of her
aching heart. 'It's such a fantastic outfit...'

Maybe, even if Santino believed that she looked ridiculous, he would at least smile at the effort she was
making, Poppy thought when Dulcetta had left her.
Tears prickled her eyes as she removed her make-up
and freshened up with a bath. Only a few days before
her wedding, she ought to be the happiest woman
alive. After all, she was about to marry the man she
loved...but a man who would not be marrying her had
it not been for their daughter's birth. Santino adored
Florenza though, and he would make a wonderful father. It was just selfish of her to want the moon into
the bargain.

Santino had already been alienated by her foolishness over the letter and it had finally occurred to her
that he might even have got the impression that what
she had written was unpleasant in some way. His unashamed anger with Craig, his belief that the other
man had cost them the chance of happiness the previous year, had shaken Poppy when he'd voiced it, but
at the time she had been too enervated to appreciate
what Santino had *really* been telling her. Too busy
conserving her pride and protecting herself from embarrassment, she had neglected to note that Santino
had been making no such pretences. It shamed her that
he should be so much more open and unafraid than

she was. He had told her how attracted he was to her, shown her in his anger what he believed Craig Belston had stolen from them, for without his spiteful interference they might have been together much sooner...

And what had she done? Let Santino continue thinking that the valentine card had been a joke. She had saved face at every turn and given not an inch because the memory of her own adoring generosity the night of the party still mortified her. Yet it had been a wonderful night of love and sharing and wasn't it time that she acknowledged that? It didn't matter that he didn't love her. He cared, he certainly *cared*. From now on, she swore that would be enough for her.

While Poppy was anxiously owning up to her sins of omission, Santino, who had just arrived in his own suite next door, was confronting *his* as well. He needed to squash the conviction that he deserved a woman who saw him in terms of being the sun around which her world resolved. Poppy was not in love with him but that was only the beginning of the story, *not* the end. Ego might urge him to play it cool, but playing it cool was not advancing his own cause in any way, was it? For a start, he had been downright childish about that letter, he conceded with gritted teeth. Her determination to prevent him from accessing material that would damage their present relationship had been sensible. Just as Santino *still* recalled every word Poppy had affixed to that valentine card almost twelve months earlier, so he knew that he would have been haunted for ever more by the accusations he imagined had to be contained in that letter.

Anchoring the glorious feathered head-dress to her upswept Titian hair took Poppy some time. Dulcetta and Arminio had invited her to dine with them and a maid was to come upstairs to sit with Florenza. Poppy attached the glittering diamanté-studded mask to her eyes and surveyed herself. The emerald-green gown had theatrical splendour and the neat low-cut bodice flattered her lush curves in a way that made her blush. Yet she felt her own mother would not have recognised her, a stray thought that hurt just a little for she had decided not to tell her family about her wedding until after the event. At such short notice and with flights from Australia and accommodation in Venice during the carnival being so expensive, it would have been impossible for her parents to attend their daughter's special day. But in her heart of hearts, Poppy had also feared to put what she deemed to be already strained affections to the test.

When the knock on the door sounded, Poppy hurried to answer it before Florenza, who had just gone to sleep, could awaken again.

Disconcerted that it was Santino, whom she had believed might not arrive much before midnight, she fell back an uncertain step. Intent golden eyes pinning to her, he murmured something in husky Italian and his heartbreaking smile slowly curved his handsome mouth. As ever, he looked devastatingly dark, vibrant and attractive.

Her breath caught in her throat, for she had truly wondered if Santino would ever smile at her again. Her heartbeat picked up tempo and a flock of butterflies flew free in her tummy, but she held her head high, firmly convinced he would not recognise her at first glance.

'Poppy...' Santino said without a second of hesitation.

'I thought you wouldn't know it was me!' Poppy wailed in helpless disappointment.

As he closed the door his wonderful smile deepened. 'I would know you anywhere. In any light and any disguise.'

'You'll be able to dine with your mother and stepfather, after all.' Feeling foolish, Poppy reached up and unfastened the diamanté mask to set it aside.

'No. I called them from the airport and expressed our mutual regrets.' Santino's expression was now very serious. 'We need to be alone so that we can talk.'

Poppy tensed in sudden apprehension. It was as if he had pushed a panic button. Suddenly she feared he was as keen to cancel the wedding as he had been to cancel the family dinner. 'Santino...'

'No, let me have the floor first...' Santino dealt her a taut look from his beautiful eyes, his raw tension palpable. 'I haven't been straight with you. I haven't been fair either—'

'You're stealing my lines...' Poppy sped past him to snatch up her handbag and withdraw the much-abused letter, which she thrust at him in near desperation. 'I didn't think how it must've looked when I wouldn't let you read it, but it is *your* letter—'

'Stuff the letter,' Santino groaned, not best pleased to have been interrupted just when he had got into his verbal stride and setting it straight back into her unwilling hand. 'It's unimportant. What matters is that I tell you how I feel...but you're not likely to be impressed by the news that you had blown me away in Wales before it dawned on me that I was in love with you.'

In the act of ripping in frustration into the envelope

for herself to produce a thick wad of notepaper, Poppy stopped dead and viewed Santino with huge, incredulous blue eyes. She couldn't possibly have heard *that*, she told herself. In fact she must have been dreaming...

'*Porca miseria*...in advance of that day, strange as it may seem,' Santino disclaimed with touching discomfiture and a look that was a positive plea for understanding in his strained dark eyes. 'I just had no idea why I was always coming down personally to the marketing department, why the day seemed a little brighter when I saw you, why I just *liked* you, why I started finding fault with every other woman I met...have you anything to say?'

In shock, Poppy shook her head.

'Your very first day when I took you to hospital after you hurt your finger,' Santino reminded her doggedly, lean, strong features taut, 'I demonstrated how macho I was by passing out at the sight of the needle coming your way. Yet even though you were a real chatterbox and all my staff would have fallen about in stitches had you told them about that episode, you kept quiet. That was remarkably restrained of you...'

'I wouldn't have d-dreamt of embarrassing you at work.' A great rush of answering love was surging up inside Poppy and playing havoc with her speech.

'I know, *amore*...' But his shapely mouth only semi-curved. 'I was furious when my marketing head overreacted to that stupid cup of coffee. I was so protective of you, and then at the party, when Belston was scoring points off you, I could've ripped him apart! And when we were together in my office and I finally had you all to myself, it was more temptation than I was capable of withstanding—'

'I felt like I'd thrown myself at you...' Poppy shared painfully.

'Who stopped you from leaving? Who kissed you? Who made all the *real* moves?'

Only then did Poppy appreciate that the prime mover had been him. 'But you had been drinking—'

Santino groaned out loud. 'I was just making excuses for myself. That night nothing had ever felt so right to me and I knew exactly what I was doing, but the next day I felt appallingly guilty for seducing you—'

'I sneaked off because I thought it was all my fault—'

'And I was furious about that. I called round at your bedsit that afternoon—'

Poppy winced. 'Oh, no...you just missed me...'

'I suspected you were home and just not answering the door because you didn't want to see me—'

'I wouldn't have done that.'

'Then I had to phone round half of Australia to track down your sister-in-law, Karrie, to find out where you were. Didn't she tell you about my call?'

Even though her heart was singing, Poppy had paled. 'Yes, but I just assumed it was because you were really worried I might be pregnant 'cos at that stage I still believed you were engaged to Jenna. Santino...I think you ought to take a look at this letter of mine before I get so mad with myself that I scream!'

But Santino had other ideas. She was still listening and her lovely eyes were soft and warm and it had been a day and a half since he had last touched her. Tugging her into connection with his lean, powerful length, he brought his mouth swooping down with unashamed hunger and urgency on hers, and for timeless minutes she clung, every fibre of her being alive with joyful excitement and the wondrous relief of knowing herself loved.

Pausing to snatch in a ragged breath, gazing down into her shining eyes, Santino muttered, 'Sooner or later, I'll find the magic combination of making you love me back…if only you hadn't hated me when you were in Wales—'

'I didn't—'

'I was devastated for weeks after that. I tore up the belated valentine card I had searched high and low for—'

'You bought me a card?' Poppy was touched to the brink of tears.

'Signed it with an unadventurous question mark… the guy with few words. All I could think about was getting you back to London. I didn't understand I loved you until that day…'

Her throat thickened. Stepping back, she handed him the letter. 'Well, I always knew how I felt about you, but I'll forgive you for that.'

With perceptible reluctance he accepted the letter, and then as he scanned the first few lines with a frown such a stunned look began to form on his lean, strong face that she had to suppress a giggle. Suddenly he was glued to every page with total, focused concentration.

'It's a…it's a love letter…a wonderful, fantastic love letter,' Santino finally vocalised with a roughened edge to his deep voice.

'It wasn't meant to be, but when I learned I was expecting your child I wanted you to know that my card hadn't been a cheap joke—'

'I should skin you alive for having lied to me, *amore*.' But as at that point Santino was looking at her with wondering, loving intensity, she was in no danger of taking offence. 'I *still* have that card you sent me locked in my office safe. I pretended it wasn't there so that I didn't have to dump it!'

He followed that confession up with a beautiful sapphire engagement ring that took her breath away. Then he looked in on their infant daughter and smiled at her peaceful little face before he strode into his own suite next door to don the very rakish matching eighteenth-century outfit his romantic mother had laid on for his use that evening. The burgundy velvet surcoat, lace cravat and tight-fitting breeches and boots gave him an exotic and dangerous appeal that thrilled Poppy no end. For a while, all he wanted to talk about was what it had been like for her to carry their daughter during those months apart from him. Then they ended up in each other's arms again and Santino pulled back and announced that they were dining out.

'Oh...' Poppy mumbled in surprise.

'We're not going to share a bedroom until we're married, *amore mio*,' Santino swore. 'It's the only way I can *ever* hope to live down that sofa.'

So he took her out into the city where he had been born and they dined in an intimate restaurant by candlelight, both of them so busy talking, both of them so incredibly happy that they had a glow about them that drew understanding and envious eyes.

On Poppy's wedding day, the early morning mist was lifted by sunlight.

She had actually forgotten that it was Valentine's Day, but then a giant basket of beautiful flowers and a glorious card covered with roses and containing a tender verse arrived. Inside, Santino had written those three little words that meant so much to her, 'I love you', and even *signed* it. So, it started out a fantastic day that just went on getting better and better.

She had only just finished her breakfast and was feeding Florenza when someone knocked on the door and her whole family—her mother and father and Peter and Karrie and her little nephew, Sam—trooped in. She couldn't believe her eyes. Santino had flown them out at his expense and they were staying in the same hotel. He had arranged that in secrecy for her benefit and she loved him even more for that sensitivity. All the awkwardness she might have felt in other circumstances with her family evaporated straight away and, watching her mother's eyes glisten over Florenza and enveloped in a hug by her father and her brother, Poppy was content.

Her mother and her sister-in-law helped her dress, enthusing over her exquisite ivory gown with its hand-painted hem of delicate pastel roses. A magnificent tiara and drop earrings arrived with a card signed by Santino. Tucked into a velvet-lined gondola for her passage to her wedding, Poppy felt like a princess. But when she saw Santino turn from the altar in the wonderful old church, that was when her heart truly overflowed with happiness.

The reception was staged in a superb ballroom and there were masses of guests. The bridegroom and the bride were so absorbed in each other that their guests smiled and shook their heads in wonderment. They watched them dance every dance in a world of their own and then depart for their honeymoon.

Late that night in Santino's hideaway home in the

wooded hills of Tuscany, Poppy lay in their incredible medieval bed draped with crewelwork drapes and surveyed her new husband with an excusable degree of satisfaction.

'Just to think you were falling in love with me all those weeks I worked for you...and I hadn't the foggiest idea.' Poppy sighed blissfully and reckoned that low self-esteem was likely to be a very rare sensation in her future.

'Neither had I,' Santino quipped, dark golden eyes resting on her with adoring intensity as he gathered her close again. 'But I missed you so much when you weren't there. I love you, *amore*.'

'I love you, too. But just to think of *me* almost breaking *your* heart, it's heady stuff—'

'You are revelling in your power,' Santino groaned in teasing reproach.

Wearing an ear-to-ear grin, Poppy nodded in agreement, for finding out that he had never, ever been in love before, no, not once, made her feel that providence had kept him safe for her. They chatted about whether or not they would return to Venice for a night or two, checked on Florenza and congratulated each other on having created such a truly wonderful baby. All too soon they melted back into each other's arms and kissed and hugged, both of them feeling as though they were the very first couple ever to discover that amount of love and revelling in their happiness.

Kim Lawrence lives on a farm in rural Anglesey. She runs two miles daily and finds this an excellent opportunity to unwind and seek inspiration for her writing! It also helps her keep up with her husband, two active sons, and the various stray animals which have adopted them. Always a fanatical consumer of fiction, she is now equally enthusiastic about writing. She loves a happy ending!

Look out for the next book from Kim Lawrence:
AT THE PLAYBOY'S PLEASURE
on sale May 2003, in Mills & Boon®
Modern Romance™

RAFAEL'S
PROPOSAL
by
Kim Lawrence

CHAPTER ONE

THE door of the lift was just closing when Maggie Coe slipped in.

'I've been trying to catch you all day, Rafe!' she cried breathlessly. 'I want to run something by you.'

Rafael Ransome didn't consider a lift a suitable place to conduct business conversations, especially when he was on his way home after working twelve hours straight to persuade the intransigent CEO of an ailing electronics company that awarding himself and the senior management team a fifty-per-cent pay rise while simultaneously laying off production staff wasn't the best strategy to ensure the long-term future of the firm!

Ninety-nine out of a hundred people would have been able to deduce his feelings from the discouraging expression on his striking dark features, but Maggie Coe was not one of the ninety-nine.

Rafe ran a hand over the dark stubble on his normally clean-shaven jaw and grimaced. Her tunnel vision made Maggie an asset professionally, but it was a real pain in the rear when all you wanted was a hot shower and a cold drink.

'It looks like you have me for the next sixty seconds.' Coincidentally the same time, according to his disapproving mother, of his longest *relationship* to date.

Despite the shaky start, about thirty seconds into her pitch Maggie had his full attention.

'So effectively all she'd be doing is sorting mail.' Typically Rafe cut to the chase. 'Is that right—?'

Maggie Coe nodded, too pleased with herself to note the steely tone of disapproval that had entered his deep voice. 'And licking the odd stamp,' she added with a smile of satisfaction.

She looked up with every expectation of seeing her boss looking dumbstruck with admiration that she'd come up with the perfect solution to a troublesome problem—the problem in question being Natalie Warner, a young woman who couldn't seem to get her priorities right.

They didn't need an employee who was going to turn up late if her child had a snuffle, even if she did always scrupulously make up that lost time and more. The fact that moreover she didn't complain when she was regularly allocated an unfair proportion of the tedious, boring tasks didn't cut any ice with Maggie. As far as she was concerned, if they tolerated such a *laissez-faire* attitude they were at risk of setting a dangerous precedent, and, as she had told Mr Ransome, before long everyone would be strolling in when it suited them.

In short, anarchy.

Even though she couldn't see his expression Maggie had no doubts that a man who valued efficiency as much as Rafael Ransome, and who furthermore was capable of being as ruthless as he deemed necessary to achieve it, shared her view.

The silent lift came to a halt at the required floor, but Rafe pressed a button to prevent the door opening and turned back to the woman beside him.

'Do you not feel that opening envelopes is a waste of someone with her qualifications?' he questioned his zealous subordinate mildly. Those who knew him best would not have been fooled by the casual tone, but Maggie was blissfully blind to any signs of danger in the cold eyes or in the nerve pulsating in his lean cheek.

'Well, I'm hoping she'll think so,' came the smart reply.

Rafael's eyes narrowed thoughtfully. Maggie was prone to seeing things in terms of black and white, but she was a normally fair-minded person. Her hostility for this young woman seemed almost personal, which wasn't like her.

Natalie Warner, he reflected grimly, seemed to have a knack for aggravating people. She had certainly got under his skin...not in a personal way, of course—he made it a rule never to mix business with pleasure. It was just he hated to see talent wasted and Natalie Warner had buckets of the stuff, even though she seemed determined not to use it.

'So you're hoping that she'll be humiliated and re-sign...?' A child could have seen exactly what Maggie's tactics were.

'That's her choice, but let's just say I wouldn't try and stop her.'

She sounded so complacent that it took Rafe several seconds to control the sharp flare of fury that washed over him. It was ironic that the person on whose behalf he felt so angry wouldn't have felt even slightly grateful if she'd known she had aroused his dormant protective instincts.

An image of a heart-shaped face floated in the air before his eyes, a rare distracted expression entered the densely blue—some said cold—eyes of the man who was famed for his single-minded focus. Natalie Warner barely reached his shoulder and looked as fragile as delicate china, but the likeness was highly deceptive. Any man whose chivalrous instincts were aroused by her appearance would be well advised to repress them unless he fancied an earful of abuse for his efforts—he'd seen her in action and had felt sympathy for the man foolish enough to imagine she needed any special favours.

Rafe admired independent, spunky females—*admired* but avoided involvement with. At this point in his life he wasn't into high-maintenance relationships. But Natalie Warner wasn't just self-reliant, she was the sort of prickly, pigheaded female who wouldn't have asked for a glass of water if she were on fire just to make a point.

'Have you considered that she could have a good case of constructive dismissal if she wanted to take it farther?'

Maggie quickly assured him she had covered this. 'Her job title will be the same, and there will be no drop in her salary. The content of her job would even be the same on paper.' The older woman shrugged. 'So she can't claim she's been demoted.'

'This is in fact a sideways move,' Rafael mused drily.

'Exactly.'

So much for the sisterhood he was always hearing

about. 'It doesn't bother you that she's a single parent with a child?'

This time even Maggie couldn't miss the steel in his voice. She blanched as his long lashes lifted from the sharp angles of his razor-sharp slanting cheekbones to reveal disapproval glittering in his deep-set eyes.

'Bother me?' she echoed, evincing confusion while she did some fast thinking. It was becoming clear that, far from being pleased with her ingenuity, Rafe was inexplicably furious—in that quiet but devastating way he had. 'In what way?' she questioned, desperately trying to retain her composure in the face of the displeasure of a man she deeply admired and whose approval she craved.

'Don't play the innocent with me, Maggie,' he drawled, an expression of simmering impatience stamped on his classically handsome features.

'You say yourself that there's no room for sentimentality in the workplace,' she reminded him with a hint of desperation.

'I rather think you might be taking that quote out of context,' he returned drily.

Maggie flushed. 'So you want her to stay where she is?'

Do I…?

Ironically his life would be a lot more comfortable if he let Maggie install the distracting thorn in his side in some dark cupboard. He sighed; as tempting as it was, he couldn't let her do it. God, sometimes he wished he weren't a good guy.

'You will not hide Natalie Warner away in some God-forsaken back room, Maggie.' Firmly he spelt out his instructions so there would be no convenient misunderstandings. 'Neither will you move her anywhere without my *personal* say-so.' He saw the alert expression appear on Maggie's face and wished he had omitted the *'personal'*. The last thing he wanted was that sort of rumour starting up again.

A while after Natalie had started at Ransome it had come to his attention that there had been whispers that he'd been taking a particular interest in their smart new recruit. He blamed himself for not having foreseen his actions could have been interpreted that way—he knew all too well how people's minds worked.

He could still remember the hurt look of surprise on her face when she'd come to him excited by an idea she'd had, and he had cut her dead—he had made sure there had been plenty of people to witness the snub. It had been a case of being cruel to be kind. Even if the affair had been fictitious, the rumour that she had made it, not on talent, but because she was sleeping with the boss, would haunt a woman through her career.

'You will carry on treating her exactly the same way you do all the other trainees,' he elaborated quietly. 'Do I make myself clear—?' He lifted one brow questioningly and the woman beside him gulped and nodded.

Having made his point, he allowed the door to open and stood aside to let her pass. 'Incidentally,' he called after her, 'there's a meeting scheduled next month to discuss flexible working hours.' Or at least there would be once he'd asked his PA to organise it. 'You might like to ask around to see what the level of interest would be in a crèche.'

*   *   *

The last of Natalie's co-workers had left an hour earlier, laughingly predicting how many valentine's cards they would receive.

'Are you doing anything special, Nat?' asked the young woman who had just boasted that her boyfriend had booked them a table at a really swish restaurant—and was pretty sure he was going to propose.

'I'm going to a wedding,' Natalie explained.

'How romantic, getting married on Valentine's Day!' someone exclaimed enviously.

Then someone else asked the question Natalie had hoped they wouldn't.

'Anyone we know, Nat?'

'Mike, my ex-husband, is getting married to his girlfriend, Gabrielle Latimer…the actress.'

'Your *ex*!'

'Oh, God, she's *gorgeous*!' someone else breathed, only to be elbowed by the guy standing beside her.

'Personally,' someone else remarked, 'I don't think she'll age well—now, if she had *your* cheekbones, Nat…' Everyone looked at Natalie and nodded. 'And I read the other day she's had a boob job.'

Natalie smiled. She appreciated the loyal attempt to make her feel better but, like the others, she knew that when it came to looks she couldn't even compete in the same league as the younger girl.

Natalie would have actually preferred to spend Valentine's Day having root-canal work than attending the wedding of the century, but her daughter, Rose, who was to be a bridesmaid, had flatly refused to attend if Mummy wasn't there, too.

At least Luke would be there for moral support.

With a sigh she set about reducing the pile of paper on the desk. When half an hour later Luke Oliver put his good-looking blond head around the partition that separated her from the rest of the large office she had made good inroads into the backlog.

'You're working late, Luke,' she observed as the rest of his body followed suit.

'I'm not the only one—after Brownie points?' he teased lightly.

'There wouldn't be any point, would there?' Natalie felt guilty when Luke looked embarrassed by her dry observation. 'I'm making up for a late start,' she admitted hurriedly. 'Rose had another asthma attack last night.' Natalie pinned an upbeat smile on her face as Luke's good-looking face creased with sympathy. 'Fortunately I managed to get her an early appointment at the doctor's this morning, but they were running late and by the time I'd finally got her settled with Ruth it was almost eleven.'

'How is she?'

'She's loads better this morning, thanks.' Even so it had torn Natalie apart to leave her fragile-looking daughter. It was a guilt thing, of course. Rose had been more than happy to stay with Ruth, who doted on her and was more than capable to cope with any crisis.

'So now you're working twice as hard as everyone else to prove you don't expect any special favours just because you're a single mum,' Luke suggested perceptively.

Natalie gave a rueful smile and rotated her head to relieve the tension in her neck and shoulders. 'You know me so well, Luke.'

Luke's glance dropped to the delicate, clear-cut features lifted to him—features made nonetheless attractive by dark smudges of fatigue under the wide-spaced, darkly lashed hazel eyes and lines of strain around the wide, softly curving lips.

'Not as well as I'd like...' he sighed huskily.

Natalie's smile morphed into a wary frown as she registered the suggestive warmth in his expression; she'd thought they'd got past all that stuff. 'You know that I'm not...' she began wearily.

Luke sighed and held up his hand. 'Sorry, I know I said I wouldn't go there, Nat, but...' his attractive smile flashed out '...you might change your mind?'

'No, I won't change my mind.' Natalie hardened her heart against Luke's hurt puppy-dog look. 'And anyway, you know as well as I do that office romances never work.' She smiled to lessen her rejection. 'Besides, there's no room in my life for a man.' Or for that matter much for anything but work and sleep, and not too much of the latter when Rose wasn't well!

'Have you told little Rose yet about Mike moving to the States?'

Natalie rubbed the faint worried indentation between her feathery eyebrows and shook her head. 'Nope. I suppose I should before the wedding?' What am I doing asking a childless bachelor advice on child-rearing when I already know the answer? she thought begrudgingly. 'But I just don't know how she's going to react.' *Liar!* She knew Rose would react like any other five-year-old when she learnt the dad who spoilt her rotten every other weekend—when he turned up—was moving halfway around the world—*badly*!

Luke shifted uncomfortably. 'Actually it's about the wedding I wanted to have a word, Nat.'

His next words confirmed that the shiver of apprehension snaking down her spine was justified.

'I hate to do this to you, but Rafe has put me on the Ellis account; he's sending me to New York for a couple of weeks.' He tried to sound casual about this amazing opportunity and failed miserably.

'Congratulations.'

'Thanks, Nat. It should be you that's going, though.'

Natalie shook her head and pinned on a smile. Only a real cow would begrudge someone as nice and genuinely talented as Luke a break like this. 'You deserve it, Luke,' she assured him warmly.

'I'm afraid it means...'

'You won't be able to come to the wedding with me,' she completed, unable to totally disguise her dismay behind a sunny smile. 'That's fine, don't worry,' she added stoically.

She wasn't surprised that Luke had said yes; when Rafe *asked* hungry young executives like Luke they never said no. In fact, she brooded, people in general don't say no to him...*except me*.

These days she didn't rate cosy chats with His Lordship, as the blue-blooded heir to a baronetcy was called—sometimes affectionately, sometimes not!—behind his back. Which just proves, she told herself wryly, that there is a bright side to having a career that's going nowhere.

On paper she and Luke had the same qualifications, they had even begun working at the top-notch management consulting firm within weeks of one another, but ten months on Luke had his own office and she was still sitting at the same desk doing routine stuff that she could have done asleep.

Things weren't likely to get better either. You didn't get offered a chance at Ransome twice and Natalie had, after much soul-searching, refused hers. Luke, who hadn't had to weigh his desire for promotion against the problems of child care, had not said no to his.

The rest, as they said, was history. She'd made her choice; she didn't consider herself a victim—lots of women managed to have high-flying careers and babies. Clearly she didn't have what it took.

'God, Nat, I'm really sorry.'

'It's not your fault,' Natalie soothed a guilty-looking Luke. 'It's *that* man,' she breathed, venom hardening her soft voice as she contemplated the grim prospect of attending the marriage of her ex to the glamorous Gabby without the support of a passable male to give the ego-bolstering illusion she had a well-rounded life. 'I don't suppose it even occurs to Rafael Ransome that some people actually have a life outside this place!'

'*Nat*, he's not that bad.'

'*Bad!* The man's a cold-blooded tyrant! I'm surprised he doesn't make us sign our contracts in blood,' she retorted with a resolute lack of objectivity. 'Forget all that stuff you read about him in the glossy supplements,' she advised Luke, imaginatively expanding her theme. 'He might have turned this place into one of the top management consulting firms in Europe virtually overnight—the success of the nineties...'

To Luke's amusement she proceeded to dismiss one of the most spectacular financial successes of the decade with a disdainful sniff.

'And have every top company beating a path to his

door, but I've always reckoned he was born in the wrong century.'

Luke looked amused. 'Sounds like you've given the subject some thought?'

'Not especially,' Natalie responded hurriedly. 'It's just obvious that underneath the designer suits—'

'You've not given that much thought either, I suppose.'

'Most certainly not!' Natalie denied, insulted by the suggestion she was in the habit of mentally undressing her boss.

'*Sure* you haven't. So what *do* you think goes on under his designer suits, Nat?'

'I think there lurks the soul of a feudal, your-fate-is-in-his-hands type of despot. I can just see him now grinding the odd handful of peasants into the ground.'

Her voice lost some of its crisp edge as an intrusive mental image to match her words flashed into her head. In her defence, Rafe Ransome, his well-developed muscular thighs covered by a pair of tight and most likely historically inaccurate breeches, was enough to put the odd weak quiver into the most objective of females' voices.

Unlike Natalie, most women were not normally objective about her employer's looks; his mingled genes—Italian on his mother's side and Scottish on his aristocratic father's side—had given the man an entirely unfair advantage in the looks stakes.

'*Nat!*'

Natalie was too caught up in her historical re-enactment to hear the note of warning. 'On his way to burn down his neighbours' castle and ravish the local maidens…'

Like the modern-day equivalent, his victims probably wouldn't have put up much of a fight, she
thought, contemplating with disapproval the inability
of her own sex to see beyond a darkly perfect face of
fallen angel and an in-your-face sensuality.

It struck her as ironic, when you considered he was
set to inherit a centuries-old title and the castle that
went with it from his Scottish father, that Rafael
Ransome, all six feet three of him—and most of it
solid muscle—looked Latin from the top of his perfectly groomed glossy head to the tips of his expressive tapering fingers.

Even she, who wasn't into dark, dynamic, brooding
types, had to admit that if you discounted his discon-
certingly bright electric-blue eyes Rafael looked like
most women's idealised image of a classic
Mediterranean male. Dark luxuriant hair that gleamed
blue-black in some lights, golden skin stretched tautly
over high chiselled cheekbones, and a wide, sensually
moulded mobile mouth…just thinking about the cruel
contours caused a shudder to ripple through her body
and she hadn't even got to his lean, athletic body!

'Natalie!'

It was Luke's strangled whisper that finally made
her lift her unfocused angry eyes from the computer
screen, filled by now with row after row of angry exclamation marks.

Oh, God!

Even before Natalie heard the inimical deep mocking drawl the back of her neck started to prickle and
her stomach gave a sickly lurch. Why, she wondered
despairingly, hadn't her selective internal radar, selective as in it only spookily zapped into life when His

Lordship was in the vicinity, kicked in a few moments earlier?

Her wide eyes sent an agonised question to Luke, who almost imperceptibly nodded.

I must have done something really terrible in a previous life, she thought.

CHAPTER TWO

'EMPLOYMENT law being what it is these days, I generally have to satisfy myself with the odd formal written warning, Ms Warner.'

As an alternative to ravishment?

The unbidden image that accompanied her maverick and fortunately silent response made Natalie's skin prickle with heat. She shook her head slightly as if to physically dislodge the breathless, tight feeling that made her head buzz. Being ravished, even hypothetically, by the owner of the most blatantly sensual lips she was ever likely to see was somewhere Natalie was not going.

'See you, Nat! And good luck,' Luke hissed.

And I'll need it, she thought wistfully, watching Luke making one of the fastest exits she'd ever seen—discretion obviously being the better part of valour as far as he was concerned, and who could blame him?

Still, at least there would be nobody to see her grovel, she thought dully. She took a deep breath and, squaring her slender shoulders, resolutely pushed aside a tide of self-pity that threatened to engulf her—she only had herself to blame. If you were going to bad-mouth your boss a sensible person took a few basic precautions first, such as checking he wasn't within hearing distance!

I can do humble…I *can* do humble, she silently mouthed. Even, she mentally added, if it chokes me! If I feel myself getting bolshy all I have to do, she told herself, is think about that enormous electricity bill I found sitting on the doormat yesterday.

Maybe she was worrying over nothing—for all she knew he might see the funny side to this. Did dynamic workaholics have a sense of humour?

Gripping the arm rests of her chair so hard her knuckles turned white, she slowly swivelled her chair and raised a weak smile. Underneath she felt the same prickly feeling of antagonism she always did when in his vicinity.

'Oops! You weren't meant to hear that.' She heard with dismay a high-pitched giggle emerge from her lips. You're meant to be upbeat, not manic, she berated herself silently. God, why do I always act like a total idiot when he's around? Perhaps it was a case of doing what he expected? His attitude said he expected her to do something stupid, and she generally obliged—even if it was only tripping over her own feet!

Rafe, his beautiful mouth set in a stern straight line, raised one dark, slanted brow; beneath his heavy, half-closed lids his eyes glittered like cold blue steel. He was looking down his aristocratic nose at her because, along with the fearfully smart brain and the incredible film-star looks, Rafael Ransome was also arrogant and élitist. With his pedigree, she reflected sourly, it was not to be wondered at.

The silence was shredding her nerve endings. If he didn't say something soon she might start confessing to stuff she hadn't done! Say something even if it is sneery and sarky, she quietly muttered to herself.

Her wish was almost immediately granted.

'Such flights of fantasy, Ms Warner...' he drawled in a voice that was both sneery and sarky enough to satisfy the most demanding consumer. 'Should you ever decide to commit them to paper I have a publisher friend who would be happy to cast a professional eye over them.'

Was that his way of saying she was in the wrong job? No, a brutal 'you're not up to it' was more his style.

'I really don't think they'd be that interesting,' she replied, quieting a fresh spasm of panic... *Fantasy*, he said—he couldn't possibly know about the dreams. She broke out in a cold sweat just thinking about him being privy to her nocturnal fantasies. Not that she was going to start feeling guilty—a girl couldn't be responsible for her subconscious.

'Though if I'm going to be cast in the role of villain, litigation-wise it might be a sensible precaution if you changed a few details. Change of eye colour, make me a blond...'

Giving his character a hint of human warmth would definitely work, she thought grimly—then *nobody* would recognise him! 'It was a joke,' she insisted hoarsely.

Though if anyone had been born to fulfil the role of a ruthless criminal, she decided, sneaking a covert look through her lashes at his cold, classic profile, this was the man—it didn't require much imagination to picture him in the role of the cold-eyed assassin who aimed a gun at his victim's heart without any sign of emotion. Her own heart, perhaps in sympathy for the phantom victim, began to behave in an erratic manner, which made her feel breathless and a little light-headed.

'If you find me such an oppressive monster,' he mused, ignoring her hoarse interjection, 'I'm surprised you're still with us.'

Appealing to his sense of humour had always been a long shot.

'And at such a late hour, too...' He glanced point-edly at the metal watch on his wrist. Natalie was al-most as conscious of the light dusting of dark hair on his sinewed forearm as she was of the sarcasm in his voice. Her stomach did a slow backward flip. 'Such dedication...'

She felt the colour deepen in her already pink cheeks, the sarcastic implication that she did what she had to and nothing more had enough truth in it to make her angry and defensive.

'I do what you pay me for,' she returned, success-fully keeping her growing antipathy from her voice. Her control didn't stretch as far as her eyes but her antagonism did—it shone brightly in the clear depths.

This fact was not lost on Rafe, who was not dis-pleased by the results of his calculated baiting. He reasoned that she'd eventually have to defend herself and then he might finally learn the real reason that she'd knocked back his promotion offer. He hadn't swallowed the lame 'I don't feel I'm ready' for a sec-ond.

'And not a jot more,' he completed smoothly.

Natalie's bosom swelled; smug, hateful pig! It was becoming increasingly difficult to recall her resolve to take what he threw at her and smile. I'd like to see him cope with the demands of a child and work for just twenty-four hours, she challenged mentally, allowing her gaze to sweep with simmering resentment over his tall, immaculate figure.

She exhaled noisily and tried to take control of her erratic breathing.

'Have you had any complaints about my work?' she demanded, quietly confident on this point at least. Sure, she was frequently frustrated by her inability to put more hours in at the workplace, but she also knew that she actually contributed as much and more than other people doing the same job as herself—she earned her salary.

Something that looked like amusement appeared in his eyes but it was gone so quickly and it seemed so unlikely that Natalie assumed she'd been imagining it.

'On the contrary.' One corner of his mobile mouth dropped as his eyes moved over her tense figure. 'Everyone goes out of their way to cover for you.'

In reality the simple fact was that if Natalie Warner's work hadn't been adequate she wouldn't still be at Ransome. Margaret had been right about one thing: Rafe was not sentimental about such things— when such a lot had been riding on his making a success of Ransome, he couldn't afford to be.

Quite a few people had known his own father had been behind the damaging rumours that had circulated just after the launch of Ransome, but he was the only one who knew the reason behind the old man's actions.

'If you're so damned confident how about a wager?' James Ransome had suggested when his only son had remained unmoved by the direst of his threats. 'Put your money where your mouth is, boy. If you don't make a go of it within twelve months you'll quit this nonsense and come home to run the estate.'

'*Twelve months!*'

'Well, if you don't think you're up to it, boy?'

Failure had not been an option.

When he looked at Natalie Warner, he saw potential going to waste—actually it wasn't the only thing he saw, but it was the only thing that had any relevance in the workplace.

'I don't need anyone to cover for me,' she gritted.

'Don't get me wrong, you're to be congratulated.' Natalie's teeth clenched at the patronising drawl, which it seemed to her he kept just for her and bad weather. 'Overplaying the single-parent card could have caused resentment amongst your childless colleagues, but you seem to have the balance just right…plucky, but fragile.'

Not so fragile that she couldn't land a pretty good punch if you stepped out of line—she sure as hell looked as if that was what she wanted to do right now. At least that would be some sort of reaction, and preferable to the meek and mild, fade-into-the-background, yes-sir–no-sir attitude she had adopted even before she'd refused the promotion offer.

The line between his dark brows deepened as he compared this Natalie with the one who had arrived bubbling with enthusiasm and raw talent, displaying a fresh and exciting approach and causing ripples with her willingness to speak out of turn.

The sheer injustice of his accusation stunned Natalie into silence. Chin up, she met his scornful scrutiny head-on and refused to respond to the provocation. To her surprise it was Rafe who dropped his gaze first.

'For God's sake, woman,' he snapped irritably. 'You look terrible. Do you even own a mirror?'

Aware that her automatic female response to his criticism had been to lift a hand to her hair, Natalie frowned and pulled it angrily back to her lap. Rafe Ransome thinks I'm a dog... This should come as no great surprise—she'd seen the type he dated. A man who could probably emerge from a hurricane without a hair out of place was never going to feel anything but disgust for someone who looked messy as soon as she walked out of the door.

The unexpected urge she felt to burst into tears just went to prove she had more vanity left than she had thought.

'Well, you've no room to talk!' Rafe looked so astounded by her sharp retort that Natalie almost laughed. It was probably the first time in his life anyone had implied there was any fault in his appearance. He might be a nicer person if they had, *and* he might be a little more tolerant of those who didn't possess his physical perfection—like her!

'When did you last shave?' she demanded with a disdainful nod towards the dark, incriminating shadow. Actually the look of dangerous dissipation it lent him was not unattractive.

Rafe lifted a hand to his jaw and looked amused. 'I had an early start,' he admitted.

'That's fine, because *I* don't judge people on appearances,' she informed him piously. 'And, just for the record, I hardly think my looks or lack of them are relevant to my ability to do my job.' And until you drew attention to it I hadn't even thought about the way I looked, she thought, angling a look of seething dislike up at his face.

Not true, the irritating voice of honesty in her head piped up—you started thinking about the way you looked the moment you saw him. It was at times like this, she thought with a sigh, that self-deception was infinitely preferable to the truth. Not that there was any sinister significance in her bizarre reactions to his presence, neither was it unique she'd seen the way other women in the building acted when he was around—God, but it must be awful to be married to someone all other women regarded with lust.

Oh, sure, Nat, a fate worse than death!

Just because you caught yourself wondering what undies you'd put on that morning when you saw a man didn't mean you were contemplating him or anyone else seeing them. Rafe was the sort of man who would be pretty knowledgeable when it came to women's underwear, she mused…or at least removing them. He was just the sort of man that made women conscious that they were…well…women! Possibly because he was so obviously and in-your-face *male*!

'Granted, but your ability to do your job is compromised if you're too tired and run-down to work and an ill-kempt appearance is hardly professional.' Neither was it professional for him to want to unfasten the piece of velvet ribbon that held the hair she'd scraped back from her face in an unattractive ponytail.

Natalie, teeth clenched and head bent over her desk, was unaware that her boss was finding the exposed nape of her neck strangely attractive. Calling her physically repulsive was one thing, but calling her unprofessional really hurt, especially when his accusation had some foundation. Uncomfortably she glanced down at her crumpled skirt and the run in her tights; he was right, she was a complete mess!

'Linen is meant to look crumpled.'

'If crumpled was the look you were after, congratulations, you've succeeded.'

Though she looked as though she'd been dragged through a hedge backwards, her nut-brown hair looked smooth and glossy. Rafe felt confident that it would feel like silk if he let it fall through his fingers.

'Are you wearing *any* make-up…?' he rasped suddenly, exhibiting what seemed to her to be a peculiar preoccupation with her appearance.

'I'm not sure,' she responded without thinking. She found this conversation, like his critical scrutiny, was getting far too personal for her taste.

'You're not sure!' he ejaculated, looking at her with the sort of expression she suspected he reserved for females without lipstick and Martians.

'Did someone die and make you the style police? Or is it now office policy not to appear without lip gloss?' she grunted with a belligerent frown.

He shook his head. 'Don't be ridiculous!' he snapped impatiently.

She wasn't even beautiful, he thought, examining the too-sharp contours of her pale, pinched face. Actually, though her features lacked symmetry they did have a certain charm and her smooth skin, though as pale as milk, was amazingly blemishless. So she was attractive, he conceded, but beautiful—no, and either she had no fashion sense at all or for perverse reasons known to her alone she went out of her way to wear things that didn't suit her. Take today's offering, for instance…he looked and barely repressed a shudder.

Natalie hunched her shoulders and lifted her chin as she registered the pained expression on his dark, saturnine features. She could have explained that she'd had things other than colour co-ordinating her outfit on her mind that morning. Things such as hoping Rose wouldn't end up being hospitalised *again*, but that explanation would no doubt elicit another accusation of her using her daughter to get special treatment—and no way was she going to give the smug ratbag the satisfaction.

Is it against your precious principles to say something that might make him *not* want to dispense with your services? Or is an apology too much like good sense? the exasperated voice in her head pondered.

'I'm sorry you heard what I said. I was upset…'

'Sorry I heard, or sorry you said it?'

Rafe, it seemed, was not in the mood to be placated.

She eyed him with escalating irritation. 'Well, if you're going to be pedantic…' She closed her eyes as she heard the snippy words slip from her lips. God, I'm doing it again! She opened her eyes and pinned a bland smile on her face. 'I wasn't being serious, it's just Luke had just told me something a bit upsetting.'

'I'm so sorry that work interferes with your social life.' Natalie's bewildered eyes locked with his; the depth of smouldering anger in the deep, drowning blue only deepened her confusion. She couldn't imagine what had put it there. 'You weren't happy Luke was going to New York…' he reminded her in a terse, clipped voice. 'Couldn't you bear to be parted from him that long?'

'You were standing there all that time!' she gasped without thinking. 'Well, I call that plain sneaky not letting on,' she told him indignantly.

She was actually more indignant than she might have been because there was a grain of truth in what he'd said. Of course she was pleased for Luke's good fortune, but she could still guiltily recall the wave of shameful envy that she'd felt for a split second when Luke had told her his news.

For a moment he looked taken aback by her indignant cry, then she saw his electric-blue eyes fill with laughter. His mobile lips twitched, and Natalie, who normally had no problem laughing at herself, especially when she said something spectacularly stupid— and that little gem *definitely* qualified—felt more inclined to lie on the floor and scream.

'I wasn't actually trying to hide and if you hadn't been so absorbed by pulling my character to shreds you would have seen me...or at least seen the message Luke was desperately trying to signal.'

The mention of Luke reminded Natalie of his original accusation. 'I was not upset because you gave Luke a great job!' At least the notion that she had a social life at all was funny. 'And I'm happy for him,' she insisted sturdily.

Even as she spoke she saw herself, not Luke, striding confidently into the New York office. Even Rafael would have found no fault with this glossily groomed other her, she thought, releasing the image. A realist, she was impatient with herself for indulging in this romanticised daydream.

'If you don't mind a little bit of advice?' Rafe suggested, watching the revealing expressions flit across her face with narrowed eyes.

'Do I have any choice?'

She instantly regretted her childish retort as his perfect profile hardened with displeasure. Do you actually want to lose your job, Natalie? The problem with men like Rafe, she told herself, was they could dish it out, but, surrounded by people who constantly told them how marvellous they were, they bleated foul if anyone gave it back.

'I think that it's possible you might find that your relationship with Luke would stand a better chance in the long term if you actually support his efforts to promote his career rather than trying demotivate him.' The condescension in his voice made her teeth ache and her fingers furl into combative fists. 'Some people are not happy to drift along without any real challenge.'

No need for him to add that he considered her one of this breed he evidently despised when the scornful expression on his dark features said all too clearly he thought she was.

'How dare you?' His smug, sanctimonious attitude made her long to beat her hands against his broad chest, though he'd probably emerge from the attack without a hair out of place and she'd have bruised fists and no job!

Quivering, she rose to her feet; even then she barely reached Rafael's broad shoulder. As their eyes locked a wave of dizziness hit her, making the room tilt and everything but his dark, devastating features shift out of focus... They seemed to sharpen until they filled her vision; similarly the subtle male scent of his body filled her nostrils...

'Are you ill?'

Only in the head. Natalie closed her eyes and took a deep, fortifying breath. Actually this close it wasn't possible to pretend even to herself that the damage was restricted to her mental capacity, not when her body started responding in some very embarrassing ways to the man.

She had no illusions, she could have dressed up the effect he had on her in all sorts of painless ways, but what would be the point? It wouldn't change anything. He was an outrageously attractive, sexy guy—in a dark, predatory way that wasn't to her taste, at least not on an intellectual level. Problem was it wasn't her intellect that was in action here, it was her indiscriminate hormones that were responding to his raw animal magnetism.

She could be a victim of her hormones or she could rise above them.

Her knees were trembling—in fact her entire body was quivering as she tried to shake off the last remnants of the red blur before her eyes.

'If I did have a relationship with Luke, which I don't—*I don't!*—' she enunciated grimly from between gritted teeth in response to his blatantly sceptical smile '—the last person I'd take advice from would be someone with the emotional depth of a puddle! Luke is my friend.'

'But he'd like to be more?' He scanned her face as if he suspected to find a guilty secret written there.

CHAPTER THREE

NATALIE'S jaw tightened as she glared at Rafe belligerently. 'Would that be so amazing?' She was too angry to wonder at the personal comments coming from someone who was not exactly a touchy-feely boss. You did your job and didn't bring your personal problems to work at Ransome. 'Well, maybe he doesn't have *your* high standards!' she snarled waspishly.

The faces and figures of the women in Rafe's life could have been neatly superimposed by a computer on top of one another with no overlapping edges. Long, leggy and decorative, even the ones who weren't looked like models. Thinking about them made Natalie feel unaccountably angry.

'Or maybe he doesn't know a lost cause when he sees one,' Rafael suggested provocatively.

Natalie's nostrils flared as she took a wrathful breath. 'As for me being happy with a job that I could do in my sleep…*you think I like that*?' she quavered incredulously.

His wide shoulders lifted as he leaned towards her and his compelling eyes collided with hers before dropping to her quivering lips. He swallowed, working the muscles in his brown throat. 'Tell me what you would like,' he instructed tersely.

Tell me what you would like?

In her mind Natalie heard those words spoken in a way that changed their meaning dramatically. Her soft lips parted as a sigh snagged in her dry throat. Mike had never asked her what she'd wanted, and even if he had—an unimaginable scenario!—she doubted she could have told him. There had always been a restricting self-consciousness in the physical side of their relationship.

Natalie had sometimes wondered a little wistfully if the mind-blowing sex of legend, the sort where you forgot where you ended and your lover began, actually existed. She had come to the conclusion that if it did she was not likely to experience it. Self-awareness was a good thing, but it was still dreadfully depressing to acknowledge that you were just too inhibited to ever experience the pleasures of head-banging, no-holds-barred sex.

Though he hadn't come right out and said so, Mike had managed to reinforce this belief with the few things he'd casually let slip about his vastly improved love life with the sexually insatiable Gabby. It was impossible to avoid coming to the inevitable conclusion that the fault must lie with her.

I'm just not a sexy, throw-caution-to-the-wind woman, which is probably why I married the first man I slept with who was my childhood sweetheart to boot!

She sighed, a dreamy expression drifting into her eyes as they dwelt speculatively on the strong features of the man who had spoken…the sensual curve of his mouth did not suggest he was overly encumbered with inhibitions. Looking at it made her breathing quicken and her tummy muscles quiver in a painfully pleasurable way.

Would Rafael be the sort of lover who would...?

With a horrified gasp Natalie pulled a veil across that dangerous line of speculation. Her neatly trimmed nails pressed half-moons into the soft flesh of her palms when, despite her best efforts, tantalising little glimpses of what lay behind that veil kept intruding in a deeply distracting manner.

In an angry gesture she flicked her head, sending her pony-tail whooshing silkily backwards. 'So that's what *this* is about!' she cried contemptuously.

Rafe watched, his blue eyes unwillingly held captive as her explosive action dislodged several more silky strands of hair from her pony-tail. If he had his way she'd never tie her hair back but wear it loose. In his mind he saw it lying straight and fine down her narrow, naked back almost reaching a waist he could span with his hands—though to know this for sure he'd have to put the theory to the test...

He cleared his throat and reached up to loosen the tie at his throat. 'Define ''this''.'

As if he didn't know! Maybe it was time they got this out in the open even if it did mean she lost her job.

'I turned down that stupid offer of fast-track promotion...' she continued carelessly, brushing a stray section of hair off her face with the back of her hand. She could see a vee of brown skin where he'd undone the top button of his shirt. She ran her tongue over the dry outline of her lips as she watched his long brown fingers release the second button.

She released her baited breath in a gusty sigh as the fabric parted.

And I'm the one who always wondered what

women get from watching men strip…hell, I'm getting hot and bothered over an innocent extra square centimetre of bare flesh! I've clearly lost it.

'*Stupid…?*' Rafael shrugged. 'I suppose,' he conceded wryly, 'in retrospect it was stupid, but at the time I actually thought I was giving you an opportunity most people in your situation dream about.'

His scornful tone made her flush angrily. 'Out of the goodness of your heart, no doubt,' she sneered irrationally—since when had business been about kindness? 'What was I meant to do with a young child when I got the word to hotfoot it to New York like Luke…shove her in my hand luggage?'

Rafe looked taken aback by her aggressive question. The line between his dark brows deepened as he shook his head. 'If *that* was the only problem why didn't you say so at the time?'

Only problem? That he could imply she was making a fuss about nothing added insult to injury.

'Why? So you could tell me you're not a social worker.' That had been Maggie's response when she had attempted to explain her dilemma to the other woman. She had gone on to warn Natalie that Mr Ransome would not be interested in her lame excuses either.

You girls these days expect it all ways. Natalie had been deeply humiliated by the contemptuous criticism; she had vowed never to give anyone the opportunity to level that accusation at her again.

His dark brows knitted. 'Social worker?' he repeated, looking genuinely perplexed. 'Being a single parent is hardly so unusual these days, is it? In fact,' he added drily, 'it's almost the norm. Half the people I know are on their second or third marriage.'

But not him. Rafe seemed one of those men who were allergic to marriage. 'More fool them.'

'You sound bitter,' he observed.

'I'm not bitter, just cautious,' she countered.

'Cautious about what?' he persisted. 'Men or marriage?'

'One is a nice idea, the other...well, just look at yourself.' The righteously indignant expression faded from her face as she followed her own advice. She stifled an appreciative sigh; he really was the *most* stunningly perfect male imaginable.

'*Me...?*'

'Well everyone knows you have the staying power of a two-year-old when it comes to women. Yet I suppose one day you'll meet the *right* woman and get married,' she predicted sourly. 'It's just not logical to suppose that your personality will change overnight...' Her voice faded as she encountered the blankly astonished expression on his face. It occurred to her that her evangelical enthusiasm for the subject had made her go too far. 'Well, it seems that way to me anyhow...' she added with a touch of husky defiance.

Rafe inhaled deeply and rocked back on his heels. 'So it *seems* to you I am a shallow womaniser, who will sleep with the maid of honour at my own wedding.' Cold ice scanned her dismayed face. 'Have I got that right...?' he enquired in a cuttingly satirical drawl.

'Oh, dear, I've upset you.' An understatement, she thought, regarding his taut expression with growing dismay. Well, at least there was no need to watch what she said any more—she had obviously talked herself out of a job.

Rafe brought his teeth together in a wolf-like smile. 'How long did you say you were married for?'

'I didn't, but it was two years.'

'*That* long?' he drawled insultingly.

'There's no need to be personal.' He released an incredulous laugh and she blushed. 'I'm just trying to say that a lot of men are…'

'Congenitally incapable of fidelity,' he finished smoothly. 'Whereas women never stray.'

'Of course they do.'

'Did you?'

'Chance would be a fine thing!' she snorted. 'When Mike walked out Rose was three months old.' As far as *straying* went, any idiot could figure out that this ruled out the twelve months prior to their separation. And afterwards, well… 'Would *you* want an affair with a woman who had a baby or young child?' she added cynically.

'Some people seem to be able to combine being a mother and lover…'

The fact he had avoided the question was not lost on Natalie. 'Whereas I can't even combine it with a career.'

Rafe released an exasperated sigh from between his clenched teeth. 'Self-pity doesn't suit you,' he observed drily. His brow creased. 'Wouldn't a nanny solve your problem? Or an au pair?'

Natalie gave an incredulous snort of laughter; nobody was that naïve, surely! She searched his face—he was serious! What world did this guy live in? Not one where you juggled half a dozen tasks simultaneously and did your supermarket shopping with a fretful child dragging along at your side.

No, Rafe lived in the glamorous world of the élite, flash cars, and flashier women, film premières and weekend skiing trips. It was hardly surprising that it was his world that sold newspapers and magazines to people whose own lives, like her own, were humdrum by comparison.

'Oh!' she cried, lifting a hand to her brow. 'Why didn't *I* think of that?' Her eyes narrowed. 'Maybe,' she added crisply, 'because I couldn't afford to pay for a full-time live-in nanny or even half a full-time nanny,' she added thoughtfully. 'The fact is you have it in for me,' she spelt out before he had a chance to respond, 'because I had the temerity to turn down that job offer!'

'*Have it in for you?*' he echoed incredulously. His narrowed eyes homed in on the accusing finger she was waving in front of his nose and with a grunt of sheer exasperation he caught the offending digit and, folding it into her palm, covered her small fist firmly with his own. Her hand was lost within his.

His grasp was firm but not constricting; Natalie could have pulled away, but she didn't. The blood drained from her face as, almost fearfully, she stared at the long, elegant fingers that looked very dark curled against her fair skin. Illogically the contrast excited her...a furtive excitement that she dared not admit even to herself.

His thumb began to move against the blue-veined inner aspect of her wrist and she let out a sharp gasp. A heat that began low in her belly suddenly flared hot and spread through her body invading every cell with a strange, enervating weakness. She raised her shocked eyes and Rafe smiled, a smile that held a terrifying mixture of sexual speculation and understanding as if he knew exactly how she was feeling. *Well, at least one of us does.*

'I was meant to be overcome with gratitude—' Natalie could barely hear her own hoarse whisper above the heavy throbbing beat of her heart.

'*Gratitude…? You…?*' he interjected with a wry laugh. 'I'm not *that* unrealistic.'

She continued as though he hadn't spoken. 'And I said no.' His skin was cool against her overheated flesh and there was controlled strength in his light touch that she found deeply exciting. 'You took it as a personal insult, that's why I've been given every crummy job going!' The moment the words were out of her mouth she wished them unsaid.

Determined not to lay herself open to an accusation of asking for preferential treatment, Natalie had consistently refused to complain…until now.

With an angry cry she wrenched her fingers away from his grasp and, covering them with her uncontaminated hand, nursed them against her chest.

'*Personal…!*' A feral smile illuminated the darkness of his face. He could have told her about personal—personal was wanting to take her face between his hands before kissing her senseless, the kind of kiss that might go some way to relieve a little of the frustration being around her filled him with. The errant nerve in his lean cheek began to pulse erratically as he visualised the pleasure of her willingly opening her lips to offer his tongue access to the soft sweetness of her mouth. His body reacted to the erotic imagery that filled his mind with all the subtlety and control of an adolescent boy.

Natalie was almost relieved when he frowned and suddenly barked, 'And what do you mean every crummy job going?' For a moment there the way he was looking at her had been almost frightening—not that she could ever have been *physically* scared of him, but there had been a combustible quality to his fixed stare that had been deeply unsettling.

By way of reply Natalie picked up a pile of documents from her desk and held them out to him. 'The perfect cure for insomnia,' she promised him.

'I don't suffer from it,' Rafael replied as he took them from her. He didn't look at them or—much to her relief—appear to notice when she snatched her hand away as if scalded when their fingertips accidentally brushed. 'I'm sorry if you feel your talents are being underused,' he replied, replacing the stack on her desk. He was detecting Maggie's handiwork here.

'Do you think I have any?' she exclaimed in mock amazement.

'You have a remarkable talent for making me lose my temper,' he told her drily. 'As for personal, you underestimate my ego…I have it on excellent authority that it is Teflon-coated.' The memory was one that seemed to entertain him—at least his expression had lost some of the edginess of a few moments ago that had made her feel uneasy. 'Apparently nothing short of a nuclear explosion could dent it.'

Natalie would have liked to meet the person who was daring and perceptive enough to tell him this to his face.

'My mother.'

Natalie's eyelashes swept down as she averted her gaze from his face; either she was awfully obvious or he was scarily perceptive. With my luck probably both, she concluded wryly.

'I hate to disappoint you, Natalie, but my job is to look at the big picture. I have neither the time or the inclination to exact revenge upon some junior members of staff with a lack of ambition.'

Well, that puts me firmly in my place, she thought bleakly. This seemed as good a time as any to remind herself that her position in the scheme of things at least at Ransome was a small and insignificant cog.

'I have ambition,' pride made her insist stubbornly. She lowered her eyes. 'But I also have other responsibilities,' she admitted with a rush. Her head came up. 'But that doesn't mean I'm asking for any special favours.'

'Why not?'

Natalie was perplexed by his unexpected response. 'Oh, sure, you're really geared up to parents...'

Rafe inhaled sharply and his hard-boned face darkened with annoyance. 'I don't think it's unreasonable to expect the people I employ to be capable of sorting out their personal lives without my unwanted interference, but that doesn't mean I'm unsympathetic when there's a problem.'

'I don't think anyone would want to invite you home to tea...' If they were talking beds she might be on shaky ground. The thought of the female staff who lusted after their good-looking boss brought a disgruntled frown to her smooth brow. 'But something as basic as a crèche and more flexible working hours might be appreciated.'

If she ever heard Mandy, his PA's scheme for a back-to-work package for new mums that included a voucher for a health spa he was in serious trouble! 'And you, I suppose, have been nominated to speak on behalf of this dissatisfied section of the workforce?' he interrupted smoothly.

'Not exactly,' she conceded, shifting her weight from one foot to the other under his ironic gaze. Not only did he make her feel like a gauche schoolgirl, now she was acting like one, too, she thought, only just stopping herself before she began to chew on a loose strand of hair—she hadn't done that since she was twelve, but at twelve she hadn't needed to distract herself from tender breasts that ached and tingled as they chafed against the fabric of her thin top.

Her chin lifted. 'A happier workforce makes for a more productive workforce...' she began defensively.

'Well, that's just fascinating. Have you any other little gems of management theory you'd like to share...any other little pearls of wisdom? You know I really ought to introduce you to the guy who drove me to the airport last week—he had some great ideas about how to run the country.'

CHAPTER FOUR

WHY am I even trying? Natalie wondered. The man is never going to take advice from anyone, least of all me. Hell, he made it pretty clear that I'm too low down the pecking order to even approach him directly!

Even now the memory of Rafe's bored, 'Send my PA a memo, Ms Warner,' had the power to send a flush of mortification over her skin. It had been especially hurtful because before that he had seemed perfectly happy when she'd approached him; in fact she had found herself looking forward to their conversations as the highlights of her days.

She had been deluded enough to think they'd been friends, and had even—God, she cringed to think about it now!—spun romantic little fantasies about them being more. That was why him cutting her dead publicly had hurt so much. Since then she had always been guarded and circumspect in front of him…until today!

People had been very sympathetic, assuring her they'd never seen him act like that before; the popular theory was he must have been crossed in love. This explanation didn't seem at all likely to Natalie as he seemed to change the women in his life almost as frequently as he did his shirts and, as far as she could tell, with about the same degree of emotional attachment.

'There's no need to be so damned patronising!' she exploded. 'I don't suppose it's your fault,' she added bitterly. 'It's probably genetic.' The same genes that had made him the most physically perfect specimen of manhood imaginable had also made him an élitist sod. 'God, I bet you hate children!' sheer frustration made her accuse wildly.

'Genetically impossible. My mother is Venetian and the—'

'I know your mother is Italian!' she snapped. '*Everybody* knows that,' she added quickly—the last thing she wanted was him to run away with the idea she took a personal interest in him. 'You're *famous*.'

Rafe had heard people say serial killer with the same distaste Natalie Warner managed to inject in 'famous'.

'My mother's family come from Venice. I make the distinction because she likes to—it's a regional pride thing. As I was about to say, the Italians adore children. I have a nephew and several godchildren...'

'And you think that makes you an expert?' Natalie laughed, blinking to clear her head of the image of Rafe with a golden-skinned baby in his arms...the irony was she had no doubt Rafe would be as exceptional at fatherhood as he was at everything else. In short, he'd be the sort of dad that Rose would never have. The thought brought an uneasy mixture of guilt, sadness and envy—*envy*...? Her smooth brow wrinkled as alarm shot through her. 'You'll find being a parent is quite different,' she told him with a superior sniff.

'I have no plans to find out any time soon, but you may be sure that when I do have a child I will be financially able to support a family and in a stable relationship.'

'Unlike me, you mean.'

'I have no idea of your personal circumstances.' Except that most of the unmarried men in the building would like to change them—and a number of the married ones, too, he thought grimly.

Natalie smiled. 'True, but don't let that stop you making judgement calls, will you?' Dark colour appeared across the crest of his sharply defined cheekbones; she was pleased to see that her jibe had found its mark.

'A child needs two parents.'

Natalie released an incredulous laugh…he thinks *I* need telling this? 'Did you read that somewhere or is this original thought we are hearing?' She shook her head in disgust. 'And what will you do if the other half of this *stable* relationship decides that she isn't ready after all for parenthood…or, for that matter, marriage? What if she packs her bags and says she has to leave because living with you is stifling h…her artistic creativity? That …she doesn't love you any more and thinks maybe he never did!'

Natalie froze in horror as the lengthening silence continued to echo with the acrid bitterness of her last throbbing announcement. She was totally aghast at what she had said.

Why not just strip your soul bare, Natalie? Oh, I forgot, you already did! Her head sank to her chest as she closed her eyes. She couldn't bear to see what he was going to make of that. Her performance amounted to handing your enemy a loaded gun. *Rafe being the enemy and this being war?*

War...? The analogy struck her immediately as being on the extreme side. Why when Rafe was involved did she lose all sense of proportion—why did she go off the deep end so dramatically? Was this just a clash of personalities or was it a symptom of something much worse?

'I think I would consider myself well rid of such an idiot.'

Natalie was startled by this objective pronouncement, and her troubled gaze fluttered to his face. The bad news was he had seen through her hypothetical scenario; the good news was that nothing resembled the 'pity poor dumped wife' expression she hated so much in his face.

She gave a sigh—under the circumstances there didn't seem much point continuing the pretence. 'It wasn't really Mike's fault,' she protested. 'We were too young, and before we got married him being an artist unwilling to sacrifice his artistic integrity seemed quite romantic.' It had seemed a lot less desirable when they'd had rent to pay.

A spasm of distaste contorted Rafael's austerely handsome features—in his eyes a man who deserted a wife and young child was the lowest of the low.

'My God, I never took you for one of those pathetic females who defend the shiftless bastards who abuse and leave them!'

The lashing virulence of the anger in his voice took her aback almost as much as his accusation. It seemed she wasn't the only one in danger of going off the deep end.

'Mike wasn't abusive!' she protested. Her slender shoulders lifted. 'Just immature,' she judged generously.

Rafael raked a hand through his dark hair and gave vent to his feelings in a flood of musical Italian. It was the first time she had heard him revert to his mother's native tongue and, even though she doubted if the passionate invective translated into anything she'd like to hear, Natalie was spellbound.

Italian was not only beautiful to listen to, it was a very passionate language, she thought as his words flowed over her, smooth as warm honey. Did people who were bilingual find one language more appropriate than another for different activities…say English was good for booking theatre seats and Italian might be better for, say, making love?

'And I'm not pathetic,' she asserted, her voice rising to a panicky pitch as she tried to dispel from her head the shocking image of pale limbs entwined with dark gold. She closed her eyes in disgust and opened them with a snap when she felt the light touch of his fingers slide over the curve of her jaw. Her startled gaze collided head-on with burning blue eyes.

Natalie was too shocked by the casual physical contact to do anything but stare wide-eyed back at him like a night creature caught in the glare of headlights— and any headlights paled into insignificance beside his compelling cerulean gaze. There was no respite, no place to hide from the raking scrutiny of his lustrously lashed eyes.

Her lashes fluttered as the corners of his sternly beautiful mouth lifted; the action lessened the severity of his expression quite dramatically. His smile could have melted stone and Natalie's heart was not made of stone, and, though she liked to pretend otherwise, neither was it immune to this man's charismatic charm.

'No, not pathetic.' The half-smile reached his eyes and Natalie felt bathed in the warm glow of his approval...this was ridiculous!

It's not as if I care what he thinks of me! she thought. Care or not, she was mightily relieved when his hand fell back to his side. Are you so sure about that, Nat? Isn't there some secret part of you that wanted to prolong the contact...?

Rafe saw the tiny negative shake of her head and raised an interrogative brow.

The fight abruptly drained out of Natalie, leaving her feeling too weary to sustain her anger or resistance—Rafe was the most exhausting man to be around for any period of time. Or for that matter to be around period!

'Oh, for God's sake, if you're going to sack me or something get on with it.' She sighed, wearily sinking back into her chair.

She would have spun away from him but Rafe caught the back of her chair and turned it back towards him. Hands on the arm rests, his body curved over hers, he was an extremely big, powerful man and the action could have been intimidating, but it wasn't—it was exciting.

Natalie pressed a nervous hand to her neck. She could feel the dull vibration of her heartbeat in the hollow at the base of her throat. She was discovering that underneath his northern Celtic cool Rafe Ransome had inherited more of his mother's volatile Latin temperament than she had suspected. She might have been able to predict what Rafe would do in a given situation, but not *Rafael*, and the man who towered above her looked all Rafael.

'Or something.'

Natalie, who had forgotten what she'd said, didn't respond to the husky murmur. He was so close now that she could see the fine lines radiating from the corners of his eyes and the gold tips on the ends of his long sooty eyelashes. Through the dark concealing mesh she could see the shimmering summer-blue of his eyes. The tension in the air was so pronounced that she could almost see the invisible barrier that stood between them.

He appeared to be breathing hard; she could hear the soft, sibilant hiss of each inhalation and feel the intimate warmth of his breath whisper along her forehead and across the curve of her cheek. She found herself wondering what the texture of the dark shadow that emphasised the hollows of his cheeks and ran along his angular jaw would feel like if she ran her fingers over it... The achy, empty feeling low in her belly intensified as, unable to trust herself, she locked her fingers together tightly to prevent them doing something she'd regret.

He had angled his dark head so that the fragrant warmth now fell directly against her parted lips. The possibility he was going to kiss her no longer seemed so remote. Dizzy with anticipation, Natalie stopped breathing and closed her eyes.

It seemed like a long time later that his lips finally brushed against hers; Natalie's body stiffened, then relaxed. The pressure was light. It wasn't a lightness that could in any way have been construed as accidental; this was a leave-you-wanting-more, mind-blowingly erotic lightness.

And his technique worked. It worked like a dream. Maybe it was a dream...that was the only place she'd been kissed in a long time. She half wished it were a dream; people could behave irresponsibly in dreams and there were no consequences.

If this is a dream, don't let me wake up just yet.

'You're going to hate me in the morning,' he predicted throatily as his mouth moved with tantalising slowness down the slender curve of her throat.

'I already do,' she rebutted huskily.

'How much?' he asked, kissing her closed eyelids.

'You talk too much,' she complained.

Rafe laughed huskily, but there was nothing amused about his taut, driven expression. She looked into his smoky eyes and whimpered as his teeth gently tugged at the soft flesh of her lower lip. She bit him back and felt the purr of husky laughter in his throat.

'And there isn't going to be a night before to regret.' There wasn't; she was going to put a stop to this any minute now...any minute...

Well, what harm could another couple of minutes do? she told herself as she felt the pressure of his skilful lips subtly increase. It was just kissing.

Releasing a long, shuddering sigh, she ignored the alarmist voice of caution in her head that was insultingly suggesting she couldn't stop even if she wanted to, and instead responded to an instinct that impelled her to clutch at him to intensify and prolong the delicious experience. Weaving her fingers into his lush dark hair once she had done so seemed equally instinctual and very satisfying. If this went on for ever it wouldn't be too long, the dreamy thought drifted through her mind, before she gave herself up totally to the hedonistic pleasure of feeling his hard, rampantly male body pressed up against her.

Natalie hadn't known that kisses so addictive you couldn't walk away from them existed. Totally submerged by a tide of longing, she hooked her arms tightly around his neck. Rafe responded by encircling her narrow waist with his hands. With effortless ease he drew her upright, causing the chair he lifted her from to spin backwards until it collided noisily and unobserved into a filing cabinet.

Natalie wasn't even conscious that her shoes had slipped off as her toes lost contact with the floor.

'What if someone comes in...?'

Her agonised whisper caused him to pull back slightly. The flicker of cold reason in the passion-darkened eyes that swept over her flushed face brought the stupidity of what she was doing crashing home.

Her cheeks heated with mortification. 'This is really stupid.' She shook her head. 'We shouldn't be doing this.'

Rafe let his head fall back and she heard him exhale noisily. 'Sure,' he agreed, lifting his head and pinning her with a feverish cerulean stare. 'But think,' he advised her throatily, 'of the alternative.'

Natalie blinked in confusion.

'*Not* doing it.'

'*Oh!*' Every cell in her body screamed in protest.

'Precisely.'

Natalie was transfixed by the dark need stamped on his hard features.

'That would be...?'

His eyes slid to her mouth, then back to her eyes. 'Unthinkable,' he completed. Still holding her eyes, he parted her lips once more and with seductive skill slid his tongue between her trembling lips.

'Yes!' she whimpered, giving herself up to the craving she could no longer pretend didn't exist. *'Oh, yes, please!'*

Her fractured sob ached with longing. It was too much for Rafe's iron self-control, self-control she naïvely hadn't been aware existed until it was no longer there. A shudder rippled through his lean, powerful body the moment before he claimed her lips. His hungry lips had barely covered hers before his tongue stabbed deep again and again into her mouth.

Natalie was swept up into a maelstrom of pure sensation.

CHAPTER FIVE

NATALIE felt bereft and dizzy when Rafe abruptly put her from him.

'The phone is ringing.'

There was not a trace of the raw, driven hunger he had been exhibiting moments before in the hard planes and hollows of his face.

Natalie shivered, she suddenly felt very cold. He was going to pretend it hadn't happened... That was good, that was excellent—well, as excellent anything connected with kissing your boss with all the finesse of a sex-starved bimbo could be!

Just why had kissing him seemed a good idea? When she thought about how she had... Don't think about it, she instructed herself firmly. It didn't happen. If it works for him it works for me, she told herself angrily. It's just easier for him, she thought, sliding a resentful sideways glance at his darkly impassive face.

Rafe intercepted the look and exhaled loudly. 'This,' he grated, raking a hand through his hair in an exasperated manner, 'is *exactly* what I've been trying to avoid. Getting involved emotionally at work is a recipe for disaster.'

Wasn't that just typical of the man, acting as if he were the innocent victim of her shameless lust when he was the one who had started it? And that in itself was confusing. Why would a man who had spent the previous few minutes pulling all aspects of her appearance and character to shreds want to kiss her? Well, whatever the reason she wasn't going to accept all the blame.

'Afraid it wouldn't be good for your reputation if it got around you'd kissed someone with an inside-leg measurement of less than thirty-four?'

Initially Rafe looked startled by her caustic taunt, but within a matter of seconds an amused glint she didn't like appeared in his eyes.

'Or are you worried I'll play the sexual harassment card? Don't be!' she advised, determined he would not be left with the impression she envied in any way those blonde clones. Her small bosom heaved as she sought to control her strong feelings. 'Do you think I *want* people to know you kissed me?' She gave a very expressive little shudder.

'It's not *my* reputation I'm concerned about.'

'What are you talking about?'

'Have you any idea what people think about ambitious young women who sleep with their bosses?' He paused to let his point sink in. 'It doesn't matter how talented you happen to be, people will always assume that you slept your way to the top.'

Natalie flushed. 'Some place I'm not likely to get!' she gritted.

'If you stop bleating and start actually being positive, it's not totally impossible,' he declared callously.

Natalie glared at him with loathing.

'The phone is ringing again.'

'I know the phone is ringing, I don't need you to

tell me,' she snapped back childishly. 'Hello!' she snarled down the line.

'Is that you, Nat?' a puzzled voice the other end asked tentatively.

It was hardly surprising, Natalie reflected grimly, that she didn't sound like herself—she certainly didn't feel like herself! And as for the way she'd been acting! How could you loathe someone and want to rip their clothes off at the same time? She turned her back on the tall, silent figure but it didn't stop her being painfully aware of him in every cell of her body.

'Natalie?'

'Yes, it's me,' Natalie replied, recognising the familiar voice of Ruth the child-minder. Alarm bells began to ring in her head—Ruth never rang her at work unless there had been a disaster of some sort. The last time Rose had been inconsolable because she had lost her favourite teddy.

'Don't panic, Nat.'

Nothing, in Natalie's experience, was *less* likely to soothe than a telephone conversation that began with these words, but this was especially true if they were closely followed by a horrifying, 'I'm ringing from the hospital.'

Not a lost teddy this time.

This was the sort of phone call that every parent dreaded getting. An icy fist of frozen fear closed around Natalie's heart as a dozen scenarios, each one more catastrophic than the one preceding it, chased rapidly through her head. The panic racing through her veins made it hard for her to think straight. Her lips felt stiff and reluctant to form the question she knew she had to ask, but desperately didn't want to.

'Is she...?'

There was a gasp the other end. 'Oh, God, no, Rose is fine!' The child-minder sounded horrified. 'Well, not *fine*, obviously, or we wouldn't be here, but she will be, they say.'

Natalie's shoulders sagged. *'Oh, my God!'* She was not conscious of Rafe retrieving her chair and sliding it behind her knees at the crucial moment they gave way.

A strange numbness spread through her body while in her head she could feel the dull throb of her own heartbeat.

'After you left Rose seemed a bit feverish,' Ruth relayed hurriedly. 'And later when she started wheezing the inhaler didn't work. I thought the best thing was to get her here first and then ring you.'

'You did the right thing, Ruth.' Natalie caught her trembling lower lip in her teeth. 'I should have listened to my instincts,' she gulped. 'Oh, God, I knew, I just *knew* I shouldn't have left her...but the doctor said she was fine this morning, just a cold...' She stopped, her expression one of grim self-condemnation. She couldn't pass the buck. Nobody had forced her to come into work; that had been her own decision. Because I have a point to prove—namely that a single parent can be just as good...no, *better* than everyone else.

And while I was busy proving my point my daughter was... She shook her head in disgust. What sort of parent does that make me?

Ruth's sensible voice injected a note of practicality into the endless flow of bitter self-recriminations.

'Natalie, dear, if you listened to your instincts you'd never leave Rose at all.'

'Maybe that isn't such a bad idea,' Natalie replied heavily. 'Listen, tell her Mummy will be there soon...yes...all right, Ruth, and thank you,' she said, placing the receiver down and rising urgently to her feet.

Her eyes drifted over him, but from the vague, unfocused expression in them Rafe doubted she had even registered his presence.

He watched as she opened her handbag and, extracting a wallet from the depths, began flicking through the contents with an expression of fierce concentration on her pale features. Her hands were trembling but he doubted she was aware of it; she was displaying all the classic symptoms of shock.

'Where are you going, Natalie?'

Natalie swung back and as she saw him standing there Rafe saw a flicker of shock replace for a moment the fretful expression in her wide, darkly lashed eyes—clearly she had forgotten he was there. This female, he thought wryly, seemed to be determined to single-handedly supply the dose of humility his mother—not a person exactly renown for modesty herself—liked to say he needed so badly.

'You called me Natalie,' she heard herself say stupidly.

'It's your name,' he reminded her gently.

'It sounds...different when you say it,' she observed in a distracted voice. 'My daughter is in hospital.' She looked around the familiar room as if she was surprised to find herself still there. 'I have to go...' She glanced briefly towards the mess on her desk and then back at him. *'Now,'* she added, dealing him a ferocious frown.

Clearly she thought he was an inconsiderate louse who would demand she cleared her desk before she went to her sick child, which was a great basis for a relationship. *Relationship…?* First you break the 'mixing business with pleasure' rule, which is bad, but not as bad as wanting to break it some more. Now you're thinking *relationships*! he derided himself. What next…?

'Which hospital is she in?'

Natalie told him because it was easier than telling him to mind his own business and because he was blocking her way. Actually his calm voice helped her focus her thoughts. Rafe was the sort of man that women less able than herself to take care of themselves would have automatically leaned on in a situation like this.

Natalie was fully awake to the pitfalls of leaning on a man…when they walked away you either fell flat on your face or learnt how to do things for yourself. Of course, Mike had never exactly been a pillar of strength to begin with, so it hadn't been so difficult for her. In fact the gap he'd left in her life had been pretty insignificant all things considered… Rafe Ransome, on the other hand—her wary glance flickered to his tall, vital person—well, nothing about him was insignificant!

'Give me a minute and I'll take you.'

Natalie stared at him incredulously. *'You?'*

'It's on my way.'

She looked up at him, a sceptical line between her dark, feathery brows, clearly trying to figure out his ulterior motive. He couldn't help her out; he still wasn't sure if he had one himself.

'On your way where?'

'I can give you a detailed run-down of my itinerary or I can take you to the hospital.' He gave a very Latin take-it-or-leave-it shrug. 'Unless you prefer to take your chance with public transport?'

Natalie's thoughts turned to the empty condition of her wallet. If anyone had asked her earlier that day she'd have stated with total confidence that nothing on earth would have persuaded her to accept a lift from Rafe Ransome...the man who had just kissed her—*and you kissed him back*!

If her lips hadn't still felt bruised and swollen she would have imagined it had been another of those erotic dreams that woke her up more nights than she cared to admit.

Impatiently she shook her head; she couldn't think about that now.

Swallowing her pride, she lifted her eyes to his. 'Thank you.' It wasn't, she told herself, as if she were sleeping with the enemy, just riding with him. 'Don't be long!' Her anxiety and impatience made the request emerge as an imperious command.

Rafe turned, looking about as surprised as it was possible for someone like him to look. It occurred to Natalie that he wasn't used to being on the receiving end of yelled orders. Not, she acknowledged, that he did any yelling—he didn't need to. He could silence any would-be dissident with a look.

'You did say you'd only be a minute,' she reminded him, moderating her tone. 'You might forget I'm here...' she added defensively.

For a brief moment his narrowed eyes scanned her face. 'I've already tried to do that...and failed,' he revealed cryptically. A rather grim smile lifted the corners of his mouth as she looked back at him warily. 'Don't worry, Natalie, I'm renowned for my attention to detail and timing.'

This time his grin was frankly wicked.

True to his word, he was back within the minute. He walked towards her, shrugging on a dark, loose-fitting suit jacket, and the expensive fabric fell smoothly into place across his broad back. That never happens to me, she thought as she fell in step beside him. She quickly got breathless trying to keep up with his long-legged pace.

'Is there anyone you want to contact...to meet you at the hospital...?' he probed when they reached the underground parking area.

'No.'

'A friend, relation...your daughter's father, perhaps?'

Natalie, her mind on more urgent matters, was exasperated by his persistence. 'My grandmother is my only relation and she lives in Yorkshire. Hospitals freak Mike out.'

And she couldn't cope with a man who went catatonic when he saw a white coat as well as a sick and almost certainly fretful child. Mike would appear when Rose was back home, bearing expensive and often inappropriate gifts. He meant well, she thought indulgently, now she didn't have to contend with her ex-husband's foibles on a daily basis.

Rafe was not inclined to be so generous. It seemed pretty obvious to him that there had been two children in her marriage. He found it inexplicable that women were frequently attracted to the inadequate types who traded on their boyish charm.

'And is your daughter...?'

Natalie's expression softened. 'Rose.'

'Is Rose ill often?'

'No more than a lot of children,' Natalie replied defensively. 'Well,' she conceded, her eyes falling self-consciously from his, 'I suppose she is. She's asthmatic. She's fine normally with the medication. Only winter's not a good time...a cold or virus can trigger a nasty attack in some sensitive people.'

'I've heard that pollution from exhaust fumes and so forth can make matters worse.'

His depth of knowledge surprised her. 'It doesn't help,' she agreed, nodding her thanks stiffly as he opened the passenger door of a black Jag. She slid inside the luxurious interior, her tense back remaining a good two inches clear of the backrest as Rafe belted himself into the driver's seat.

'Haven't you considered moving out of the city— if it would improve your daughter's health?'

Natalie tucked a strand of hair behind her ear and threw him an impatient look. 'Some of us have to live where the work is.' She gave a dry laugh. 'Always supposing I still have work. Does it feel good to hold my fate in your hands?'

Dark colour scored the slashing angles of his high cheekbones as he turned the key in the ignition. The powerful engine came to life. 'You've got me—we egomaniacs just love wielding power.' He turned his head and his dark lashes dipped as his glance moved with deliberation over the length of slender body.

'Only actually in this instance it felt even better to hold your body in my hands.' A firm, supple and surprisingly strong body that had proved amazingly responsive to his lightest touch.

For the briefest of moments their eyes collided. The anger in his made her recoil, but it wasn't the anger that made her look away, her heart thudding hard against her ribcage. The message in his smoky eyes had been explicitly sexual in nature…and worse was the fact her entire body responded to what she had seen.

God, she despaired, I am obviously a desperately shallow person and a terrible mother to boot to be feeling this way when my daughter is lying sick in hospital.

'I think we should discuss what happened back there…'

Natalie shook her head. 'As far as I'm concerned it didn't happen.' If she told herself this often enough, maybe she would even start believing it herself. She thought for a moment he was going to contest her statement, but after a brief nod in her direction he returned his attention to the road.

It had taken Rafe several frustrating minutes to find a parking space, so when he walked into the busy casualty department he had no expectation of finding Natalie still there.

She was.

He summed up the situation at one glance. Natalie was standing at the back of a queue several people deep that had built up behind an aggressively awkward drunk who was giving the young woman at the reception desk in the busy casualty department a hard time.

'I know my rights!' the dishevelled figure slurred loudly enough for Rafe and everyone around to hear.

Natalie, who was struggling to contain her impatience, heard the subdued murmurs of complaint as someone shouldered through the people who were waiting ahead of her, but didn't pay much attention. It wasn't until a few moments later when she glanced up that she recognised the tall, broad-shouldered figure. She cringed with embarrassment when she saw what he was doing!

Typical, she thought angrily. Rafael Ransome thinks he's too damned special to wait his turn. As she watched he began to speak in a low voice to the befuddled guy who had been holding everyone up. There was nothing threatening about his body language and the conversation, considering the older man's loud hostility, seemed to be perfectly amicable. Possibly too amicable for Rafe, she thought as the drunk suddenly threw his arms about the younger man's neck and announced to everyone that this was a good guy!

Natalie watched in disbelief as the man let Rafe lead him back to a seat in the waiting area and bring him a drink from the vending machine. It would seem that *nobody* was immune to Rafe's charm and persuasiveness.

By the time the overtaxed security team arrived the queue was moving smoothly and Rafe had, much to Natalie's discomfort, joined her.

'Did you have to interfere? What if he'd got nasty? You could have made things worse.' She heard her voice rise to an unattractive, shrill accusing note. 'You should have left it for the people who are paid to deal with that sort of thing,' she gritted. 'The ones who know what they're doing.'

One of that number chose that precise moment to approach them. 'Cheers, mate,' he said, slapping Rafe on the shoulder. 'Understand we owe you one. Old Charlie's a regular,' he explained, nodding in the direction of the old man who was now snoring happily away. 'But he can get nasty. Last time he took a swing at a nurse.'

'See, you shouldn't have interfered,' Natalie insisted, glaring up at the modest hero. 'Have-a-go heroes usually get themselves or someone else hurt.'

'Well, I didn't.'

Natalie, who was feeling physically ill visualising a scenario where he had got injured, didn't reply.

'I just need to find out which ward they've taken Rose to,' she explained hoarsely. 'You don't need to hang around,' she added pointedly.

Rafe smiled down into her face but didn't budge.

To Natalie's intense annoyance, when it was her turn and she enquired about Rose from the pretty girl behind the desk it was to Rafe the young woman replied.

'Your little girl has been taken up to Ward Six. If you and your wife—'

'She's not *his* little girl and *I* am not his wife!' Natalie snarled before she stamped away. 'That should make you happy,' she added under her breath. It just made her sick that some women were so *obvious*, and some men just lapped it up.

'You think I'm in with a chance there, then?'

He must have incredibly acute hearing. 'Listen, I'm

grateful you got me here,' she said, sounding anything but, 'but, like I said, there's absolutely no need for you to stay.' As she spoke they came to another intersection; Natalie took the right turn without looking at the direction sign overhead.

'I take it you've been here before,' Rafe observed drily.

'Why *are* you still here?' she puffed, genuinely puzzled by his continued presence.

'It would be like walking out before the end of a film if I left now…I'd be wondering all night what happened.'

They had reached the door to the ward. Natalie pressed the buzzer and waited. Still slightly breathless from the brisk jogging pace he'd set, she tilted up her head to the man beside her—it went without saying that he wasn't out of breath. Just looking at him standing there in his designer suit with not a hair out of place made her bristle with antagonism. How had she ever imagined they could be friends…?

'I'm so glad we are providing some entertainment for you!' she exclaimed bitterly. 'Better than interactive telly.'

A muscle clenched in his lean cheek. 'For God's sake, woman, it was a joke. I know you think I'm some sort of heartless creep…' It was pretty hard to miss the fact—she didn't fall over herself to deny this estimation. 'What is it with you? Why can't you accept people want to help? Why do you throw their concern back in their faces?'

The anger faded from his face as he looked into her pale, upturned features—too-bright eyes looked back at him. He judged that she was keeping going on nervous tension alone. Take that away and she would shatter like a piece of the fragile porcelain she reminded him of.

Natalie blinked. '*You* want to help…?'

'I'd like to stay until you find out how your daughter is.' Rafe's frustrated urge to protect her from deadbeat ex-husbands and her own stubborn independence found release in a fresh burst of anger. 'You'll drive yourself into the ground with this I-don't-need-anyone stuff,' he predicted grimly. 'Who's going to look after your daughter then?' Natalie winced at this brutal observation. 'Your loser ex…?'

Her eyes filled with tears. Nice one, you always have to go too far, don't you, Rafe…?

'If you want me to go, just say so and I will,' he grunted.

Gold-shot green locked with electric-blue and Natalie's mind went a blank, then from out of nowhere she heard herself say, 'No! No, I don't want you to go.'

Natalie saw some emotion, strong but unidentifiable, flicker in the back of his eyes and she went pink. Her no hadn't been a laid-back, if-you-like sort of no, more a raw, you'll-leave-over-my-dead-body sort of no. Another of those silences filled with dangerous currents began to stretch between them. It was broken when a crackly voice emerged from the speaker on the wall.

With a sigh of relief Natalie identified herself and the door clicked open.

She turned to Rafe and gave an offhand shrug. 'I didn't mean to be rude but I'm used to doing this alone.'

'And do you like it that way?'

'I haven't had much choice. Someone has to make the decisions and I'm the one on the spot,' she explained matter-of-factly. 'You can stay if you like, but you'll have to wait here.' She nodded towards some seats and left him. She had no expectation that he would still be there when she returned.

He was.

CHAPTER SIX

NATALIE stopped mid-yawn and stared. 'You're still here!' The clock on the wall behind him read half-past midnight.

Rafe languidly uncurled his long, lean length from the uncomfortable-looking chair that was far too small to accommodate him and stretched. The action caused his shirt to pull tight, revealing the definition of his well-developed chest muscles shadowed by dark body hair and his washboard-flat belly.

She knew she was staring but tiredness made Natalie less able to adequately disguise the effect this disturbing spectacle was having on her—if not from him, certainly from herself. Finally in a position where she couldn't hide from the truth, she could hardly believe that she'd been walking around for weeks acting as if the facts her blood pressure went rocketing and she couldn't think straight when he was around were simply a coincidence.

Talk about fooling yourself!

'Why...?' she asked, closing her eyes briefly while she regained a degree of composure. Now she had accepted how attracted to him she was, she could guard against it. If she'd been more honest sooner that kiss might not have happened.

When she opened her eyes again Rafe had fastened

a button on his loose-fitting jacket. She watched, her expression carefully neutral, as he smoothed back his thick hair, which to her eyes seemed perfectly ordered. She found herself considering how it might feel to mess it up again...to run her fingers deep into that lush— *Stop that, Natalie!*

'I had nowhere else to be.'

Natalie could not allow a lie this blatant to pass unchallenged. 'I find that difficult to believe.'

'So now you're wondering what my ulterior motives are. Actually, Natalie...I fell asleep,' he ruefully revealed in the manner of someone making a clean breast of it. 'I had a long session with Magnus Macfaden today...the usual battle of attrition.'

He seemed genuine enough and she supposed the explanation was just about plausible.

'No wonder you're tired, then.' Natalie had never met the head of the famous electronics firm but she had heard about him. 'I'm just surprised you managed to sleep through the noise.' Everyone entering and leaving the ward would have passed by him and it had been a busy evening.

'Oh, I can sleep anywhere, any time.'

'And with whoever you want, but then you already know that. Everyone who reads a tabloid knows that.' *Please tell me I didn't just say that out loud.*

'Are your objections moral or personal?' he enquired with interest.

'Neither!' she squeaked. 'Your personal life is your own business.'

'It's not nearly as...*active*, as the papers would have you believe.'

'Whatever,' she said, evincing disinterest.

'How is your daughter?'

'Rose is much better, thanks. She's finally asleep and off the nebuliser. I just thought I'd stretch my legs; if you fall asleep in one of those chairs you can't move in the morning.'

Rafe let his head fall back and flexed his shoulders. 'That I can believe,' he grimaced.

'What you need is a massage,' she observed without thinking—at least, she was thinking, but of things she had no business to be thinking about.

A half-smile played around his lips. 'Are you offering...?'

Natalie went as red as it was possible to go without spontaneously combusting. *'Most certainly not!'*

His suggestive sigh of pity combined with the lingering image in her head of her hands sliding over oiled golden flesh made her stomach muscles flutter madly. Their eyes touched and the liquid heat pooled shockingly between her thighs.

'Have you done many all-night stints in the chairs?'

Natalie couldn't look at him.

'One or two. You know, about that kiss earlier...I don't want you to get the wrong idea...' she said awkwardly.

'What idea would that be?'

'I don't...well, I don't have casual relationships. It wouldn't be fair to Rose for her to get fond of a man only to have him disappear from her life. She's already had that happen once. I'm not saying this because I think you want to...'

'Yes, you do, and you're right.'

'You w...want me...?' Her cheeks burned. 'I mean you...'

'Right first time.' Natalie's jaw dropped. 'Listen, I hear what you're saying about your daughter, but what are you going to do, remain celibate?'

'It's worked for me so far.' She saw the flicker of shock in his eyes and hurried on. 'People put far too great an emphasis on sex.'

'It's a very basic need. Sex is like any other appetite...'

'For men maybe.'

'For women, too, trust me...' he drawled.

'Do I look that stupid?'

'A lot of women don't want a deep and meaningful relationship. A hotel room and a long lunch hour,' he elaborated crudely. 'Functional sex is more to their taste. Maybe you should try and develop a taste for that if you don't want any involvement.'

Was he trying to insult her? She found the idea of the sort of cold-blooded clinical encounter he described appalling. 'Is that what you're offering me?'

'I thought it was the other way around.' He didn't have the faintest idea why the idea of sex without the complications should outrage him so much.

'How do you figure that one?'

'Well, you do want to keep your home a male-free zone...'

'How does that put me in a hotel room with you?' Natalie tried to sound amused and failed.

'You don't *seriously* expect the attraction between us to simply go away, do you? Pretending it's not there doesn't work—we've tried that! It's inevitable that we'll end up in bed at some point.'

'How dare you talk to me like that?' she gasped.

'I dare because I'm the man who wants to go home with you,' he reminded her softly.

Natalie's eyes widened; this was news to her and, maybe from his expression, Rafe, too.

She bit her lip. 'We can't talk about this here.'

'Then I hope for the sake of my sanity that you're not going to be here long?'

'I think they're going to let us out in the morning this time,' she revealed, half of her wishing it were longer if it meant she didn't have to confront the issues he had raised. 'Which is a big relief. If Rose hadn't got to go to the wedding I don't like to think what sort of fuss she'd have kicked up.'

'Wedding?'

'Yes, the one that Luke was going to come to with me. Rose is going to be bridesmaid at her dad's wedding—on Valentine's Day,' she explained with a wry smile. Mike had not been such a romantic when he'd been married to her.

'You're going to your ex's wedding?'

Natalie grimaced at the incredulity in his voice; she'd seen that response before. 'Before you ask, I'm not actually a masochist, or that forgiving, it's just Rose wants me to come and see her in her bridesmaid dress, and Mike might not be my husband any more but he'll always be her father,' she explained gravely.

The last thing she wanted to become was one of those mothers who bad-mouthed their ex-partners to the kid caught in the middle.

Despite her apparent composure when she mentioned her ex, Rafael couldn't help but wonder if she had come to terms with the situation quite as well as she liked people to think. Inexplicably any number of women nurtured passions for men who treated them appallingly. He frowned as he scanned her face for signs of the secret passion he had half convinced himself she was nursing. It was quite possible Natalie still carried a torch for the pathetic jerk.

'And Luke was going with you?'

'He was,' she confided with a sleepy yawn.

'Then you two are…?'

'Just good friends. This is so strange…' she mused.

'What's so strange, Natalie?'

'Talking to a real person…as in one who is over ten,' she elaborated, 'here.' Her gesture took in the walls, which were covered in brightly coloured childish paintings. 'The nurses are lovely but they're always so busy.' She was totally unaware of the wistful note in her voice. 'And sometimes you just want to talk to someone who doesn't consider tomato ketchup on chips the height of sophistication.'

'I will try and do my best to supply some adult conversation.'

'So long as you remember that's *all* I want.'

'How could I forget? Why was Luke going with you?'

'If you must know, I didn't want to turn up alone looking like a sad loser.'

'Why would you look like a sad loser?'

Natalie threw him a pitying look—this man knew nothing about being a single female approaching thirty or, for that matter, looking like a sad loser. She was dimly aware that a combination of exhaustion and relief was making her not just light-headed, but dangerously garrulous, too.

'Think about it,' she suggested. 'I'm a woman

whose husband left her for a gorgeous blonde and *everyone* knows a female is unfulfilled unless she is half of a partnership.'

'I hesitate as a mere man to disagree, but isn't that a slightly old-fashioned attitude?'

'It's the way it is. I suppose I should have the guts to be single and proud; asking Luke to pretend to be my lover is even more pathetic than being dumped. *Poor Luke.*'

'And I sent Luke away.'

Natalie nodded and took the cup of coffee he handed her from the vending machine. Nursing it, she sat down on one of the nasty, shiny fake leather seats. 'You could say you owe me a pretend lover.' She took a sip and winced as the scalding liquid burnt her tongue.

'Then I suppose I'm obligated to provide you with a substitute.'

'Know a good escort agency, do you? Mind you, even if you did I doubt if I could afford the rates of the sort of place you would use.' She chuckled weakly at her joke.

Rafe blinked. 'I can't say anyone has ever accused me of being au fait with high-class escort services before.'

'Gracious, I didn't mean…I don't think that you…' She gave a gusty sigh of relief. 'You were winding me up? I thought you were about to sack me for sure, or have you already done that? I forget,' she admitted with a yawn.

'No, and I have a suggestion to put to you. I have this idea about starting up a facility to offer advice to small businesses...' He stopped. 'Well, like you said, this isn't the place and you are dead on your feet.'

'I'm fine.'

'Sure you are,' Rafe murmured as he took the seat beside hers.

'I'll just rest my eyes for a minute.'

'Good idea.'

The periods her lashes lay against her waxily pale cheek before she forced her eyes open got gradually longer. For some time after her head had fallen against his shoulder Rafe stayed still, afraid to wake her. When it became obvious nothing was going to do that he shifted so that he could look at her sleeping face. It was the sort of face a man could look at for a long time without growing tired—maybe never!

Natalie woke in a strange bed. It took a few panicky moments before she recognised her spartan surroundings. She wished she weren't so familiar with the small room reserved for parents who wanted to stay overnight with their children.

Yawning, she threw back the covers. She was still fully dressed. Her frown deepened as she saw her shoes neatly placed at the bedside. She couldn't recall putting them there or, for that matter, taking them off. In fact she had no recollection of getting into bed at all—the last thing she remembered was in fact... *Good God!*

She hadn't forgotten because she hadn't done any of those things, which meant that someone had done them for her. That meant...

The nurse at the desk looked up as Natalie approached.

'Oh, you're awake.' She smiled. 'I was just going to take your boyfriend a cup of tea. Would you like one?'

'My boyfriend?' Natalie echoed warily.

'He's in with Rose. He's got quite a way with her, hasn't he?' she observed. 'Until he turned up I thought we were going to have to wake you. She was really cranky when she woke.'

'Why didn't you wake me?'

'Your boyfriend said to let you sleep.'

'He did?'

'You must have been tired,' the nurse reflected, oblivious to the grim note in Natalie's voice. 'You didn't stir when he put you to bed,' she recalled.

Natalie gulped. 'Rafe put me to bed?' Rafe, it seemed, had been busy. Not content with deciding what was best for her, he was usurping her authority with her child as well! The man just couldn't help taking charge. Well, he was about to learn that she didn't need anyone to make her decisions. She chose to forget all the occasions when the burden of making all the decisions concerning Rose's welfare had lain heavily upon her shoulders.

'Carried you like a baby,' the youthful health professional confirmed with a very unprofessional gleam of envy in her eyes.

Natalie decided it was high time she put the record straight. 'He's not my boyfriend, he's my boss.'

'*Boss?*'

'Yes, boss,' Natalie declared defiantly as she stomped off.

Rose's bed was in a bay of four but at that moment she was the only occupant. Natalie's impetuous stride halted as she entered. The main lights in the ward were dimmed but the night light above Rose's bed illuminated the area beneath. And the people.

Rose was seated cross-legged on top of the duvet and Rafe sat in an easy chair, leaning on the bed with his dark head resting on his crossed arms. She could not see his face but she could hear the deep rumble of his voice in the quiet of the room. Rose too was listening to what he was saying, her little face rapt.

An emotional lump formed in Natalie's throat as she stared at the tableau. She'd never been more aware of the things that, even with the best will in the world, she couldn't provide in Rose's life.

Suddenly Rose's childish laughter rang out and, brushing the back of her hand across the dampness on her cheeks, Natalie moved forward to reveal herself.

'Mummy, Rafe's been telling me a story about a boy who had a pet dragon but nobody else can see him.'

'Mr Ransome has been very kind, but he's got to go now and you must get some sleep, so snuggle down.'

Reluctantly the child complied. 'Kiss,' she commanded imperiously to Rafe, who complied.

'Well what have I done now?'

Natalie pulled a concealing curtain around them. 'Where to start?' she hissed. 'How about with taking unilateral decisions?'

'You needed the sleep, Natalie.'

'I need to stay in control. Listen, you've been very kind, but—'

'Butt out and clear off. Right, am I allowed to say goodbye to Rose?'

'Of course.' His swift surrender had deflated her.

'I'll see you on the fourteenth?' The curtain rattled as he pulled it aside.

Natalie frowned. *'Fourteenth?'*

The wedding.

'We agreed it was the least I could do as I had robbed you of Luke.'

'I didn't agree to anything…' Natalie's brow furrowed as she tried to think back, but her recollections were frustratingly hazy. *'Did I…?'*

Rafe smiled. 'Morning dress, right? Oh—' he turned back '—don't even *think* about coming into work tomorrow or Friday. No buts, *I'm* the one in control there.' Or so goes the rumour, he added drily to himself as he walked away.

CHAPTER SEVEN

'OH, YES, very nice,' Mike said vaguely as his daughter waved her new patent leather shoes in his face for his approval. Deliberately not looking at his ex-wife's angry white face, he bent down awkwardly to his daughter's level. 'How would you like to come with me and Gabby to America, Rosie?' he asked the excited child in a coaxing voice.

'Will I see dolphins?'

Mike, who didn't have the faintest idea that his little daughter was fascinated by dolphins, looked momentarily nonplussed by this response. 'Sure we'll see dolphins.'

'Will Mummy be coming?'

'No.'

The child's face fell. 'Well, thank you very much,' she said politely, 'but I think I'll stay at home.'

Mike's smile grew fixed. 'In America we'll have a swimming pool in the garden.'

Rose's eyes grew round. *'In the garden!'* she gasped in awe. 'We don't have a garden here, but we have a window-box.'

Natalie gritted her teeth as Mike shot her a triumphant look and hissed, 'Out of the mouth of babes.'

'Rose, go and put on those pretty socks we bought

to go with your dress and then you can go with Daddy
to have the man put flowers in your hair.'

'Why can't you do that?'

'Because Aunt Gabby's friend is much better at fixing flowers in your hair than I am.' He'd have to be,
she reflected grimly, to justify the expense of Gabby
flying him along with a make-up artist across the
Atlantic to fix the bridal parties' hair and faces.

Ironically, when Mike had turned up in person to
take his daughter to the hotel suite where Gabby and
the other bridesmaids had spent the night she had actually felt touched by the gesture. *How naïve does that
make me?*

She waited until the little girl had danced away before turning furiously to her ex-husband. Without pre-
amble she grabbed him by the lapel of his morning
suit—that got his attention.

'Good God, Natalie, there's no need to get physical!'

'That just about sums up our marriage.'

Mike coloured. 'What's got into you, Natalie?'

'You can ask that? You come here on the *morning*
of your wedding,' she began in a quivering voice of
disbelief, 'to tell me you're going to apply for full
custody of Rose. What do you think has *got into me*?
You must be insane if you think I'm going to allow
you and Gabby to take Rose out of the country!' she
hissed. 'Besides, no court in the country would give
you custody just because Gabby doesn't want to risk
stretch marks,' she mocked, releasing him and press-
ing a hand to her trembling lips.

Was there…?

Mike looked shaken but stubbornly determined as

he smoothed the fabric she had released. 'Our lawyer doesn't agree with you, Nat. He says we have a very good chance. What can you offer Rose compared with us?' He looked around the neat little room with distaste.

'*Love...?*' Natalie suggested ironically.

'Sure, sure, we all love Rosie, she's a cute kid.'

'And she's house-trained.'

'It's the quality of life we can give her,' Mike insisted piously. 'She needs a proper family life.'

'Pity, you didn't seem to think so when you walked out on us.'

Mike flushed angrily. 'You're a single parent, Nat, living in a poky little flat. You're always saying how you struggle to make ends meet.'

'That could have something to do with the twelve months you didn't pay me child support.'

'Yes, well, things have changed. Since the exhibition I'm doing very well and, besides, I'd have thought you'd have been grateful to have someone else take the burden off your shoulders.'

'Rose is not a burden and if you ever say that in front of her I'll make sure you regret it.'

'For God's sake, Nat, what do you take me for?'

'A selfish, insensitive prat...shall I go on?'

'There's no need to get abusive. With us Rosie would have all the advantages and opportunities money can buy.'

'Money can't buy everything.' It could buy lawyers, though; lawyers who could twist the facts to suit their clients.

'*And* we're a married couple.'

Natalie felt a fresh flurry of uncertainty. He might

be bluffing, but then again perhaps such things did still weigh heavily? 'Nobody cares about that sort of thing…?'

Mike heard the uncertainty in her voice and smiled. 'I know this is hard for you—' he placed a hand on her shoulder '—but you have to think about what is best for Rosie, Nat.'

Eyes flashing fire, Natalie angrily shrugged off his hand.

'Am I early?'

The couple, who had been too engrossed in their argument to hear the approach of the new arrival, turned towards the figure in the open doorway.

'And who the hell are you?' Mike demanded.

Rafe unhurriedly transferred his attention from Natalie's tense face. He did not feel very well disposed towards the man who had put that shadowed look of distress in her eyes and he saw no reason to disguise the fact.

'I'm Rafael Ransome,' Rafe announced, giving himself his full title. 'And you,' he observed, managing without changing expression to convey that he wasn't overly impressed with what he was seeing, 'must be the bridegroom.'

Natalie, who had never seen Rafe conduct himself with this particular brand of chilling hauteur before, wasn't surprised that Mike looked uncomfortable and angry to be on the receiving end of such studied insolence.

Identification established, Rafe seemed to lose interest in the other man almost immediately. He turned to Natalie, the warmth in his eyes a stark contrast to the dismissive contempt of moments before. He opened his hand and revealed a bunch of keys before placing them beside a colourful pot plant on a leather-banded ship's chest that had been a junk-shop find.

'I thought I'd lost them!'

Before Rafe had arrived she'd thought that Mike looked pretty impressive in his expensive morning suit and handmade shoes. Now that he stood beside Rafe she could see that she had been mistaken. Even if they had been dressed by the same tailor Mike would always have looked like a pale imitation standing next to this extraordinary man.

It wasn't just the fact that Rafe had a body that was better than incredible—anyone with enough discipline could achieve a six pack, she thought, eyeing his flat belly and feeling her own stomach muscles tighten. No, what made Rafe was that extra special ingredient that separated the leader of the pack from the common herd. He didn't have to try, he just had...well... *presence*.

Worriedly, she examined her reaction when she'd seen him standing there. Casting herself on her boss's broad chest every time he appeared was not the best way to hide the fact you were having an affair with him—or were about to. She wondered what Rafe would say if he knew that she had decided to...to...sleep with him. Hell, I can hardly think it, let alone say it. Do I have a problem!

Of course you have a problem—you're in love with the man. You could only ignore something that was staring you in the face for just so long.

'You should be more careful with your keys,' he chided.

Natalie gulped and nodded. Oh, God, you don't

know the half of it! Sure, he wanted an affair, he'd
made that plain, but a clingy woman who wanted to
offer him her heart—that really wasn't Rafe's style.

Mike, who had been watching this interchange with
a sour expression, cleared his throat.

'Listen, if you don't mind, Nat and I were having
a *private* conversation.' His hostility was still there,
but it was not so overt now he had had the opportunity
to fully take in the size and quality of the new arrival.

Rafe didn't even look at the other man; his steady
gaze remained fixed on Natalie's face. 'Do you want
me to go, Natalie?' In contrast to the intense expression in his eyes, his tone was light.

Natalie took a deep breath and turned to face her
ex-husband. 'I don't have any secrets from Rafe,' she
claimed.

Mike frowned. 'Since when?'

Probably something Rafe himself was wondering,
too. Natalie didn't dare check out his reaction, sure
that if she did her resolve would fail. She took a deep
breath and plunged recklessly onwards.

'Since we decided to get married,' she announced
casually.

A stunned silence followed her words.

'Well, now, isn't that convenient?' Mike drawled,
quite obviously, despite his amused tone, thrown by
her declaration.

Natalie was excruciatingly aware of the still, silent
presence of the man beside her; she could only imagine how shocked Rafe had been to hear he was going
to get married. She turned warily to look at him; with
one word he could blow her out of the water. She had
no way of knowing from his expression if the silent

message she was desperately trying to telegraph him
had been received.

'Not had time to buy a ring yet, then?'

Natalie flushed and tucked her bare left hand under
her right.

Observing her action, Mike regained his confidence.
'You don't really expect me to believe it?' he asked,
shaking his head. 'I mean, *you*, married…?'

His incredulity stung. 'Why not *me* married?' she
demanded dangerously.

'Well, you're just not the type, Nat.'

Something inside Natalie snapped. 'Not the type to
what? Need a hug occasionally, need someone to
laugh at my jokes…need sex…?'

'Natalie!' Mike exclaimed in a shocked tone.

She gritted her teeth and planted her hands on her
hips. 'Sex, sex, sex!' she parroted defiantly. 'Just because you don't fancy me, doesn't mean other men
mightn't!'

'Well, you haven't had a boyfriend for the past five
years—I'd say that speaks for itself.'

Natalie's shoulders slumped in defeat as the fight
drained out of her. Of course he didn't believe it, who
would? Sheer desperation had driven her to attempt a
rash bluff and all she had done was make a total fool
of herself. Rafe was never going to back her up—and
why should he? If she was going to claim a fiancé it
would have been wiser to chose a more plausible candidate.

'Well, she's got one now.'

The air rushed out of Natalie's lungs in one startled
gasp. Her eyes flew to Rafe's dark, autocratic face.
Even though she knew the possessive warmth in his

eyes was for Mike's benefit, her responsive stomach muscles quivered.

'I don't believe it. You're just saying this to stop me getting Rosie,' Mike accused, sounding like a truculent child. 'It won't work.'

'Get Rosie?' Rafe frowned.

Natalie cleared her throat. 'Gabby and Mike want to take Rose to the States...' her face crumpled '...and I'll never see her again.' The disastrous wobble in her voice made her words barely intelligible but Rafe appeared to get the gist.

'Is that some sort of joke?'

Natalie blinked back the tears. '*He* says that they—'

'*He's* talking through his...' Rafe cast the other man a look that caused the shorter man to blanch and withdraw behind a chair '...armpit,' he finished acidly. 'And I suspect he knows it.' He lifted a strand of hair from Natalie's cheek and brushed away a tear with his thumb. 'He's trying it on, sweetheart,' he promised her.

'Now, you listen here...whoever you are...'

An ebony brow quirked. 'Natalie has told you who I am. I am the man she is going to marry.'

If it weren't for the possessive arm that snaked around her waist Natalie would have fallen in a heap. Instead she turned her face into the broad chest at her disposal. There was something very soothing about the steady thud of his heartbeat, as there was about the hand that came to rest on the back of her head.

'*You can't!*'

'I think you'll find I can.' While continuing to stroke the back of Natalie's head, Rafe lifted his eyes to meet the indignant face of the other man. His lips curled contemptuously. 'I appreciate that it must be hard for you to see the woman you lost with another man. I suppose,' he added thoughtfully, 'that it's at times like this we realise what we have lost—or in your case thrown away. There really is no mystery here. We've kept our relationship under wraps because it's a bit difficult as I'm Natalie's boss. We're off to visit my parents this weekend so if you don't mind we'd like to keep it quiet until then.'

Natalie admired his ability to improvise but she wished he'd keep things simple—Mike wasn't stupid.

'Then that makes you...?'

'Quite disgustingly rich,' Natalie supplied helpfully. She knew how Mike's mind worked. Despite his avowed contempt for money, he was always in awe of people who had it. A really horrid part of her was beginning to enjoy the sick expression on Mike's face.

'You've been sleeping with your boss?'

His tone of shocked disgust made Natalie flush.

'Well, actually, we haven't been getting a whole lot of sleep.' Rafe cupped her chin in his hand and tilted her flushed face up to him. 'Have we, angel?'

She was grateful that he'd decided to play along, but she wished he weren't doing so with quite this much relish. Already pretty messed up by the contact of his hard thigh against her own, her nervous system went haywire when he looked at her like that.

'I love it when you blush and, darling, happy Valentine's Day,' he told her in the manner of a man who found her totally fascinating and completely ir-resistible.

Natalie knew it was a lie but she was still mesmer-ised by the caressing light in his eyes.

Rose entered the room at that moment and her face lit up when she identified the tall figure standing there. 'Rafe…Rafe!' she cried, bounding across the room towards him.

'Rose…Rose!' Rafe echoed, releasing Natalie.

Well, if nothing else had convinced Mike their daughter's rapturous greeting would have swung it. Natalie was concerned by the child's enthusiasm; now with Mike about to leave it was even more important that Rose didn't grow attached to a man who wouldn't be around for long. Natalie had no illusions—she didn't have anything that could keep a man like Rafe interested for long. It was something she'd have to deal with when the time came.

'Have you brought me a present?' the little girl demanded with innocent avarice.

'*Rose!*' Natalie cried in a scandalised tone.

Rafe didn't seem bothered. 'Next time,' he promised with a grin. 'Wow, cool shoes!'

'I look pretty.' Rose preened complacently.

'Beautiful,' Rafe agreed.

'You look beautiful, too,' she observed. 'Doesn't he, Mummy?'

A choking sound emerged from Natalie's throat. As hard as she tried to avoid looking at Rafe, like a compass needle finding north her eyes seemed irresistibly drawn to his.

'Men are handsome, Rose, ladies are beautiful.'

Rose shook her head. 'No,' she persisted stubbornly, 'Rafe is beautiful.'

Natalie could only agree with her daughter's assessment of the man whose startling blue gaze was melded with her own. Her voice thickened emotionally. 'Extremely beautiful,' she agreed huskily.

'Well, I think it's time that we were going,' Mike interrupted stiffly.

It was difficult to persuade Rose it was time to go, but eventually the time Natalie had been dreading arrived—she and Rafe were alone. There seemed no point delaying the inevitable; she took a deep breath and got straight to the point.

She shot a wary glance at the tall figure who was examining the books in her bookcase. He didn't *look*, but it was reasonable to suppose, despite his performance, that he wasn't too happy with her.

'I think Mike's in a bit of a huff.'

Rafe slid a copy of a paperback thriller back; he ran a finger slowly down its spine before turning. There was a hard light in his eyes. 'I don't think I'll be losing any sleep over your Mike.'

'He isn't my Mike,' she replied irritably.

Rafe's eyes narrowed as he looked searchingly at her. '*No...?*'

'He's getting married today.'

'Most people would consider him pretty good-looking,' Rafe remarked casually.

'Fortunately Rose took after him in the looks department...'

'So you *do* think he's good-looking...?'

Natalie gave a bewildered frown. 'Look, just how are Mike's looks important to anything?' she demanded.

'If he decided not to get married, if he asked you to take him back—would you?'

Natalie coloured angrily. 'What do you take me for?'

His smile was cynical. 'A woman in love?'

Natalie's eyes slid from his. 'I am not in love with Mike,' she replied guardedly. Now that she knew what being in love actually felt like she knew she had never loved Mike in that way.

Rafael gave one of his inimical shrugs. Natalie studied his face. 'You didn't like him, did you?'

His jaw tightened. 'I didn't like the number he was trying to do on you,' he revealed grimly. 'Give him custody? No lawyer, no matter how well paid, could persuade a court in the country to take Rose away from you.'

'You don't know all the facts.'

'I know you're a good mother.'

The conviction in his tone brought an emotional lump to her throat. 'But I'm stony-broke. It's ironic, really Mike has never been able to pay child support. Now he's marrying a rich woman, his uncle has died and left him a property worth over two million and the critics have decided he's the next Warhol! I, on the other hand, expend more than I earn.'

'What I said still stands—you're a good mother and that's all any judge would be interested in.'

'You're sure?' Natalie said wistfully; she really wanted to believe him.

'Totally,' Rafe confirmed.

Normally Natalie found his immutable confidence irritating, but this was one occasion when she welcomed it. 'Did you go along with...?'

'Go along with...?'

Cheeks burning, she lifted her head. 'Me saying we were engaged. Was it because you didn't like Mike?'

'I expect that had something to do with it,' he confirmed.

'I suppose you expect me to apologise for...'

'Well, going on your track record I'm not expecting it any time soon.'

Natalie's head came up, she set her hands on her hips and glared up at him. '*I* don't have a problem apologising when I know I'm in the wrong—even to you!'

One dark brow lifted. 'Meaning I do?'

'You made me feel about so high,' she said, holding her forefinger and thumb a whisper away from one another. 'And,' she added bitterly, 'if you wanted to put me in my place you didn't have to do it in front of everyone! You didn't have to...' She broke off, dismayed to feel her eyes fill with tears. 'You probably don't even know when I'm talking about.' Why would he?

'I know.'

'I was stupid enough at the time to think that we were friends,' she added in a small voice.

'Yes, you were stupid,' he agreed. 'We could never be friends,' he added harshly.

To hear him spell it so brutally hurt more than she would have thought possible. 'What's wrong, Rafe—is my hair the wrong colour?' Rafe's eyes followed the movement of her fingers as they slid through the silky strands of her long brown hair. 'Or am I from the wrong social background?' she suggested scornfully.

'Your hair...' He cleared his throat and removed his

gaze from her hair. 'Your hair is beautiful.' The forceful nature of this raw declaration made Natalie look at him sharply. 'And who our parents were has nothing to do with it.'

'Pooh…says you!' She sniffed.

His nostrils flared as she turned away from him. 'Yes, I do,' he rebutted in a driven undertone. 'And I say we couldn't be friends because there's too much chemistry between us and there has been from day one.'

Natalie spun back, her face flushed, her mouth slightly ajar. She could feel her fragile grip on reality slipping as she focused on his lean dark face. 'You're my b…boss.'

'I don't need reminding of that,' he promised her.

'*Day one!*' she breathed in a stunned undertone. 'You liked me…?'

'I don't think *like* is the correct term. Changing the subject slightly, which believe me I don't do out of choice…I was wondering…?'

'Yes…?'

'Are you going to the wedding like that?'

'*Like…?*' Frowning, she followed the direction of Rafe's gaze and gave a cry. 'Oh, God, what time is it?' she cried, drawing the gaping lapels of her thin, loose-fitting robe in her fist.

'Relax, it's early yet.'

'You wake up looking drop-dead gorgeous; for me it requires a little more time.'

'I think you look gorgeous like that.'

'If you're going to lie, try for something a little more believable.'

Rafe shook his head. 'My God, I've never met a woman as hard to be nice to as you.'

CHAPTER EIGHT

NATALIE smudged a little soft brown shadow on her eyelids and smeared some clear gloss on her lips. A quick flick of blusher completed her hastily applied make-up. It was ironic that the one time she had planned to really go to town with the warpaint she was in even more of a hurry than usual.

'Well, they do say the natural look is in this season,' she reflected, eyeing the result in the mirror as she fought her way into the simple soft apricot shift dress she'd decided to wear. It bore the label of a chain-store brand; Natalie had decided it would be foolish to try and compete on her budget.

She slipped her feet into a pair of high-heeled sandals that emphasised the shapely length of her slender calves and smoothed out a wrinkle in her fine lace-topped hold-ups she wore underneath. She glanced at her watch; it was the only jewellery, besides a pair of antique drop pearl earrings, she wore.

All I have to do now is something with this hair, she thought, frowning as she slid her fingers through the silky mass that fell river-straight almost to her waist. That was always supposing she *ever* got this darned zip up! She grunted softly and grimaced as she twisted around in an effort to see what the recalcitrant fastener had snagged on.

While in a position that would only be considered comfortable by a contortionist she lost her balance and stumbled against a lamp. She lunged for it, but her reflexes were not sharp enough to stop it falling off her bedside table, taking with it her alarm clock, which hit the metal bed frame and catapulted like a thing possessed across the room where it hit dead centre the cheval mirror, which shattered before her disbelieving eyes.

The noise as the glass showered onto the bare wood of the stripped floorboards was so loud that she wasn't aware of the door opening until Rafe was actually inside the room.

'I heard a noise.'

'I think they heard a noise half a mile away.' The wry smile that invited him to share the humorous side to this situation faded as her eyes encountered no reciprocal amusement in his—on the contrary Rafe's expression was unexpectedly severe, his entire manner off-puttingly grim as he stood there not reacting to the disorder around him.

Perhaps it was the thought of acting as her fiancé at the wedding that was making him look so bleak—now he'd had a little while to reflect he could be questioning if his acting ability was up to carrying it off.

Natalie was wondering if she ought to do the decent thing and give him the opportunity to back out gracefully when she caught sight of the neat stack of freshly laundered undies that were waiting to be put away on the bottom of her bed. Instinctively she reached across and drew the chenille throw that was folded across the bed over them. She realised immediately that all her prim action had done was draw his attention to them.

He probably thought it hilarious that she imagined the sight of her white cotton knickers would inspire uncontrollable lust.

In your dreams! Maybe his too—*he* was the one who had mentioned chemistry. Lust at first sight, no less.

'Well, I suppose this means seven years' bad luck.'

'Are you superstitious?'

'Not especially—I have my fingers crossed.' So the joke had been pathetic, but a polite smile wouldn't have killed him! A frown deepened the line between her arched brows as she studied his enigmatic dark face. She was beginning to get the distinct impression that he hadn't heard a word she had said.

'My zip jammed,' she began to explain. When she was nervous she babbled and his silence and the growing tension she sensed in him made her *very* nervous. Also this whole bedroom thing was something she wasn't comfortable with. 'I guess it's a classic case of more haste, less speed. I was trying to unstick it and I knocked the lamp off.' She gestured to the lamp lying on the floor. 'It was sort of a chain reaction after that—you should have seen it.'

'Is it still stuck?'

His abrupt question made her start. 'What? Oh, yes, you have to be a contort—'

'Turn around,' he instructed brusquely.

'Oh, I'll manage.' She forced her lips into a smile.

'Turn around,' he repeated in a tone that suggested he was getting bored with the subject—and, for that matter, her.

Natalie bit her lip. If she persisted in resisting his perfectly unexceptional offer it might give rise to awkward questions, such as for instance why did the idea of him touching her skin have her in such a blind panic? After all, she planned on letting him do so as much as he liked.

'Thank you.' Taking a deep breath, she turned around to give him access to the zip.

Nothing happened; nothing happened for so long that she almost turned around.

Just as she was deciding enough was enough she felt cool air touch her skin as he lifted the mesh of her loose hair off her neck. A shiver slithered softly down her spine as she felt his fingertips lightly graze her skin. At that point Natalie realised this was going to be every bit as bad as she had imagined and more...*pure torture*!

Rafe eventually managed to gather all her hair in his fist. 'There's a lot of it,' he murmured, laying the heavy swathe over her shoulder. Displaying a meticulous attention to detail, he brushed the few stray strands that clung to her neck to join them.

'Did you say something?'

Natalie closed her eyes tight shut. 'Not a thing,' she assured him brightly.

There was another agonising pause before he reapplied himself to the task in hand. The zip was jammed just below her bra strap, and Rafe's fingers slid under the lacy hem to give himself better access to the problem.

'Stop fidgeting!' he snapped tersely as she shifted restively in a frantic effort to lessen the contact that was sending ripple after ripple of hot sensation through her body. Her skin was so hot and sticky he had to have noticed.

'Then hurry up,' she retorted thickly.

'I'm going as fast as I can.' He gave a grunt of pent-up frustration. 'Damned...stupid...!'

His touch had a frightening addictive quality. 'For pity's sake, it's not brain surgery!' she gasped, desperation in her voice. 'I have a wedding to get to.' And if she did or said what she actually wanted to she was pretty sure they wouldn't!

She heard him mutter darkly under his breath and felt his warm breath stir the fine hairs on her nape as he bent closer to his task. A faint whimper escaped from between her clenched teeth.

'You all right...?'

If she hadn't been so far from all right Natalie might have noticed that Rafe's normally assured voice held an unfamiliar strained note. 'Absolutely fine!' she heard herself lie breezily.

'I'm getting there.'

So am I—she was at that very moment hovering on the brink of a precipice; one little shove would have her turning around and begging him to take her. Exhaling gustily, she dabbed her tongue to the film of moisture above her upper lip. The debilitating weakness that was already severely affecting her limbs had obviously begun to cloud her mental judgement as well. Her suspicion was validated by the next uncensored idiot observation that spilled from her big mouth!

'Dear God, if you take this long to undress a woman the poor thing is probably asleep by the time you actually get started.'

'So far that hasn't happened; slow but thorough, that's me.'

The fiery blush travelled all over her skin, but underneath the embarrassment she was getting even more excited thinking about Rafe being thorough and slow with her.

Not now, there's a wedding to go to and all sorts of ground rules to figure out.

'Got it, I think...?' Holding the fabric taut, Rafe forced the zip upwards, it gave, and when he pulled it down again this time it slid smoothly—very smoothly all the way down.

All the way!

With a silken rush the peach-coloured fabric of the dress parted from her neck to the top of her tight buttocks and revealed the entire length of her satiny slim back, plus the interesting little dimple just above the soft curve of her peachy skinned bottom.

'Oh, *my God*!' The pressure inside Rafe's head was now so intense he knew something had to give. 'Oh, my God,' he repeated in a fainter but no less impressed tone. 'You're absolutely perfect.' He ran a fascinated finger down her straight spine, feeling the evenly spaced bony projections, letting his exploration widen to take in the elegant definition of her elegant shoulder blades.

With a mumbled imprecation that concerned his sanity, Rafe spun her around.

She stood there, visible tremors running through her slim body, eyes wide, lips parted. In the front the dress was hanging onto her slender shoulders—*barely*. One judicious tug and it would... Her wide eyes looked up at him; she was scared stiff he'd take the next step and scared stiff he wouldn't. Having suffered a similar ambivalence for weeks and months, he could readily identify with what she was feeling.

The dress fell with a sexy, silken slither to pool around her feet and Natalie stood there clad only in her minuscule lacy bra and matching pants; the stockings and high heels that completed the outfit she wore couldn't really be classed as clothing—more provocation!

Less is quite definitely more, Rafe decided, unable to stop staring like a kid at a sweet-shop window. No window...no door—in fact there was nothing keeping him away from her except his disintegrating willpower—an overrated virtue if ever there was one.

Natalie wanted to tell him that he really shouldn't have done that, but her vocal cords were paralysed—as she was—with lust. She waited for her protective reflexes to kick in, but they didn't. But then no man had ever looked at her the way Rafe was, and she felt her legs tremble.

'I've wanted you for weeks,' he confided, laying his hands heavily on her shoulders. 'I've fantasised about what you had on under those hideous, baggy clothes you wear.' He wasn't sure she was ready to hear what he had fantasised about doing once he had removed those clothes...fantasised about doing right there in his office.

Desire was like a fist clutching low in her belly. 'I dress for comfort.' She was surprised to hear an unfamiliar breathy voice emerge from her lips. 'Well, thank you for fixing my zip.' And blowing my mind into some lustful other dimension. 'But I really should be getting ready now.'

Rafe heard her out politely before he laughed scornfully and closed his hand possessively over her right breast. From the expression in his eyes it seemed to Natalie that he found the sight of her small breast covered by his big hand as stimulating as she did.

'I know a short cut to the church, we have at least forty minutes to spare.' He appeared to consider the problem. 'What do you suppose we do with that time?'

As he spoke he was scooping her straining breast out of the flimsy bra cup with practised ease. A sibilant hiss escaped through his clenched teeth as he watched the already engorged pink bud swell and harden. Natalie cried out and grabbed him by the front of his shirt.

'You are probably the smuggest, most conceited man that ever lived,' she accused shakily.

Rafe swallowed hard and dragged his reverent gaze to her face; there was not a trace of the smugness she accused him of in his raw, driven expression. Her stomach flipped.

He gave a strained, crooked grin. 'But sexy with it, *right*...?' he croaked hoarsely.

A laugh was wrenched from Natalie's dry throat—laughter and sex had never seemed compatible until now. 'It isn't your sex appeal that's in question here, it's my sanity—' She broke off mid-complaint as she felt the catch on her bra unclick.

With a smile Rafe chucked her bra over his shoulder. 'In the interests of symmetry,' he explained, admiring the perfect symmetry of her unfettered breasts. The thought of taking those straining peaks into his mouth aroused him unbearably.

Natalie could smell the warm male scent of his body. She wanted to touch him, wanted to so badly it

blocked out every other thought. Feeling bold and
reckless, she laid a hand flat against his chest; through
his shirt she could feel the heavy thud of his heartbeat.
His body was solid muscle and bone, a long, lean and
lovely body. She gave a shudder of sheer heady anticipation and let her hand slide boldly to his flat belly.
She felt the sharp contraction of his stomach muscles
as he sucked in his breath.

'Sorry, I'm messing up your lovely clothes.'

She went to lift her hand but he caught it hard and
held it there. His shimmering blue eyes scanned her
flushed face. 'To hell with my lovely clothes!' he declared, releasing her, but only to tear the tie from
around his neck. This followed the same path as her
bra.

'There's glass everywhere—this is dangerous. You
could cut yourself.'

No, you're the dangerous one, she thought, looking
at his stern, predatory profile. Desire kicked hard in
her molten belly, she shivered and her eyes darkened
dramatically.

Without saying a word and correctly taking her
compliance as written, Rafe swept her up in his arms,
and picked his way through the shattered mirror towards the bed. Before he placed her down he removed
the top cover, which was covered in tiny fragments of
glass, and flung it to one side.

'Where are you going?' she asked plaintively when
he didn't join her.

'I'll be right there,' he promised. His bright-burning
eyes didn't leave her face for an instant as he stripped
off his clothes with flattering urgency.

Natalie stared. She couldn't help herself—he was

beautiful in a way that made her throat ache. His skin was an even dark gold dusted lightly in significant areas by erotic drifts of dark hair. The impressive strength of his upper body and magnificent, tightly muscled shoulders was perfectly balanced by a hard, washboard belly and long, long legs. Greyhound lean, he moved with the perfect co-ordination and fluid grace of a natural athlete.

He certainly had a turn for speed—in a matter of seconds he was standing there in just his boxers. As he stepped out of them Natalie caught her breath. She looked away, feeling like a guilty schoolgirl caught peeking.

Rafe gave a wolfish grin of predatory satisfaction. 'Don't mind me, I like you looking,' he confided with shameless candour.

The bed springs creaked as he landed beside her. There was no trace of laughter in his face as their eyes locked. Without saying anything he fixed his mouth to hers; it fitted perfectly. He continued to kiss her, deep, drugged kisses that sent her spiralling out of control and kept her there.

Natalie clutched at him, revelling in the smoothness of his skin and the hardness of his muscle. She didn't connect the soft guttural sounds that she could hear with herself.

Hands cupping her buttocks, Rafe drew her body into his. 'You can feel how much I want you...?'

Her body reacted as much to the sound of his voice as the erotic pressure of his arousal against her soft belly. Giving a fractured little sigh, she opened her eyes and tried to focus on his face...the outline was blurry.

'Are you crying?' Concern roughened his voice.

Natalie blinked and shook her head. The combination of lust and love was something she had never been exposed to before; she had no defences against the heady cocktail. 'I want you, too,' she whispered, touching him because she quite simply had to—*not* touching his silken length was no more an option than not breathing!

He groaned greedily and pulsed against the confines of her trembling hand. His uninhibited pleasure encouraged her to continue her erotic explorations.

It was Rafe who eventually stopped her teasing caresses.

'My turn, I think,' he announced throatily as he flipped her over onto her back.

Still ahead every step of the way, still anticipating what she wanted before she knew it herself, he slid down her body, caressing her with his hands, tasting her with his lips.

Her swollen, tingling breasts felt as if they were on fire after he had applied his clever tongue and hands to each quivering, pink-tipped mound in turn. She closed her eyes as he licked his way lower and when he reached the hot, drenched, sensitised region between her pale thighs her back arched, lifting her hips clear of the mattress.

Natalie hooked her fingers in his hair.

Rafe lifted his head. There were dark bands of colour high across his cheekbones. He took one look at her face and groaned. 'When you look at me like that I just want to...'

'So do I,' she moaned. 'So do, Rafe. Do it right now, you beautiful man!' she cried brokenly.

He kissed her neck as he settled over her. 'Oh, my God!' she moaned as he slid up into her, hard and hot. 'Oh, this is…is…' he rocked higher into her and she bit into the damp skin of his neck sobbing softly '…good…very, very good.'

'It will be…' he promised, thrusting hard. 'Just let go, let it happen,' he instructed, continuing to build a smooth, fluid rhythm.

Natalie didn't know what he was talking about, but she did know that she wouldn't mind if he carried on doing what he was for ever. A little while later she found out this wasn't true—in fact she couldn't bear it any longer. Just about that moment she discovered, in the most earth-shattering way, what he had meant—*it* happened!

In the aftermath of a climax that had involved her entire body from her toes to—well, she couldn't discount the possibility her hair follicles had been involved—she lay there in a dazed glow, curled up like a sleepy, sexy kitten in his arms. The only sound was her occasional murmur of, *'Wow!'* which made Rafe, who had his chin propped on top of her head, grin.

'I think I'm going to fall asleep,' she confided.

'Nice idea, but we might miss the wedding photos.'

With a horrified cry Natalie leapt out of bed, ignoring his warning cry of, 'Watch the glass!'

'Oh, God, we'll be late. Why didn't you remind me?' she remonstrated severely as she struggled into her clothes.

'I had other things on my mind.'

*   *   *

They weren't late and Natalie got to cry a little, seeing Rose looking sweet walking up the aisle behind the bride.

There was a certain novelty value attached to being the centre of attention. It aggravated the bride, too, which was a definite plus, but Natalie knew it wasn't her stunning good looks or sparkling personality that were the draw. No, it was the man beside her. That Rafe would inevitably know and be known by people on this sort of celebrity guest-list had not even crossed her mind.

She had reached the point, after two glasses of champagne, where she was actually enjoying herself when Mike introduced her as Rafe's fiancée. He did so in front of half a dozen people Rafe knew, one of whom, an opera singer of international fame, turned out to be one of his mother's best friends.

'Oh, Luisa didn't tell me and I only spoke to her on Thursday!' she exclaimed, kissing first Rafe and then Natalie on both cheeks.

'Actually, Sophia, we haven't told the families yet so I'd be grateful if you could keep it to yourself for a couple of days,' Rafe requested smoothly.

'But of course,' she promised immediately. 'And do your family know yet, Natalie?'

Natalie got the impression those bright, curious eyes were missing not a detail of her outfit.

'There's only my grandmother.'

'Oh, how sad, but you have a little girl, I believe…? A ready-made family—how nice for you, Rafe…but you have such a big family. Have you been to the *palazzo* in Venice yet?'

Natalie shook her head. *Palazzo!* That figured— blue blood on both sides.

'We'd planned to spend our honeymoon there,' Rafe slotted in smoothly.

'Oh, you will love it. Come along and tell me all about yourself, my dear,' she urged, drawing a reluctant Natalie away.

'I have never been so glad for Valentine's Day to end.' Natalie sighed later as she kicked off her shoes in the comfort of the car. Rose was already fast asleep in the back. 'I am so sorry!'

'About what?'

'About the fiancée stuff in front of your mum's friend. What'll you say to them?' she asked worriedly.

Rafe dismissed them with a shrug. 'Oh, I'll deal with them, don't worry.'

'You're being awful nice about this...?'

'I'm a nice guy,' he revealed modestly. 'Once you get to know me.'

Natalie lowered her eyes to her hands, which lay primly in her lap. 'I was wondering...' Was she making a terrible mistake?

'You were wondering what?' he prompted.

'I was wondering if you'd like to stay the night with me...if you've no plans, that is...'

There was a charged silence.

'If I had any I'd change them,' he told her with a grin that revealed his even white teeth. 'You have absolutely no idea how happy I am to hear you say that.'

'Well, I'm pretty happy to hear you say yes,' she admitted. 'The only problem is...I mean, I know that it's inevitable this thing between us has a relatively short shelf-life...'

'Is that so?'

His weird tone made her glance across at him sharply, but his profile was unrevealing.

'Well, of course,' she confirmed, determined to show him she didn't have any unrealistic expectations. 'I'm afraid...' she cast a worried glance at the child asleep in the back seat '...that Rose will get too fond of you. Perhaps you should keep your distance,' she suggested doubtfully.

'And how do you propose I do that?' he grated, not looking amused by her suggestion.

'I see what you mean. It's a pity you get on so well...'

'I can see how it might be more convenient if your child and boyfriend hated the sight of one another,' he drawled. 'For the record, I don't think it's a helpful thing to decide a relationship is doomed to failure before it's even started.'

Natalie blinked. Surely he wasn't suggesting they could have something long term!

He took his eyes briefly from the road. 'Why not see how things develop?' he suggested in a more moderate tone.

'That's fine by me,' she replied, trying to keep the jubilation and hope from her voice.

CHAPTER NINE

THE following Friday a week later Natalie was outside Rafe's office. They had arranged at breakfast to have lunch together. They had *done* lunch together twice already that week, and breakfast every day! A smile appeared in her eyes as her thoughts dwelt on an unshaved Rafe sitting at her kitchen table with tousled dark hair falling in his eyes... Sometimes she had to pinch herself, it seemed so unreal. But there was nothing imaginary about the growing selection of male toiletries crammed on the shelves in her dinky bathroom or the pair of black men's socks that had turned her white delicate wash a dirty grey.

The changes weren't restricted to her flat. Natalie felt a different person from the one she had a mere week earlier: happier, more carefree—simply more alive!

She had her moments of doubt. It wasn't just that Rafe had quickly become part of her life—he had become part of Rose's, too.

'Things are moving a bit fast,' she suggested tentatively to Rafe after the sock incident.

His deep blue eyes lifted from the journal he was reading. 'Do you mind?'

Natalie thought about it. 'No, actually, I don't,' she revealed with a silly grin.

Rafe responded with a grin of his own—one that was not at all silly. His grin made her heart race and her knees turn to cotton wool. He didn't raise any objections when she took the magazine from his hands and climbed onto his lap—none at all!

When she had asked Rafe what she ought to tell people at work, he had shrugged in the way only a Latin male could and said, 'Whatever you like,' —which was no help at all. On reflection Natalie had decided not to volunteer anything, but if anyone asked she would tell them the truth, though sometimes she wasn't sure what that was, or where they were going.

She was totally, deeply, deliriously in love with Rafe, but how did he feel? Though expressive in many ways, shockingly so on occasions, he never once said 'love'. He told her how beautiful and sexy she was, but never once did he say he loved her. His restraint on the subject made her shy of expressing her own feelings, even though sometimes she *ached* to do so.

She was about to knock when she saw the door was ajar. She had pushed it open a little when she heard Rafe's voice inside; as she paused he switched seamlessly from Italian to English.

'Hold on, Mother, I'll put you on the speaker.'

His mother! Natalie, who had been about to move away, couldn't resist the opportunity of listening a little longer.

'Rafael, you don't call, you are never at home when I call and I've been so concerned ever since Sophia contacted me.'

The husky voice the other end was attractively accented.

'I asked her not to, so I was fairly sure she would.

Why are you concerned, Mother?' Natalie could hear
the sound of Rafe moving about the office—a drawer
opening, paper rustling. She really ought to go—if he
found her standing there eavesdropping it might be a
little embarrassing.

'Do not be so obtuse, Rafael! Why do you think I
am concerned? I know you were a little annoyed with
your father...'

'*Annoyed!*' Natalie heard the sound of Rafe's harsh
laugh. 'Why should I be annoyed? My father thinks
he can arrange a marriage to suitable breeding stock,
he puts me in an impossibly embarrassing situation...what is there to be annoyed about?'

'You know your father, he means well, but he—'

'Is a snobbish, manipulative, unprincipled... Do you
suppose he's *ever* going to learn he can't run my life?'

'I know you're angry, I know you want to punish
him, but really this isn't the way to do it!'

'What are you talking about, Mother?'

'I'm not stupid, Rafael,' came the impatient maternal reply. 'Remember what you said when I asked you
about marriage—you told me then what the girl you
married would be like. From what Sophia tells me this
girl is the exact opposite.'

There was a short pause, during which Natalie held
her breath; any desire to leave had vanished. 'You
know, I haven't actually thought about it, but I suppose she is.'

'Add that to the fact this girl you so suddenly get
engaged to just happens to be everything your father
would dislike—divorced...with a child...from a totally different social background to your own... Am I
supposed to think this is a coincidence? I know you

want to teach your father a lesson, Rafael, but you have involved another person,' the husky voice remonstrated worriedly. 'Have you thought how this young woman is going to feel when she realises you are using her? I am assuming you are going to call a halt to this thing before you get as far as a church...?'

Natalie could have told her how *this girl* would feel—how this girl *was* feeling: numb. There was a total absence of feeling; she felt dead inside.

She turned and began to walk away, slowly at first and then quicker until she was running full pelt, oblivious to the startled glances she attracted. It all made sense, of course. That was why Rafe hadn't been angry when she had claimed he was her fiancé. He had seen it as the perfect opportunity to teach his interfering father a lesson—and the sex had been good, too.

My God, he must have thought it was his lucky day! She felt used and grubby and very, *very* stupid. She dashed a hand across her face as the tears started in her eyes. The numbness was beginning to fade, leaving a knot of pain that was lodged like a fist behind her breastbone.

'And all the while I was dreaming my silly dreams like the besotted idiot I am!'

'Ms Warner...Natalie...?'

'Yes, Maggie,' Natalie replied as she continued to empty the contents of her drawers into a bag.

'I just wanted to say...I'm sorry if...'

God, is this Maggie trying to be friends because she thinks I'm the boss's girlfriend? Ironic under the circumstances. 'Honestly, Maggie, you don't have to bother.'

'Oh, but I do, I *want* to! I think I might have treated

you unfairly,' she began awkwardly. 'No, I *know* I did.'

'It's not nec—' Natalie began tiredly.

'I need to say this,' came the taut response. 'You made me feel guilty.'

Natalie straightened up. *'Guilty...?'* she echoed with a frown.

The older woman nodded. 'I had a baby, you see. I wasn't married and I gave him away...'

The simple statement hid half a lifetime of pain. Natalie's eyes filled with tears as her tender heart ached with empathy for the pain etched on the other woman's face.

'Oh, I'm so sorry, I didn't know.'

'Nobody did,' Maggie told her thickly. 'I made a choice, I chose my career over my baby. You didn't and, seeing you doing both so well, it made me ashamed that I had never even tried. Every time I looked at you I...' She shook her head and when she continued her voice was thick with emotion. 'I'm sorry I gave you a hard time.'

Natalie shook her head. 'It doesn't matter,' she told the other woman wearily. Nothing mattered any more, but Maggie's poignant tale had reminded her of something she still had—her daughter—and for that reason if no other she had to carry on. It didn't matter how bleak her personal future seemed, the luxury of falling apart was not an option.

'What are you doing?' Maggie seemed to notice for the first time that Natalie was removing her belongings.

With her forearm Natalie brushed the entire contents

from her desktop into an open bag. She fastened the bag and straightened up. 'I'm leaving.'

Staying after what had happened was clearly out of the question. The idea of seeing Rafe on a daily basis made her blood run cold. She would take Rose for a holiday to her grandmother's, and when she was there she could sort out her options, such as they were. Maybe she would stay in Yorkshire? It had a lot to recommend it, the biggest selling point being the number of miles that separated it from Rafe Ransome. It was cheaper to live in the country. Grimly determined to be positive even if her world was falling apart, she told herself the country air would be good for Rose.

'Leaving! But I thought that you and...' Maggie stopped, colouring under Natalie's wry gaze.

'I thought we were, too, but I was wrong.' Natalie clamped her trembling lips together and, brushing past the other woman with her head downbent, fled.

Natalie found herself back at the flat; scarily she had no memory of how she'd got there. Once inside she began to put her plan—such as it was—into action. It was unlikely that Rafe would follow her, but if she was wrong, however, she had no intention of being here when he arrived. She gritted her teeth and blinked back the hot tears that filled her eyes as she haphazardly piled some of Rose's clothes and toys into a suitcase. She would pick Rose up from the childminder and go straight to the railway station—yes, that was the best thing to do.

She was struggling as she lugged the second over-full case into the living room, when she hit her shin a painful glancing blow on a low table. If anything the

pain was a useful distraction from the other pain...
Sniffing defiantly, she placed her burden by the front
door and looked around, trying to focus her thoughts.
Had she forgotten anything vital? Mentally she ticked
off items on her list of necessities. Her gaze fell upon
an open book. It lay where Rafe had left it after Rose
had climbed off his knee the previous evening.

'Tomorrow,' he had promised when she had begged
him to continue. 'You heard what Mummy said—it's
bedtime for you, young lady.'

An overwhelming sense of loss washed over
Natalie, followed by a violent wave of anger. Rafe
could have argued he had never lied to her—never told
her he loved her—and it would have been true. She
was willing to take a proportion of the blame herself,
blame for falling in love with him. As far as Rose was
concerned *nothing* could excuse his behaviour. That
little girl adored him and she was going to be desperately confused and hurt to have him vanish from her
life.

For that Natalie would never forgive him!

The sound of the key turning in the lock was very
loud in the quiet room. Natalie mastered her panic and
lifted her chin as she turned to face the door.

Rafe stepped into the room. Tall, devastatingly
handsome and very, *very* angry. Anyone with normal
co-ordination and reflexes would have fallen in a
graceful heap over the pile of cases that lay there, but
not Rafe. Without pausing, he sidestepped the obstacle
without removing his burning gaze off the slim, rigid
figure who stood in the middle of the room.

Lips compressed, nostrils flared, his powerful chest
rising and falling as if he'd been running, he scanned

her pale, hostile face with his brilliantly compelling gaze.

'Going somewhere, Natalie?'

Natalie gave a contemptuous little laugh. 'Anywhere you are not.' Her antagonistic reply was rewarded by his sharp inhalation. 'How did you know I was gone? No, don't tell me—the loyal Maggie. You really do seem to inspire selfless devotion in women, Rafe, but consider yourself with one less devoted slave.' She placed her splayed fingers flat on her heaving bosom just in case he was in any doubt of whom she referred to. 'You can leave the key on the table when you leave.' She spoilt her dignified dismissal by adding childishly, 'I suppose you'll be relieved not to be slumming it any longer!'

Rafe shook his head impatiently. '*Slumming it?* What the hell are you talking about?'

'I did wonder that you never invited me to your place, but it all makes perfect sense now. How would you explain me to your friends?' With curious objectivity she observed the effect of her words on his composure as the nerve beside his mouth jerked.

'How could I suggest you spend the night with me when you kept telling me how you wanted to keep the disruption to Rose's routine to a minimum? Dear God, woman, you acted as if I was trying to move in when I left a toothbrush in the bathroom!'

His ability to come up with a plausible excuse and then turn the tables so that *she* was the one at fault was staggering and probably, she thought angrily, the secret of his success.

'Sure, you're Mr Considerate!'

'Stop this, Natalie,' he pleaded in a low, impassioned voice.

'Stop what?'

The calculated obtuseness of her comment drew a harsh Italian curse from him. Swearing fluently, he crossed the room. As he reached her side Natalie was extremely conscious of his sheer physical power, of his tall, tightly muscled frame—he was a man in the peak of physical condition. In the past awareness of this strength had excited her; even now her stomach lurched as he approached. Contemplating the thrill it had given her to surrender to that strength increased her sense of self-loathing. With provocative deliberation she turned her head and looked away.

'What's going on here, Nat?' Rafe took her chin in his hand and tilted her head up to him. 'This morning things were fine, lunchtime you clean out your desk and walk out without a word...now I find you about to leave. Were you planning to give me any sort of explanation?' The screaming tension on his taut features brought his cheekbones into sharp prominence.

'No.'

Her monosyllabic response had much the same effect on him as a red rag did to a bull. 'Good God!' he thundered. 'You are—' He bit off the words he was about say and inhaled, breathing deeply as if he didn't trust himself to respond. When he did speak his low tone was flat and expressionless. 'Do you not think that I deserve to know what the hell I'm supposed to have done?'

Natalie gave an enraged yelp and tore her face from his grasp. 'You deserve—you deserve!' she yelled, her voice rising to a shrill, accusing shriek. 'You deserve to rot in hell, Rafael Ransome!'

He recoiled as if she'd physically struck him. If she hadn't known better she'd have bought that look of bewildered confusion on his dark face—if, that was, she hadn't heard that incriminating conversation and if she hadn't subsequently had her heart ripped out.

'I know, Rafe. I know.' She waited for him to at least acknowledge he had been caught out, but he didn't even have the decency to do that! 'So you can imagine why I find it a bit laughable you acting like the injured party here. I'm an adult, I should have known better,' she acknowledged, 'but I'll never forgive you for Rose. It was cruel, Rafe—you made her love you!' She pressed a hand over her mouth as a sob escaped.

'And I love her.'

Natalie gasped wrathfully. 'Why, you callous bas—!'

Rafe caught her hand mid-swing and brought it firmly down to her side. 'Now you will tell me what I am supposed to have done.'

Breathing hard as if she had been running Natalie raised her bitter eyes to his. They shimmered with unshed tears. 'There's no need to pretend, Rafe. *I know.*'

As if he could compel her to speak by sheer force of will, his piercing blue eyes narrowed on her face. '*You know...?* I'm glad one of us does, because I haven't the faintest idea what you're talking about. You know what exactly? Speak to me, Natalie, because you're killing me here.'

For a moment she hesitated; surely nobody could fake the raw emotional intensity and anguish she heard echoed in his voice. Then she remembered that damning conversation she had overheard and her face hardened.

'I know that you had your own reasons for pretending we were an item.'

Natalie hadn't known that she was secretly harbouring a crazy hope that this would all prove to be some horrible mistake until she felt it die. It died when he couldn't meet her eyes.

'And you think you know what those are?' he hedged.

'I know why you weren't bothered if your parents got to know about our fake engagement—you wanted them to.'

He shook his head, his brows drawing together in a puzzled line. 'Wanted them to what?'

Natalie gave an exasperated sigh. 'I heard you on the phone with your mother.'

A flicker of comprehension appeared in his strained eyes. As she watched his head fell back and he exhaled noisily. Bizarrely his attitude seemed one almost of relief.

'I took the call on the speaker phone…' He ran a hand across his jaw.

Natalie knew that by this time of day he would be able to feel a faint stubble. Only yesterday she had complained about it when he'd kissed her in the office lift and he had laughed. Actually she enjoyed the abrasive roughness against her soft skin. The flood of heat that washed through her body was mingled with anger and shame.

'Don't bother trying to remember what you said,'

she advised dully. 'I heard enough to make me realise I've been a total fool to fall in love with you.'

Rafe's head jerked up sharply; his iridescent blue eyes scanned her face. Whatever he saw there made the blood drain from his face, his normally healthily golden-toned skin looking greyish.

'You fell in love...?'

Clearly this was news to him and not welcome news. Maybe he had a conscience after all? Well, that was good, because if she felt this wretched it only seemed fair that he should feel a little bit bad, too.

'So sorry if you didn't bargain for that, but don't worry, I've woken up, I won't be proclaiming my feelings from any high buildings.' The way I've been acting, I probably don't need to. 'I know that this has all been about you wanting to teach your father a lesson. Everything falls in your lap, doesn't it, Rafe?' she reflected bitterly. 'You needed an unsuitable sort of girlfriend and who comes along but the definitive version—*me*? The sort of girl your father would cross the street to avoid being contaminated by!'

'So *that's* it. You think...!' He shook his head and drew an unsteady hand through his dark hair. Then unforgivably he laughed—he actually *laughed*. This fresh proof of his heartless callousness made Natalie feel physically sick. 'You were eavesdropping! Actually, Natalie, my father has been known to cross the street to get a closer look at a beautiful girl but never the other way around.'

'That only works if the girl is beautiful and I'm not.'

Her statement brought a stern, disapproving frown to his wide brow. 'If I say you're beautiful, you are,' Rafe pronounced with breathtaking arrogance.

'I have to be beautiful because you deigned to sleep with me, is that how it works? And don't expect me to apologise about eavesdropping—if I hadn't been I'd still be walking around thinking I was living out some sort of romantic fantasy.'

His eyes dropped to the lush curves of her full lips and then lower to the firm, uptilted outline of her small, pert breasts. He swallowed hard.

Seeing the contraction of muscles in his strong brown throat was the key that unlocked the door to forbidden memories. Memories of other muscles in his lean, firm body contracting and quivering beneath the glistening surface of his sweat-soaked skin and all in response to her touch.

She had almost succeeded in locking away the steamy memory when his heavy, darkly fringed eyelids, lifted revealing an expression so hot it could have started a forest fire. Natalie's pupils dilated until they almost obliterated the iris; similarly, the hormonal rush in her blood had a dramatic effect on her ability to think rationally—as in she couldn't! Sweat broke out over her entire body as she tried to drag herself clear of the sensual vortex that was sucking her deeper with each passing second.

'All my fantasies have you in,' he told her simply.

Goose-bumps broke out over her body as she suffered yet another dramatic shift in temperature. *If you believe this it'll hurt, Nat…don't believe…don't…!* She didn't allow herself to respond until she had regained some sort of control over her emotions.

'What is it with you?' she grated, trying to frame a reply that would make him realise he no longer had anything to gain from this pretence. '*I know*, Rafe, you don't have to keep up the act.'

'The only thing I've ever pretended with you, Natalie, is that I could control the way you made— *make* me feel,' he gritted with a self-derisive grimace. 'If you'd stayed around to hear the rest of my conversation with my mother you'd have heard me say as much to her. I left her in no doubt that she'd read things wrong.'

His hard jaw clenched as his brooding glance paused hungrily on the outline of her soft, quivering lips.

'The reason I didn't object when you introduced me as your lover was I liked the way it sounded.' Natalie's fractured gasp was clearly audible in the short pause that followed his words. 'As for playing your future husband, I had this idea that if I played the part really well you might decide to keep me on permanently.'

The blood drained from Natalie's face. '*Permanently?*' she parroted weakly. 'As in living together!'

'No.'

God, Natalie, will you never learn? 'Right,' she said, fighting for composure.

'As in married,' he slotted in coolly.

Natalie looked at her hands. They were shaking; so was the rest of her. This was all happening too fast for her to take in. 'But you said…'

'No, Natalie, my *mother* said. Think about it,' he suggested.

She did.

An arrested expression crossed Natalie's face. *Rafe* had never actually said…had he…? Could she have jumped to the wrong conclusion?

'My mother is legendary for reading situations wrong.' His brows lifted. 'Now that I think about it, you two should have a lot in common,' he mused drily. 'Of course, if she had actually met you she would never have made that mistake. One look at you and she'd have seen that I'd be the luckiest man alive if you'd have me. Will you have me, Natalie?'

Natalie's heart was trying to batter its way out of her chest; the tight feeling her racing pulse created made it hard to breathe, let alone speak.

'What are you saying exactly, Rafe?' This time she wasn't going to jump to any premature conclusions.

A spasm of raw frustration flickered across his handsome, drawn face. 'Do I need to spell it out?' he asked thickly.

'Well, yes, actually, I think you do.'

'Marry me, Natalie.' As her silence grew so did the tension in him. 'I think we make a pretty good team...'

Natalie widened her eyes innocently. 'So this is by way of being a business merger?' she queried pertly.

Their eyes touched; when Rafe saw what shone in hers the tension seemed to drain from his body. A fierce grin spread slowly across his dark face. 'Like hell it is!' he growled, reaching for her. 'Come here, you stupid woman.'

Resistance didn't even cross Natalie's mind as she walked into his open arms—where she belonged. His muscular arms tightened around her as his mouth found hers. The masterful kiss was raw, hard and hungry. Natalie's lips parted eagerly beneath the pressure. When they finally broke apart she was dizzy and insanely happy.

'Don't you ever, *ever* do that to me again! Do you

hear me? I've aged about twenty years in the last hour.'

Natalie touched the raven hair at his temple. Despite his claim there was no sign of premature greying. 'Well, I wouldn't have jumped to the wrong conclusion if you'd told me how you felt,' she chastised him reproachfully.

One dark brow lifted. 'Like you did…?'

'I was afraid if I said anything I'd scare you off,' she admitted.

'And I felt that every time I tried to get closer you pulled back.'

'I was trying to be what you wanted—a low-maintenance girlfriend who didn't make demands…' She intercepted his wry look and grinned. 'Except in the bedroom,' she admitted guiltily.

'Let's leave the bedroom out of this for a few minutes,' he pleaded throatily.

'That's a first for you!'

Her saucy jibe earned her a long, lingering kiss.

When his head finally lifted Natalie gave a languid sigh and ran her fingers down the hard curve of his cheek. Rafe's eyes darkened as he caught her fingers and brought them to his lips. Quite deliberately he kissed each individual fingertip—Natalie found it incredibly erotic. He pressed an open-mouthed kiss to her palm before returning her hand to her.

'Is this real?' The air left her lungs as his arms tightened about her ribcage before dropping to the small of her back. The firm pressure brought her up onto her tiptoes and sealed their bodies at hip level so that she could feel—as he intended her to—the very real state of his arousal. 'You've convinced me,' she admitted with a husky chuckle.

'You see why I wanted to keep the bedroom out of this. I need to say stuff and I can't think above the waist when you're like this.'

Secretly delighted at the image of herself as some sort of irresistible Jezebel, Natalie gave a sexy little sinuous wriggle that drew a deep groan from Rafe. She gave a regretful sigh and drew back.

'You're right, we should talk. How about if I sit over there—' she pointed at the sofa against the wall the opposite side of the room '—and you sit here.'

Rafe caught her arm. 'Too far.'

'And this is too close?' she asked huskily.

'It wouldn't matter to the way I feel if a thousand miles separated us,' he declared in a deep, throbbing accent. 'Oh, my love!' His blue eyes glittered down into hers as he laid his big hands on her shoulders. 'I think I loved you right from the beginning. When I told myself I was protecting you by keeping my distance, in reality I think it was more about protecting myself—I just wasn't ready to admit what I felt for you.'

'Are you ready now?' she whispered, hearing the thud of her own heartbeat in her ears.

She watched a slow, incredible smile spread across his face. 'Ready, able and very, *very* willing.'

'Oh, Rafe, I love you so much!'

The warm, sensuous impression left by his lips made her own tingle even after he had lifted his head. While she was smiling a little stupidly up at him he slid his hands down her arms until their fingertips were touching.

'I think this is about as far as I feel safe letting you go away from me…' he confessed.

'I'm not going to run away again, but…'

Rafe groaned. 'No more *buts*, please!'

'I love you but I don't want to be responsible for some sort of family rift. Your mother said your father would hate me,' she added worriedly.

He took her face between his hands needily. 'My father is many things, but stupid is not one of them.' The uncomplicated love revealed in his expression made Natalie's eyes fill with tears of sheer joy. 'It'll take him about two seconds to see you're exactly what he's been telling me I need for years. Within half an hour he'll have convinced himself it was all his idea.'

Natalie laughed. His certainty went a long way to easing her concerns.

'Forget my father, forget everyone, this is about us. We're a package deal: you, me and Rose,' Rafe declared proudly. 'Is that all right by you?'

'I think I might get used to the idea.' She laughed, throwing her arms around his neck. 'Given forty years or so.'

And Natalie was looking forward to every second of those years beside the man she loved.

Modern Romance™
...seduction and
passion guaranteed

Tender Romance
...love affairs tha
last a lifetim

Sensual Romance™
...sassy, sexy and
seductive

Blaze Romance™
...the temperature's
rising

Medical Romance™
...medical drama on
the pulse

Historical Romance™
...rich, vivid and
passionate

27 new titles every month.

*With all kinds of Romance for
every kind of mood...*

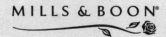
MB2 V2

MILLS & BOON

dark angel
LYNNE GRAHAM

Knight in shining armour
or avenging angel?

Available from 21st March 2003

*Available at most branches of WH Smith,
Tesco, Martins, Borders, Eason, Sainsbury's
and all good paperback bookshops.*

0403/135/MB68 V2

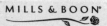